WICKEDNESS & WONDER

SHAELYNN LONG &
BRITTANY MCMUNN

Wild Ink Publishing LLC

wild-ink-publishing.com

Editors: J.K. Raymond, Brittany McMunn, & Fatimah Jan

Designs & Layout by: Abigail Wild

Contents

My Daughter's Favorite Heroine

By Kristen Argyres

I WILL GO GREY by year's end, and I have no one to blame but myself. The daughter of a shapeshifter will inevitably favor her faerie father. I should have known.

But can one blame me for my vexation when my child avoids scolding by hopping away with the hares? Or when she melts into a puddle when she does not wish to be whisked off to bed? I will never rest easy when my daughter throws herself from the treetops, though she flies as well as any bird.

Tamlin dotes upon her as any loving father ought. Their bond is special; they match their forms to swim in the stream as fish or chase the wind sprites in the meadow as stag and fawn. My heart swells with joy at the sight.

But in the wake of their laughter, I am left hollow. With no faerie blood of my own, I struggle even to alter the color of my eyes or curl my hair. I cannot join them as I am.

Yet each night, as the blushing pink sky fades to starry black, my daughter nuzzles my shoulder. "Mama, will you tell me how you saved Daddy from the Faerie Queen?"

Tamlin grins. "You're always the heroine of her favorite tales." He scoops us both into bed, cuddling close.

I chuckle and muss our daughter's hair, touched by their words. "Very well." Eyes closed, I bask in the warmth of their love.

"Once upon a time..."

The Little Siren

By Amie Glazier

AFTER THE GLITTERING RAINBOW and happily ever after subsided, the fear of the sea remained. The image of the sea witch being lanced by a ship was rooted in the psyche of all the sailors, and it was reputed her wrath had quelled when she had possession of a woman with red hair. There were some who thought the sea witch truly died at the hand of a human, but no one was willing to gamble their life on it.

Sailors came to believe that when the storms raged and the sea swelled with anger, it meant the sea witch was hungry and demanded a mortal woman to devour. So, it was Talina's terrible luck she was on a ship with the most superstitious crew in the twelve seas when the cyclone struck.

"Bind her hands!" The sailor's words were as poisonous as his breath as he wrestled her to the rain-slicked deck.

"No!" she shrieked.

Four brusque men grabbed her bound limbs and heaved her across the deck. The pelting rain slicked her skin, and the men struggled to hold her tightly. Her head lolled and crashed into a barrel as the ship pitched over a furious wave. Her long, red hair danced in the violent wind. The men's shouts were barely audible over the roar of the sea as they approached the plank and readied to hoist her overboard.

Talina snuck onboard to escape the sale of her body to a husband twice her age. The ship was supposed to be her freedom, but her imminent death was a cruel irony. Drowning in an angry sea, she thought, would be far kinder than a lifetime forced to bed a drunk, old man. Even in death, her agency was stolen.

"Oh, mighty sea witch," they shouted into the churning storm, "accept our offering. Take this bitch to the depths and leave us be!"

"Waaaait—" But Talina's words were cut short as she fell like a stone through the surface of the waves. Her lungs capsized from the cold. Her green eyes grew wide and panicked as she wriggled and fought to free her limbs. She sunk into the inky depths of the tumultuous water as tiny bubbles escaped from her mouth unbidden, like foam upon the sea.

Please.

The simple plea echoed from her heart as her eyes squeezed shut to brace herself against whatever spirit would bring her into the afterlife. What Talina didn't see was how her plea became a prayer that rippled through the stormy waters. It undulated in concentric circles as if she were a star exploding in the night sky. Fighting the urge to gag, she opened her eyes to see a bright light racing toward her. Death. As her lithe body seized and begged for air, she surrendered, and her world went black.

When Talina awoke, the first thing she noticed was how her body thrummed with energy. Her breath was even and calm, and her throat no longer felt raw from screaming through the violent, salty air.

"Hello." A woman's voice vibrated through the water and sounded as bright as a summer's morning. But Talina opened her eyes to find only darkness. She must have grimaced in confusion, because the woman replied, "Give your eyes a moment to adjust."

Talina blinked rapidly as the world around her slowly came into focus. But the more she saw, the more her heart fluttered with panic. The woman was a gruesome beast: half-fish and half-monster. Her hair was red and wild, undulating gently around her spiked teeth and gilled neck. Opaque scales peppered her abdomen and funneled into a shimmery, black tail that forked into two sheer fins. Talina's shock was palpable. But as her hands scanned her own body, she realized this woman mirrored her own, new reality. A wave of apprehension washed over her.

"Welcome to our shoal." The woman's accent milked the vowels and sharpened the consonants. "We are all discarded women who have been thrown to the beast of the depths by ignorant and superstitious men." She lifted her clawed hand to the space between her large, bare breasts. "I am Eleni."

"I am Talina," she replied, eyes wide with shock that her voice felt like honey dripping lazily down a sweet cake.

One side of Eleni's lip curved up; her green eyes glowed against her sun-kissed skin. "There are many things about your new body that will take time to adjust."

"Am I dead?" Talina struggled to remember.

"No. You cried out, and The Mother saved you."

"Who?" Talina's confusion only grew.

Eleni chuffed. "How ironic that men sacrifice us to the one who transforms us into their demise, eh?"

Talina flicked her shimmery, black tail through the water and watched the ripples with awe. "How many of us are there?"

"Our shoal is 150. But there are twelve seas filled with men who fear the sea witch." Eleni spat the last words as if they were bile. "But," she continued with a smirk. "We have never gone hungry. So, there is no need to swim elsewhere."

At that, a grumble grew somewhere beneath Talina's black scales. Hunger. But in this new form, it felt dark and foreboding and more like lust. One last question lingered like fire on her tongue. "What do we eat?"

A malicious grin spread across Eleni's features. "My mother was a pious woman who said that forgiveness is the sweetest nectar." She lifted a talon to her teeth and flicked away a piece of debris. "But, down here, we know nothing is sweeter or more satiating than revenge."

Talina wanted to balk at Eleni's insinuation, but she couldn't. Her blood thrummed in agreement as if vengeance was as essential to her now as air to a human.

Just then a shadow of a ship passed overhead, and a growl tore from Talina's lips unbidden. Eleni laughed wickedly. "Come, my little siren," she said. "Dinner awaits."

Breaking and Entering: A Modern-Day Retelling of Goldilocks and the Three Bears

By Lindsay Schraad Keeling

Goldie Luxe—or, as her family affectionately called her, "Go," —hated being the new girl in school. An Army brat since birth, she couldn't count how many schools she'd attended as her father was deployed to city after city, even overseas. Her mother had told her she would someday appreciate the well-roundedness that came with knowing cultures all over the world but Go did not care. She just wished to have a normal high school experience. And that wish was what got her into this predicament in the first place.

Go found herself with a ski mask on, her hood pulled up over her head, donned in all black clothes as she struggled to hop the chain link fence that backed up to a house owned by the Bears - the wealthiest family in Chanhassen, Oklahoma. Her newfound friends—a rough-around-the-edges, coed group who came to Go's rescue when she couldn't find anyone to sit with at lunch that day - sat in a dark blue Honda idling quietly at the street corner. It was 11:00 pm on a Friday.

Rumor had it, thanks to the loudmouth of William Xavier Bear II (who also attended Go's school), the Bear family was going to be in Texas for the weekend for a football game.

"Just go in and see what kind of pills and stuff they have," one of Go's new friends, a girl named Raven, had forcefully suggested earlier that day. "If you want to fit in around here, stealing from the Bears is the way to go. You get everyone what they want and the Bears won't notice a thing."

"Yeah," a guy named Davier said as he nodded his head. "They're stupid rich. They have everything."

"And depending on what you find, we can either share it or sell it," Raven added.

"We'll be in the car the whole time, watching for any cops," Davier assured her.

Goldie was seventeen. She desperately wanted to fit in somewhere. Anywhere.

Go was able to find a forgotten window in the house facing the backyard, open by only two inches. She shoved her fingers underneath and lifted up, using all of her upper body strength she could muster until the window slid upward enough for her to fit in. She took the knife that Raven had given her to slice the screen open and placed it back in her pocket as she delicately made her way inside the enormous house.

She was inside, her heart beating erratically.

Not knowing the layout of the home, Go used her gloved hands to make her way, feeling the walls and the furniture until her eyes adjusted to the darkness. She found a hallway with three bedrooms and entered the first one.

This must be Mr. Bear's room, she thought, as it was the biggest. (William Xavier Bear II had also glumly announced at school one day that his parents "no longer shared a room," which made sense as he often talked about his parents' constant arguing). She looked around the darkened area and saw an enormous king-sized bed, a single nightstand, and guns hanging up all around the walls.

These guns are way too big, Go thought. I can't sneak these out to the car.

She entered the master bathroom—a complete mess if there ever was one—and rifled through the medicine cabinet above the sink. The only bottles were for high blood pressure and something to do with diabetes (a quick Google search on her cell phone of the names of these assisted in her quick decision to abstain from stealing them).

Using the light from her cell phone, Go walked out of the bathroom, through the master bedroom, and back down the hallway until she reached the second biggest bedroom. As she walked in and saw the pink comforter and fancy throw pillows, she thought, This must be Mrs. Bear's room.

A vibration from her phone told her she had a text from Raven saying, "Hurry up," which made her want to vomit. She quickly explored the bureau and the night-stand but didn't find any guns (or anything other than unmentionables, for that matter).

Go walked into the darkened bathroom that connected to Mrs. Bear's room. It was completely spotless with salmon-colored tile and cabinets. She opened up the medicine cabinet but found nothing but antidepressants.

Glancing at the time on her phone (11:23 pm), Go briskly walked back down the hallway and into the third and smallest bedroom, which was obviously William Xavier Bear II's. It wasn't quite as messy as his father's room, but not nearly as clean as his mother's.

Go took a different approach to her classmate's room. Not only did she rifle through the chest of drawers and the bathroom medicine cabinet, she also checked under William Xavier Bear II's bed. There was a shoebox covered in dirty laundry, and when she pulled it out to open it, she saw a small, shiny pistol.

Just right, she thought.

Her heart skipping a beat, Go realized there was much more in the shoebox than just the gun. Little baggies of powders and pills filled the shoebox to the brim, along with a wad of cash. Was poor little rich boy William Xavier Bear II a drug dealer at school?

This is perfect—a goldmine, Go thought, and shoved the gun back into the shoebox and covered it with the lid. Hugging the box to her chest, a small click of a lock could be heard in the foyer, but it was too quiet to be heard among the rustling in the bedroom Go was in.

Go emerged—prideful and beaming, excited to show Raven and Davier her loot—into the darkened hallway when she saw the lights flick on.

In front of her was the Bear family.

Go dropped the box to the ground, the gun and baggies of drugs spilling out everywhere, as she made eye contact with Mr. Bear. He was standing in front of his wife and son, guarding them, as he pulled something from his waistband.

Time stopped.

The first **BANG!** didn't register in Go's ears. All she heard was ringing, then the sound of a car screeching off in the distance. She collapsed to the floor. The bullet hit her leg and missed a major vessel—just barely.

The second **BANG!** grazed Go's arm—a slice of her black hoodie shaved off as the bullet hit the wall behind her. Go leaned over, desperate to shield herself from the oncoming bullets.

The third and final **BANG!** was the perfect shot. As Go ducked down, the bullet entered the crown of her head, bouncing around her brain and severing her brain stem.

Just right, thought Mr. Bear.

Goldie Luxe hated being the new girl in school. And now she wasn't anymore. She would never be the new girl again.

Following the police investigation, the Bears were found not culpable for Go's death due to the "Stand Your Ground" law and their use of deadly force on a threat on their lives. However, under Oklahoma law, Raven and Davier—who were caught on a neighbor's camera fleeing in their car once they heard gunshots and eventually apprehended—were both charged with first-degree felony murder as accomplices to Goldie Luxe.

Goldie was cremated, a private family service held at the funeral home, and the ashes were given to her parents. The Luxes first placed her urn on the mantle in the living room but moved it because they couldn't bear to be reminded of their daughter's death and final decisions when they walked through the door. They then placed it on their dresser in their room but cried every night when they went to bed. And so they put it on a shelf in the closet of their daughter's old bedroom, where they could access it and think of it whenever they wanted to—which was not often.

It was just right.

A Letter for Linette

By Erin Jo Eldry

To my darling, Linette,
On this night, before our elopement,
I whisper through the flow of my quill
So you may read in secrecy what I've been shown by
Heaven

What curious things do happen in the world, my love,
That I dreamt of a life together
Not of boorish days as orthodox wives
But of who we were, before flesh and bone

I was once a boyish soldier
Made with twenty-four others in my likeness
Cast to bear arms in uniforms of red and blue
My queerness tailored in one limb's absence

You, a paper ballerina, unique in stoic virtue
Poised high in your castle where I could not reach
Fair maiden on one leg, I beheld you in adoration
Where in doting upon your beauty, I attracted scorn

What a bewildering creature, that Dreamweaver,
A harbinger of God's visions, yet corruptible by Lu-
cifer
Knitting your father's wickedness into that of a troll
Where even in dreams, I was exiled by his abusive
campaigns

Down I fell, Linette, into chasm of rotting darkness,
Sealed in the belly of a fish that was sure to be my
coffin
Yet by faith's great miracle, and Heaven's presence in
my heart,
Lucifer's minions be damned, I returned to my fair
maiden

As such, I saw our death from that lifetime ago
Engulfed in flames to please the contemptuous eyes
of your father
But also where God's winded sigh delivered your body
unto mine
Where we both succumbed, reborn as the women we
are

When we abandon this desolate place tomorrow,
And forsake our families who do not understand us,

If your father, that troll, should hunt us with lighted torch,
May the passions of his disdain warm us as we burn to ash

No other love but ours could ever sear as bright
For when we melt away and our bodies intertwine,
In any existence, of dreams or other worlds to come,
To you, my sweet Linette, I'll always remain steadfast

Until the Last Petal Falls

By Kendra Keplinger

THE STATUES HAD SINCE left. The spell was broken, yet she remained in the halls. Fragments of stems and torn rose petal corpses scattered across the castle. The vivid decor of gold gilded. Only the light of the Dark Moon illuminated the emptiness now. Still, a darkness lurked from within the walls, tormenting Beauty while she reflected.

Her chance to escape was but once to see her father. Being true to her word, she returned under the impression reciprocal love awaited her. "I do" was the final enchantment to her demise. The words sealed her into a forever fate not even death could part. As the prince, he treasured her and delicately nurtured her heart. He professed his care and devotion night after night, but deep down she knew something wasn't right.

Each time she closed her eyes and drifted into dreams, an enchantress appeared before her, entrancing through a piercing stare with onyx eyes clouded in darkness except for her golden irises. The enchantress levitated in a midnight forest of bare trees and pure ice. A black, lace gown covered her slender frame and flowed around her with the wind. Long strands of loose blonde curls billowed around her face with the gusts and faint smoke that swirled around her. An aroma of burning pine overwhelmed Beauty's senses as the sorceress before her lifted her delicate hands to her sides. Flames engulfed surrounding branches, blazing toward the sky as if they were trying to reach the untouchable heavens. Their hissing and crackling steadily grew louder until it was nearly deafening. Beauty fell to her knees on the frozen ground in pain, but the enchantress's gaze didn't falter.

"Not all is as it seems," she warned. "Your prince is not as pure as snow, and the rose is as red as blood." Suddenly, the ground beneath her turned to a blanket of snow and a macabre splatter of crimson, staining the hem of Beauty's nightgown and the palms of her hands.

Beauty awoke on the last night to a burning sensation trailing down her spine and an overwhelming metallic taste. The prince wrapped her in a secure embrace and nuzzled her until she rested once more, but even his body tensed this time. Something tormented him as well, but he never would say. So, Beauty kept the nightmares to herself, wishing to know just what haunted both her and the prince. The curse had lifted, and happily was forever after, so why was there a sinister presence?

The next evening, Beauty followed a trail of cream-colored rose petals in the west wing that led to the prince standing by the bay window in his study. The setting sun streamed through, illuminating a room full of freshly trimmed roses in crystal vases. The enchanted rose remained encased on his desk as if it were a centerpiece for an elaborate arrangement only its color had changed to a cream color like those from the trail, and the tips had traces of black and crimson.

"My love," she called, reaching out to him. "What is the meaning of this?"

He tensed at her touch and strengthened his grip on the desk, digging his nails into the wood and leaving claw marks behind. "You'll never be free, Beauty, unless you leave now," he replied in a strained voice.

"I—I don't understand," she said, unsure of how to console him.

The prince turned around and faced her. His eyes clouded in darkness just as the enchantress's had in her reoccurring dream. Beauty stepped back, managing only to allow small, shallow breaths. He picked her up by the throat, slamming her against the opposite wall. Her vision faded in and out on his vacant eyes that turned ocean blue but for a moment. The prince clenched his jaws, and his grip loosened temporarily before his gaze flickered back to the darkness. With a strengthened force, the prince lifted Beauty in the air one last time before slamming her down into a bed of roses and broken glass. The searing pain penetrated from her shoulders to the small of her back. As the pain ravaged her entire back, she began to cough up blood.

The enchantress appeared in the room beside the prince, gazing over Beauty's final moments. His blue eyes met Beauty's as he cried out in agony. The enchanted rose in his hands, now wilting, was left with the last petals becoming a more vivid red as if painted by her blood.

"I warned you, Beast," the enchantress said, gazing down at Beauty and shaking her head. "You need only blame yourself."

The prince charged toward her, but she held up a hand which sent him flying backward against his desk. "It IS true love. The curse was lifted," he said. "You should have no power here!"

"Did I forget to mention as long as that love was mine? Pity," she scoffed, waving her hand at the prince as if he were some nuisance. He then transformed back into the beast Beauty had first met. He cautiously held the rose closer to him.

"Beast..." Beauty uttered before closing her eyes.

"Beauty!" he shouted back, but she was gone. The last petal fell.

With another wave of her hand, the enchantress levitated Beast and threw him through the bay window and onto the lawn, rendering him unconscious. When he awoke, he no longer saw the castle. A midnight forest with bare trees had taken its place.

Inside the castle, Beauty slowly sat up and rubbed her temple, trying to piece together what had transpired.

Broken glass and roses covered the room, but there was no sign of Beast nor the enchantress.

"I do love the beauty of irony," the enchantress whispered in her ear. "You thought you spared your father and saved your precious Beast from a cursed castle but instead cursed yourself to eternal damnation within these walls never to be discovered and too late to be saved. Happily. Ever. After."

Lil' Red

By Bruce Buchanan

"How many times do I have to tell this story? You've already made up your mind that I'm a murderer."

"Just one more time." The police detective presses a button on his digital recorder. "Subject: Raylene Houlde. Age 20. 120 W. Greene Court, Lot 2. Charge: First Degree Murder."

The 100-watt spotlights burn my eyes, forcing my gaze to the plain wooden table between the detective and me. Under the lights is a wall-to-wall mirror—undoubtedly concealing an observation room where more cops are watching my interrogation. I squirm in my seat as the hard metal chair digs into my back. But I can't go anywhere—not while my right hand is handcuffed to the table. Besides, a man is dead.

"Okay, it all started two days ago—Friday night. I was working the evening shift at the Wagon Wheel...

"Just called to tell you not to wait up, Grandma. It'll be a late night at work. We've got a hot new band on stage tonight—Demi & the Butterflies. So, the Wagon Wheel will be hopping."

Pushing a pile of long, fiery red hair from my face, I click off my cell and get out of my ancient Honda Civic. A gentle voice calls from across the gravel parking lot before I make it to the employee entrance.

"Um, hey—Lil' Red!" I look up to see a tall, gangly young man in a red buffalo plaid flannel shirt. He holds his hand in the air as if he's hailing a cab.

"Michael! You're here early. D'Andre doesn't fire up the grill for another half-hour." I straighten up to my full five feet in red-and-white cowboy boots. It's the "Lil'" part of "Lil' Red," my nickname since childhood.

Michael is a right-out-of-college park ranger at the U .S. National Forest just outside Sherwood, N.C. He's also become a regular patron at the Wagon Wheel—even though he's more into alt-rock than country.

Rubbing the back of his neck, he looks down at his hiking boots. "I... I know you've got to get to work. And I've got a Scout group coming in for a workshop. But I just thought if you weren't busy tomorrow night...I mean, if you are, then no worries. I was hoping... that, well, maybe..."

I rock back and forth in my boots, smiling as my pulse speeds up. Michael and I have hung out a few times; he listens when I talk, loves animals, and respects boundaries. Plus, for a guy with an X-Men logo tattoo, he's pretty cute, even when he's hopelessly tongue-tied.

"Michael, I'd love to go out with you!" I give him a playful swat on the arm. "I'm working an early shift tomorrow. Maybe we could get some dinner? Just pick me up at my place around six."

He breaks into a broad smile and laughs. "Yeah! That sounds great. Thanks, Lil' Red!" He waves goodbye and practically floats back to his truck. Once he's out of sight, I give a discrete fist pump and say "Yesss!" to the empty parking lot.

I've got a date tomorrow. Wait until Grandma hears about this!

The Wagon Wheel is Sherwood's go-to spot for live country music, cold beer, and the best burgers between Charlotte and Asheville. Okay, that last part might be an exaggeration. But the food is good and so are the people.

"Jolene" flows from the bar's loudspeaker. Despite the heavy tray on my shoulder, I sing along with Dolly, as I've done for as long as I can remember.

I don't even realize I'm doing it. But my singing gets the attention of Angie and José Gomez, a couple of Wagon Wheel regulars. They look up from their burgers and beers to send a round of applause in my direction.

"Lil' Red—you've got the voice of an angel!" Angie points up at the stage. "When are you getting up there again?"

"Um, soon—I hope." My cheeks flush and I look down at the worn hardwood floor. This isn't a topic I want to discuss.

José nods. "I hope so, too. We've all missed hearing you sing. You have a gift, Lil' Red."

I smile. I don't have the heart to tell them I won't be on stage in the near future—if ever.

Grandma got me my first guitar when I was eight, and I never put it down. In high school, I dreamed of being the next big country star.

But two years ago, right before graduation, Grandma's health took a downhill turn. She had to quit her job at the hair salon. And that meant goodbye college and so long Nashville for me. Grandma is the only family I've got, and I'm going to take care of her.

I head back to the kitchen, but I don't feel much like singing anymore.

"Lil' Red! Order up for table four!"

Tucking the pencil behind my ear, I load my tray. "Two cheeseburgers well done, jalapeño poppers with ranch, and two draft Coors Lights. Looks good, D'Andre!"

"Well, come on back and we'll do it again. If the dude in the Wolfpack cap at table six doesn't get his order soon, he might get hangry—and that is not on my agenda tonight!!"

I chuckle, then hustle off for the umpteenth time tonight. Not that I'm complaining. Busy nights like these mean good tips, and my Civic needs a new set of tires.

"Hi, folks. Sorry for the wait. Just let me know if you need anything else and hope you enjoy." Greedy hands reach for the froth-topped beers and steaming basket of poppers. I set the rest of the food down, then half-walk, half-run back to the kitchen when I hear a sound that pricks up every hair on the back of my arm.

"Wassup Wagon Wheel? Ladies, feast your eyes and fantasize!"

A tall young man in tight Wranglers and a sleeveless T-shirt struts into the room, trailed by four hangers-on. Tucking his Ray-Bans into the neck of his shirt, he winks at a woman sitting at the bar. She giggles and blushes, despite her husband nursing a beer beside her.

The guy with the gun show man sprawls at the first open table, puts two fingers between his lips, and whistles for someone to take their order. His buddies laugh, as they always do. Dogs howl in the presence of a wolf.

Leonard "Lobo" Hamrick is an old classmate from Sherwood High School. We didn't run in the same packs then, to put it politely. He was the golden boy quarterback and the son of the biggest commercial real estate developer in the county. The only times he ever spoke to me was to make gross, suggestive jokes at my expense. Sherwood is a small town and I know just about every person in it. Lobo is undoubtedly my least favorite.

I push open the swinging doors to the kitchen. Jerry, the Wagon Wheel's grease-soaked manager, flips three more expertly grilled burgers onto plates and sends them down the line.

"Jerry, I gotta switch off table seven. I can cover twelve and fifteen for Rhonda."

He shakes sizzling grease from a basket of French fries, not even bothering to look up. "Anything I need to know about?"

"Not really." I sighed. "It's just... an old classmate of mine came in. He used to give me a hard time and—"

"Rhonda! You're up on table seven. Lil' Red's got twelve and fifteen now." Jerry gives a generous shake of salt crystals, which coat the fries like January ice.

"You're a sweetheart, Jerry!" I grab my next order and hit the dining room floor full speed.

I get tables twelve and fifteen settled in record time. Hustling back to the kitchen, I think I'm home free when a booming voice makes me wince, to the point I nearly drop my tray of empty glasses.

"Raylene Houlde! Dynamite comes in small packages, don't it? Sashay your fine self over here, girl!"

Oh, geez. I roll my eyes and silently groan. Then, I conjure up a fake smile and turn to face table seven.

"Hey, Lobo! Didn't see you. Look, I need to get back to table twelve, but Rhonda will be glad to take care of you." No—I'm not throwing Rhonda to the wolves, pun intended. I wouldn't do another woman like that. But her son played football with Lobo, so he treats Rhonda with respect he doesn't afford the rest of us worker bees.

"Screw table twelve! C'mon, Lil' Red. Don't tell me you're too good to talk to an old friend." Lobo pats the empty chair beside him and grins. His eyes linger well below eye level, and my skin crawls.

My instincts tell me to run. But Jerry's number one rule is, "Treat the customers like family." So I force my mouth into a smile. "Oh, nothing like that, Lobo. We've just got a full house tonight and—"

My smile turns into a gasp as Lobo grabs my upper arm and jerks me down into the chair. He's been out of football for a year, but he's every bit as strong as in his playing days. My arm instantly throbs under the pressure of his fingers, while my legs tremble with weakness. But he can't do anything bad to me in public, right?

"Look at you, playing hard to get. Always have, Lil' Red." As he leans into my face, his hot, beer-scented breath stings my nostrils. I turn away, trying to de-escalate the situation and not finding the words.

"N-no. I mean, I..."

Thankfully, one of his cronies interrupts my stammering with a cackle. "Aw, you've got Lil' Red shook up, Lobo!"

"I reckon you're right." Lobo reclines in his chair and puts his hands behind his head. "Go bring us another pitcher of draft, Lil' Red. We'll catch up some other time."

Shaking, I stand up and dash to the kitchen before my legs give out. I'm out of the woods for now.

D'Andre picks up on my discomfort as soon as I walk through the swinging doors. "Lil Red, what's wrong? You're even whiter than normal!"

"It's nuh–nothing." I tilt a plastic pitcher at an angle and fill it with light beer from the tap, trying not to let D'Andre see how badly my hands are shaking.

"It's that Lobo character, right? He's giving you a hard time? I'll get Jerry—we'll throw that creep out!"

"No! I mean, I've got it covered... but thank you."

Exhaling deeply, I carry the pitcher back to Lobo's table, where he's regaling his friends with stories of his State Championship glory days.

I lean forward to fill his friend's glass. "How 'bout a little love over here, hot stuff?" Lobo says. Before I can respond, Lobo's hand smacks the seat of my cutoff jean shorts!

My face turns the color of my hair. As my head spins, I try to exhale the anger through my nostrils.

That stupid grin is back on his stupid face. He looks at his giggling dudebro friends. "Told you I know how to get a girl's attention. That and—!"

That's when a full pitcher of beer cascades down Lobo Hamrick's head.

His friends erupt in laughter. Other diners join in, pointing at the suds-soaked ex-jock, who sputters as cold beer drips down his face. Me? I just stand there, empty pitcher in hand, in disbelief over what I've just done. Disbelief—but not regret.

"Damn! She got you good, bruh!" Lobo's friend cackles so hard he nearly chokes.

Lobo jumps up from the table, aggressively knocking his chair to the floor. He's got beer on his clothes and fire in his eyes. I shudder when I look into them, but I don't take a step backward.

Thankfully, Jerry and D'Andre rush into the dining room and to my side. "Lobo, I need you to leave. Go cool down, okay?"

"You need to fire her, Jerry. Look at me!" He angrily snatches a wad of napkins and blots the beer from his face.

I jab a finger in his direction. "Yeah, I dumped a pitcher on your head—after you put your hands on me!"

Jerry nods. "Sounds like you had it coming, hoss. I don't want trouble, Lobo, and if you leave, there won't be any." He gestures toward the front door.

Lobo throws the beer-soaked napkins on the table and stomps away. But halfway to the front door, he turns back to me and scowls.

"This ain't over, bitch."

I slump through the door of our single-wide trailer just after 2 a.m. Man, I'm way too young for my back and feet to ache this much.

The trailer is dark. Maybe Grandma actually went to bed for once, rather than waiting up for me. I sure hope so. I ease my boots off so I can tiptoe to my tiny bedroom when the lamp by Grandma's recliner flicks on.

"'Zat you, Raylene?" Grandma shakes her head to wake herself up, but her eyelids stick together like magnets.

"Yeah, the party people didn't want to go home early tonight. 'S'okay, though. I got a couple hours of OT, and we could use it." As if to underscore the point, I spot the power bill with "PAYMENT OVERDUE" stamped in red block letters on Grandma's TV tray.

So long, new tires. But I pretend I don't see it and fake a smile for Grandma's sake. I'm sure not going to mention my dust-up with Lobo. "What are you doing up, anyway? I figured you and that stud in Trailer 18 might be hooking up while I'm at work!"

Her easy laugh spills across her wrinkled face. "Lord, child! You know I'm seb'ty-three—too old for foolin' around. Besides, the guy in 18 ain't my type. I may be a senior citizen but can still pull a fella with all his own teeth!"

Now, it's my turn to laugh. "I'm sure Channing Tatum will text you soon, Grandma. Now c'mon—we both need to go to bed."

At 5:33 the next evening, I pull into our gravel driveway. My house key in my left hand, I fish my phone out of my back pocket with my right and hit FaceTime.

RING! "Hey, Michael!" His grinning face pops onto my screen. I have to say, he looks pretty hot in a button-up green shirt. My stomach flutters a little.

"Lil' Red! Everything good? I mean... it's okay if you..." His face drops a little, and his eyes widen.

I shake my head and laugh. "No, dummy! I'm not canceling on you. Work just took longer than I thought.

Can you give me an extra 30 minutes to get ready? I mean, it takes us girls a while to look pretty."

His sigh of relief comes through the phone. "Oh... I think you've got that part covered, Lil' Red." Michael turns away from the camera, blushing slightly.

The lights are off in the trailer. Stepping inside, I flick them on... but no Grandma in the living room. Her full bowl of ramen soup is on her TV tray and it's cold. Maybe she's taking a nap. But why didn't she eat her soup?

"Michael, I'll be right back. Just lemme check on Grandma..." I prop the phone up beside the microwave on the kitchen counter.

"Grandma...?" Our bedrooms are on opposite sides of a ridiculously narrow hall off the kitchen/living room combo space. Like the rest of the trailer, the lights are off back here.

I poke my head in the cracked door of her room. She's sitting in the dark looking out her tiny window, her favorite hoodie draped across her hunched shoulders. With her back to the door, her white mop of hair sticks out around the edges of the hood.

"Is everything okay?" I flick the light switch, but the overhead light doesn't come on. Did the power company shut us off? No—the kitchen light is still on. "Why are you sitting in the dark?"

She doesn't turn around. Just mutters something too low for me to hear.

"What's that, Grandma? I can't hear you." I rub my hands on the legs of my shorts. She's normally at the door, ready to meet me with a hug and a laugh. Is she upset about something?

I step inside the cramped bedroom. Grandma's twin bed sits pushed against the left wall, with a small table and lone wooden chair under the window on the opposite side of the room. Framed pictures—mostly from my singing days—cover the wood-paneled walls. Grandma just continues to stare out the window, not turning to face me. My heart sinks—something is wrong. She needs me.

"Come closer." Her voice is so raspy like she's got a cold. But Grandma was fine this morning.

"Grandma, are you sick?" I take a step forward—then pull my foot back. Something's not right here. Call it intuition, but a strange feeling takes residence in my gut. I bite my lower lip. "Is everything okay?"

She leans forward, holding the hoodie tight around her neck. "Lil' Red, c'mere. Hard to talk."

My hand shoots over my mouth to cover a gasp. Grandma is the only person who always calls me "Raylene." Never "Lil' Red."

Leg muscles tensing, I get ready to run.

"If you won't come to me, I'll have to come to you!" And Lobo leaps out of Grandma's chair, her sweatshirt and a white wig dropping to the floor!

He lunges at me. I barely avoid his powerful grip and slip out of the room just inches ahead of frantically grabbing hands.

My heart rate spikes—and not just out of fear for my own safety. What has he done with Grandma? Oh God please let her be okay.

"Told you this wasn't over. You made the biggest mistake of your life when you embarrassed me! The last mistake of your life!"

Lobo grabs the back of my shirt and pulls me down. The wind leaves my lungs as my back slams against the hallway's dingy short carpet.

His weight presses down on me as he continues his assault. A fist, launched with full force, barely misses my bobbing, squirming head. His hand slams into the floor. Lobo just grunts, seemingly oblivious to the pain. He's too strong—if he gets a hold on me, I'll be at his mercy.

So, I reach up and dig my fingers into his face, going straight for his eyes. I don't get lucky enough to blind him, but he leans back. That gives me a chance to scramble to my feet.

I race toward the kitchen. Lobo has to run sideways up the narrow hall, allowing me to get a couple of steps ahead of him. And I've got to stay ahead for a few seconds longer. For Grandma.

But exiting through the front door isn't the answer. I can't outrun a star athlete in an open field. Fight, not flight, is my only salvation.

Just when I reach the kitchen counter, Lobo grabs a handful of my long red hair. He's going to pull me to the ground and... I don't want to finish that thought.

Looking into the eye of my cell phone's camera, I stretch my hand to the wooden knife block and pull out the butcher knife.

Lobo jerks me back. I spin toward him—and lunge forward with the knife, adding his momentum to my own.

The eight-inch blade goes into his chest all the way to the handle.

For a second, he freezes stock still. Did the knife somehow not hurt him? But then he wobbles like a Jenga block tower. Blood bubbles from his lips.

He falls face forward. Lobo Hamrick is dead before he hits the floor.

My hands shake and sobs erupt from my mouth. I... I didn't want to kill him. I'm the girl who catches bugs and sets them outside because I can't bear to squash them. But Lobo gave me no choice. If I hadn't killed Lobo, he would've killed me.

I'm not relieved, though, I can't be until I know Grandma is safe.

I bolt to her bedroom and find her in the closet, gagged and tied up with electrical tape. "Ruh-Raylene! I... I was so scared for you!"

She's shaken up and sore but not hurt. Thank God she's not hurt. Exhaling deeply, I cut her free and she grabs my neck in a tight hug.

Only then can I allow myself to cry. I sit on the floor beside her, sobbing into the shoulder of her warm sweater.

The Sherwood Police Detective's face doesn't change. He sits, arms folded across his chest staring at me.

"So, is that the story you're going with, Lil' Red?"

"It's the truth!" I don't mean to yell at a cop. But the frustration spills out in my voice.

The detective stands and paces the cramped, windowless interrogation room. "Tell you what I think happened. A rich, good-looking guy has an argument with a poor girl. She thinks, Maybe I can play this to my advantage. So she invites him over to her place. Maybe he'll make an apology worth her time. Maybe she can even string him along and get her ticket out of the trailer park."

"But it doesn't go the way she planned. The argument continues, tempers flare, and...well, you know the rest. Tell you what, though—you confess, and I bet we can bump this down to voluntary manslaughter. Good behavior, you're looking at being out in 10 years. What do you think, Lil' Red?"

But thinking is the last thing I'm capable of at the moment. Prison? What would happen to Grandma? My brain whirls and my vision blurs as I hyperventilate. I grab the edge of the table with my one free hand.

"I didn't do anything! Grandma told you the same thing I did!"

The detective just shakes his head. "Or maybe she's lying to protect you. You're her only family, after all."

He's never going to believe a trailer park girl. Not when the dead man is a football star and a rich guy's son.

As I try to regain control of my racing heart, a uniformed cop knocks on the door. The detective waves him off. "Not now, Clemmons."

"Sir, I think you'll want to see this." The police officer steps into the room—and someone is with him.

"Michael!" My vision and brain start to clear; my breathing slows a bit.

He gives me a quick nod but says nothing. Instead, he holds up his phone and plays back the video of our call. A video that shows everything—Lobo pulling me to the floor, his guttural threats, our desperate chase, and finally, me protecting my life by taking his.

I choke back a sob, both at reliving this horrible moment and realizing Michael had come to help.

"Detective, I think this video clearly shows Lil' Red acted in self-defense. If you disagree, I know a lawyer. One who won't hesitate to file a wrongful imprisonment lawsuit." I smile. The sweet, shy woodsman has a backbone, too.

The detective sits down. "No... that won't be necessary. I'll file the report tonight—this case is closed. Ms. Houlde, you are free to go."

He doesn't have to ask me twice. And I'm not alone.

"Lil' Red, I'm sorry I'm just now getting here. When I saw what that creep was trying to do, I called the police and raced to your place. But by the time I got there, they had already taken you to the station. They didn't want to let me see you, but I wouldn't take no for an answer."

I take Michael's hand in mind and lean my head against his arm. "On the contrary, you arrived right on time! If you could give me a lift home, I just want to spend some time with Grandma. And you, too, if you've got it."

One month later...

I've spent hundreds of hours in the Wagon Wheel over the past couple of years. But I've never been quite so nervous in a place that normally is a second home.

"Ladies and gentlemen, one of our own is making her return to our stage tonight! Give it up for Raylene 'Lil' Red' Houlde!"

I tentatively step into the spotlight, then lock eyes with Michael—correction, my boyfriend, Michael. He's brought me a bouquet of flowers, which he unsuccessfully tries to hide in his lap. Of course, he brought Grandma, too. She turns and says, "That's my granddaughter!" to a total stranger at the next table.

Clearing my throat, I step to the microphone, strum a D chord, and sing. An "Oooh!" ripples through the crowd, and my nerves fade. They are replaced by a wave of energy, carried to the stage by the crowd's enthusiastic cheers. Boots scuffing on the dance floor, the amp's reverb, the bright overhead lights, the weight of the guitar in my hand. These sensations flood my senses and fill my soul.

I smile—and this time, it's genuine. I've found my happily ever after.

Once Upon a Mold Spore

By Jade Lebzelter

<u>Content Warnings:</u> This poem contains themes of poverty, mental
  deterioration, and death by fire.

This is the house the witch built
with magic, spells, and tricks.
It wasn't meant to be a home
for famished little kids.
But the witch's stolen jewels were spent,
And landlords came in search of rent.
So Hansel and Gretel fled.
Back to the home where their terrors unfolded,
where gingerbread walls webbed over with mold and
spores that messed with their heads.
Winter stretched longer than taffy drapes.
Cracked sugar windows siphoned out heat.

With tattered clothes and frozen hopes,
Ovens seemed a nice place to be.
Finally warm, as the fierce fire blazed,
Away with the witch, they went in a haze.

A Dove, A Bell, and A Lily

By Erica Duarte

May 1875

Mother said not to go, but Katherine went anyway, curious to see the man who'd suddenly appeared on the other side of the river.

"Katherine! At least put on your shoes! And stay in the trees, don't let him see you!" Macette called from the porch.

There was no way, on this green earth, Katherine was going to stay after learning someone had moved to the valley. A man no less. A young one, she imagined, with dreams and aspirations. A strapping man, in need of a young wife.

Some girls, at eighteen, hated the idea of finding a husband, but not Katherine. She was ready for it. Ready for love, for adventure, for a life outside this lonely vale where nothing ever happened. Where days were spent with her mother doing chores, reading alone, or practicing magic.

The river was icy, like always, but she was scorching with anticipation and barely felt the cold on her hot skin. Scanning the rocks for snakes, she tiptoed through long grass to a meadow clearing where sawing could be heard. Crouching in the sage, she took the hem of her green dress and pulled it over her auburn hair.

In the far corner of the meadow, he'd erected a canvas tent. On the lowest slope, stood a small outhouse, and on the rise there he was, building a log cabin. The springtime sun was climbing, and he was baking in it already. His skin, where he'd rolled up his shirtsleeves, was red. He could use some sun salve.

Katherine made a mental note to find a way to bring him some.

It was difficult to tell what exactly he looked like from this distance, but one thing was certain, he was tall and broad of shoulder, with a slim waste, and arms that hued bark from the logs with practiced ease. He would do well in the field, able to plow and raise good crops, clear pasture for horses and cows. She pictured a small kitchen garden in the lovely sunny spot near where the front door would be. A small fence would look nice and keep out the deer and smaller critters of the woods. And the river was nearby, easily accessible for bathing or having fun. Perhaps playing with children when the time came.

It was a good dream, a fairytale dream of love and marriage, and happily-ever-after. The only dream a magical girl of eighteen, living secluded in this valley, and raised on tender fairy godmother stories, could dream. Katherine picked a small, purple flower, crushed it in the palm of her hand, and whispered words that brought a bit of cloud cover to the man's meadow. A little spell to block out the harsher rays of the sun, to better help him work, to keep him safe. Katherine was enamored by the way he moved, by the quiet things he said to himself, by the way he whistled, and sang songs she had never heard before, hymns from a faraway, mysterious land that spoke of awe and wonder. She watched him until the witching hour when the sky grew orange, and she knew her mother would be wondering. Reluctant, Katherine rose, splashed across the river, and ran through the long field back to her home.

Macette was indeed waiting for her in the kitchen, not idle, but stoking the fire and putting the stew on. "Have you got your fill?"

"He's building a cabin." Katherine plucked a carrot from the sideboard and crunched it between her teeth.

"You've been gone for hours, he couldn't be that interesting to watch." Macette arched her pretty brown brows at her daughter.

"But he is! I can't wait to see him again. To talk to him and know where he came from and why he chose this land?"

"You are too curious for your own good. I've allowed your indulgences because it's always been just us here, but be careful, Little Dove. We don't always get to control our fate." Macette patted her daughter's cheek. "We'll call on him together in a few days. Let him get settled."

"He's got burns from working in the sun. I could make him a salve." Katherine was already pulling together the herbs and ingredients she would need, spooning out delicate carrot seeds and beeswax, putting them in a warm mortar and crushing them with the pestle.

That evening, Katherine slept with her balcony doors of her bedroom open, cocooned in curtains of home-spun, hung to keep the pesky mosquitos out, thinking about the man. Thinking it wasn't all that hard to control one's fate. Thinking it would be fun.

At dawn, she was greedy to see what he was up to. She wound down the wrought iron spiral stair that linked her room to the garden. There she plucked a sprig of peppermint stem to clean her teeth and chase away the taste of sleep. She detoured to the well to quickly drink then ran again through the field, across the river, and up the dewy slope.

The meadow was beautiful this early in the morning. Grass glistened like golden silk, peaking through silver fog. He was just waking up. Stretching near his tent, tending a small fire, and feeding the squirrels his left-over breakfast.

She ventured closer, skirting the meadow, crouching low, she scared a couple of turkeys that squawked and made him turn in her direction. He saw her immediately and Katherine quailed a little at his penetrating gaze. Her confidence skittered until his face lifted in an eager smile.

"Hello!" I was told another family lived nearby. Are you a child of Mrs. Lefay?"

Katherine stood then, and he seemed shocked so see she was not a child, but a young woman close to his own age. "I am," Katherine said as she stepped forward, wanting to see his face. From here she could tell he was handsome, but up close, she was surprised at how devastatingly beautiful he actually was.

Deep-set stormy blue eyes took her in. Long tendril of chestnut hair escaped a strap of leather at his nape. His square jaw was covered with a soft spray of golden fuzz and Katherine couldn't help but smile up at him, feeling completely awe-struck. "What do they call you then?" she asked, wanting to hear his deep voice again.

"Hastings Bell the second, after my uncle," he said, stretching out his hand, "and you, my lady?"

"Katherine Lefay, the first." She mimicked his strange grammar and gingerly took his hand. It was callused and strong, but gentle. "I have a salve that'd keep the sun from burning your arms, if you'd like?" she said, which seemed to interest him.

"I'd like that very much, thank you." His eyes fell to the red skin of his arm then scanned down to his hand still holding hers and pulled away. "It's very nice to meet you, Miss, or is it Mrs.?"

"Miss. I've no husband, yet." She laughed. "And you, Mr. Bell. Are you married?"

"Not yet, Miss. Not yet. But I do have a lot of work I must complete, so I will take my leave." He backed away, the golden hairs of his beard shimmering as he said, "Until we meet again. Farewell, Miss Katherine."

A warm wind blew tendrils of auburn hair across her face, and to Katherine, it was the beginning of her very own, most extraordinary, fairytale.

Katherine walked slowly back to the small Victorian her mother and father built before the war, before he became a soldier and set her and her mother up here, in this hidden glen. Before he went off, never to return. She carried a bucket of water from the well. She didn't want Macette to think she'd openly disobeyed her and made a ruse with the water.

"Thank you, Dove. You're up early."

"Thought I'd get a jump on my chores," Katherine's exuberance was an attempt to hide her real motivation and Macette didn't seem to notice, so she continued on with her work. Half-heartedly milking the cow, weeding the garden, picking the ripe beans, and sweeping the porch. After tea, when a woman from town arrived wanting to purchase a coughing tonic and a love potion, Katherine again stole away.

From the trees, she studied him. He was meticulous in his work. Going over and over the logs, freeing them from every bit of bark. She watched as he ran his fingers atop the smooth surface he'd been working on and a rush of sensation skittered across her skin as if he were touching her. She felt suddenly flushed. Picking the delicate petals off a white Bloodroot blossom, she willed a cool breeze to blow. Looking to the sky, Hastings closed his eyes and let the cool tendrils of her magic dry the perspiration from his brow. She couldn't tear her gaze away but had to when he started to walk right toward her, presumably heading to the river. It was where she would be, if she were not here, on a hot evening such as this. She dashed, quiet as a hare, through the trees and across the river, back to her side of the glen only to stop in her tracks when she chanced a glance back through the thick wooded trees and saw him removing his cloths.

Crouching low with the green hem of her dress covering her hair she watched. She had seen men naked before, the old and dying, the feeble one's who called on Macette to heal or help them pass to the other side, but never before had she seen a man as beautiful as this. Every muscle strong and taught, skin stretched tight over his stomach, and when he dropped his trousers, Katherine's eyes drank him in, filled with delight. He was like the Roman statues in the books Macette made her read. Only more endowed, more thrilling, more everything. The sight sucked the breath from her lungs. She closed her eyes for long seconds and when she opened them again, his eyes were wild on hers. She felt the forest contract. The elements spun as her heart thundered in her breast. As if he could hear it, feel it. She leapt to her feet and fled.

Never to return.

She wanted to return.

She would return.

That night, wearing her dark blue dress, the one that almost matched the color of his stormy eyes, Katherine mixed the nectar of honeysuckle, seeds from a ripe strawberry, and the last petal of a red rose she'd imbued with magic into the sun salve. Then into an earthen jar, she poured the melted liquid and left it to set up beneath the crescent moon.

Rising early the next morning, her dress rumpled from bed, hair as wild as her spirit, she padded quietly down her steps with the potion in hand. She caught him at breakfast, by the fire, looking bedraggled and beautiful. Again he was feeding the squirrels. Stepping out of the trees with purpose. She no longer felt the need to hide.

The sight of his shy smile, a blush nipping his cheeks, galvanized her. "I brought you a salve to keep the sun from burning your skin."

"Katherine," he said, his voice a throaty rumble.

Heat coursed through her veins, a deep primordial magic that begged for release. She gave it to the wind. Trees swayed and leaves spun. Her dress clung to her legs. The flame of his small fire ignited, fueled by her released magic.

"Looks like a storm's headed this direction." Hastings scanned the sky.

Katherine laughed. "Not today."

As the wind died down, she sat in front of him, close enough to feel his breath. "May I?" she reached for his arms. His eyes darkened. She rolled up his sleeves. Tiny blisters had formed over red, raw skin. "This will help," she said, gently rubbing in the salve.

He sucked in a breath when her fingers lightly touched his and she knew, in that moment, she had him. For several minutes they sat like that, her fingers roaming over his skin. His eyes searching her face. "You're very beautiful, Miss Katherine," he said, his voice a whisper, "and kind, but I—" His gaze drifted over her shoulder.

Turning, Katherine saw Macette sitting perfectly put together atop their dappled mare, cantering toward them. Hastings pulled his arms away. Rolling down his shirtsleeves, he stood, cleared his throat, but said nothing more.

Straightening her back, Katherine watched her mother dismount elegantly, in a practiced way she had mastered years ago. Macette was a master of many things. A powerful witch, she was a force to be reckoned with, and yet, kept it well hidden.

"Hello, Mr. Bell. I am Macette Lefay. It's so nice to finally meet you. I see you've met my little dove, Katherine."

The scent of rose filled the air and magic rolled in waves around them. Katherine gathered it and used it to calm the electrified current that was her mother.

"Yes, Mrs. Lefay, I have. She's been kind enough to come to my aid. I had not realized the sun would be so magnanimous here. The summer is not so hot, where I am from."

"And where is that, Mr. Bell?" Macette's mouth tilted in the hint of a smile and Katherine could tell her mother was having fun making poor Hastings ill-at ease. "England, Mum. A village called Uffington in Berkshire."

"And what brings you to this far, forgotten place?" Macette's voice was a gossamer sound mixing with the early morning bird-song.

"It's a long story, I'm afraid." Hastings's small self-effacing laugh, was slow, cautious. Katherine looked at him. He clasped his hands, but did not look away from Macette.

"Well, we've all the time in the world to get to know one another, Mr. Bell. We are neighbors after all. And by the looks of it, you plan on settling down as a young man should, but this place, so far gone and such a long way from your home, it must feel quite overwhelming at times for one so young. But you seem to be doing well."

"I am, Mum. I find this land to be, more myself than I am." Hastings said simply, and Katherine gasped when his eyes met hers for the briefest second.

That line. He'd read Wuthering Heights.

Macette lifted her chin, looking at him kindly. "I can see it must indeed feel that way, but take care, this place has a wild heart and at times can be uncertain. If you should ever need assistance, please feel free to call on me, and you must come tonight for supper to tell us more about how you came to be here. We don't get many visitors and stories are always a welcome evening."

"Thank you, Mum. This evening would be most agreeable."

"Come now, Dove, let us leave Mr. Bell to his work. I foresee a lovely cottage in his future."

"Yes, a lovely cottage." Katherine beamed, overjoyed about the prospect of a whole evening spent with this beautiful, intriguing man.

Katherine spent the rest of the day getting ready. Dusting the house, sweeping the porch, making bread, all while Macette butchered a rabbit for a hearty stew. Then, she took her time bathing in the river behind the house, dressing in her favorite yellow dress, and pinning up her hair. Finally, as the sun began to dip behind the horizon, Katherine lit the lamps, hands jittery with anticipation. The oil infused with Macette's special blend of lavender created a calming aura. When the knock on the door came, Macette flashed her daughter a sidelong glance, one that said, no magic, and then opened the door.

"Mr. Bell, so nice to see you again. Please, come in." Macette, polished in manners, set Katherine instantly at ease. With a deep breath in, she smoothed down her dress.

"Thank you, Mrs. Lefay. I'm sorry I don't have much to offer, but these grow in the field and are quite lovely." He handed Macette a small bouquet of orange daylilies and then handed another one to Katherine.

Katherine sighed, touching the tips of the lilies, and bringing them to her nose. They were fresh and earthy and in them she saw herself in Hasting's arms followed quickly by an undercurrent of sorrow. But just as quickly as it had come, it was gone as if it had never been.

Macette touched Katherine's arm, handed her the bouquet. "Thank you, Mr. Bell. Please sit, make yourself comfortable. Supper is nearly ready."

"It smells delicious, and I've not had fresh bread in an age."

Katherine moved around the room, put the flowers in a vase, and smiled over at Hastings as she sat across from him at the table.

The beer was a strong brew and Hastings seemed to enjoy it, drinking his fill, and eating two helpings of stew with nearly a whole loaf of bread.

Macette kept the conversation light and Katherine hung on his every word. "While attending Rugby school,

I met a man called Thomas Hughes who spoke of this land in great, aspiring detail, and I soon came to realize emigrating to America was the best course of action for me. You see, my brother, Robert, will inherit my family's estate, but as a second son, I'm free to find my own way in this world."

"Sounds poetic," Macette mused.

He bowed his head to hide a smile. "I suppose I am a hopeless poetic."

"As am I, Mr. Bell." The knowledge made Katherine's heart pound harder, but she kept her voice steady.

"Please, call me Hastings."

"I will. It is a suitable name."

Macette glanced between them, a hint of cautious amusement in her eyes. "Do you think your love of books will translate to the field? I assume agriculture will be your next endeavor, will it not?"

"Absolutely, I was raised to be a gentleman, but I strive to engage myself in a trade. There is nothing for me in Britain, but here, I see this place as my opportunity to forge a new way."

"Poetic and passionate, two fine qualities. Hard work will come easily indeed to a young man such as yourself. And will anyone be joining you out here?" Macette asked matter-of-fact which had Hastings averting his gaze.

"Mother, I fear you embarrass our new friend with such personal talk."

"No, Miss Katherine. I only just, it's been a while since I had such fine food and strong beer. I'm afraid, I'm not worthy of such gracious company." Something wistful and yearning was in his stare as he watched Katherine rise from the table.

"We cannot send you off without a cup of tea." Katherine's face filled with delight as she scooped, and poured, and served.

"I must insist." Macette agreed.

Hastings held a look in his eyes, like there was something he wanted to say, but didn't. He simply nodded. Then sipped until the tea was gone and took his leave.

As soon as the door closed behind him, Katherine hastily swept up the cup, only to have her thoughts scatter. "Mother, do you see it. Do you see? Mother?" A grin that couldn't be contained spread across her face as she read the leaves that clearly showed a dove, a bell, and a lily.

Macette leaned over her shoulder to look. "I see your fates are entwined, but not in the way you may perceive, Little Dove."

The words Macette spoke were left to hang in the air. Katherine picked up the vase of flowers and carried them up to her room. Electricity crackled through the night, mixed with the scent of lilies. Katherine lay awake in bed unable to stop her thoughts from thinking on and on and on about Hastings. His lovely mind. His graceful face. His strong body. His stormy eyes. All of him finding a way into the deepest depths of her soul and taking root. She would for all time remember Hastings just how he was on this night. Happy, passionate, free.

When the sun rose, she plucked a sprig of mint and crossed the river to where he was, whispering into the wind to stop time and speed up the work on his cottage.

"Sunrise to sunset, hands hard at work, complete this cottage, he has begun before the day is done."

The trees were felled one by one, the bark reduced to dust. He moved like the insect buzz, buzz, buzzing from tree, to wall, to timbered roof.

Hastings closed his eyes and brightened when he saw her standing near his completed home. Hair blowing in the wind, bathed in the orange witch light of the setting sun. She called to the butterflies and swarms filled the meadow.

He turned, arms reaching out to them. "I never knew this place could hold so much wonder." He looked confused, but rightly so.

Katherine giggled, taking his hand. "This is part of the fun," she said and felt him tremble.

"What have you done?" His eyes widened at same time his fingers tightened around hers.

"Walk with me." She led and he followed her into the forest. Not yet ready to reveal her secret but close enough to take him to the stone circle that surrounded the sacred spring. Steam rose from the water in clouds around the clearing.

"Katherine." Hastings's fingers were warm and steady against her chin. "Katherine," he said again, this time, sounding breathless. His voice deep and gravely sent shivers down her spine.

On tiptoes, she reached up and kissed him. Eyes wide open, she held her breath. His lips parted. He pulled her against his hard body and hers cracked at the seams. He took his time, distracted by her curves. Long, chaotic kisses. His hands entwined in her hair. Breathe a moan.

"Katherine," he said half gasp, all heated pleas. He stared down at her as if she held the key to his happiness, to him, to everything. And a storm erupted inside her. She had never kissed a man like this. So wanton and bold. His fingers bruising her hips, holding her close to deepen the kiss and she became the thunder following the lightning. Chasing his need until he pulled away breathing hard, eyes holding the same faint trace of surprise as hers. He fell quiet. Traced her swollen lips with the tip of his thumb. Her heart beat against her sternum. "What is this place?"

"Everywhere and nowhere," Katherine murmured. "Ancient and sacred."

"And who are you?"

Katherine swallowed, searched his eyes. Storm and wind and lightning, a mirror of her own. His heart pounded under her palm. Unable to say the word, she led him back to his meadow. Up the stairs to his cottage that was now filled as if it had been lived in for years, with a wood burning stove, a table and chairs, a cupboard, and large four poster bed. She laid him down and touched his eyes. "Sleep," she whispered, letting the heavy magic dissipate. She too felt tired from the day's exertion.

She stood, but he grabbed her wrist and losing her balance she fell onto the bed. "From the moment I saw you, I haven't been able to stop thinking of you." Then his hand fell to his side, and he was deep asleep.

Part of her wanted to curl up against his side, another part of her wondered how much of this was the magic, and a third hoped it was just him, feeling as she felt, hopelessly and irrevocably in love.

"I'd ask where you've been, but I know." Macette eyed her daughter, suspiciously, as soon as she walked in. "Do you think it wise to use so much magic in pursuit of your own happiness?"

"It's not just mine. It's for him as well."

Macette sighed heavily. "You barely know him?"

"I did it to give us time together." Katherine yawned, heading for the stairs and her bed. "Don't worry mother, I know what I'm doing."

"Are you sure about that, Little Dove?" Macette frowned, but Katherine was already halfway up the stairs, the words barely reaching her ears.

Sleep was bliss, heavy and uninterrupted by dreams. Birdsong woke Katherine. It was late morning. Stretching, she pushed sweat-dampened hair off her forehead. Sometime in the night, mid-summer heat had settled like a quilt over the valley in an intricate pattern. Macette was in the garden, tending crops that weighed heavy on delicate vines.

With a basket of biscuits and butter, Katherine emerged from the house refreshed. She picked a handful of cherry tomatoes, scanned the fruitful garden. "What's happened?"

"It seems the energy of the valley has shifted. You've also been asleep for several days. Heavy magic does that, if you recall."

"I do." Katherine plucked several crisp cucumbers. Admired their quality. "See, mother, it's meant to be."

She stepped lightly, hugged Macette, and set off. "I'm going for a picnic."

"Just be careful, Little Dove. If you need me, call out my name," Macette urged as Katherine skipped through the overgrown field, her mother's voice reaching her in a whisper.

Knocking on his door, she eagerly waited and waited some more. She knocked again then tried the latch. It was unlocked. "Hastings?" She poked her head in and was taken aback at the sight of him on the bed. He was bare to his waste, sound asleep on his stomach, his head propped atop his folded arms. His breath moved his strong back and the muscles of his shoulders. "Hastings?" Katherine set down her basket and kneeled beside the bed. She ran a single finger along the bridge of his perfect nose. "Hastings, wake up, my sweet."

He shifted, his eyes blinked open, pupils blown wide with sleep.

"Hastings, it's me, Katherine."

"Katherine," his voice was low and deep and warmed the pit of her stomach. "Katherine," he said again almost disbelieving. "I had the strangest dream." His eyes moved then, to take in the cottage, the ceiling, his hand fisted in the linen beneath him. He sat up. "I dreamt, I had only just got here, had only just begun building."

Katherine pressed her lips together to suppress a smile, "Dear Hastings, let me make you some tea. I brought breakfast." She turned to light the fire and put the kettle on. She heard him moving around behind her, cautioned a glance as he pulled on trousers and a white shirt. He came up behind her and she felt weightless.

"You shouldn't be here, alone with me."

"Why is that?" She breathed, unable to turn around to face him. Was he going to ask her to leave? Had all the feelings been in her heart alone?

"It's not proper, your reputation."

"My reputation," she giggled, "Hastings, there's no one here to see."

"Katherine."

The way he said her name heartbreakingly soft and eager, raised the hairs on her skin.

"Hastings?"

"Katherine—"

"Was I also in your dream?"

His answer was a tug on her sleeve, turning her, wrapping her in his arms, his nose in her hair, nuzzling her neck. But the joyful embrace also felt sad until he whispered, "Always. You are always in my dreams."

Scorching heat consumed her. Air, she needed air. A fierce wind blew open the door, finding a way in. It startled him. It cooled her. She closed her eyes. Sunk deeper into his tight embrace. "Hastings, does this mean, we'll be married now?"

"It's all happened so fast, but my time here has felt slow. I know not the day nor the month. I must send word to my brother." He pulled away from her, reached for his jacket and hat and was gone.

Time stood still. She felt cold without him. Shivering, she walked outside and sat in the sun. Gazing out over the meadow, she blew a kiss to the wind and tiny purple flowers bloomed. After a while, her bones thawed, and she returned to help Macette in the overgrown garden.

They were busy for several days, picking and canning, putting up food for the winter. Katherine immersed herself in the task like never before, delighting in the idea that she would spend the winter with Hastings. Married and doing all the things young married people in love did. Just the thought made heat pool between her legs. Would he be gentle? Kind? Would he know how to please a woman? Yes, of course, and if not, she would show him.

Macette rapped lightly on the ground with a stick. "And what would you be thinking about, looking like a cat that caught the blue jay?"

"He wants to marry me, Mother? He went to town to send word to his brother." Macette's smile widened. "Of course he does. And he is lucky to have you. He seems kind. Do you find him to be so when it is just the two of you?"

"Yes. He feeds the squirrels. It is a funny habit. He should snare the squirrels and eat them for breakfast. But he loves their company."

Macette smiled, then caught a sound on the wind, and turned to see what it was she heard. "I think your young man has returned and he has company."

Unable to keep from grinning, Katherine put down her basket, hiked up her skirts, and ran through the field.

"Be careful, Little Dove," she heard her mother whisper.

At his cottage, she slowed, used the wind to cover all sound, and slowly crept up to an open window. She wanted to know who else was here, before making her presence known.

A man was with Hastings. His voice was similar, but deeper, older sounding.

"Brother," he was saying. "You must see reason. A promise got you this land, bought the supplies you needed to build this cottage, now you have to honor that promise."

"Robert, please. I can't—"

"You MUST!" Robert interrupted. "Don't allow yourself to be bewitched by a nobody!"

Katherine's hand flew to her mouth. Did he mean her? No. Surely not. Hastings would tell him. She waited and waited some more, but his words never came. She crept quietly around to the front door, smoothed down her dress, ran her fingers through wild hair, and knocked.

"Hastings, may I come in?" she questioned when he answered the door, her eyes moving past him to his brother seated at the table.

"Katherine, Little Dove," his use of her mother's pet name for her sent shivers down her arms, "not at the moment. I have business with my brother. I'll come find you."

Katherine blinked up at him, her eyes hot with unshed tears. "Of course, my sweet." She took a breath, backed off the porch, and returned to help her mother in the garden.

For three days, she waited. Macette looking at her with a sad expression. "He'll come for me," Katherine said, turning away, blinking. "He said he would."

"Of course, Little Dove. Here, drink this."

Katherine drank down the tonic and for a moment felt at peace, but it was short lived. She stared out the window. Wishing, calling to the wind to bring her her love, but he did not come. Biting her lip she steeped rose and lavender blossoms imbued with her kisses in three drops of orange oil and added water to make a cologne. Then, as the sun sank into the western sky, she set out across the field and through the river to his perfect cottage, where her own tiny garden would be one day, just outside the front door, with a fence to keep out the deer and tiny rodents. To the porch where he would sit and feed the squirrels. She knocked and waited and was not shocked when Robert answered the door.

Katherine smiled prettily; she'd worn her berry print dress, brushed and styled her wild hair, put on her high lace boots. "Good evening, you must be Hasting's brother, Robert. I am Katherine."

Robert pursed his lips. "It's a pleasure to meet you Miss Katherine, but Hastings is not here."

"I have a gift for him. If you would please..." She handed over the package she'd wrapped in muslin and tied with a vine of ivy, speaking slowly, pronouncing every word, as Hasting did.

His brother scowled, took the package, and shut the door. Cold wind blew, invaded her chest, pressed against her sternum. She snuck to the window, watched Robert move around the cottage. He stopped before the fireplace, built up a fire, added kindling, and logs, waited until the flames danced shadows on the hard lines of his face, then threw her present in. The cologne exploded on impact. Katherine's vision blurred and a scream escaped her lips. "No!"

Robert turned and she fled. The waxing moon rose as Katherine sat on her balcony, letting the mosquitos swarm, staring out at the distant, empty forest. Sometime in the days past, the cicada's had emerged, their pulsing buzz an insidious sound, matched the ache in her heart. Thunder rumbled long and low overhead and she was overwhelmed with the urge to reach out to him. Pulling magic from the light of the moon, she chanted into the wind. "Brother Robert, leave him be. Let sweet Hastings come to me."

Raindrops hit the dry ground, steamed in the hot night air. Leaning her head against the cool iron railing, she waited and waited and waited some more. Until a dense fog rose and out of it, he was there.

"Katherine," Hastings said, winding up the spiral stair to face her. "I can't stay long. He's gone to town but will be back."

"Why do you do as he asks? And not follow your own heart? Is that not why you left England?"

His eyes were full of some unrecognizable thing, something fragile, delicate. "I am bound by duty to him, to my family, too—"

"To yourself?" Katherine interjected. "To me?" she added softly.

He searched her eyes for a breath then he nodded, "Yes. I want to be."

"He said I was nobody." Her voice turned dreadful, and she swallowed hard, tears prickling her eyes. "Am I nothing to you, not the right kind of person to be in your world?"

"No, that's not it. You are perfect." His voice was low and rough, making her insides like the storm building around them. "I have never met anyone like you. Never knew this, this feeling of being so utterly bewitched."

"Because I am a witch," she said plainly.

Terror and intrigue flitted across the features of his face. His hand cupped her cheek, his thumb caressed her lips. "You must be," he leaned in close. "Because I can't stop myself. I don't know how to not do this." He kissed her hard and fast then slow and deep.

Katherine was suffocated by how much she wanted him. Climbing into his lap, she dragged her teeth over his swollen lips. Giving herself over completely to the sensation of him holding her, pressing her hand to his heart, feeling the thundering beat that matched her own. She tingled with greedy excitement. She pulled him to his feet, led him to her bed.

Pulled the homespun curtains, kicked up the sound of the cicadas, to cocoon them in privacy and noise so they could do whatever it was they wanted to do. "Hand to hand. Bound blood and bone," she chanted under her breath as magic swirled between them.

"When you make those sounds," he growled into her ear. Kissed her neck. Intertwined their fingers. She vibrated with excitement. Heat filled her body, cheeks flushed and for a sudden desperate second, she thought she was dreaming, but he was here, and she was his, bound now and forever with a witch's magic and a lover's kiss.

Morning dawned gray and still. The only sounds were the cicadas. He was beautiful in sleep. Lips parted, eyes closed, breath slow and languid. She snuggled up next to him and he pulled her in, tucking her close to his body.

"Good morning," she whispered.

"It's not morning," his voice was gravelly with sleep.

The corner of her mouth lifted. "It is the best kind of morning."

"Come with me," he breathed. "We'll tell him together."

"Tell who what?" she giggled.

He held her down, kissed her nose her cheeks, bit the lobe of her ear. "Tell Robert, you will be my wife."

Her racing heartbeat thrummed in her chest as he kissed her and kissed her and kissed her.

Dragging themselves from the bed, she pulled him to the river to bath and dress. Glimpsing Macette out of the corner of her eye, she saw her mother casually sitting, quietly hidden, tying up tomatoes with a sad smile touching her lips.

Katherine felt the pin prick of sadness too. This was it. She would leave her mother's home. But she would not go far. She brushed out her hair and pined it in place. Chose her most beautiful white lace and linen dress but left her feet bare. Together they walked hand in hand through the field, across the river, and up the small rise to the cottage in the meadow.

At the door they exchanged a glance, breathed a shared breath. Katherine trembled and Hastings squeezed her hand. "It will be alright."

Lifting the latch, they entered. Hastings dropped her hand, and her heart tumbled down the walls of her chest.

Cold infiltrated her bones. Robert was there, but also seated at the table was a young, very beautiful woman.

"Hastings?" the woman questioned, upon seeing him, her eyes darting from him to Katherine and back again.

"Robert," Hastings growled.

Robert narrowed his eyes, "Brother, I brought your betrothed, as you always intended. This is her land, after all, and you made her a promise."

Katherine swallowed, ice in her blood, gaze unfocused.

"Hastings?" the woman's lips quivered. "Who is this?"

Hastings stepped away, leaving Katherine to stand alone. "Lily. My Lily, I–I—"

"Who is this?" she asked again.

"Nobody," he said, and time stopped.

A rose gold engagement ring shined in the dappled light on Lily's left hand and Katherine shuttered. She looked from Robert, to Lily, to Hastings. His stormy eyes told her everything. He looked calm, but he wasn't calm. My Lily, he'd said.

No, she blinked. No. It couldn't be. He was tied to her and yet. She reached for his hand, but he pulled away. She felt lightheaded. Needed air to breath. Wind, she thought but Robert was in her way, making excuses for his brother.

"It's been a long time coming. Perhaps you should leave."

Hastings cleared his throat. Robert put his hand on her back, and she recoiled spinning to face him. One look and he backed away.

"We are bound blood and bone," she whispered but Hastings would not meet her gaze. Staring at her palms, stomach in knots, she backed away, walked slowly down the steps, down the dewy slope, across the river, and through the field, flowers wilting in her wake.

Reaching the garden she sank down to the earth, trying to break through the crushing, cold in her chest, but her breathing remained shallow and uneven, her eyes a fixed stare at nothing. He'd said she was nobody. She was nothing to him, not good enough to be part of his world. It was nothing for him to disregard her. He'd done it without hesitation when faced with his true intended.

Lily.

The trembling started in her hands. She clutched her arms to her chest, unable to control the cold that engulfed her. Ice in her blood, in her bones. The vegetables withered and died on the vines, turning black. Nobody. How could that be? After all the beautiful things that came before. It was impossible. He was lying. He would return to her. He would marry her. "Hastings, please, please come to me. My heart is breaking." The sun disappeared, and still she sat in the garden, waiting for him to come, but he never came. She laid her head on the cold, cold ground and wept into the dirt until the veil of sleep claimed her.

She woke with Macette kneeling next to her and a quilt warming her cold body. "Your tears made it snow, Little Dove. Do you want to tell me what happened?"

"His Lily came," her voice trembled, and more snow fell.

"I am so, so sorry, my Little Dove. I know this hurts, but I promise, you will find love again."

Katherine shook her head, clutched the quilt around her shoulders, and stood on shaky legs. "He loves me. He's lying to them. Why? Why would he do that?"

"We all have many reasons for the things we do, many of which are incomprehensible to people we love."

Katherine's jaw tensed and she looked out over the snow-white field considering her mother's words. No. She would not accept this. Her gaze sharpened as she strode through the winter landscape of her vale, across the frigid river, and emerged on the other side where his land remained cloaked in summer.

Laughter rose and fell on the warm breeze as she crept up to the tree line outside the cottage. Lily was sitting in a rocking chair on the porch sewing and Hastings... Hastings was plowing the perfect, little square of land, near the front door where he too thought a garden should be. Silent tears rolled down her face as she watched them until the sun fractured the western sky in shards of pink and violet. Lily stood and went inside. Hastings wiped his brow. And Katherine stepped out of the trees.

He saw her immediately and immediately strode in her direction. Katherine waited until he was almost to her before she turned and motioned him to follow.

He did.

She took him into the woods to the stone circle, to the sacred spring where her magic was most potent. When she stopped, she was unable to face him. "I want to know why?" she finally said through the soreness in her throat.

Hastings stepped closer. She could feel him, his warmth through the heavy quilt close behind her. The buzzing cicadas roared in her ears.

"I promised her. She has no one else. Her father is dead and if I don't marry her, her fortunes will be——" he stopped short, but Katherine understood. He wanted her money. "You'd rather have her money than me?"

"There's more to it than that. You couldn't possibly understand. You've never been in society. You are blessedly ignorant . . ." He went on and on and Katherine felt stupid and small. "I was born into a different world, I have duties that are hard and harsh that I must accept as my reality."

She turned to face him. "And I am nobody."

He looked at her intently, his eyes never leaving hers. "No, Katherine, you are my beating heart, but I can't marry you. Please, accept it. Please, forget about me. Forget I ever existed."

Hot tears pricked her eyes, and she swallowed them down. A full moon was rising. Katherine gathered it's magic into herself. "You have a choice. You can choose me. Please, choose me." The quilt fell from her shoulders as she reached for his beautiful face, her fingers brushing the fine golden hair on his cheeks.

He pushed her hands away, his eyes trained on the ground. "No Katherine, I can't. Lily and I were married yesterday evening," he said, and she shattered.

Blood pounded in her ears. Magic shimmered. She fixated on the moon, magic consuming her. "Monster," she chanted. "You are a monster, bound blood and bone, everything you are, and everything you will become. I tie you to this land, to me, to the inescapable moon. Forever shall it be."

A knife appeared in her hand. In one swipe, Katherine cut her palm then slashed across Hasting's chest. Blood seeped from a wound above his heart, and she began to chant again, faster and faster until bathed in silvery moonlight, he shifted into the monster she saw him as, a creature of inexorable ugliness, fur and teeth and claws. A woman screamed.

Katherine's head snapped to the sound.

Lily.

The monster leaped and was on her in a second. Tearing at her dress. Goddess above, what had she done. The air cleared but panic rose.

"Mother! Mother!"

Macette stepped out of the shadows. Took in the seen in a single glance and froze everything. "What has happened?"

Katherine, crumpled in on herself, clutched at the quilt on the ground, shaking.

"Katherine," Macette's voice was stern.

"I–I cursed him." The words quivered out of her. "Change him back, Mother. I didn't mean to. I didn't mean to. I was angry he married Lily even though he loves me. He loves me. He loves me."

Macette knelt next to her daughter, wrapped her arms around her. "Little Dove, we do not get to choose our fate. He made his decision, and you made yours, and some things cannot be undone."

Katherine shook her head. "What will happen to them?"

"I will try to lessen it." Macette looked around, dipped water from the sacred spring. Poured it on the monster and Lily. "Blessed mother, hear my plea, take this curse away from he, when the moon is full, give it back, but just one night is what I ask."

Wind swirled as the whispered words were chanted over and over until the monster, Hastings, saw what he had done. He released Lily who panted on the ground, eyes wide with terror and disappeared into the forest.

"What was that?! What did you do!" Lily screamed, scrambling to her feet.

Macette approached her as if she were a wounded animal, magic wafting in waves all around. Katherine took it in and created calm.

Lily physically softened. "He'll return in the morning, a man again. But by the light of the full moon, he will be this." Macette's voice was a primordial whisper, a soft chant to magic the innocent woman who was now forever tied to the monster, to the man, to the witch, and to the land.

Days passed, weeks, the sun shifted in the sky. Summer turned to fall and fall to winter and Katherine knelt on the ground near a tree by the sacred spring erecting an altar. She was performing a memory charm using heavy magic. Digging a hole, gathering the life force of the earth, she planted a sapling heart-leaf birch, a tuft of roughish witchgrass, and a single lily of the valley. Pulling in the magic of the waning moon, she felt her skin tingle and imagined a time in the future when perhaps the magic would find a way to return, but for now she wished it gone.

Gone from herself and gone from all blood kin who came after. She swept a hand over her eyes and all knowledge of witchcraft and curses and men who were monsters disappeared from her mind. Everything, but the stormy eyes of gentle young man, laughing at her dinner table as he told her the story of how he came to be in this place with his young wife, Lily.

The Fairest of them All

By Maple R. Nowark

Lady Fair's return to the kingdom was a grand celebration. The townspeople held a parade in her honor, singing praises for their beloved princess who had overcome such darkness. Her gentle gaze touched even the coldest hearts, radiating warmth and hope to all who gathered to welcome her. But there was something that lingered beneath her smile, a festering dread that gnawed at her soul. As if a shadow clung to her heart, filling her with an unshakeable sense of unease, even as she stood at the center of her kingdom's adoration. In every laugh, every empowering cheer, she felt hollow, something fleeting, as though the celebration around her was a mere illusion teetering on the brink of shattering.

The dread was a silent specter that haunted her in the quiet moments, creeping up on her in the stillness of her chambers. Every time she made attempts to retire to her chamber, she could feel a ruinous, oppressive presence fill the room. She could see shadows stretching across her bed, creeping closer with each passing hour, as she lay down. As she drifted into sleep, her dreams turned to nightmares, vivid and unrelenting.

Lady Fair found herself wandering through an endless, twisted forest where the trees towered like silent, menacing sentinels. Shadows gathered around her feet, pulling her deeper into the murk undergrowth, her steps growing heavy, as though invisible hands were trying to drag her down. Faces peered from between the trees, hollow eyes watching her, filled with malice and resentment. She tried to turn away, but the forest shifted, trapping her, forcing her onward as her pulse quickened with terror. And always, in the distance, she heard a voice—cold, familiar, beckoning her toward something inevitable, a fate she could feel tightening around her like an invisible chain. The voice grew louder with each nightmare, taunting her, reminding her that her victory over the dark queen was not complete. Her stepmother's spirit clung to her, an unshakable shadow within her mind, binding her to a curse she could not escape.

Lady Fair woke each morning drenched in sweat, her heart pounding. No matter how far she had come, the shadows of her past loomed ever closer, a haunting reminder that the darkness she presumed defeated might still consume her. She hears her stepmother's chilling laughter echoing in empty corridors, her whispers creeping into Lady Fair's thoughts, venomous suggestions that slowly poison her mind. They will betray you.

They're all the same. Show them the power they feared in her. The voice urges her to look deeper into her own reflection. Her moments of clarity grew fewer, replaced by bouts of paranoia and anger. She finds herself lashing out at the servants for minor slights--a missing shoe, a broken plate--and though she hears their fearful whispers, a dark satisfaction fills her at the sight of trembling hands and lowered gazes, leaving her face twisted into a malevolent smile.

The townsfolk soon notice the change, too, gossiping about how the kind, gentle princess has turned cold, sinister. Some speak in hushed tones of a curse; others dare to wonder aloud if Lady Fair was ever truly freed from the queen's spell.

One evening, she receives a letter from an old ally of her father's, a seasoned advisor who once helped lead the kingdom. He expresses concern for her wellbeing, urging her to remember her father's legacy of compassion and wisdom. The letter, meant to console, only feeds her rage. She tears it to shreds, her hands shaking with fury, feeling her stepmother's laughter ripple through her mind like a sinister echo.

They don't respect you, the voice hisses. They think you're weak. Show them what it means to be a true ruler.

Lady Fair's eyes grow in fury, she demands a meeting with her council, staring them down with a coldness that chills the room. Her voice, once warm, is now edged with iron, each word a threat cloaked in formality. She declares her intent to impose stricter laws, to stamp out any whisper of disloyalty. The council members exchange wary glances, but no one dares

challenge her.

Late that night, alone in her chambers, Lady Fair feels a strange pull toward the mirror. Her reflection is barely recognizable now; her eyes are shadowed, her cheeks hollow, her expression almost cruel. She leans closer, the candlelight flickering, casting shadows that twist her face into a mask of malice. And then, from the depths of the mirror, her stepmother's face emerges, faint but unmistakable, her eyes alight with triumph.

"Look at you, my sweet," her stepmother's voice coos, smooth and mocking. Her figure looms behind Lady Fair, caressing her cheek with her ghostly hands, "You're just like me."

Lady Fair's skin crawls, a creeping horror at the realization that she has become her stepmother's reflection. But even as a part of her recoils, another part feels exhilarating. A dark and wrathful energy she cannot deny. The power, the control, the fear she commands... it all feels intoxicating.

Unable to tear herself away, she watches as her stepmother's reflection leans forward, smiling with a familiar, malevolent smirk. "Don't fight it," the reflection whispers closely in her ear. "This was always your fate."

"I am nothing like you," Lady Fair hisses, her voice barely above a whisper, but the conviction wavers, hollow and weak. The reflection only laughs, a low, chilling sound that fills the room, crawling up her spine.

"Oh, but you are, my sweet," her stepmother murmurs, her voice a dark lullaby weaving through Lady Fair's thoughts. "Do you think kindness alone could ever rule a kingdom? Do you think innocence could command respect, inspire fear? No, my dear." Her stepmother's voice sharpens, filling Lady Fair's head until it's almost deafening. "Weakness is a luxury you cannot afford. Remember, power is the only truth, and now... now it has fallen right into your hands."

With a sickening thrill, Lady Fair feels the truth in those words coil around her heart, like a snake killing its prey. The memories of the pitying looks, the whispers of doubt behind her back, the dismissive glances from her council, all the moments when her kindness was seen as weakness. A hot, unfamiliar anger rises in her, mingling with a twisted sense of vindication, a need to seize the respect she has craved. As if reading her thoughts, her stepmother's ghostly form leans closer, her voice now a soft yet piercing whisper in her ear. "They're afraid of you now. And fear, my darling, is loyalty." The ghostly fingers brush her throat, a cool caress that sends shivers through her, though a part of her feels drawn to the embrace, drawn to the power it promises. Listen to my hum and fall to my command.

Lady Fair's hand rises to her throat where her stepmother's touch had been, feeling the lingering ghostly fingers on her skin. She stares into the mirror, into the reflection that is both hers and not hers. Her once-soft face now holds a severity, her eyes sharp and calculating, her lips curved into a faint, sinister smile she doesn't recognize.

"They **will** respect me. They **will** fear me." The words leave her lips with an unnatural ease, as if someone else were speaking them for her.

In that moment, something shifts within her, and Lady Fair feels herself embracing the darkness that has taken root. She stands taller, her shoulders set with newfound resolve, her eyes reflecting a fierce, unyielding determination. She no longer shies away from her reflection but studies it with a cold, unsettling calm. Her stepmother's face gradually fades from the mirror, yet the smirk remains. Not as a haunting shadow, but as her own expression, her lips curling in a subtle, knowing smile.

The next morning, the castle feels her transformation like a dark wind sweeping through the halls. Finally, the Prince confronts her, his voice filled with a mixture of desperation and sorrow. "What has happened to you, Lady Fair?" he asks, his eyes pleading. "Where is the kind, innocent girl I married?"

But Lady Fair only feels a surge of anger, the accusation piercing through her like a blade. She can barely contain the venom that rises within her, twisting her thoughts with suspicion. Innocent? Kind? The words sound hollow now, like a distant echo from a past life. She feels her lips curl in disdain, her heart hardened by a sense of betrayal that gnaws at her. Somewhere in the depths of her mind, her stepmother's voice whispers encouragement, feeding the flames of her wrath.

"You think me weak, don't you?" Lady Fair sneers, her voice cutting through the air like ice. "You think me a fool, the sweet girl you can manipulate and control."

Her gaze sharpens, and her voice lowers to a dangerous whisper. "You have betrayed me, all of you have."

The prince steps back, stunned. "Lady Fair, this isn't you," he insists, a tremor in his voice. "You're becoming—"

But she cuts him off, her voice rising with a cruel authority she barely recognizes as her own. "Silence!" she snaps, her eyes cold and unforgiving. "You will pay for your betrayal." She gestures to the guards who stand by, shocked and uncertain. Her next words seal her transformation, her command echoing through the silent hall.

"Take him to the dungeons," she says, each word a ruthless pronouncement of fate. She looms over him, her eyes cold and unwavering as the prince cowards. "At dawn, he is to be executed."

The guards exchange glances, but none dare defy her. The prince is dragged away, his protests falling on deaf ears as he calls her name, pleading with her to see reason. Lady Fair stands unmoved, her expression hard and unyielding. Her heart feels nothing, no sorrow, no regret, only the faint, perverse satisfaction of having silenced another threat to her rule.

Days pass, and Lady Fair's grip on the kingdom tightens. She ascends her throne, looking out over the subjects who once adored her, their eyes now filled with fear and unease. They stand before her in silence, a gathering of souls too frightened to speak, their gazes averted, as if to avoid the darkness that now cloaks their queen. She surveys them with a slow, chilling smile, savoring the power she holds over them. Their adoration has turned to terror, and instead of wounding her, it fuels her, stoking a fire within that she cannot, and does not wish to, extinguish.

Her stepmother's voice echoes in her mind, soft and approving. You have done well, my child. Fear is the key to loyalty. Now, they are truly yours.

Lady Fair realizes then, with a final, irrevocable clarity, that she has become the very monster she once feared, the embodiment of her stepmother's twisted legacy, a tyrant. She feels no sadness, only a dark, consuming satisfaction. The throne that once symbolized purity and justice now belongs to a queen cloaked in shadow, her heart hardened by betrayal, her soul entwined with the spirit of the woman she once hated. She sits back, her fingers tapping lightly on the throne, her gaze unyielding.

The Evil Queen has returned, reborn in Lady Fair's form, and she revels in the horror she has become, knowing that no one dares to challenge her reign again.

Gretel to Her Therapist at Forty

By Colleen S. Harris

There never was a tasty
candied forest house, no
breadcrumbs in pockets, no
evil woman, no boiling
cauldron, only a boy with tall
tales, meaty fists, a ferret
mind, and a lenient
father. Only a boy's shark-
toothed grin, a brother
who told me my crib
was an oven because
he liked to hear me
cry. He liked the breathy
sibilance of *Hansel*

when I whimpered
in the dark. He said
"Gray hair on a woman
is the sign of witchery
and death," and I cowered
behind him when
Nana approached.
Now I spend my nights
strumming each strand of
my own, scissors
honed, ready to slice
the first sign of strega
from my head.

That Cottage in the Woods

By Charlotte Bennardo

Even in daylight, the cottage cast menacing shadows. Vines crawled over most of the walls, the door hung crookedly on one hinge, and a shutter lay on the ground. Missing roof tiles added to the ramshackle and despairing look.

"I don't like this," grumbled Hansel.

I spun, threw up my hands, and glared at him.

"We have NO choice! Would you rather stay here and freeze or starve? Maybe you'd rather be eaten by wolves?"

He stopped, crossed his arms over his chest, and stuck his chin out in that mulish pout. Even though firstborn, he was the follower. I was the bolder one. Someone had to be.

"Maybe we could make it to the next village."

I tilted my head. "Don't you think word has spread, and that we won't be run out there too?"

"This place gives me nightmares!" He rubbed his face. "She was fattening me up to eat next."

"I had to kill the witch! You don't think I get nightmares??" I left him standing there and thrust the door aside, anger fueling my strength. Leaves, dirt, branches, and animal nests lay in piles. Somewhere in the dark, a critter skittered across the floor. Spiderwebs hung from the rafters like macabre garlands. The sight of the black cauldron hanging in the fireplace, which she used to boil the bones of the children she beguiled, made me shudder. That would be buried in the woods, never to be used again. The oven, unfortunately, had to stay. Hansel was not going to like it, but we would need it to cook.

Her bones might be in it still.

A shuffle behind me announced that Hansel finally found the courage to come in. I pointed to the door.

"First thing, fix the door so the wolves can't get in. I'll start cleaning in here." I dropped my knapsack on the dirty table. I would have to sacrifice a piece of clothing to make a cleaning rag. In the corner, I picked up a bucket and tipped out the dirt. Her broom stood nearby.

"Don't," Hansel whispered.

"I know!" I snapped. No one would touch a witch's broom any more than their wand. "I'll make one from some pine branches." I threw open a window so some of the stale air could escape, but under the dense forest, not a breath of wind moved. Hansel would have to cut down trees that were too close to the house. "Unless you want to sleep in a tree again, get started, it'll get dark quick."

He left without a sound and my shoulders slumped. I had to think of everything; food, shelter, and escaping from the villagers when they turned on us. Hansel provided the strength when, where, and how I told him.

I was so tired.

But there was work to be done.

With a sigh, I headed to the creek.

After four days of hard, grueling work, Hansel had repaired the door and roof, hauled out piles of debris, and trimmed back the overhanging branches. He'd discovered an axe dropped in the overgrown weeds, so we had a nice stack of firewood. The inside of the cottage I had scrubbed clean until blisters on my hands cracked and bled. The chimney was still sound and a merry little fire crackled, roasting a freshly caught rabbit which filled the cottage with a tantalizing aroma. While Hansel tore down the vines that sought to pull down the cottage, it was time for me to look inside the oven. Once the oven was cleared and enough wood burned, Hansel wouldn't complain if it filled our empty bellies with baked bread or meat. Not that he had a choice.

Steeling myself, I lowered the oven door.

Chunks of bones nestled in the ashes.

I had been prepared for that, but I'd hoped she'd burned to nothing. Maybe if I'd stayed and kept the fire stoked after I pushed her in, she would have. But terror had driven me to free Hansel and help drag him as far as I could—to the same village that now scorned and drove us out. First, one farmer's cow died. Then the cabbage crop became diseased. When the baker, who'd taken us in when we escaped, discovered weevils in his flour, fingers pointed and accusations arose that we were to blame; we were the witch's minions.

We ran for our lives.

So here we were, in the one place no one should be, trying to hide and survive. Using a short piece of firewood, I scraped the skeleton and ash into the bucket. Who knew what evil remained in her bones; I would not touch them and find out. When the oven was mostly empty, I closed the door and put fresh pine branches over the bucket, which I shoved into a dark corner. If Hansel saw the bones, he would rebel and nothing I said would change his mind; he would refuse to live here and we'd be at the mercy of the forest and the weather. I quickly busied myself with cutting up some wild onions Hansel found while hunting for the rabbit which was now our dinner. He grunted by the door as he ripped down a rope of vines.

The door squeaked. He came inside, swiping the sweat and dirt from his face with his arm.

"Here," I held out the cup. Before we ran from the baker, I swiped a cup, a small pitcher, some bread, and a knife, nothing that would be immediately missed, hoping the baker wouldn't chase after us if and when he discovered the pilfered things. I prayed he would be content with us being gone.

Hansel drank the tepid water deeply, tipping his head back. Exhaustion left dark smudges under his eyes. Soon though, when winter snows blanketed the forest and the days were short, he could sit by the fireside, whittling and repairing things we needed at his leisure.

I needed an excuse to get him out of the cottage so I could bury the bones. "Do you think you could get more of the onions? I can store them for winter."

His shoulders drooped. "Sure. Give me some time, okay?"

"Of course, but I don't want you out there when it starts to get dark."

He nodded, grabbed the knapsack, and headed out. I watched him from the doorway and as soon as he disappeared from sight, rushed to grab the gruesome bucket and slip away.

I ran through the woods, low-hanging branches tearing at me, my feet pounding on the ground. An outcrop of granite lay ahead. There was a small crag, big enough to dump the ashes and bones in without having to touch them. I emptied the bucket and then pushed rocks and dirt until the crag was filled with a mound on top. No animal should disturb the bones now, and maybe the earth would cleanse the evil. Using sand, I scrubbed the bucket and rinsed it many times. Still, I would only use it for cleaning water; neither Hansel nor I would drink from it. We may be poor, but we weren't stupid.

I was back at the cottage no more than a few minutes when Hansel returned. He handed over the sack, fairly filled with wild onions and some herbs.

"Sit, I'll bring you dinner."

He shook his head. "I need to wash, I can't stand my own stink. Where's that bucket?"

"No!" I yelled. He drew back. "It was hers, and we don't know if she used it for some dark potions. I only use it for cleaning. Go to the stream and wash up, here's a cloth."

He glowered. "It's going to be cold! There was frost last night."

I nodded. "Yes, Hansel, I know, but I don't want anything to happen to you. I have to wash the same way."

With a resigned sigh, he grabbed the cloth and headed out toward the stream.

The next morning when Hansel ate the cold last bits of the rabbit, I sat next to him at the table.

"Maybe you could fish for our dinner?" I wanted him away from the cottage so I could fire up the oven.

He looked up from his too-small portion. He was a boy doing a man's work and he needed more food, so I'd taken as little as I could.

"I should burn the debris we took out. I'll feel better when we get rid of as much as we can. Bad enough we're in her house."

"That can wait, you've been working so hard. When it snows, we'll burn it. There will be less chance of the fire accidentally spreading. We need food, and you need a rest. Put in a line and just sit for a while." I laid a hand on his arm. It seemed more muscular to me, but then it would with how much work he'd done.

He ate the last bite of rabbit and threw down the bone. "I guess you're right. Don't want to sleep on an empty belly. It's just that there's so much to do."

"Before you come back, get some river mud. I want to make some bowls and see if they can be hardened in the fireplace. Then we can have plates, too."

"That's a good idea. Hand me the bucket."

It would only hold mud; surely no evil would come of that. After all, I'd had my hands in the bucket many times as I cleaned the cottage. I retrieved it from the corner.

"As many fish as you can. You need to eat more."

He grinned. It was the first in a long time. I smiled back.

"You're so bossy." He stood, stretched his back, and yawned.

"That's because I'm good at it. Take the cup in case you get thirsty. I have the pitcher."

He bent over to kiss the top of my head. When had he gotten taller?

"I'll be a few hours."

"I've got things to do, so no hurry, but back before—"

"Dusk, yes, I know, Miss Boss. What are you going to do?"

Uh...

"I think I'll plan out where I want to put in a garden next spring. Sweep the floor because you tracked in dirt, you know."

"Stay close to the house." He closed the door quietly. I swept the room so that when he came back, he would see at least that accomplished chore.

I stacked dried twigs and leaves to start the fire in the oven. Once they caught, I put several small branches. When the fire was hot enough, I put in three hefty logs. The oven burned so hot I had to open the cottage door and the windows. If Hansel smelled the smoke, maybe he would assume it was the fireplace.

Close to the cottage, I scavenged more wood so I wouldn't use all of the stack. It also gave me time to think about where a garden would go if we survived the winter. I stuck a few sticks in the ground, giving the impression of a fenced area. Carrying in my load of wood, I stoked the fire again, careful to stand back from any blast of smoke or heat. I would do this several times to make sure every bit of her was gone before I cooked our food in there.

I sat at the kitchen table, wondering what else I could do when a shaft of sunlight shone in through the open door. Dust motes danced on the beam and it lightened my heart. My eyes followed the trail to the opposite wall. A knot hole in the wood was missing. I remember cleaning the walls and feeling it. In the light, something about it was peculiar. It looked too perfect, like it wasn't the odd shape that knot holes were.

It looked like a finger hold.

The sun went behind a cloud and I shivered.

Curiosity drew me. Lighting a twig from the fireplace, I held it up. I grabbed another twig, about as thick as a finger, and poked it in the hole. Levering it, a section of the wall popped out, revealing a compartment in the wall.

In it rested the witch's grimoire.

I jumped back in horror.

I refused to touch it so I could not remove it. If Hansel saw it, he would drag me away from here, and with the cold nights, we would surely freeze.

I jammed the piece of wood back.

Over the days, while I thought about the grimoire, I was not tempted to use it. If a witch did something that seemed good, it was only to deceive and corrupt something else.

But winter set in and Hansel had little success hunting rabbits or birds or anything else for us to eat. It seemed as though the forest and the stream were barren. I'd made an onion broth, but it was watery, with few onions and a sprinkling of dried herbs. And now it was gone. We would starve if we couldn't find something to eat.

"I'm sure I'll catch something today," he mumbled, a sad smile pulled tautly across his drawn face. It had been at least five days since we'd had something more than onion broth.

My smile was shaky. "Oh, I know so! I'll keep the fire going so we can put it on the spit as soon as you get in!"

He trudged out to check the various traps that had so far proven to be useless, along with his lines in the river.

Hunger pains gnawed at my stomach. Drinking water to hold them off only worked for so long. A light snow dusted the ground, except under the trees, so maybe Hansel could still find more onions or mushrooms, something.

But if he didn't...

My eyes darted over to the grimoire's hiding place. I chewed my lip with indecision. The oven was clean. We could roast anything Hansel caught.

If he caught anything.

I'd just take a peek, but I wouldn't touch it. Using my cleaning rag, I pulled off the panel and lifted out the book. There was no surge of malice; it felt like an ordinary book. I set it on the table. The cover was a dusty dark brown leather. I was not fooled; it was human skin. That was another reason not to touch it. Witches each made their own grimoire. Who was the poor soul who'd lost their skin for this one?

Shuddering, I forced myself to open it. The script was long and elegant, almost beguiling to the eye. Her name, I dared not repeat it, flowed across the page. The next page was a table of contents. Quickly I scanned down the list. There was no spell for how to find food. The closest I could see was how to beguile animals. If I could get one animal every few days to go near or in the traps, while we'd still be hungry, we wouldn't starve and it wouldn't raise Hansel's suspicions like a pot of stew that never emptied.

I turned to the numbered page, my cloth-covered finger gliding down the list of ingredients. If I wanted rabbits, I needed a rabbit's bone. I could dig one up from the refuse pile we buried. Black spider carcasses were no problem, they were always coming in to escape the cold. I could find some grass as snow didn't fall under the denser trees. The other ingredients were just as easily found.

I took a deep breath. I could do this, but I would have to hurry in case Hansel got lucky and came back. I gathered all the ingredients and put them in a crude clay bowl I'd made. It was very fragile, as I couldn't get the fireplace hot enough to set the clay. But that would change as soon as I stoked up the oven and fire several. Tonight would be good; we'd be warm and have dishes.

Hansel would balk, but if I was only baking clay bowls... What could be the harm? I set the bowl on a shelf in the kitchen, under others so if Hansel grabbed one he wouldn't see my ingredients and ask about them; there was no good recipe using black spider carcasses. The last thing I needed was a cup of water poured under the new moon. That wasn't for at least two days. Somehow, we had to hang on. If there was no food until then, I might have to tell him about the grimoire. Maybe Hansel would be desperate enough and urge me to use it—but he'd be angry with me for concealing it all this time.

At the stream, I filled the bucket and the little pitcher. I walked back taking a different route and stumbled upon both black walnuts and acorns. I dumped out the bucket to hold all the nuts. We could eat the meats. Tomorrow, I would collect more. With enough dried, I could grind them into flour for bread. How many other things had Hansel passed without knowing they could be eaten? I couldn't blame him, he didn't know.

But we would still need game meat.

Hansel was there when I got back, a scrawny rabbit stretched out on the table, ready for the spit.

"Nice! Look what I found!" I showed him my treasure, but the smile didn't reach his eyes.

"It's not enough. I had to hike really far. Maybe tomorrow we should return to the village and beg for food."

I slammed the bucket onto the table and grabbed the gutted rabbit. "No! They will either kill us, or chase us down, then kill us!" I placed the rabbit on the spit and hung it over the fire. "We're good for a few days. I'll go back out tomorrow and see what else I can forage."

We wouldn't need the grimoire just yet, but maybe I should check for what other help it could render.

When Hansel left to check the traps again, I drew out the book. In the back was a list of edible roots, nuts, leaves, and fruits available through the various seasons. This could be a lifesaver, provided I could find anything on the list. I memorized the drawings.

By the river, near the swampy area, I dug up curly docks and cattail roots, and then on the ground under the trees, dandelions. All these we could eat. As I roamed in an ever-widening circle, I discovered a few wild berries and gathered all the nuts I could find that weren't rotted or chewed. The last discovery near a moss-covered fallen tree was mushrooms. Such a savory stew I could make, if I only had a proper pot. Just the thought made my mouth water.

I hauled my loot home.

"What do you have?" Hansel peered over my shoulder as I dropped the bag on the table.

I jumped. How could I suddenly explain that I knew which leaves and roots were safe to eat?

"I remember the baker's wife showing me plants that were safe to eat," I lied. "And I gathered all the nuts I could. I can dry them out and if I grind them into flour, I can make bread. See?"

"Bread!" A greedy look crossed his face, it had been so long since we'd had any.

"Well, it won't be like the baker's, I don't have any yeast."

"When can you make it?" He sounded like an eager boy and it almost made me laugh.

"As soon as you find me two stones big enough to grind the dried nuts." I looked toward the fireplace; no game hung on the spit. I didn't let him see my disappointment. Tonight we'd eat dandelion leaves with some onions.

A pained look crossed Hansel's face. "I'm sorry I didn't bring anything back."

My smile was overly bright as I patted his arm. "Things will change, don't worry." I hid the trepidation that churned within my breast.

When Hansel snored deeply on his pallet, I snuck out the door with the pitcher of water and my knapsack. Without moonlight, all I had was a small burning stick from the fireplace to guide me—and warn me of any approaching danger. We hadn't seen any wolves, deer, squirrels, or even an owl, which surprised me. Did the evil still linger? Trees and plants thrived, I saw no shriveled or blackened areas except for where we burned the witch's things. But there was... a feeling of something not... as it should be. I couldn't put my finger on it. There was no dread or fear, just a sense of unease, waiting? I shook my head to clear the unsettling thoughts and walked to a small clearing open under a starry sky.

Sinking the stick into the ground, I poured water from the pitcher into the cup. It was the final ingredient for the spell to draw rabbits to Hansel's traps. I made the potion in the rough bowl and hesitating only a moment, said the inscribed words that I'd memorized.

Nothing happened. Not a bubbling or puff of smoke or even a spark of color. I had no way to know if it worked. And now, I had to find a way to get Hansel to put a few drops in the traps. I couldn't say it was simply water, and I couldn't find them in the dark by myself. I'd have to go with him tomorrow when he checked.

"Hansel, I want to go with you when you check the traps. Maybe there are more nuts or mushrooms, things we can eat."

He'd been cutting firewood. I held out a cup of water to him. He set aside the axe and drank. "I'm almost done." He smiled at me. "It will be nice to have company."

I returned his smile but I felt like a schemer for not being completely honest. Yes, I'd forage, but I'd also put the potion on the traps. Inwardly, I sighed. I had to use the potion. Hansel's gurgling and sunken stomach, so like my own, only confirmed my belief.

We left soon after. I trailed a little behind, carrying the bucket with some of the potion, but covered over with a cloth. The first trap, the closest to the cottage, was empty. He shook his head and waved me away.

"See if there's anything around here to eat."

I made a pretense of looking since a quick glance told me that there wasn't anything to gather. When he took off for the next one, I hurriedly dripped a few drops in the trap and then ran to catch up. I only had enough of the potion for three traps, but on the fourth, a distance from the cottage, I found more nuts and dandelion and sassafras leaves.

"Look, Hansel! I can make us some tea!"

He grunted. "We have no pot to boil the water."

I tramped behind him, silent, for the rest of the traps. All were empty. It was a tense walk back to the cottage.

Now was as good as any time to bring up using the oven.

"NO!" he screamed after I explained.

I waited patiently while he ranted, storming around the place. He threw himself into a chair, one he'd fashioned from branches himself.

"Hansel, I cleaned it out. Her bones and ashes are buried in a rock hole. I've burned wood in there seven times, a lucky number. It's safe to use for firing clay plates and bowls."

"Does it matter if we have plates and bowls when we'll starve in the next few days?" His tirade, as well as the trek to check the traps, left him exhausted. I was too, but I couldn't let him see that. I set a fire in the oven and dragged down the roughly fashioned pottery. With a growl, Hansel stormed out the door.

I rubbed my tired eyes. He needed time to accept our dire situation. While I waited for the oven to heat, I ground nuts with the large flat stone and smaller rounded one Hansel found near the river. Maybe he went to fish or wandered the forest. He was gone long enough that the first bowls were cooling when he returned. They looked to be serviceable, and I now could make more. If we survived.

Hansel didn't talk to me that night and refused to eat anything I put in the newly fired bowl. He grabbed a handful of the dandelion leaves and nuts, then stormed out.

He was gone the next morning when I awoke. I cleaned the cottage, laying in fresh pine branches for our beds, and then ground more nuts. I had a small mound of flour but would need a bit more for even a tiny loaf.

The door flung open. I jumped. Hansel stood there, a triumphant gleam in his eye. He held up his hands holding a clump of rabbits.

"Look, Gretel! And this is just from the first two traps!"

Thanks to magic, we wouldn't starve.

"Oh, Hansel, I'm going to make the best meal you've ever had!"

"I'll clean them outside. One for each of us!" Beaming, he turned around and went outside.

I closed my eyes in relief.

"I don't understand why suddenly there are so many rabbits! For weeks, nothing, now, they fill the traps!" Hansel opened a trap and let the rabbits scamper away. We couldn't eat them all.

"Maybe just leave one trap open every other day?" I suggested, dropping my eyes so he wouldn't see my panic. "Maybe they were frightened this way by... wolves. Or a fire in another part of the forest."

He shook his head, confused. "Maybe." His sudden smile startled me.

"I can take them to the other village and sell them! Then we could buy the things we need, like clothes, pots, a grinding stone for the ax!"

I was leery going to any town and he must have seen it on my face.

He grabbed my arms. "The people in a village in the opposite direction of where we were wouldn't know what we looked like, and I've grown since then. If I go alone, they shouldn't think of us."

He was so excited that I didn't want to turn him down, and we did need things like a cooking pot, since we couldn't use the witch's. I chewed my lip, undecided.

"Come on, Gretel. I can get you sewing needles, warm gloves, and a thick wool shawl. And blankets!"

Now he was tempting me.

With a sigh, I nodded. He whooped and I forced a smile.

He set all the traps and fashioned a cage that he could wear on his back. He collected as many as he could. The next day he would leave just after sunrise to sell as many as he could, maybe trade with the others.

We awoke early.

"Well, I'm off!" He carried a stout walking stick to fend off any danger.

"I'll walk with you to the stream."

He rested a hand on my arm. "You'll be all right alone?"

I nodded. "After I get water, I'll go straight back to the cottage. Bring back a pot if you want stew. And see if you can get any vegetables."

I waved goodbye at the stream then bent to wash up and fill both pitcher and cup.

"Gretel!"

My head jerked up. Hansel strode toward me and I rose. "Why did you come back, is something wrong?" He had no wounds. He could not have reached the village and come back that quickly.

"Why are you following—How did I get back here?"

"Did you get lost?" That was silly, Hansel never got lost; he got us out of the forest when we escaped from the witch.

"I've made a circle..." He shook his head. "I made a wrong turn somewhere. I'll try a different way."

Two more times he ended up back at the stream.

His eyes darkened with fear. "It's the witch's magic! It's made us prisoners!"

I grabbed my skirt. "But we escaped before!"

Deep in my heart, I knew I was to blame. I had to check the grimoire.

He turned in circles, squinting into the distance.

"Come back to the cottage, Hansel." It was my tone of voice that gave me away.

"What did you do, Gretel? Tell me!"

I took a deep, steadying breath, but still, my knees shook. "We were starving, I had to do it!"

He shook me. "What did you do, Gretel?"

The words rushed out. "I used the witch's grimoire to lure animals to the traps."

His bellow echoed in the forest, but it disturbed no birds.

"Maybe I can undo this, let me check the grimoire again."

He stomped away, not waiting for me. When he reached the cottage, he opened the cage, setting the rabbits free. We both knew the traps would be full again tomorrow. Inside, I pulled the book from its hiding spot. As usual, I did not touch it with my bare hands. He watched me flip the pages, reading.

I dropped into the chair.

"Tell me what we need to do, then we are going to burn that evil book!" He slammed his fist on the table, making the bowls and plates jump.

My voice was a whisper. "It says that once anyone uses the magic, they are doomed to remain here unless one person is sacrificed, and another takes their place."

Hansel was to have been the sacrifice, I would remain, bound to this place, which would set the witch free. But she had become the sacrifice, and the magic lured us back.

Adults knew better than to approach a strange cottage in the woods, but children...

If we ever wanted to be free, we would have to lure children.

Just as she had done.

THE LAST BITE

BY ADELE LILES

HAPPILY EVER AFTER WAS the cruelest lie she ever believed.

She shuffled past the smooth glass, intricate carvings snaking around its gold frame. The heirloom once belonged to her stepmother, its magic silenced long ago. Now, it was her own—another reminder of the life she inherited.

She avoided her reflection. A familiar stranger would peer back at her, and she didn't want to greet her. Withering emptiness stole the bloom of youth, her innocence swallowed by the crown. The wide, bright eyes that enchanted the prince dulled, weighed down by a decade of disillusionment. Dark circles clung to her eyes, and her lips pressed into a thin line as if smiling required too much effort. She didn't need the mirror to show her that.

Hers was the face of a caged animal—albeit a gilded cage—not of a woman in love. She had once been a girl full of life, radiant like a spring blossom. The fairest of them all, they had called her. But now, that girl had long since wilted, replaced by a woman worn down by the life she had been given but never wanted.

She threw a glance at their bed. The side opposite hers was empty, the sheets cold and unwrinkled. Florian left before dawn as he always did—without a word, without a touch. He had important duties to attend to. Councils to command. People to lead. There was no room for intimate mornings shared between the two of them anymore.

Their passion shriveled, and the distance between them was more suffocating than the glass coffin. The vibrant promise of love decayed and left behind brittle, lifeless leaves.

The fairy tale had lost its luster.

Snow White let out a quiet breath, a small surrender to the loneliness that took root inside her heart. This isn't how it was supposed to be, she thought. The girl who had once been saved by true love's kiss became a woman drowning in the solitude of a loveless marriage. Florian rescued her from death, but who would save her now?

For the first time in days, she made her way outside for some fresh air. She moved slowly through the palace garden with steps soft against the stone path. Each one felt heavier than the last as the earth itself seemed to pull her back. The gentle rustling of leaves and the faint melody of birds filled the air. The garden bloomed in vibrant reds, yellows, and pinks. The apple trees towered above her, their branches bending under the weight of ripe fruit.

None of it seemed real to her.

The world had turned into a blur of color and sound, obscure and muted, as if she were walking through a dream she no longer wanted to be in. Her hands grazed the velvety pink petals of a rose, its thorns biting gently at her fingertips. She didn't flinch. Instead, she let the sting ground her.

It was supposed to be forever. Her heart sagged with the heaviness of that promise. She exhaled. Happily ever after. But no one warned me that after the fairy tale, life goes on... and on.

She never considered what came after the prince's kiss, after the celebrations, after the heavy castle doors closed behind them. She had been saved, yes—pulled from death's cold grip and given a new life, but no one told her what that life would look like. No one told her "forever" was a long time to fill with a husband who was always somewhere else, with days that stretched on endlessly, barren, each one the same as the last until it became an untended garden overgrown with bitterness and regret.

Her footsteps slowed, and she stopped beneath one of the largest apple trees. Her eyes traced the familiar shapes of the red fruit suspended from the branches. Polished. Perfect. Tempting. The sight of them brought a glimmer of something inside her, a shadow from her past.

Funny. The thing that almost killed me is the thing I miss the most. Danger. A fight. Something to feel.

Snow White's hand hovered near a low-hanging apple, and her fingers brushed against its sleek surface. It shone beautiful and perfect like the one her stepmother offered her all those years ago. She plucked it from the branch and held it in her hand, staring at the vibrant, crimson skin.

Now, it's just this. This empty existence. This endless cycle of pretending. Pretending to be happy. Pretending to be in love. Pretending to be the same girl who once believed in fairy tales.

In her palm, the apple was cool with a comforting weight. She rolled it between her hands as her thoughts darkened. The world around her remained so still, so peaceful. But inside, everything was rotting.

What happens when the story ends, but you don't?

She raised the apple to her lips, enjoying its smooth skin against her mouth, inhaling its sweet scent. She closed her eyes as the breeze caught her hair and sent a shiver down her spine.

I didn't ask for this. No one warned me what "happily ever after" really meant. That forever would feel this lonely.

Her eyes fluttered open, and she lowered the apple, a cold clarity settling in. As the garden continued to sway and sing around her, Snow White felt more isolated than ever before.

A thought coiled through her mind, dark and uninvited. Perhaps, after all these years, there was only one way out of this life. A way to cut the thorny ties that bound her to a fate she hadn't chosen.

She reentered the peaceful palace and made her way down the corridors with purpose. The few servants she passed along the way offered polite smiles, and their faces lit up at the sight of their sovereign moving through the halls after days of seclusion.

She stopped one of the servant girls near the entrance to the kitchen. "I'll be preparing dinner tonight myself."

The servant blinked in surprise. "Your Majesty? But we—"

Snow White raised a hand, her delicate smile almost apologetic. "It's our anniversary," she explained. "I want to do something special for him. Just the two of us. You understand, don't you?"

The servant's face softened with understanding. "Of course, Your Majesty. How thoughtful! I'll make sure the rest of the staff knows not to disturb you."

Snow White nodded, offering another weak smile before watching the young woman disappear down the hall. As soon as she was out of sight, Snow's face fell, the mask of pleasantness slipping away, leaving her features blank and unreadable. She turned toward the empty kitchen, where everything was set out in perfect order. Rows of silver pots and pans gleamed on the shelves, and the smell of freshly baked bread lingered in the air like the last breath of summer.

She returned to her chambers to retrieve another heirloom, something she'd buried in the floorboards, deep like a seed waiting to sprout. She pushed aside a heavy rug, loosened the board, and pulled out a worn book of spells and potions. She tore out the page she needed and tucked it into the pocket of her dress. Then she hid the book away again, pulling the rug back in place.

Back in the kitchen, she gathered the required ingredients. As she chopped vegetables, the rhythmic noise of the blade meeting the cutting board filled the room. Its soothing sound took her back to a happier time when she'd cared for the seven brothers in the cottage in the woods and every meal had been a labor of love.

As she moved from task to task—seasoning the meat, thickening the sauce, arranging the side dishes—her mind remained calm, her thoughts white noise. The familiar actions of preparing food lulled her into a quiet focus while under the surface, something poisonous simmered.

With a practiced hand, Snow White selected a pristine apple from the basket on the counter. She held it up, turning it in her fingers, inspecting its vibrant red skin. It was impeccable—glossy without a single blemish. Using the recipe folded in her dress, she prepared it carefully. The fruit's flesh greedily absorbed the special concoction, and the exterior gleamed brighter, unmarred by the dark secret inside.

She carried everything to a table in the garden dressed with white linens and candlelight that danced gently in the breeze. It was the kind of scene that would look beautiful from the outside—romantic, intimate, everything a loving wife would prepare for her beloved husband on their anniversary. The palace staff, no doubt, would talk later about how thoughtful and devoted their queen was. A surprise, they would say. A sweet gesture of love and tenderness.

She placed a pair of polished apples on a silver tray in the center of the table. The final touch. She stepped back and surveyed her work. The setup was charming and flawless, like the life she cultivated—the perfect facade of a fairy tale.

But in the quiet, beneath the stillness of the air, something waited like a weed ready to choke the life out of everything around it. Even the roses held their breath, waiting, their petals quivering.

Winter settled deep within her soul. This dinner, this anniversary, was supposed to be a celebration of love, a tribute to the happily ever after they once shared. But tonight would be something else entirely.

A different kind of ending.

Snow White admired the apples one last time, sitting like crown jewels, gleaming in the golden sunlight filtering through the vines draped over the garden trellis. With their ripe and lethal beauty, they looked as though they had grown from the earth for this moment.

The preparations were finished. All that was left now was to wait.

As the afternoon stretched on, the light in the palace began to soften, and long, pale shadows scattered around the room where Snow White sat at her writing desk. Subtle notes of lilac trickled through her open window, tickling her nose, reminding her of the life outside these prison walls. Her hand inched across the parchment, each word deliberate. Only the soft scratching of the quill filled the silence, and even that felt distant as if it belonged to another time, another life.

She paused to stare at the words she penned. The letters were neat and elegant, the message clear. They held despair, entwined like roots strangling the heart. She dipped the quill into the inkwell once more, signing the bottom with a slow, heavy hand, the ink like sap, sticky and reluctant to let go.

With a sigh, Snow White folded the letter carefully. She slid it into a small envelope, pressing the wax seal closed with the emblem of the royal family.

For a moment, she allowed herself to imagine someone finding it later, eyes widening as they read the letter, hands trembling as they realized what it meant. Would sorrow flower in their chest? Regret? Or would life simply move on, as it always had, rooted in the kingdom and too caught up in its demands to understand the depths of despair?

None of it mattered now.

She changed into her dinner gown and tucked the letter—its wax still warm beneath her fingers—into her bosom. She moved to her vanity and painted on her mask before picking up a gold hairbrush. She ran it through her tresses as if this were a ritual she needed to complete—a final act of care before the frost claimed everything.

"I never asked for this," she whispered, her words tainted with bitterness, burning her lips like the poison before had done.

She set the brush down gently on the table and locked her gaze on the hollow figure in the mirror. There were no tears, no sign of the emotions left to harvest. Only a cold, steady resolve, like the hush of winter before the first snowfall.

Escape. Release. The words echoed in her mind like a bell tolling in the fog. This was the only way she could see. The only way to cut herself free from the pain rooted in her heart, growing with every passing day. She tried to live in this story, tried to make sense of it, to thrive in it, but it became too much.

She leaned forward and brushed the edge of the mirror, her reflection warping slightly under her touch.

"This wasn't supposed to be my story." Her voice was low and filled with finality, sharp like a broken branch. She stared into her own eyes, searching for a spark of the girl she used to be.

But there was nothing left.

Snow White straightened and turned away from the mirror with a heart as cold and still as the winter's night she had been rescued from all those years ago. The preparations were complete. The letter was written. The stage was set.

Now all that remained was to wait for the prince's return. And when he did, everything would be over.

Florian arrived home just as the last traces of daylight were fading, the sky painted in deep shades of purple and gold. He stepped through the gates, tired from the day's meetings and negotiations, but as he caught sight of the palace garden, his mood shifted. Candlelight flickered in the dusk, throwing a warm glow over the intimate table set among the roses, and the savory aroma of a home-cooked meal wafted through the air.

He smiled, pleasantly surprised. "Snow," he called as he approached. "What is this? What have you done?"

She stood waiting by the table, her white gown ghostly and luminous in the twilight. With the hint of a smile, she turned toward him. "I wanted to do something special," she said, her voice barely audible, as if the words were only meant for her.

The prince beamed as he took her hand and lifted it to his lips in a quick kiss. "It's beautiful." He glanced around the garden and took in the details. "You needn't have gone to so much trouble, though. After the day I've had, I would've been happy with bread and cheese."

Snow White's smile remained, though it didn't reach her eyes. "It wasn't any trouble."

Florian pulled out a chair for her and settled into his own with a contented sigh. He marveled at the meal laid out before them and praised the tender roast glistening with a glaze of golden honey and the delicate aroma of rosemary and thyme. Snow White deftly poured two glasses of wine, the deep burgundy liquid swirling in the crystal goblets like crushed petals in a spring rain.

"You've outdone the palace chefs." He reached for a piece of bread and dipped it into the fragrant stew. "You must have been working all day."

She took a sip of wine, her gaze lowered, only offering a small nod in response. His words whispered past her like white dandelion fluff in the wind, insignificant in the grand expanse of her thoughts.

As the prince ate, he launched into stories from his day. "The council meeting was unbearable," he said with a chuckle, barely noticing her silence. "More talk about the neighboring kingdoms and treaties—none of it exciting, of course. You wouldn't believe Lord Ecclestone. He fell asleep halfway through the discussion. If only I could have done the same."

Snow White glanced down at her plate, the food untouched, her hands resting lightly in her lap. She listened but slipped further away from the conversation. His voice was a faint echo of a forgotten season, the words losing meaning as they reached her ears.

Oblivious to her detachment, he continued. "And then there was the matter of the trade routes. We've been negotiating for months, and I think we've finally come to an agreement. You should've seen the look on the king's face when he realized we had outmaneuvered him."

She gave a practiced smile and nodded along, but her mind wandered like wild ivy, coiling inward. He has no idea, she thought. No idea of the roots of sorrow digging deeper with each passing year, strangling her spirit.

The prince took another sip of his wine, and his eyes flicked to the candlelight dancing on the silverware. "It really is incredible what you've done here," he said between bites. "You should do this more often. It's like I'm seeing the old Snow again. The one who used to make me feel like the luckiest man in the world."

Her smile faltered as the words cut deep. The old Snow. As if he weren't the reason that girl died long ago. She wondered if he could even remember that bright-eyed girl who believed in love, in happily ever afters, in the promise of forever. Did he know how far away she was from that dream? Did he see how her eyes dimmed, how her spirit withered beneath this life?

But the prince, still lost in his own musings, didn't notice. He reached for the goblet again, lifting it in a toast, his smile wide. "To us." He raised the wine to his lips. "To our happily ever after."

Snow White raised her own glass, and her gaze collided with his. She clinked her glass against his, her hand steady, her eyes unwavering with asp-like watchfulness.

"To us." The crystal touched her lips, but she didn't drink. She observed him, her thoughts tangling with intensity, her mind already far beyond this moment, beyond the garden, beyond him.

They finished the main course, and when the prince drained the last of his wine from his glass, she poured him another. The candlelight shivered softly between them, casting delicate shadows on her pale face. She folded her hands under her chin, and for a long moment, she said nothing, simply watching the man she once believed would be her savior.

Florian slouched back in his chair, his expression relaxed, his smile easy. He seemed content, utterly unaware of the tension curling around them. His mind was still filled with the day's mundane politics, the comfort of home, and the belief that this dinner was merely a romantic gesture, a celebration of their love.

Her tender voice broke the silence. "It's been a long journey, hasn't it?"

"It has." The corners of his mouth turned up. "But it's been worth it, hasn't it?"

Clouds darkened Snow's eyes. She inhaled slowly, steadying herself as her gaze drifted to the table. "I've been thinking about what this day means," she continued, "and I've come to realize something important."

The prince raised an eyebrow, still oblivious to the growing weight of her words. He leaned forward, waiting for her to continue, a trace of amusement on his face as if expecting her to share something sweet and reminiscent of the love they once shared.

She gestured toward the sparkling rubies at the heart of the table.

"For our anniversary," she said, her tone laced with finality.

A chuckle escaped Florian's lips. He'd assumed it served as part of her romantic surprise, a symbol of their history, of how far they had come together. "Snow, you really didn't have to—"

But he stopped short when he saw the intensity in her eyes. He reached for an apple, taking the brightest one, as she knew he would.

As he held it in his hand, turning it slightly, admiring its flawless skin, Snow White leaned back in her chair, her breath steady. She watched him, her eyes never leaving the fruit. Her hands rested calmly in her lap once more, and the impact of the moment settled between them like an unspoken truth.

Florian raised the apple to his lips with a grin. "You certainly do have a way with these little touches," he remarked, his tone full of affection.

"You deserve it, after everything we've been through."

He brought the apple closer, preparing to take a bite.

Her eyes followed every movement with a viperous stare. Inside her, there was no regret, no hesitation. Only the cold certainty of the inevitable. As the apple neared Florian's mouth, Snow's lips parted ever so slightly, but she kept quiet.

There was nothing left to say.

In silence, she watched him. And waited.

He bit into the fruit, breaking the skin with a crisp snap like a branch cracking in a field. As he chewed the next bite, something shifted. His expression changed—a wink of discomfort that bloomed into confusion.

Snow White spoke again, her voice soft, measured. "Sometimes," she said, "endings are a release. A way to find peace. After all, how long can a story last before it becomes unbearable?"

He blinked, his vision blurring. The conversation around him, the soothing cadence of Snow White's voice, began to feel remote as if the world were pulling away from him.

His hands trembled. He put the apple down, reaching instinctively for the glass of wine beside him, but as he did, his fingers fumbled. The glass tipped over, spilling its deep red contents across the table, the liquid staining the white linen.

"Snow..." His voice was shaky now, uncertain, but she didn't react. She eyed him, her face a perfect mask of calm.

Florian's breath quickened. His chest rose and fell with growing difficulty as dizziness swept over him. The garden around them began to spin. He clutched the edge of the table for support, knocking a fork to the ground as his body struggled to maintain control. The muscles in his arms tightened, his hands gripping the wood so hard his knuckles turned white.

His breathing came in sharp, ragged gasps. "What... what's happening?"

But Snow White didn't answer. She sat still, her eyes fixed on him, her expression serene, as if this moment had been written long ago, as if she knew all along this was how their story would end.

The prince's body convulsed, and his limbs failed him. His heart pounded in his chest, each beat erratic, painful. His vision darkened at the edges, and his mind began to slip into a fog, panic engulfing him as he realized something was terribly wrong. His hands slid from the table, his body folding forward as he collapsed into his chair.

With the grace of an unfurling primrose, Snow White stood and left her seat. Across the table, Florian struggled to remain upright, his once confident posture now faltering with the deadly nectar twisting through his veins. Horror widened his eyes in his pale face, and his hands shook uncontrollably as they grasped again for the table's edge. He attempted to stand, but his legs buckled beneath him.

"Snow," he gasped, choking on the panic bubbling in his throat. Each breath was a battle as the poison tightened its grip. His eyes searched hers, hunting for mercy but finding only frigid indifference.

Snow White stepped closer, her expression unflinching as she peered down at him. There was no trace of the sorrow she had worn throughout the day, no hint of the melancholy that had clung to her. Now, there was only cold resolve in her eyes, stark and unyielding.

Florian's eyes glittered with confusion and desperation as his mind raced to make sense of things. His fingers scraped against the tablecloth as he tried to push himself up, but his strength was fading quickly. His body, once so full of life, was betraying him. A broken stem.

His breath came in shallow gasps, his chest heaving as he fought to stay conscious. "Why?" he croaked, the question trembling on his lips.

Snow White crouched down to him. "Because happily ever after was never real," she said, her words a venom stinging through him. "It was just a story—a story I no longer wished to live in."

Florian's hand reached out weakly toward her, but it fell short, his fingers brushing against empty air as his vision blurred again. His last breath rattled in his throat and his body slumped and slid from the chair, landing in a crumpled heap as the poison claimed him.

Snow White stood with Florian's lifeless body at her feet, the half-eaten apple resting beside his limp hand. His face, once flushed with vitality, was drained of color, his features frozen in confusion and horror like a crumbled dahlia unable to understand its decay.

She gazed down at him, her decision setting in the stillness of the night like dew on silver leaves. The garden, so carefully prepared for this final act, was now a hollow stage that served its purpose. Despite the gravity of her actions, there was no sign of hesitation or regret in her eyes. She made her choice, and the burden of it—though heavy—seemed not to trouble her.

She gathered the remnants of the dinner and hid them in the garden. She would retrieve them in the morning. From her bosom, she pulled the letter. Florian's letter. Penned in his darkest moment. How he felt trapped, his love for her twisted into an obligation he could no longer bear. How he was crushed under the weight of the crown, of responsibilities he was never meant to carry. She tucked it into his hand. The servants would find him the next day.

She stepped over Florian's body, leaving him behind without a second look, the silence of the night enveloping her as her footsteps echoed softly against the stone pathway.

The palace remained silent as Snow White made her way inside. The grand halls and towering ceilings stretched endlessly before her like canopied trees. The servants were gone for the night, unaware of the fate that had just befallen their prince. All that filled the space was her calm, unhurried steps as she climbed the stairs to her private chambers.

Her hand brushed the banister lightly. With confident strides, she ascended as if she were rising from the earth toward something purer. There was no rush, no urgency—only the slow, deliberate climb to the sanctuary she always sought but never truly found until now.

When she reached her chambers, she paused, resting her hand on the door. She pushed it open and stepped inside, the room welcoming her with its familiar, noiseless solitude. She closed the door gently behind her to seal herself away from the world beyond.

Alone, at last, she stood in the tranquil room. She allowed the cool night air and jasmine drifting in through the open window to wash over her like a balm. She inhaled deeply, filling her lungs with the crisp air, and for the first time in years, she could breathe.

It was over.

The weight she carried, the facade she wore, the suffocating expectations of the fairy tale life, all of it fell away. She exhaled slowly, her shoulders easing, the tension releasing from her body as she sank into the peace of her own decision.

Snow White stood before her mirror, the gold frame gleaming in the dim light of her chambers. She gazed at her reflection and rested her fingers on the edges of the mirror's cool surface and a long-lost part of herself. The image staring back at her was familiar yet transformed. The softness that once defined her features hardened into something stronger, more assured. The helplessness that haunted her eyes disappeared, replaced with unshakable conviction.

She smiled with deep satisfaction and acknowledgment of the choice she made. The life that trapped her, the fairy tale that suffocated her, was over. She was no longer bound by the happily ever after that never truly belonged to her. The prince was gone, and with him, the life she had never wanted, the role she had been forced to play.

She had uprooted herself and was reborn. Wild. Untamed. Free.

The poison that once threatened her life had, in the end, given her the power to claim her own destiny. No longer the helpless princess in a glass coffin, waiting for someone to save her, she had rewritten the story.

And for the first time, she knew the story was truly hers.

THORNS

BY REBECCA MINELGA

A YOUNG GIRL, PALE and pink and fragile as a petal, softly wrapped in gauze and gold, bright hair cascading down her back and wide, sea-green eyes. She watches the world, first with wonder, then warily as she withstands her cruel brother's pokes and prods, the complacency of her mother, and the weighted crown of her father. It will never be hers. Second in line, and a girl besides, she's destined for a foreign land and a foreign prince.

Is it any wonder she grows thorns?

When he comes, dark and dangerous astride a stamping steed, she casts her eyes down. When he studies her, sneering, but accepts her anyway, she presses her lips into a thin line, biting her tongue. Biding her time.

Now a woman, his heavy hand reminds her she's always been owned. First by her family, now by her fiancé. His ring is a shackle around her finger, but no less binding. It is an anchor dragging her down to the depths of despair, but still, she does her duty.

Her thorns have been scraped away.

A boy, dark like his father, a perfect heir. Then a girl, hair bright as her mother's and eyes like the sun on the sea. History will repeat itself, and her daughter's story will never be told.

When war comes, her warrior spirit is all but broken.

Her husband is vicious. And victorious. Vivats drown the screams of stolen sons, widows weeping at their windows as his parade passes beneath the portico. With sharpened nails, she combs through the strands of her daughter's hair, braiding an intricate coronet, then gathers herself to welcome him home with a hunt.

Accidents happen. A boar for a boor, a son silently slips away, slashed and slaughtered, but hardly missed. Like his father, he was cruel and callous, condescending and cold. It is a just recompense for the many sons his father stole.

The king is too busy clothed in his crown, lamenting his loss. Finally free, she rides every day, cantering along the cliffs and trailing along the tarns, always escorted. Her captain preserves and protects her person. Soon, she is delicate, but no longer breakable, and when another son is born, this one with eyes dark as chocolate and hair streaked madrona red, her spouse stalks the stag in celebration, but a soldier stalks him.

She weeps crystalline tears, prism prisoners on her lashes. Heavy is the head which now bears hope, but she has climbed the walls of this palace, pricked its panels and palisades, punctured its portcullises. Stems spiked with spines and stained scarlet, she persists.

Braids and buds twine in her daughter's hair, a diadem of dreams.

And they live happily ever after.

The Ghost of Birkerød Sø

By Erin Jo Eldry

IT WAS TERRIBLY COLD in Birkerød. A fresh coat of frost that came in overnight covered the last snowfall from Christmas morning, enough to freeze the clocks and church bells that sat dormant in their towers. Houses along both the newly paved roads and old cobbled streets settled in with tender breathing from smoke puffs from their chimneys. They billowed out through the winterscape of the small Danish hamlet, lingering below the clouds with an aromatic assortment of holiday feasts.

On that last night of the year, a little girl walked along a low stone wall of Søholmsvej, a street near the northeastern end of Birkerød Sø.

Tracing lines along the wall with a stick, she was on her way to the lake. A place she often visited in the summer months when her father was home from duty.

For now, it was only her on the road, in a new pair of slippers she'd received on Christmas night and her older sister's brown riding hood. It kept her blonde curls tucked in place behind her ears and dry from the bitter windchill.

While the lake was iced over that deep December, no one was expected to be about socializing or skipping rocks along its banks. That was more than fine with her. She needed a moment of tranquility after such a festive week. Out of her mother's careful watch and far from her boisterous siblings. They, and her cousins visiting from Hillrød, felt the need to occupy their home with as many loud noises as they could from their brand new toys and musical instruments.

Despite the delicious smell of roasting meats and baked sweets in the air, the girl was not hungry as she passed house after house. Each, with a cozy scene of holiday comfort inside the golden glow of their dining rooms, complete with twinkling lights from Christmas trees and advents *julestage* candelabras displayed in their windows. It was well past dinner in her own house, and her belly was still full of her mother's *flæskesteg*, *rødkål*, and *brunede kartofler*. Delicious roasted pig, red cabbage, and caramelized potatoes.

Although, the warmth did look quite inviting as she trekked further down the street.

The chill of the air was quite a contrast to the kitchen she had abandoned back home. Especially when her sister was hard at work baking that night. By now, she imagined her family was enjoying a second batch of her *tebirkes*, her special sweet pastries topped with poppyseeds. She didn't blame them a bit for wanting more. In fact, before she snuck out, she slipped a few into a cloth to tie around her waist. They would make for a delicious treat once she got down to the shoreline.

No one in her home witnessed her departure that late evening except for her younger brother, a boy no older than five.

He stood behind the counter as she prepared herself for the elements, peeking around its corner as she tied the riding hood around her collar.

"Where are you going?" he asked.

"To the lake," she replied.

He furrowed his eyebrows in confusion, stepping around slightly as if to stop her, yet held back.

"That place is haunted this time of year," he warned. "Why would you go there?"

"For peace away from the lot of you. If there's a ghost down at that lake, at least he will be quiet."

She left quickly after that, without so much as a threat toward him to keep her outing a secret from the rest of the family. If he protested her decision at all, his voice died among the wind, never to reach her ear.

She knew her older brother's stories about the lake well, but they did not frighten her the way they did her younger one. What she knew to be true was the Ghost of Birkerød Sø was not even a ghost at all.

There was an old man who lived alone at the north end, and his odd eccentricities were where those old stories came to life in their sleepy, little town.

He had to be a man close to a hundred years old with hair as white as the snow on the trees and old, shriveled skin that clung to his veins. They protruded and branched out along his wrists and temples, causing him to look as pale blue as the ice on the lake whenever the sun went down. For anyone who dared get close enough, they often described his dark, sullen eyes about as low-hanging and dreary as a thick winter fog.

But to the girl, The Ghost was just a sad, old hermit. Nothing more than an unfortunate man who never married and spoke in cryptic messages about the stars and the planets. To some, he was rumored to be a warlock who could predict the future, but to her, he was just an odd end result of a long, sad, and lonely life.

And there was nothing to be scared of about a man like that, except maybe to lead a life as he had.

The crunch of snow beneath her feet softened as the girl's stick found the far side of the stone wall. The end of the road. Ahead of her was the dirt path leading down to the open shoreline, and she sighed a breath of triumph.

Finally.

While in the summer, this wide pathway was full of greenery and neighbors on their bicycles, in the fresh snowfall, all human intervention of paved sidewalks and benches were covered in white. There was no echoing laughter, only the roaring whirl of the open wind. The girl's footprints were the only evidence of any human life as she walked along the frost near the bank.

Nestled in the treeline, speckled homes on the horizon were alive with the comradery of their families. Distant music, silenced by the song of nature, and the orange glow of fire ablaze in a pattern of stars through the hazy overcast above the ice. Yet, where she was standing, there was no sound but the crunch of snow beneath her slippers and no heat but what she could hold inside her hood and scarf.

A few steps further and she found what she was looking for. Her favorite bench near the bank with a panoramic view of the landscape. Eventually, she'd wipe the seat and sit, but for now, she leaned over to pick up some stones by her feet. She threw them as far out as she could, listening for the cracks. Judging by the lack of such sound, it was evident the lake was in a deep freeze below the surface.

It wasn't surprising, given the several nights of storms, but it did give her a challenge to try and break it before settling down to relax in her peaceful meditations.

She needed a bigger rock down by the shoreline. Those that were heavy, more dense, and stacked along the roots of an old tree that lay frozen near the sand.

Perhaps her mind wandered a bit too far in imagining the best way to pull them from the ground, not paying attention to where she stepped, but she slipped. Hard. On a sheet of black ice, her slippers gave way from under her, and she threw out her hands to break her fall as she fell over forward.

She hardly registered her own scream that echoed in the vast dreariness of Birkerød Sø.

On her knees, she hunched over to shelter her hand from the wind. It picked up in a roar as she inspected the damage of a searing pain coming from it. A sticky red smudge stained the lines of her palm, as it did on her clothing when she pressed her hand against her sleeve to protect her wound.

So much for a quiet evening alone. She'd have to go back home and get this bandaged.

As she stood to make her way back, she stopped, blocked by a sudden presence.

In front of her was a large figure in black and something she mistook for another tree at first. It moved forward, like the shadows she'd watch on the wall at night when a car passed by her window, and she dreamed of who it might be.

She didn't have to dream about who it was in front of her. Those veins on his wrist caught her eye and the chill of knowing replaced the chill of gust around them. Legs as stiff as the frozen tree roots, she made no sudden movement as that bony hand took hold of her shoulder.

With a nudge from him, and without the will to run from her, the Ghost of Birkerød Sø led the girl toward his cottage.

Between an old stove and the walls of his home sheltering her from the wind, the warmth came back to the girl's cheeks as she sat on a torn-up ottoman in a dim, humble living room.

The Ghost removed his scarf and coat to set on a hook before retrieving a tin box from out of a cupboard.

"You shouldn't be out so late after a blizzard," he told her. "Children have been known to freeze to death in such conditions."

The girl said nothing as she kept her cut pressed against her sleeve.

"I'll doctor you up," he said, "but you should go straight home once you leave here."

It was easier to disobey rules when none were specifically given. To be caught by an adult and given instructions meant respect was in order, else she'd get in trouble with her father when he returned home in the morning. So, she nodded.

The Ghost's home was one she'd heard about in her older brother's stories, but nothing she cared about enough to see in person. It wasn't much at all what she'd expected as she held out her hand and looked ahead to the mantle.

In her home, old photographs of her family and a military portrait of her father sat above the hearth. There, upon his, was just an old slipper. A vintage-looking thing that made sense to keep packed away in a basement, much less in a prominent space.

While it was an odd trinket to keep on a mantle, the fact it seemed to be dusted and kept clean in comparison to the rest of his house was something to note. Much like how the snow covered the lakeside, the dust here too coated everything in a desolate state. All but that slipper.

She still didn't look at him as he cleaned up her cut with a warm, damp rag.

"How come people call you The Ghost?" she asked. Better to have something interesting to return home with if she were to divert her family's attention away from her injury after sneaking out.

"I imagine it has a lot to do with being a hermit," he said.

"You're not a very good one," she said rather bluntly. "If I were a hermit or a ghost, I wouldn't invite any people into my house."

"Well, I'm sorry to disappoint you." It sounded as if he were smiling as he carefully dabbed her cut dry with a lump of cotton.

Her head still turned away from him, her gaze wandered to his stove.

"You should add more coals to that," she said. "Your fire's almost out."

"I don't have many coals left," he replied. "Besides, when the fire's low, you can see dancing pictures in the embers."

She saw nothing but the dying, burnt orange of their glow. Not even the moving shadows of its crackling gave her imagination much to work with. And she considered herself a girl with a rather enigmatic imagination.

"Here you go." The Ghost wrapped a bandage around her palm and gave it a pat for good measure. "I'm sure your mother could do a better job, but I've done my best."

"Thank you." She inspected it for a moment before looking back at him. He didn't seem so ghoulish in the soft lighting from the stove. At least that night, he looked less like a corpse and more like a human, albeit an extremely ancient one.

She pulled back her riding hood at the hip and brought forth the cloth around her waist.

"Since I'm going home, I won't need this if you want it."

She reached in to hand him her sister's pastry.

He looked down on it in his open palm with a large smile, several teeth missing.

"Thank you very much. I'll give you something to take back to your family as well."

The Ghost shuffled off into the kitchen, leaving the girl to rub the bandage again with her thumb.

Maybe she could lie to her siblings and tell them she snuck inside the Ghost's cottage. That could be where she got her injury from. And whatever it was he wanted to give her, she could say she stole it. She'd have actual evidence, and she'd know what his house looked like if they ever wanted to sneak in and see it for themselves as proof.

There was the old slipper on the mantle she could describe to them, but there wasn't much else that stood out to be quite as unique. There were hardly any family trinkets. Not even a single photograph on the wall.

When The Ghost returned, without hesitation, she asked, "Did you ever have a wife?"

He held a cheesecloth of his own, cradling within it a few balls of powdered *æbleskiver*. Without hesitation himself, he replied, "No, I never did."

"Why not?"

"It just never happened. Why?"

"Just wondering. If you've been a hermit your whole life, does that mean you're sad and lonely?"

"That's nothing to worry about." He kept his gentle smile. "I'm not the only one who lives the way I do.

When you're older, you'll see there's plenty of us everywhere. Some even in homes with spouses and children of their own."

"I don't understand that."

"That's a blessing you should cherish. You'll figure it out someday, and when you do, you'll find sitting alone is a lot better than vapid distractions from other people. Especially when you're alone in the winter, and there's no one around to bother you."

"That, I understand." She perked up. "I like sitting alone by myself, but I don't think it's lonely."

"Then do you think I'm lonely?"

"No. Just a bit dirty." She paused. "And you smell funny."

He laughed, and her lip curled into a smile.

"My family can be very loud and noisy," she went on. "My mother always makes too much to eat, and we have it for weeks at a time. It gets boring. And my siblings and cousins are so loud and nosy about my business. I blend in too much to stand out, but they still bother me like I do. I think I'd like to be a hermit like you."

"Is that so?"

"Yes, and I think it would be nice to have stories made up about me that make me seem mysterious."

That gentle laugh returned as he asked her, "Do you believe those rumors?"

"No, but everyone else does. Maybe, if once in a while you waved at me, my family and the neighbors could gossip about me, too. Maybe they'll think I've made friends with The Ghost and stop bothering me but just talk about me instead. And if the rumors about you are true, maybe you can teach me about the stars and planets, so I can be special."

"You're already special. I can tell you're curious and imaginative, and an imagination is good to pass the time."

"I can't see dancing pictures in old coals, but I do like to daydream. Oh!" She sat up straight as The Ghost closed the tin box to place on top of a dresser. "Can you really see the future? I want to learn how to do that."

"I don't predict the future; I just notice patterns when the stars and planets are a certain way." He turned back to her, keeping a distance as he held the dresser corner to keep his balance. "But, I do talk to a ghost of my own, and sometimes, she tells me things in my dreams."

"A ghost of your own?" she clarified. "You mean a real one?"

"Yes. One of a little girl about your age."

"What's her name?"

The Ghost shrugged, crossing the room to be near her again.

"We didn't know each other very well when we were children. I was a troublemaker back then, much like your brothers, I'd imagine. She was a quiet, passive little thing and sold matches in the town square to make money for her family. One night, I stole one of her slippers to taunt her, and when I went to return it the next day, I couldn't. The townspeople gathered at the mouth of a dark, narrow alley where she was found. She'd frozen to death sometime in the night."

"Oh." The girl's shoulders slumped, and she rubbed her bandage again. Looking past him, she fixated on that old slipper on the mantle. That was surely the evidence of his story as far as she knew, and adults didn't make up such wild, macabre stories like children did. Right?

Maybe she could test it to be sure.

"Well, will you ask your ghost if my father will be long in Copenhagen this year? He's gone a lot with the military, and when he's home, my mother's not as moody, and my siblings bother him instead of me. He's home tomorrow for a short while, but each time he goes back, it feels longer and longer."

"That's a pretty big question. I'd need time to think about it, and you need to get back home. Here."

He walked over to the mantle, and the girl watched as he removed the slipper. Inside, he set the cloth of *æbleskiver* from his kitchen and handed them to her.

"You want me to carry them home in this?"

"Yes. It's my present to you and your family."

"This isn't a very good present," the girl remarked, even dismissing its interesting, possible origins from his boyhood. "My family makes prettier treats than yours, and we usually gift them in blue and white porcelain."

"It's all I have that's of great meaning." He folded the cheesecloth over the balls of dough and sugar to keep them warm inside the slipper.

"If your story's true, then I don't see how it's meaningful if a little girl died without it. For all I know, it's haunted, and you're passing a curse of it onto me." Suddenly, she lit up with a spark of her imagination. "Oh, can I pretend that you stole it from King Christian? It can be a haunted shoe that curses you to live a lonely life, and the only way to break it is to give it to someone else, full of sweets like you're doing now."

That would surely frighten her brothers.

"What would happen to your family then, if you took it home with you?" he asked.

The girl thought for a moment, her lips rolling as she glanced around the rest of the room for another idea.

"Well... I haven't gotten that far yet, but I'll think of something on the way home. I'd like to keep the bit about you stealing from the king, though."

"Then how about this: You heard it from me that his father, King Frederick, was a warlock. He cast a spell over this slipper, that whoever eats *æbleskiver* from this shoe has to leave Denmark forever."

"That's it? Just leave Denmark?" She pouted. "That's not very exciting for a spell."

"I suppose not, but it could be as true as the story of my ghost. How would you know the difference?"

The girl hummed to herself, thinking about the rest of the story if she were to tell it that way. "Where does the family who eats out of it have to go? The bottom of the ocean? To the top of a mountain?"

"Nope, just another country. Perhaps England, or better yet, farther west to the Americas."

"That's dumb."

"Well, too bad. It's how the spell works."

"It would be better if I could scare my siblings instead with an ocean or a mountain. England isn't scary, and I don't think my family is allowed to leave with my father's status as an officer."

"Well, if you'd like it to be scary, then I'll tell you this."

He crouched down in front of her, placing the slipper on her lap. He carefully took hold of her hands to give her a solemn warning.

"When your father comes home in the morning, ask him to bring the slipper back to me. If I've died here in my home upon his arrival, then that's a warning that you must leave Denmark."

"That's still boring." Although his deeper tone was a bit unsettling, she wouldn't give him the notion. "Why do you want us to leave? Do you want our house instead of this one?"

He chuckled, easing her nerves. "No, not at all. I think you're a very bright young lady with a promising future. If I can fix any wrongs from my past, I'd like to think that by helping you and your family, that might be the best I can do for now."

She eyed him. "Have you seen something in the future? Something terrible that's coming to Denmark?"

"Yes. You can tell your parents that if I've died by tomorrow morning, it's a sign from God to leave before the end of winter. Do not go south, or east. Only go north or west."

"What's coming that you won't tell me?"

"Something horrible I wouldn't dare mention." He stood, offering his hand to walk her to the door. "Besides, you wanted the story to be scary, didn't you? What's more terrifying than knowing something is about to happen, but you don't know what?"

The following morning, the girl waited at sunrise with the old slipper nestled in the nook of her arm. Behind her, her mother with a protective hand on her shoulder. Anxiety pulled the woman's lip into a scowl.

Surrounded by her siblings, they waited for the military truck to roll down their street and drop off their father out of the passenger side door. The girl waited behind with her mother, the last to greet her father as he made his way through his children, one by one.

Finally, he homed in on his youngest daughter.

"*Skattepige!*" he announced to her with affection. "How's my little treasure?"

He gave her a warm, tight squeeze, some of the left-over powdered sugar spilling out from the slipper still held to her chest. The treats themselves, long since eaten by her siblings and cousins.

Her father pulled away to look down at his uniform and the dusty remnants that soiled it.

"What's this?" he asked, patting it with curiosity. "Why are you holding that old shoe?"

"She got it from The Ghost!" her little brother shouted.

"Be quiet," the girl snapped at him, and she turned back to her father. "I got it last night from the old man who lives by the lake. He's not a bad man, he—"

"—*Min elskede?*" her mother interrupted. Her voice shivered in a frightful tremor.

Wrapped in a blanket against the cold, her mother stepped forward to block her from her father, and she whispered into his ear. Worry painted her face in a ghastly mask, and the longer she spoke, the more her father's face came to match it. The girl knew her mother was only filling her father's head with the same outrageous fears she expressed to her the previous night. When the girl came home, cold and wet with a bloodied palm, holding that slipper full of sweets with an unnerving tale to pair with it.

"Stop!" the girl shouted to her mother. She turned to her father. "Whatever she says, it's not like that!"

"What's this about you being alone with that man?" he demanded of her. "What have I told you about going out at night and talking to strangers?"

The harsh tone of her father put a stopper in any act of argument or disobedience on her part. The inviting emotion of love he expressed only a moment ago was replaced with vivid parental concern and anger.

Her mother took a step back, head down, her job complete as her father kneeled in front of her. He held out his hand for the slipper.

"Hand it to me," he ordered.

The girl stood frozen, unable to obey but unable to find the whimsical tone of the night before when met with such authority.

Without a second request, her father snatched it from her hold.

In calling her eldest brother to accompany him, her father wasted no time in their march toward the old cottage at the north end of Birkerød Sø.

Despite his demand that she stay behind in the house, the girl ran through the front door and fled through the kitchen to catch up to them around the back way.

"You should have been watching her," her father barked at her sixteen-year-old brother. Their voices grew louder as she trailed behind. "The world's gone mad these days, and we're not about to let any of our own be part of it by having some old man fill her head with nonsense, and God knows what else."

By the time they reached the front door, her father banged only twice upon it, announcing his presence as an officer of the Danish Royal Army, before entering inside.

By the time the girl reached the front of the cottage, she slowed her run to a cautious approach.

The Ghost of Birkerød Sø was not in his bed but curled up by the stove. The embers had long since turned to dust and ash before sunrise, the room about as chilled as the air outside, without the sun to mend it.

Her heart sank to her stomach at the sight of it all. Even her brother seemed unnerved as he held himself and kept his distance, just inside the foyer.

"What's happened here?" he asked their father.

The girl's father kept steadfast, removing his officer's hat as he crossed over to check the body hunched over on the dusty old floorboards. He kneeled to observe him as the girl pressed herself to the frame of the doorway.

She stared past her brother at the scene unfolding before her. Two fingers, pressed to the veins of his neck, and her father's eyes, looking for the rise and fall of a chest that would never come again.

And the slipper dropped from her father's hold onto the floor beside The Ghost.

"He's dead." Her father studied the room for any signs of a struggle before standing upright. He placed his cap back on and stared down into the empty stove. "Looks like he couldn't keep warm with this old thing." He knocked it slightly with his boot.

The girl stepped forward and held onto her brother who placed his hand on her shoulder for support. In looking upon the stillness of the old man's body, there was a slight curl of a smile there on his cracked lips. One that saw the end of the last night of 1939 before the dawn of a new, uncertain year.

She held her brother closer, staring at that old slipper left abandoned by the stove, and wondered.

What dancing pictures had he seen before the last of those embers burned out?

The Birth of the Morrigan

By J.K. Raymond

Sweat covered Rigan's brow as she startled from her sleep. It was the story of her life, same shit, different night. Rising from her bed, her legs twisted in a tangle of bed sheets and night clothes causing her to fall flat on her face.

Head in her hands, Rigan whispered, "Three, two, one." As the door to her bed chamber flew open.

"'Tis almost the witching hour, my lady."

"You think I don't know that, Three!" she answered from the floor on the far side of the bed, opposite the chamber door.

"I only mention it as it is my duty. I assure you, I don't like it any more than you do, my lady."

"Stop it with the 'my lady!'" Rigan yelled.

She was exhausted, sweaty, and tired of Three's shit. Completely frustrated she popped up to her knees and gave the mattress a good hard smack for emphasis. "It's been three hundred and seventy-four years, I know the drill."

"Forgive me for being impertinent my lady, but if that were true you would already be at the computer sorting spell requests and not... What is it you are doing exactly?" Three cocked his head in the way only a smart-ass raven could. "Praying, are you..." he asked, cocking his head to the opposite side. "How odd." Adding insult to injury by narrowly escaping the pillow she just threw across the room.

"Wake up on the wrong side of the bed my lady?" Three asked, landing unphased on the perch beside her desk.

She didn't answer him. There was no point. Almost four hundred years had taught her that Three would be happy baiting her for an eternity. And he might get the chance.

"Ugh. I'll be right there," Rigan said as she stood to change. With a flick of her hand, the sweaty night dress and bedhead were gone. Traded in for jeans and a t-shirt that said, "Murder shows and comfy clothes."

"Classy."

Ignoring the quip, Rigan walked past the snarky bird and sat in her chair. The bubble at the bottom of her computer screen let her know she already had over three thousand spell requests waiting for a response. Most of them were going to go straight to her spam folder but she was going to have to open every single one just to be sure she didn't miss something really important.

Rubbing at her eyes she reached for her coffee and got to work for the next hour.

"Anything today?" Four asked as he landed on the windowsill in perfect time with the fourth chime of the clock.

Rigan shook her head. "Nope. Nothing."

Four flew to her shoulder where he would remain perched for the next hour. Four was the sweet brother. His simple two-word question had been heavy with empathy, understanding, concern, and a dash of hope. At least the curse only affected her brothers for only an hour each day. Unfortunately, she didn't get so lucky.

It's funny now, looking back on all of those years, thinking she had saved her brothers from her father's curse that had turned them all into ravens. She'd had gone through hell to find them, save them, and bring them back whole. There had been so much joy, for such a small amount of time.

Then one by one, to the chime of the clock from the start of witching hour until the late morning sun sat high in the sky, each one of her seven brothers turned into a raven at their assigned time. But the phenomenon only lasted one hour per brother. Even worse, they had each come with an assignment. The little scrolls attached to the foot of each raven brother may as well have been a chain.

When she'd opened the scrolls and read the instructions of what she must do in each brothers' specific hour to keep them all alive, all her hopes and dreams fell away. They had all been cursed to a life of misery. And it was all her fault. If she hadn't been such a sickly baby, her brothers would never have been sent to the spring to gather water for a baptism. Her baptism. A haphazard ceremony rushed for fear she would die before she could be "saved." And look at them now. Damned. Every last one of them. Even father, who'd slit his throat to escape it all, was surely in a hell of his own making on some other plane of existence.

"Race ya!" Four yelled as Rigan's human body morphed into a she-wolf in the early morning darkness.

This was the very best part of her day. Four always knew how to brush away the worry that weighed on her. And the she-wolf she became in the Hour of the Wolf cared little for guilt. Ruminating over doing whatever you needed to do to survive was just plain dumb as far as her wolf form was concerned and Rigan was more than happy to give it up, for an hour anyway.

"Where to?" Rigan sent the telepathic question to Four.

"Somewhere new I think."

"What could be new in Grimm's Woods? We've covered it all a thousand times."

"Just follow me." Four sent a message back telepathically before banking a hard right, flying like wind over bramble, brush, and creek beds.

"Cheater!"

When did Four become an asshole? Rigan thought internally. This was supposed to be a friendly competition not whatever this had become.

"Oh, come on, you're doing great!" Four cheered happily.

"Your sunny nature is not going to help you get back in my good graces. I'll be picking burs out of my fur for a month!"

"As soon as you turn back into your human form they'll disappear and you know it. Now quit your bitching and get your ass up the bluff side."

Rigan dropped to her haunches making it clear she wasn't going anywhere.

"You can't do it can you?"

Because Four was her favorite; he knew all her little picadilloes. And telling her she couldn't do something was exactly how to get her to prove she could.

"Asshole." She sent the message as she circled back and then took a running jump at the cliff wall. Her paw found the footholds it needed to push off to the next and the next until she finally found herself on top of the bluff. Winded and worn with her paws bleeding, a sense of unease brought a growl to her throat.

"What is this?" Rigan whispered her message to three.

"You don't have to go inside, Rigan. I don't even want you to."

"Then why bring me here? Did you think I needed to face my demons? I face them every day, brother!"

"No. No. Not at all. You trust me?"

"I used to."

"That's not fair, Rig."

"Neither is this, Four."

The Glass Mountain standing before her seemed to exist in a liminal space. As if it was trapped between the fading moon and the rising sun. Frozen in time. Like her heart.

The door she'd used to enter almost three hundred years ago to find her brothers looked larger somehow, but the keyhole had remained the same size. Small. Just small enough to fit the bones of a child's little finger. Her finger. The one she'd cut off to use its little bone in place of the key she'd lost. Cold sweat covered her every-where as she flashed back to picking the lock. Blood coating her hands and mouth after having stripped the meat from the bones of her little finger.

"What is the purpose of this, Four?"

"You'll have to ask him tomorrow." Five's voice echoed in her mind as she twisted into her next form.

"I'm afraid he'll be too late," said a guttural voice from behind.

Standing on two legs, Rigan was now a Valkyrie. And she was canvassing the area as such. A warrior goddess who took no prisoners.

Already turning toward the new voice on the first syllable that left his lips, Rigan targeted one responsible for a strangely familiar yet foreboding voice. Automatic, her bow was already drawn. She couldn't think in this form when there was a perceived threat. The Valkyrie just acted on her behalf. It was only the small part of the real Rigan trapped deep inside the Valkyrie form that prevented the owner of the new voice from being dead already.

"You." Rigan recognized and accused the dwarf standing no more than ten feet away. The word was a combination of Rigan's memories and her Valkyrie acting as Judge, Jury, and Executioner.

The dwarf's hands were in the air as if surrendering. But his feet were slowly shuffling toward a large outcropping of boulders on the right.

"Yes me," the dwarf confirmed, keeping his eyes locked on the Valkyrie.

"One more step and you're dead."

"But, my sweet, then you would never know how I recognized you. After all, the last time we met you were just a little girl."

"It's probably the missing pinky. Don't worry, it won't interfere with my aim."

"Don't be so testy, after all, it was I who returned your brothers to you."

"No, you told me they weren't home and baited me with poisoned food."

"I did no such thing. I sat at the table for the seven ravens that would soon return home for their food. It's not my fault you sampled the fare."

"What was in it, Dwarf?" Rigan commanded with all the authority of a Valkyrie that could raze a battlefield in the blink of an eye.

"Only the ties that bind," the dwarf answered, but this time he almost sounded ashamed.

"Too vague." The Valkyrie in her took over and shot the pinky finger clean off the dwarf's left hand. The severed appendage dropped with a tiny thud into the damp early morning grass.

Screaming the dwarf clutched his hand to his chest as Rigan pressed.

"Tree dwarves can't do magic, and they certainly don't live in mountains. Who do you work for?"

"Me," said a creature who stood even taller than her Valkyrie height of seven feet.

The creature was blue like the Glass Mountain behind her. What little light the oncoming dawn cast seemed to reflect off his features, creating the illusion that he was a living breathing extension of the Glass Mountain itself. Rigan's first thought was that he was lovely. Her Valkyrie's first thought was that the blue fucker had to die.

"What are you?" she challenged. Coming to a common ground between her and her Valkyrie. Information was always the most important thing in war and she knew that her Valkyrie knew it too.

"That is just about the saddest thing I have ever heard, Morrigan. Do you mean to tell me you live in a magical forest, change forms seven times a day, and your brothers... well, I really don't get how you couldn't know of the Tuatha De' Danann. After all, you are standing at the border between our worlds. It was your pinky finger Morrigan that opened Pandora's box and let us out. Sort of. Anyway, don't get me wrong, Bru na Boinne is a lovely mountain, but no one wants to be locked away inside of it for nearly a millennia."

"You're saying an awful lot of really weird words, and I don't like your tone you, Avatar-looking asshole," the Valkyrie said, firing an arrow at the blue fuckers left pinky before the last word left her lips.

"Son of a..."

The blue creature backhanded the dwarf before the little man could even clutch his other hand.

Her arrow hit the dwarf? How did she miss? She never missed. Rigan and the Valkyrie thought simultaneously. For once they agreed on something. WTAF?

"You look shocked Morganna. Something wrong?" the Tuatha de dumbass asked. He was really getting on their moon-forsaken nerves. It took everything she had to hold the Valkyrie back. She needed more information, and she was done screwing around.

"If you want to live you best start talking," Rigan said, taking two bold steps forward as she aimed directly between the blue creature's eyes.

"I'm Fae. And I simply granted the curse your father put on your brothers for not bringing your baptism water home fast enough. It may also be the reason they didn't return fast enough, but honestly, it was just too easy to pass up."

"What was?" Rigan pulled her bowstring back two inches. She wouldn't miss this time. If he had been the one that cursed them, she would simply kill him and break the curse.

"The chance to get out from under this mountain. Your father made that possible. Well, him and little Arthur here," he said pointing to the moaning dwarf standing to his right.

"I swear to the moon if you get blood on me Arthur you'll be cleaning piss pots for the next hundred years," which brings me back to you Morganna. Kill me and you and your brothers will stay this way forever."

"Not possible," Rigan said as she let her arrow fly. She didn't miss, but she hadn't hit her mark either. She'd never met a being she couldn't take down in one shot, let alone two. Was he really Fae? She'd been told her whole life they didn't exist, but because of the curse, she could never leave Grimms Forest. It would explain why she couldn't break the curse, no matter how great a witch she had become. She'd studied for hours with Eight, Nine, and Ten by her side. Three hours a day for almost four hundred years and never once came close to breaking the spell.

"Could this asshole be the reason?" her Valkyrie thought in synchronicity with her... again.

"Feisty." the Fae said, rubbing the knick her sharp arrow had left in his ear. "Five, tell her. I've had enough of this shit and the hour grows late. We are losing liminal space, and we won't get it back for another four hundred years."

"Five?" Rigan asked, horrified. Suddenly, realizing that the most talkative of her brothers had barely said a word during the whole encounter. Never turning her head from the Fae in front of her, she said his name again, this time with the full power of a Valkyrie behind it.

"Five!"

"I'm sorry, Rigan. I wasn't allowed to tell you. I mean, I couldn't tell you. Every time I tried I..."

"Enough, Five! Just tell me! I'm not interested in excuses. Tell. Me. What. You. Know."

"Mother was promised to the king of the Tuatha De' Danann... the Fae. She was an important bargaining chip for peace between the Fae and the Witches. With her wed to the king, it would settle the three-hundred-year war between the factions."

The Valkyrie caught the slightest movement on the foot of the Fae and fired. She didn't miss a third time. The arrow shot straight through.

"Continue, Five," Rigan commanded with all the stoniness of a Valkyrie. Beneath the surface, the real Rigan fell back and let the Valkyrie overtake security while she listened and absorbed all of the terrible things that five was saying.

"Dianna... our mother. She was told she must marry the king, but she refused and ran away here to Grimm Woods with our father, a lowly warlock...one with very little power. It was an assault against both parties. The move was insurmountable. Within days the Witch and the Fae armies were closing in on the two of them. That's when Grandmother interceded and poured all of her power into casting a Mirage Spell over Grimm Woods. The witches would never remember that the woods existed. That included any being that lived within it. The Mirage Spell cut off everyone and everything existing in the woods from the outside world."

"A mirage spell wouldn't take all of her power. Not a witch as strong as our grandmother. You're lying Five."

"She used the rest of her remaining power to encase the encroaching Fae army in a mountain of glass. This mountain. And so, it had remained until you were born sick and small. You were so frail Rigan. We all knew you would die."

"But I didn't die. I saved you from this mountain, from the curse."

"Rigan, the only reason you were ever strong enough to live beyond that day is because Father cursed us. All our power reverted to you when father cursed us to be Raven's for our tardiness. You have to fix this Rigan. It's your fault we are like this."

Her Valkyrie didn't flinch. It was the only way she knew she hadn't been pierced through the heart with a knife. How was she supposed to deal with this level of betrayal? How could they do this to her? No, now wasn't the time for emotions... think Rigan... focus.

"How? How is it the fault of a child that her father was a stupid, desperate warlock? And a weak one at that! He didn't have the power to curse the seven of you. Not on his own anyway," Rigan said, releasing another arrow into the Fae still busy trying to remove the first arrow from his foot.

"That arrow won't come loose. Not until I allow it."

"That fact only remains true for the next fifteen minutes, then your Valkyrie powers will disappear, and you will become a scribe for the next three hours. Tick Tock Morganna," the Fae said with far too much confidence for her or her Valkyrie's liking.

"You must Marry Lain and end this Morganna and you must do it now or we will all spend eternity paying for Grandmother and Father's failures. If you marry Lain, it all ends. We will be free of the curse and the Witches and the Fae's centuries-old war will end with it.. You must do this Rigan."

"Who the Hades is Lain?"

"I am," said the Fae with two of her arrows stuck in him. "And you must do it now, before the hour ends or we lose our chance for another four hundred years."

The Valkyrie centered her aim on Lain's heart. The warrior queen was ambivalent. She simply wanted to win the war and she wanted to do it now. Fighting to take control over the Valkyrie's instincts took everything Rigan had.

"Be smart about this, Rigan. Do you really want to spend the next four hundred years tied to us knowing that we serve Lain? That we have since the day Father cursed us. Let it be over, Rig."

"Don't call me that," Rigan commanded. "Only my friends call me that and I have no friends."

"Do you accept, Morganna? All you have to do is say that you accept, and it's done. We will be wed and the curse brought upon us will end, the war will end, and you'll never have to see your brothers again."

The Valkyrie turned her aim on her brother as Rigan forced the words, "I accept" through her lips.

In one single, solitary moment the curse broke, her arrow flew straight through Five's now human heart, and her Valkyrie left her for the very last time.

"There now, isn't this better?" Lain said.

Powerless against the army of Fae that appeared where the glass mountain had stood just a second ago.

Rigan watched as her favorite brother took his last breath.

"Much."

An Eternal Winter

By Arwyn Sherman

1.

"Tell me again the story about the Snow Queen." Clara puts the hood of her cloak up, trying to block out the chill from the loose window.

Roan laughs, leans back into the pile of furs on his side of the room, and puts his hands behind his head. They're in the attic, a room they've shared since they were first taken to the warden. Two small kids jostled together with nothing in common but missing parents and a fear of the cold. They grew into the small space that was theirs, filled it with gangly teenage limbs, and whispered late-night stories. Clara's favorite was the tale of the Snow Queen.

"You know that one." Roan rolls his eyes. But it's all part of the game, their nightly ritual. The storyteller must be coaxed out, must feign disdain until the proper amount of begging has occurred.

"Please, Roan." Clara plays her part, bringing her safflower mittens together as if about to pray. Her auburn curls poke out from the brown canvas hood and glitter in the light of the lone candle. Crude dark stitches line all her clothes. "You tell it so well."

"Okay, fine." Roan smiles, a glittering flash in the dim light.

Many, many years ago, long before our parents or even our parents' parents were born, there used to be four seasons. Springtime, where everything rises from the mud and becomes vibrant. Summer, with its endlessly hot days and water-filled lakes. Autumn's brown leaves and cool mornings. And winter, the only season we know now. Which, I don't have to describe, because we all know it well.

One day, on the very coldest night, a girl was born. No one knew it at the time, but she was born with the magic of winter. From her very fingertips, she could conjure ice, wind, and snow; anything that froze and was cold. Her village didn't understand her and was afraid; such was the way of most folk. She was exiled when she grew up and could no longer hide. Hopeless, she went to the royal court for mercy and shelter. The king was immediately besotted with her beauty and asked her to marry him. The night before the wedding, she revealed her snow magic to him, wanting their matrimony to be based on honesty. She hoped he would respond kinder than her kin had. But the king cast her out and vowed to kill her if she ever returned. When she left, the king realized the danger he set forth and sent huntsmen to kill her. Instead of their return, a cold winter set upon the land and never turned to spring. They say it was the Snow Queen's punishment, and no autumn fire magic would undo the curse she had laid upon them.

Clara sighs contentedly and pulls her knit blanket around her, settling into the bedding on the floor. Roan holds his hand out and the flame of the candle sinks into darkness.

"Was that good enough where you'll leave me alone?" he jokes, and she can hear the smile in his voice.

"Do you think the Snow Queen is still alive?"

"I don't think the Snow Queen was ever real."

"Then what about the seasons? How do we know they existed?"

"Because they exist elsewhere. But this is a kingdom of ice."

2.

Winter magic is what they call it, the ability to call the frigid season into your fingertips. To cast it out into the world and make everything ice. Roan has autumn magic, bringing fire to his palm with a muted snap of his fingers. If the warden knew, he would send Roan to fight in the King's army and probably make a nice coin off the exchange. So, it is Clara and Roan's secret they keep together. Clara has winter buried deep inside her, coaxing icicles out of nothing and sending wind anywhere she wants.

This is Clara's secret she keeps to herself.

Clara gains another secret when she is sweeping the stone hallway on another frigid night, the moonlight guiding her movements. The warden is in the kitchen with his wife, his voice carrying out the partially open door. A chunk of light like a cut of cheese comes from the kitchen, interrupting the quiet dark of the hall.

"That girl is getting right up to marrying age." The warden's voice, low and gruff, creeps out of the room like an unwelcome rat. Clara stills upon hearing herself mentioned, the broom coming to a quiet stop against the dusty floor.

"Oh, surely not for a few more years," his wife says, timid as always. Clara can almost see her fretfully smoothing her dress as she speaks, her voice a soprano whisper.

Clara leans the broom as quietly as she can against the wall and slips over to the door to hear better. She stands against the wall, head tilted as close as possible to the entryway.

"Every day we keep her we lose money. I have someone interested, a soldier who came by a few weeks ago and took a little fancy to her."

"She does work for us. She's not a complete waste."

"Bah, barely enough to warrant the food we give her. And he's willing to pay us."

"Are you sure you can't wait another year? It is nice to have her for the potatoes."

"Woman, you don't know anything about keeping house. Let me be. The soldier gets her. He's coming in a few days to collect."

His wife is silent, as always. A battle barely fought and already lost. Clara holds a hand to her mouth, the rough yarn of her mittens pressing against her lips, the smell of nightshade and dirt still heavy on them. She thinks about leaving her little attic room, her talks with Roan, even the digging job she's assigned to, and her chest closes up. She can feel the need to cry, but it's almost as if her tears are as scared as she is, hovering at the back of her eyes. She slips away, making sure to put everything back in the closet to hide that she was ever there.

If she is going to escape, they must not know she heard their plans. And escape she will, no matter what the cost.

3.

She waits until Roan is asleep before untangling herself from her blankets. It's been two days since she heard the warden talking to his wife, and every passing hour she can feel the breath of this mystery soldier against her neck, a haunting specter that lurks in every stray thought. She thought about telling Roan, asking him for help, but every time she played that thought out in her mind, she only saw him giving up more for her than she was willing to ask of him.

He's blissful now, looking childish in his deep slumber, mouth slightly open, eyes covered by dark hair, the moonlight glowing against his umber skin. She pulls on thick leggings and a thick cotton slip before getting into her loose canvas dress she sewed from worn potato sacks. The stitches are dark and obvious, much like her cloak, which she puts on after slipping on her one sweater the warden's wife gifted her out of pity. It's cashmere, cream-colored with small, soft rose swirls embroidered at the neck.

Night is the coldest hour, dropping into a dangerous and windy freeze. Although Clara knows having winter magic makes her more resilient to it, she also knows she is not fully immune, the speck of frostbite on her right pinky a permanent reminder of that.

Her thickly knitted socks are quiet against the wood floor as she takes the ladder slowly to not make noise. A quick survey to make sure the warden has not awakened, and then she is gone, slipping through the loose window and fleeing to the woods. A tiny speck against the dark night, becoming smaller and smaller until she is nothing at all. A darkness within the darkness, a body swallowed by the woods.

Clara's plan is simple—walk through the forest to the bustling inner kingdom. There, in the city, she is sure there is an inn that needs a maid or a blacksmith wanting a shopgirl. Somewhere she can tuck herself into and remain unmarried for as long as she wants. It wasn't the safest life, but it was something better than what was coming for her.

The length of the woods is unknown; some say it's infinite, others claim it's a mere mile. Clara hopes it's closer to the latter as she tromps through the tall snow. It's the light fluffy kind that sinks under her weight, making it double the effort to move forward.

Everything is quiet, save the occasional hunting cry of an owl and thump when a tree relieves itself of a clump of snow on its branches. Clara can taste the chill on her chapped lips, the air from every exhale sucking more warmth out of her. She continues to walk, the white fluff grabbing at her boots, weighing them down with every step. One misjudged step and she ends up in a deep patch, her foot sinking into oblivion, the snow coming up to her thigh. Clara falls with a soft ooof, the chill biting her cheek as she carousauls into the snow, the taste of dirt and melting water in her mouth. She can feel the snow rolling into her boots from the top, like icicle fingers running down her legs and pooling around her feet.

She sits up and turns, sinks deeper into the snow, which circles around her waist like a frigid lover's hug. When she tries to stand, the snow weighs her down, pulling her into the ground until she's sprawled out helplessly. Looks up at the pinpoint stars, the sliced moon. Their light echoes enough off her breath so it looks like a half cloud rising from her lips.

What she wouldn't give for Roan and his ability to craft fire from nothing. She closes her eyes tightly and wills this thought away with only a single tear escaping. Every abled man in the city is drafted to the King's army unless they have a coveted apprenticeship. There wouldn't be any opportunities for an orphan like him. If she had asked, he would have gone with her. But she would never forgive herself if he were discovered and drafted. The minute anyone is enlisted, it's a slow march to death in foreign lands.

Time passes. She becomes aware she's losing touch in her fingers; her feet feel absent and heavy. Tries to clench her fist and feels like she's squeezing a lump of cloth. With a deep breath, she forces herself to sit up, then rolls to her knees and tries to stand. Her feet are foreign under her, blank from cold and unresponsive to her commands. She falls again, her hand catching her as she crashes back into the white powder.

A slow, ugly thought creeps into her mind. Uglier than regretting not bringing Roan. That the city may be too far away, that she may become a frozen corpse, hidden by layers and layers of endless winter. She would cry, but the exhaustion weighs her down and makes any strong reaction impossible. Instead, she sighs and contemplates how nice a nap would be, how she probably wouldn't feel that cold if she went to sleep.

Clara hears her first, a soft melody like a chorus of birds singing. So quiet she thinks she may be hearing a funeral song. Then she sees a small light a few moments before realizing the woman isn't holding any lantern, but rather is the light, her skin so translucent it reflects off the snow. Her blonde hair is the color of sunrise at the very brink of dawn, the beige tendrils when the beginnings of the day are barely cresting night. The woman wears it in an impressive array of braids that circle her head like a crown; bits of gold spiral and jewels flicker with every turn of her head.

Her silk dress crunches as she kneels beside Clara, close enough she can see the intricate gold embroidery along the edges. She smells of holly berries and fir, her hand warm against Clara's frozen cheeks.

"Oh, dear one," the woman murmurs. "You must come with me."

Before Clara can force her mouth to form words, she is scooped up and taken to a gilded sleigh pulled by two smoky-gray horses. She's wrapped in furs until she can barely see over them. The beautiful woman climbs in after her and gives her a tight-lipped smile.

"Who are you?" Clara finally musters the energy to ask as the woman clicks to her horses and the sled begins to pick up speed, the trees flashing past her in blurs of brown.

"I'm the Snow Queen," the woman says passively and gives Clara a look that can only be described as devilish. Even though she knows she should be scared, she feels a deep thrill of excitement as the sled barrels forward into the night.

4.

The room is too quiet when Roan wakes, absent of Clara's usual mumbling and morning protests. The sun breaks through the window, casting light on an empty space where Clara should be. In their entire childhood together, she's never woken before him, and this space of empty blankets and furs unsettles him.

In the kitchen, there's no sign of Clara. Her mug and allotted slice of bread still sit on the table, waiting for her appearance as much as Roan is.

The warden hasn't noticed she's gone yet. It's not unusual for her to come downstairs after Roan. If Clara isn't here, and she's not upstairs, then she is somewhere that she probably shouldn't be. This realization turns the unsettled feeling in his stomach sour, the tea he's drinking curdling at the back of his throat.

The warden's wife looks directly at Roan, her blue eyes holding his in a way that's unusual for her normal meek demeanor. When the warden isn't looking, she takes Clara's mug and bread and walks out of the kitchen with a long, pointed stare at Roan that he interprets as a sign to follow. A few beats later, he does, slipping out of the house. The snow crunches under his feet as he makes his way past the greenhouse, along the wall, looking for the warden's wife.

She's tucked away in a small recess between the house and a shed. The smell of wet soil is heavy as he steps into the dark and skinny corridor. He can see her breath, faintly smelling of cream and lavender.

"He hasn't noticed she's gone," the wife whispers, "but I did; she left at high moon last night."

"Why didn't you stop her?" Roan says, a little too sharply for who he's speaking to.

"And do what? Force her back? You know, the warden is going to sell her off for marriage by the end of the week. She must have heard him talking about it."

Clara hadn't mentioned any of this to him, and there's a small prick of hurt she kept this information from him. The wife pushes the staling piece of bread into his hands.

"She's probably already dead," the wife whispers. "You have a few hours before my husband figures it out. It might be good to make yourself scarce until he calms down; you know how he gets."

"I have to go after her," Roan says. "She might be in trouble."

"It's no use, you'll just get yourself killed."

"I still have to try."

The warden's wife doesn't have a response. Her large eyes just look sad as Roan turns away, walking to the back where he keeps his sled. He throws the wooden contraption over his shoulders as he crunches through the icy snow toward the woods. He knows when he returns the warden will be mad that he spent the day looking for Clara instead of working, but whenever he pauses to think about her, all he can imagine is the worst. Broken bones, stuck in a ravine, frozen. Clara bent and irreparably cracked apart.

His pace quickens at this thought until he's practically running through the thick snow, the powder surging against his trousers like water against the bow of a ship. When he crests a hill, he throws his sled down in one fluid motion and jumps on, holding the rickety wood handles as it gathers speed. He looks at his surroundings as he barrels downward, trying to see her brown cloak, and the small red cap she sometimes wears.

He is a blur through the forest, calling out Clara's name as he glides across the forest floor until he bottoms out at a plateau, coming to rest against a large evergreen. He leans against its girthy trunk and sighs, giving the area a glance over and finding nothing but green pines and snow.

A small crow hops his way to him, one foot touching the snow before quickly changing to the other. Its obsidian feathers glint in the mid-morning sun, its eyes dark but intelligent.

"Have you seen my friend, little one?" Roan asks, even though the likelihood that this is a talking animal is fairly low.

The creature proves probability is not in Roan's favor as it softly caws and cocks its head so one eye is directly upon him, but says nothing. It reaches its wings out as if to stretch them, shaking and reshuffling his feathers. Returns them to their usual spot, and gives himself another puff before settling in to stare at Roan.

He takes the bread meant for Clara out of his pocket and tears off a small piece, tossing it to the critter. She often feeds the birds with her morning slice, and he feels she would appreciate him offering the creature something.

It hops toward the bread, inspecting it with one beady eye before snapping it up off the snow. Gives Roan an expectant stare. He laughs in spite of himself and offers it another bite, which the crow eagerly takes.

"The girl," it creaks, beak up to the sky as if forming words is a monumental effort. "The girl with the dark golden hair."

"Yes, yes that's her." Roan jumps into a crouch and looks at the now-talking crow. "Have you seen her?"

"Such lovely hair." Its voice sounds like a poorly played flute, windy and barely there. "Wanted to take some for my nest, like fine jewelry or nice roasted wheat."

"Is she okay? Where did you see her?"

"Snow Queen took her, wrapped her up like a present. To the castle she goes." The crow then lets out a large caw and flies for a few beats, sending its small body a foot or so into the air before settling down.

"The Snow Queen doesn't exist," Roan sighs.

"Yes, she does!" Another hop. "Yes, she does! And your friend is with her."

"Where?"

"The castle!"

"Where is her castle?" Roan's voice is hollow, not particularly trusting this crow and its stories.

"Go to the end of the woods," it croaks. "Take the road east. I will meet you when the sun rises."

Roan gives the crow the rest of Clara's bread. Before he was orphaned, his mother had told him that one must always be polite to talking animals. He wasn't going to turn his back on that now, even if she wasn't around to remind him. The crow jumps to the stray crumbs and snaps them up, giving Roan a perfunctory nod before leaping into the still winter air.

Another sigh, deeper this time, he stands. With nothing else but a crow's word, he decides his best course of action is to try and find the road it spoke of and go from there.

He brushes the snow off his trousers and sets off toward the end of the forest.

5.

Now that the morning light was upon them and Clara was no longer on the brink of freezing, she could appreciate that the Snow Queen is incredibly beautiful. Sharp cheekbones and unfettered skin, her eyes sparkling like polished sapphires. Even amongst the brutish, hacked forest covered in snow, she is elegant. Her posture is like that of a true queen—straight and rigid. Her horses are equally regal, like puffs of smoke rearing in the frosty sun. Just looking at her makes Clara's heart beat uncomfortably fast, her palms sweating in foreign discomfort.

They ride in silence, the sled slipping smoothly and silently across the forest. Clara regards the Snow Queen with wide eyes and briefly wonders if she's died and this is just a very pleasant afterlife. How often had she wished for an incredibly alluring woman to whisk her away from her farm life drudgery? Too often to count, and now, here she is.

"You're not dead," the queen speaks as if reading her mind. "You have that stunned look about you people get when they think they've crossed over. I promise this is not the afterlife."

"Do you often put people in the position where they think they've perished?"

"Ah," the Snow Queen smiles, her lips a deep red. "Normally they have, indeed, crossed over and I am not in the position to tell them otherwise."

"I see." Clara sinks deeper into the plush furs surrounding her, "In that case, where are you taking me?"

"My castle. It isn't much longer."

Clara doesn't have a response, deciding to take in the scenery they're riding through. She isn't sure why the Snow Queen has spared her but isn't going to test her luck by getting annoying and asking too many questions.

A few minutes of silence later and the castle is upon them. They come to the large, ornate gates with golden swirls and opal inlay. The stone glints like a fresh snow cover, twinkling as the sled descends to the front. The horses whinny, their hooves prancing impatiently beside the glittering wall.

The Snow Queen lifts her right hand, her left clutching the reins, and unfurls her fingers. A ring of rainbow, the kind Clara used to catch against the wall when she played with her mother's glass wind chimes, splays outward. The air itself seems to shimmer before a gust of frigid wind blows through the gate and pushes it open. Once they are inside, she does a similar motion to blow them closed.

The courtyard is quiet, the sound of the horses clopping along the cobblestones the only noise as they roll toward the castle. Gardens flourish around them—vibrant apples ripe for plucking hang heavy off trees, a bursting greenery of squash and beans. The air is pleasant and warm, an unknown feeling to Clara, who gets feverish and quickly sheds her furs.

"It's not winter here," she says as she looks up at the fruit trees that bushel toward the sky.

"No, it never is."

"How?"

"I make the winter, and where I desire, I can make the absence of it, too."

"Then why make the rest of the kingdom an eternal winter?"

"To punish them, of course." The Snow Queen clucks her tongue to still her horses. She steps out of the sled and offers Clara her hand, which she accepts, and allows herself to be guided to the ground.

The door to the castle is heavy oak, with rusted bolts and well-oiled hinges keeping it together. It's larger than both of them and shadows the entire front step. Despite its size, the Snow Queen pushes it easily inwards. Takes Clara's hand and leads her into a long hallway lined by floor-to-ceiling shelves. A long, red carpet runs down the length of it, and Clara makes sure to step carefully to not muss it up.

"Is there a name I can call you, unless you prefer Snow Queen?" Clara steps over a wrinkle in the rug.

"Elise," she says simply. "But only when we're alone and never in public."

"Okay... Elise. Why did you rescue me?"

"You're so full of questions, little one, aren't you?" Elise laughs and it sounds like a million little bells chiming at the same time.

She stops and whirls Clara so she's facing her. Reaches out and places a hand on Clara's heart. Even through her thick cloak she can feel the pressure, the warmth. Her heart is beating out of control, her lungs folding in on themselves until she can barely breathe.

"Because." Elise smiles. "You have the same magic as me."

6.

Roan spots the main road as he breaks from the tree line of the forest. A swath of cleared snow that's turned to mud. He tries to pull his sled along behind him but it soon gets stuck, hiccupping over the rocks and sticky soil. He tries to carry it on his back, but after a few miles that becomes too much of a burden. Eventually, as his shoulders creak and neck pops with each step, he admits to himself that he must leave it behind. Finds a tree that's been split by lightning and tucks it into the empty space where the trunk parted.

Roan's chest restricts as he turns away from his sled. He swallows unexpected tears that spring to his eyes. The sled was the last vestige of his life before the warden, and watching it lay there, soon to be abandoned, twists a shard of grief that is buried deep in his heart. He remembers his mother giving it to him, her cheeks rosy and flushed, eyes filled with pride as he took it outside and flew down the hill by their cottage. And now it is nothing more than a chunk of wood nestled in the crook of a dead tree. Roan forces himself to take a breath and push his distress down until his face is placid.

Roan walks until the sun starts to set, a light orange like stained glass alight across the road. He looks back as if he can track the starting point of his journey, how far he's come. Sees only his set of footprints squelched in the mud. When Roan turns back he is stopped by a man standing in the middle of the road. He's large and brutish, covered in grime and soot. Old furs cling to his body, held together with waxed twine and luck, a large sanded club in one hand and a knife in the other.

The moment Roan stops, he is surrounded. Everyone in the group appears like the first man, unwashed and filthy like they've slept in the mud. All of them have weapons, some sharpened wood spears, others antiquated guns with rust that blooms like wisteria vines along the edges.

The man gives Roan a blackened smile and proclaims, "In case you haven't figured it out, you're being robbed."

"I don't have any money," Roan says.

"Well, that is just too bad," the man says, his gut giving a slight bounce as he grabs Roan's arm. "We don't have much use for penniless folks on the road here."

"Wait." A girl steps into the circle, leading a spotted horse behind her. She looks related to the man, same brown hair, dark feral eyes that hop around like they're constantly assessing the world. She has a singular, thick braid that comes around her shoulder and hangs to her waist, a dress of crudely stitched furs and canvas. She points a slender finger at Roan and states, "I would like him."

"Daughter, we can't just keep everyone ya fancy," the man sighs and turns to the crew.

"I would really like him," the girl says loudly before her father can speak again.

The man groans, gives Roan an eye roll as if to say, *daughters, what can you do*, and waves his hand at the rest of the crew, dismissing them.

"I guess we're taking you," he says, and Roan can only nod through the terror that's flushing through him.

Roan rides with the robber girl. The crew moves as one through the woods, abandoning the main roads and going into the depths of the forest. At first, Roan tries to not touch the girl, but eventually, the ride gets too bumpy and he wraps his arm around her waist. The patches of fur feel smooth against his wrist, her canvas-covered shoulders scratchy against his face. She smells surprisingly pleasant, like wood smoke and berries.

"You'll like it here," she says. "It's not so bad; we have a good cave that you can keep dry in."

Roan nods, unable to speak. Even though he's behind her, she seems to accept his response and reaches back, slowly stroking his jaw with her hand.

"I'm looking for my friend," he manages to stutter out.

"That's too bad," the robber girl shrugs, her whole body rolling with her shoulders. "You're one of us now. Which means you aren't going anywhere."

7.

The dining hall has high dark ceilings with painted stars that twinkle like the actual night sky. A long table made of dark wood takes up the length of the room, a single centerpiece filled with candles sits in the middle but is otherwise bare. There's a warm fire that burbles softly at the head of the room.

Clara tries her best not to stare as she walks in, the soft warmth coming over her in gentle waves with every step. Elise comes up beside her, a brief hand on the small of her back that sends trills up her spine.

"I'll teach you," Elise says. "Your magic. You've kept it hidden, no?"

Clara nods, her cheeks reddening at Elise's soft cluck of disapproval.

"It's okay." She takes Clara's chin in her hand. "You had to survive."

Clara nods again and her heart swells with the Snow Queen's touch. She doesn't know how long she's been at the castle. It feels like forever, basking in the eternal spring and pining after the frigid but kind queen. They spend every moment together, Clara lying across the lounge couch as Elise reads her fairy tales, gathering lush vegetables from the garden plots, and dining on fancy meals her invisible staff makes.

"Winter is in your heart, and all you have to do is call upon it to do your bidding. It will become your dearest friend—and the closer your heart is to it, the more you will be able to do."

Clara unconsciously puts her hand on her chest when the Snow Queen speaks. Can feel its unruly beat under her palm, always quick and erratic whenever she's near Elise.

"Here." Elise guides them to sit on the bench by the long table, takes a metal goblet filled with water, and sets it by Clara. "Ask it to become ice."

Clara stares at the tepid water rolling against the side from the momentum of being put down. A single ruby inlay beams on the side like the center of a sun. She stares at the liquid and thinks as hard as she can, begs it to become firm, to harden upon itself like clenching fists until it's immutable ice. A small film appears across the top, spider cracks throughout. Clara asks it to become colder, harder. It tightens slightly but does not go farther than the first inch of water.

"A lovely beginning." Elise claps her hands in delight. "You'll be powerful in no time."

"I fear offending, but I have a question," Clara says.

"Go ahead with it."

"I don't mean any harm, but what's the point of keeping the kingdom in eternal winter? It is a rough life to live in."

"To punish the King." Elise wraps a strand of Clara's hair in her finger and whirls it into a curl. "For banishing me when I needed help."

"That was centuries ago, the King is long dead."

"But his heirs remain. And so shall the winter until the last of them die."

"And the rest of us? That have to live with muted lives?"

Elise shrugs. "Revenge always has a cost."

"One you're not paying," Clara snaps before she can think twice. Elise gives her a sharp look, and Clara swallows in fear.

"Tell me." The Snow Queen's lips curl in disdain. "Do you love the King so much you'd fault me for destroying his corrupt system?"

Clara thinks about the castle that sits to the west, the vibrant balls run by unpaid labor. The legions of captured boys playing soldier to gain more land that quickly succumbs to winter. Her own lack of choice, being trapped between playing servant or being married off. The drudgery of surviving in the hard corners of the world. She looks at Elise, her eyes hard and fiery as if she can watch Clara's thoughts cascade downward.

"The winter affects everyone, though," she whispers half-heartedly.

Elise leans into Clara, her lips grazing her ear. "If you want spring, then make sure the line of King Eljred is dead."

Clara turns her face so her lips brush Elise's and, overcome with the intoxicating smell of berries and fir, kisses Elise softly.

"I could do that," she says without thinking, only imagining the bliss of finally seeing a warm sun.

Elise kisses her again, her thick eyelashes fluttering against Clara's cheeks.

"We could," she says. "Together."

8.

The robber girl has an oversized goat that is almost as large as the horse they road in on, the she proudly tells Roan she stole from traveling nobles. She ties both of them up at a wooden post at the mouth of the cave carved into the mountain. Roan follows her to a spot at the far end, piled in furs and a quilted blanket. The girl plops down and takes some flint, trying to spark her lantern into bearing light. After a few unsuccessful attempts, Roan leans over and touches a flame onto the wick.

"Autumn magic," the robber girl grins. "I knew there was a reason I liked you."

"It's a secret." Roan brings a finger up to his lip and smiles conspiratorially, though he knows robbers are less likely to talk to recruiters of the army than he is.

"Cross my heart," the girl giggles delightedly. "We're going to have so much fun."

Roan's heart skips a beat, a memory of Clara dancing in his mind as the robber girl pulls him into the lump of cloth. She curls up on her side and Roan mirrors her so they are face to face.

"You know I have magic, too," she whispers.

"Oh yeah? What's that?"

"I can make anything I want return to me."

"Really?"

"Robber magic." Her grin glints in the firelight. "My goat? No matter where it goes, it will come back the minute it is able."

"Impressive," Roan says, and the girl seems to blush at his approval.

They sit in silence for a while. Roan can feel the girl contemplating every curve of his face, the way the firelight dances across his angular nose.

"I have a deal," he says.

"A deal? I do love those."

"You want me to stay here. And—" he swallows before lying, "—I want to stay here, too. But I would be happier if I knew my friend was okay. What if I took your goat and found her, and that way I could return to you once I was done."

The robber girl turns so she's lying on her back and takes a few moments to think. A deep sigh turns into a softer one before she sits up.

"Under one condition."

"Which is?"

"You must kiss me first."

Roan startles and isn't sure what to make of her proposal. She is pretty enough, even with the mud smeared across her delicate nose and splattering of freckles. He wouldn't mind kissing her, if he's completely honest. Especially if it would get him to his best friend. The robber girl looks at him expectantly.

He leans in and grazes her lips. She runs her fingers through his hair and pulls him into her, pressing into his soft lips. She tastes like maple syrup and ginger. Before he can fully register what's happening, she's pulled away with a wry smile.

"Go then," she shoos him. "Take my goat. Remember to return to me."

Roan nods and gets up, forcing himself to take a few steps before running to the head of the cave. The goat looks perplexed as he unties it, letting out a soft, sleepy baaaa as Roan leads it away. He almost feels bad for not planning on coming back.

The crow swoops in and lets out a victorious CAW.

"I thought you were stuck forever!" it cries.

"You're here," Roan laughs joyously. "I thought I'd seen the last of you."

"Never! I lead you to the queen!"

And in the night, the crow flies just above Roan, guiding him and the unfortunate goat through the winding hillside until they reach the same ornate gates that he can only imagine Clara once stood before.

"How do I get up there?" Roan looks up, defeated.

"I take you," the crow says, grabbing the shoulders of Roan's coat in either claw.

Roan didn't think it possible, but the crow lifts him to the very height of the wall, where his stomach turns at the sight of how far up they are, and gently brings him down. At this point, the goat trots off, figuring it is no longer needed.

He barely notices the gardens, or the trees, as he runs toward the castle.

"Clara!" he calls out, "Clara I'm here."

Instead of Clara, though, he runs into the Snow Queen, who emerges onto the veranda from inside. She towers over Roan, who stumbles back to behold her. Tall and menacing, in a long silk robe the color of grayed snow and starlight. The small quartz pieces in her hair sparkle as she takes the steps down to the garden. Roan's mouth goes dry and he tries to swallow as she approaches.

Clara appears behind him and visibly brightens at seeing Roan. She runs past the queen to him with her arms out and they embrace.

"It's been such a journey," he weeps. "But you're here. And alive."

"How did you manage to trespass into my land?" the Snow Queen's voice is cold.

Roan goes to point to the crow but, being the smart creature it is, has made itself scarce.

"I do not like trespassers," the queen says and slowly takes her front steps one by one until she's in front of Roan.

"I-I apologize," Roan stammers, "I had only a mind to make sure Clara was safe."

"She's perfectly fine."

"I see that. Thank you for caring for her."

"Please don't hurt him." Clara turns to the Snow Queen, fear visible in her eyes.

The Snow Queen doesn't acknowledge Clara's plea, raises her hand, and unleashes a blizzard. The icy gusts push Clara back, her face hit by the chill as she stumbles into the tomatoes. The grass at the edge of the walkway wilts under the unexpected cold.

Roan's eyes are wide as he looks at the impending storm charging his way. His autumn magic erupts from inside him unbidden, the force of survival overcoming any other instinct. At the last moment, Roan is able to throw up a wall of fire, so hot the mint plants he is beside begin to curl and die. The blizzard melts around him, turning into wet soil at his feet. He faces the Snow Queen, his breath gusting in pants that are visible as they hit the cold air. Positions himself with his palms out to prepare for another strike.

Clara runs to Elise and throws her arms around her neck, whispering every frantic plea she can think of, dissolving into sobs. The Snow Queen looks to her, then meets Roan's gaze with hardened eyes.

"Autumn magic always succumbs to winter," she says, "but I have distressed my precious Clara enough. I will take one thing from you, then let you leave."

Roan is too scared to ask what she means and remains still as she detangles herself from Clara, walks to him, and places a hand on his forehead.

"In my time of isolation, I've learned many types of magic," she says. "Including the magic of memory."

By the time her palms have left his skin, Roan has no recollection of Clara.

He looks at the two women, confused, not sure how he ended up in this strange palace. One of the women screams a painful wail that makes him run from the grounds in terror. The large gate blows open as he reaches it and before he can think twice, he's running through the forest.

Back to the robber girl. Because she, too, had placed some of her magic in him.

9.

Clara turns to Elise, her face contorted with tears and rage. A slight wind picks up, pushing through her hair like a caress. She doesn't know if it's Elise's magic or a natural current which enrages her further.

"You stole him from me," she screams. "He was my best friend and you took him."

"I had to."

"No, you didn't! You don't have to do any of this, and yet you insist on it. Because you're selfish," Clara spits the last word out in disgust.

Elise's eyes are wide and, for the first time since Clara met her, she appears at a loss for words. She reaches out fruitlessly, but Clara is gone, running toward the forest with a forlorn cry.

By the time she is out of the gates, which are still blown open, there is no sign of Roan. Just a thick wave of snow and evergreen. She pauses and surveys the landscape, eyes squinting against the reflection of the sun off the white, rolling hills.

"Roan!" she screams but only hears her echo and nothing more.

She begins to run again, unbeknownst to her in the opposite direction of her friend. She runs until the woods become unfamiliar. The land warms, and she stumbles into a small square of lush greenery and warmth.

A patch of spring. An apology.

Swimming Through the Sea

By Charleigh Frederick

Five little mermaids swimming through the sea
Stick a hand out for the sailors to see
One little mermaid catches the rope
And pulls the sailor off the boat
Four little mermaids swimming through the sea
Stick a hand out for the sailors to see
A friendly sailor reaches out
She pulls that sailor down below
Three little mermaids swimming through the sea
Stick a hand out for the sailors to see
Call them by name and see their surprise
Then watch the life drain from their eyes
Two little mermaids swimming through the sea
Stick a hand out for the sailors to see
Prey on men too weak to pout

Grab some dinner for you and me
One little mermaid swimming through the sea
Stick a hand out for the sailors to grasp
She says I am the girl of your dreams
But then you'll see her with your last gasp

On the Prowl

By Matthew Crabb

MARIA TOES THE EDGE of the Fractured Forest. The long branches of the evergreens behind her sway in the wind, tapping her shoulders like an insistent child. Cold prickles run up and down her spine. She is finally back where this whole thing started. Where she lost her best friend to a curse.

"Magnificent," Prince Desiré says at her side.

She looks at the prince, then at the rocky cliff in the distance. An old castle festers at the edge of the world, looking more green than gray. Tendrils of ivy slither up the side of the ash-gray walls like snakes. Slate clouds hover over it and block out the sun.

Maria has been his squire for nearly a year, duping him by keeping her ponytail short and wrapping a corset tightly around her chest. It was only by chance that the prince chose her to fill the position. One shout for help from the noble stables as she skittered past in disguise was all it took for her to jump into action. The prince was inside, a recently purchased wild stallion bucking and pawing at the air in front of him. He jumped for the reigns, all while dodging the hooves that threatened to knock him back.

Maria had helped her father, a cavalryman for the king, break many a steed. She put her skills into action and couldn't help but feel the prince's eyes stuck on her as she worked. When the beast was back in its stall, Desiré showered praise on her. Except, he saw her as a boy. A squire.

And she'd only been dressed that way to gain access to the castle. As the closest kingdom to her and Dawn's home, she thought the gossip of townsfolk might lead her to some answers. Instead, she found Desiré and quickly learned they had the same goal. To save the princess.

The ploy has worked so far, getting her closer to finding out what happened to Princess Dawn. As her best friend and handmaiden, Maria knows it's her duty to find her. And the guilt of losing her that night still haunts her waking hours. Over time, her skills as a squire have improved. What she didn't expect was to fall for a prince in the process.

And it wasn't like Prince Desiré did anything out of the ordinary. He was charming, of course, especially at balls and social functions. Maria desperately wanted to be on the receiving end of one of the prince's bows, one he ended with a kiss to the back of the hand and a wide smile that made her legs weak. The flirtatious grins, nods, and winks. His bravery in battle and sense of justice. They're small snippets, she knows, but they must hint at his true nature in some way. And her imagination fills in the gaps.

"I was here that day, you know. Three years ago, this fortnight," Prince Desiré says. Maria knows this, of course, but she looks at him in wonder anyway. Pretending has become a part of her identity. "The ballroom was full of people. Nobles and royals, all there for the princess's birthday."

Desiré pauses and Maria leans in. It's moments like this when he's about to recount the night of the curse that Desiré always sends her away for a task or a drink. But this is different. Now it's only her. She is the confidant.

"I had courted the princess, you know," Prince Desiré says, almost offhand. But Maria knows his expressions. There's something he isn't saying. But what?

"Unfortunately, we didn't get very far before the spindle..."

The wind grabs his lingering words and pushes them toward the castle. The swirl of clouds seems more intense, and a bright flash of lightning careens to the ground.

That night has haunted Maria since the moment Dawn's finger was pierced. The girls had long since been inseparable, and the king cared not for the triviality of his fourth-born child. It wasn't until Dawn turned eleven that the King demanded the 'common girl' be gone from his princess' side. But Dawn was clever. She made Maria her handmaid, and the two worked together to conjure up the appearance of royalty. Almost as equals.

A single thought weasels its way into Maria's brain. It is not a new idea, but one she has pushed down. Because if it were true, then it would sully everything she knows of the prince. As Maria primped and dressed her friend that night, Dawn vented about a 'pushy prince' being forced on her by the king. A strategic marriage, Dawn called it. And one she desperately wanted to avoid. She would not disclose the prince's name, and there had been so many courters in recent months that Maria could barely keep track. But it couldn't be Desiré. Could it?

A fierce gust of wind makes the horses shuffle in place. The prince looks like he might say more, and Maria desperately wants him to, but instead, he dismounts his giant, tan horse and moves to the towering beast's head. His right hand caresses the white center of his steed's nose. He whispers to the horse and Maria's heart fills. She never tires of seeing his tender side. There is no way the pushy prince is Desiré.

He throws the reins over a low-hanging branch and begins his march down the hill. Maria dismounts quickly and does the same. She grabs the prince's sword and hefts her own bow and quiver across her back. She gives her small ebony horse a wave. No time for pleasantries. By the time Maria reaches Desiré, he is already holding his hand out for his sword. After a moment of waiting, he turns his head to look at her.

"I need you focused today, Max. Many princes and knights have entered this castle before us, and none of them have returned. Even a small distraction could mean the end for us." He takes the sword and begins cinching it to his side. He seems so confident, like he knows more about this place than those that had come before.

"What do you think is in there?"

"I don't know," he says, "But I've sat here many a night scouting the castle. Whatever is in there is holding onto the princess with an iron grip. I intend to stop it."

Desiré marches further down the hill. She follows him but can't seem to shake his words. Many a night? His obsession with the princess is obvious, and jealousy bubbles inside her until she takes and releases several deep breaths. As much as Maria wants to find her friend, a small part of her wants him for herself. It might actually be what Dawn wants, after all. But can she recover trust after lying to him for so long?

And how did she not know he was doing such thorough reconnaissance?

The day seems to grow darker as they approach, the sun now fully behind the maelstrom of dark clouds above. Desiré pulls his sword out, the polished metal glinting in the fading light. Maria takes this as her cue to join him. She swiftly pulls the bow from her back and plucks an arrow from the quiver. She notches it and points the tip toward the ground.

Sticks and leaves litter the bridge as they cross. Maria scans each pillar of wood as they pass, each one with a ragged line carved into it and an A or M above it. She reaches out with a rough hand and slides it across the slice. Their heights, measured each year on a new pillar with a knife stolen from the kitchen. Maria stands tall, the closest pillar only up to her shoulder, and she wipes a tear from her eyes. She hasn't seen her friend in so long.

The massive door to the castle is more than twenty feet tall and stands slightly ajar. Large grooves are cut into thick wood, like the claw marks of a desperate animal. Desiré gingerly grabs the rusty iron ring. He pulls and the hinges groan with the effort. Desiré winces, but he continues pulling. Maria's eyes dart here and there, looking behind as the squeals of old rusty metal cut the silence.

When the door has been opened far enough, Maria rushes in. They move together in the dusky light. She finds a pillar and leans against it to shield her body. Desiré does the same, only several steps ahead. This approach has been practiced and perfected, and Maria feels a rush of excitement at how much she's changed since leaving the castle.

It takes a moment, but the heavy heat of the enclosed area hits her hard. The sweet smell of rot hangs in the air and she covers her nose and mouth. Bile rises and she holds back a gag.

"Oh, god," Desiré says. He pulls his white tunic above his nose and peers through watery eyes. Maria fights the nausea and raises her bow again. She scans the cloudy twilight before her.

In the center is a fountain, its water long since gone, where Maria and Dawn would braid each other's hair on sunny days. On the far side are the stairs to Dawn's tower, where the girls would practice their sword skills. First with wooden staffs, then with actual swords. As much fun as it was, Dawn always had an ulterior motive. As the commoners chortled at the young girls and their antics, the king would fume from his throne room, watching them play at being boys, as he'd say. Dawn would always bite back, her torn and soiled dress fitting her perfectly as she discussed the merits of proper skill when needing to fight. Because why rely on the knights when we could do it ourselves?

Maria smiles at the memory as she continues to scan. She sees a dark shape in the distance. She waves Desiré forward and he follows behind her. Her steps are light and fast. She closes the distance to the fountain in the middle and crouches low. There, the head of a gorgon peers out at them. Medusa, she always assumed, because of the long slithering bodies where her hair should be. The nose is flat, sliced off when Maria's blade parried one of Dawn's attacks. They ran giggling from the courtyard, and the nose was never repaired.

She scuttles forward, Desiré right behind. The dark lump, low to the ground and unmoving, begins to come into focus.

A decapitated body leans against the wall.

Maria stops, her mouth agape. Desiré, his leather boots scuffing the dusty cobblestone, steps around her and to the dead man's side. He looks in all directions before crouching down.

"Prince Henri," Desiré whispers. Maria comes up behind him and looks over his shoulder. The head is several yards to the side and has been severely mutilated by scavengers. The eyeballs are missing, and tiny peck marks cover the gray rotting skin. Maria wonders how Desiré can identify the man, but then she notices the attire. The shield. The chainmail and the armor. Even through the burgundy blood stain, Maria can make out the emblem of the House of Pion.

"He had clear instructions. And he barely made it past the courtyard," Desiré mumbles, hand in a tight fist. "Sending him in was a waste of a fool."

Desiré moves to the side, bypassing a set of stairs that lead to the tall tower where Dawn's bed chambers are. But Maria stays at the body's side and lets Desiré's words echo in her mind. Who gave Henri instructions and sent him to this fate? And as the words fall away, Desiré's tone lingers, like an angry father cursing the failings of his son. She'd never seen outbursts like this from him before. Maria has a hard time reconciling this outburst with the image of the man she loves.

As she stands to follow, she remembers a night only a few months prior. Prince Henri visited Desiré at his castle. The visit began with merriment, but by the end of the evening, hushed whispers chased her from the room as she retired for the night.

That was the last she'd seen of Prince Henri.

"Max," Desiré says in a harsh whisper. Maria snaps out of it and joins him beside the tower. "This is no time to mourn the dead."

He lifts the sword again and disappears into the darkness of the hall. Maria gives chase, bow at the ready, but she feels like they're moving in the wrong direction.

"Sire," Maria whispers in the dark. Desiré stops but does not turn. His sword is poised to strike. "I have heard many a tale that once the death curse was converted to a sleeping curse, the princess could be found in her sleeping chambers. I believe the tower we just passed is where she lived... is it not?"

Maria hopes the prince does not perceive her confidence as impudence. She does not want to be the focus of the prince's ire, like poor Henri.

Desiré releases a great sigh and turns toward Maria. The girl is taken aback. She's never seen such a dejected face on the prince before. Every bone in her body screams at her to embrace him. But she remembers his words in front of the dead prince. He's revealing more of himself to her on this mission, and like armor with a spot of rust, Maria must decide if the whole thing is defective.

"Max, you've been with me for almost a year now. You're not a complete dullard. Prince Henri definitely was. That's why I used him to... scout things out for me."

Maria stifles a gasp and the prince continues, his voice a whisper.

"The danger here is real. And I needed to know exactly where the princess was so I could get in and get out. Henri was the least helpful of all the men I've sent in here."

Desiré turns and continues down the hall. Maria is stuck in place, the image she has of the prince slowly crumbling as they approach the ballroom.

"On the night of the curse, something strange occurred," Desiré is ahead of her, but his voice echoes in the dark. "Just like the witch said, Dawn pricked her finger. Just like the Lilac Fairy said, she wouldn't die. But something happened that sent all those people running for the exits."

Maria's mind floods with the images of that night. She'd begun to help another servant just as Dawn opened her presents. Maria was at the far end of the room when the spindle was unwrapped. She turned to see Dawn holding the present high, its point glinting in the soft glow of the torches. Her pink dress twirled around her as she spun with excitement. Then came the scream. And no matter how hard Maria pushed against the sea of rushing people, she could not get back to her lady's side. By the time the mob had passed her, the doors were shuttered, and something chased the remaining crowd from the castle grounds.

Desiré's swift movements bring her back to the present. He's at the door of the ballroom and he pokes his head in several times. He spins into the dark, sword at the ready.

"The scouts I sent in would shoot arrows from the castle with notes tied on. Several found the Princesses' bed chambers empty. And not one came back after reaching the ballroom. Naturally, this is where we need to start."

Desiré bends his knees and readies for an attack. Maria doesn't have time to process what the prince is saying. Tingles of dread creep up her back. Someone or something is watching them. The hair on her neck stands on end and she pulls the arrow back, ready to let it fly.

A bright light on the far side of the cavernous room catches her attention and she squints. It's fire, crackling in the silence of the dark. It moves up and down, then rapidly flies in their direction. Maria dives to the side, the fire narrowly missing her head. It hits a wooden pillar with a twang, the flaming arrow growing steadily with each passing second. The flames lick at a pile of dry hay sitting in the corner and it ignites. The heat is too much and Maria scrambles to her feet and shields her eyes.

The fiery hay bale banishes the dark to the corners, and it reveals the full carnage of that night. Bodies litter the floor in various states of decay. Bones lie in piles where gravity has sluffed the skin away. Other bodies seem fresh, headless corpses resting on the floor or against walls. Death hangs heavy in the air, and Maria holds her bow up, moving it in all directions. Her weapon wobbles in her shaking arms.

Something crashes near the throne, and she turns just in time to see tan fur dart to the side. The room's corners harbor large swathes of darkness, but Maria can still see movement. She moves right, her bow taut.

Desiré goes the other way, two hands on the hilt of his sword. Each step crosses over the other leg as he stares in the corner.

"Come out and fight, you monster," he yells to the dark.

A low growl emits from the shadows, and two yellow eyes blink out of the dark. A bright red tongue licks gleaming teeth and Maria finds her breath caught in her throat. The lioness, her fur shining, lunges toward the prince. Maria lets loose an arrow and it sails toward the beast. At the last moment, the lion dives for the ground and slides on the slippery floor, missing the prince. He swings his sword but the animal jumps and lunges out of the way. The lion finds solace in the shadows and both Maria and Desiré turn toward the dark.

Desiré motions for her to fire again, but she can't. Or won't. The air has shifted and the danger, at least for now, is gone.

A slow clack, clack, clack of shoes echoes through the chamber, mixing with the fury of the fire. From the dark corner comes a woman, a torn and tattered pink dress hanging threadbare from her muscular frame. Her blonde hair is up in a tight bun, a predatory smile gracing her lips. Her eyes sparkle in the faint firelight as she saunters out of the shadows.

"Desiré," she says, her voice lower than Maria remembers. "Took you long enough to get here."

Desiré is still. His sword hangs limply by his side.

"Dawn?" He says. "But, the curse... you should be sleeping."

"Should I? Is that what you got me for my birthday?"

His eyes knit together and he regrips the sword. "I don't know what you're talking about."

And neither does Maria. She has an arrow notched, but there has been no sign of the big cat since the princess emerged.

"Oh, I know about it all, Desiré. My father told me everything," she says, pointing to the wall. For the first time, Maria can see that it isn't a tapestry up there, but a person. The king. He's been strapped to the wall with rope and nails. Dried blood covers his clothes, torture wounds from long ago. Maria's stomach lurches but she does not move.

"What have you done, you monster?" Desiré says.

"I'm only what you made me," Dawn says. She passes into a shadow, the lioness emerging on the other side. She lets out a roar that rattles the windows and walls. Maria covers her ears, dropping her bow and arrow. The lion passes into the shadow again and Dawn steps forward, surprising Desiré. He holds his sword up while he takes several steps back.

"I didn't do this to you," he says, his voice shaking.

"You didn't order the witch to place a curse on me? Or convince the Lilac Fairy to switch it to a sleeping curse? All so I'd be indebted to you for waking me up? You didn't pay my father and all the nobles in the surrounding kingdoms to keep it quiet, so I wouldn't know? You didn't do any of that?"

Prince Desiré is speechless. He turns to Maria and gives her the signal to fire. But so much is happening at once. Her best friend is standing in front of her, alive and well. It's all Maria could have hoped for. But her father hangs from the wall, tortured and bloodied. Innocent people lie littered on the floor. What has she become?

"The king told me all of it, Desiré. How he wanted this marriage for the kingdom, to make the region stronger. How you convinced him that I was too rogue, too independent to follow along with the marriage. And how this was the only way to secure our allegiance. My father was a greedy fool, but in the end, your plan didn't work. Because part of me did die that day. And something wild awoke from her slumber."

"Fire, Max," Desiré says, desperation in his voice.

"And now you've brought another innocent into the castle. You've stooped to sacrificing boys now, have you?"

Maria is stuck to her spot. The two most important people in her life stand before her and violence hangs heavy in the air. They both look to her, but neither are who she believed them to be. Behind perfectly procured exteriors, darkness lurks. All Maria wanted was her best friend. And a lover. But both have disappointed.

"Will you not let your arrow fly, boy? Your prince has given you an order," Dawn's voice is sweet, but the smile is sinister. She is fifteen feet from Desiré, and Maria points the arrow in the gap between them. She can't live this lie anymore. She needs to come clean. She lowers the bow and holds the weapon in one hand. She drops the ponytail and steps forward, where the light hits her face at a different angle.

"Dawn," Maria says, the gravel in her voice set aside for her own high alto. "It's me."

There's a moment where Maria believes all is lost. Desiré stares at her in confusion. Dawn snarls, not yet understanding. Then her eyes go wide and her straight-backed poster relaxes.

"Maria?" Dawn's eyes fill and she begins to take steps toward her friend. She stops partway and looks to Desiré, who hasn't moved. She's torn between her need for vengeance and the rekindling of a friendship.

Maria picks her bow back up and points it at Desiré. He turns toward her, his sword up.

"What are you doing?" He says.

"I trusted you," Maria says, "and I was falling for you. But all you do is take. You're a parasite. Everything I saw, the flirting, charming prince. It was all a disguise."

Maria brings the tip of the arrow to her left, pointing it directly at Dawn.

"And you." Maria pauses as she chokes back a sob. "I loved you. I came back for you, and this is what I find? A murderous animal, barricaded in her past. You won't let anyone in, not even your best friend. I don't recognize you anymore, Dawn."

The princess bows her head. Maria wipes her eye on her sleeve just as a flash of movement bursts forward. It's Desiré, his sword high as he prepares to strike the princess. It's the final straw for Maria.

She turns to him and leads him before she releases her fingers. The string twangs as it strikes her wrist and the arrow flies, a little wobbly at first, but true nonetheless. As if in slow motion, Dawn backs up and Desiré tries to stop his momentum. But Maria has become quite an archer, and the sharpened metal tip slices into his quad and embeds itself in the meat. He falls to the floor, crimson blood pooling below him. He screams, and his sword clatters harmlessly to the stone floor.

Without hesitation, Maria pulls another arrow from her quiver. Dawn holds her hands up, but Maria has no intention of letting another arrow fly. At least not at the princess.

"I love you, Dawn. But I need to know that the woman I lost that night isn't gone forever. That some part of her lived through that. That she had enough toughness and smarts to live despite what had been done to her. I need to know that she still cares. Still has empathy. Can still love a simple commoner."

Desiré's wails of pain fill the room, but Maria blocks them out.

"I need to know who I'm coming back for. If you're still worth saving."

"I don't need saving," Dawn says, an edge of darkness in her voice. She softens immediately, as if instinct is dictating her actions. "I don't need saving. I need help."

For the first time since entering the ballroom, Maria sees her old friend. The one that notched the wood each year on the bridge, and the girl that broke Medusa's nose. Her best friend who took Maria on adventures and picnics and broke all the rules in all the right ways.

Maria puts the arrow back in the quiver and slings the bow over her shoulder. She runs to her friend, and they embrace; a long, hard hug that eases the rough patches of the past.

"I'm sorry I left you," Maria whispers.

"You never left me. I was just lost. And you're the one that found me."

They separate, hand in hand, and look at the pitiful prince still writhing on the floor. Without a word, the two women turn from him and walk out of the ballroom.

"Maybe one day he'll find his way home," Maria says. "But for now, let's go build our own ever after."

Dawn smiles, but her face quickly turns into a muzzle. Her skin sprouts fur and in the blink of an eye, Dawn becomes the lioness again. She nuzzles her head into Maria's hand, and the woman gives the giant head a scratch. Dawn looks back and gives one more deafening roar before they walk out of the castle together.

Out of the Oven

By Demi Michelle Schwartz

Grethel carries a tray piled high with candy to the front door of her stone cottage. The wooden floorboards groan like a slumbering monster with each wary step. Wrappers crinkle as the sweets shake and slide toward the tray's tilting edges.

No fake spider webs dangle from the ceiling. The corners are free of plastic skeletons and candles flickering atop glass tables waft the aroma of cinnamon off their wicks without a hint of pumpkin.

Another Halloween has arrived, and Grethel wishes she could crawl into bed early and turn off the lights so trick-or-treaters don't ring the bell.

But she can't. These kids deserve a better childhood than the one she and Hansel had, and if that means plastering on a smile and shoving down horrors from seventeen years ago, then so be it.

She sets the tray on the round table beside the door and wipes her clammy palms on her sweatpants. After picking up a fallen cherry lollipop from the floor and returning it to the pile, she drifts into the living room to await her least favorite event of the year.

Flames dance in the fireplace, bathing Grethel in light and warmth as she sinks into the couch. Through the circular window, the rolling mountains surrounding Sage Hollow emanate a rosy hue from the alpenglow. Soon, a full moon will rise and coat the rustling pines with a silver luster.

Grethel inhales deep breath after deep breath, but her heartbeat pounds like a drum in her tight chest. A shiver slides down her spine, and she glances over her shoulder to find nothing but the clay pot of peace lilies, a housewarming gift from her brother the year prior. The white flowers emit a celestial shine in the fire's aura, but their tranquil beauty is lost on her. She reaches for the phone on the glass table beside the couch and dials.

"Hello?" Hansel's deep voice floats through the phone.

"Hi, it's me."

"Grethel! Happy Halloween. Are you ready for the trick-or-treaters?"

"No." Grethel tries to tune out the fire, sounding like snapping branches in the woods that plague her night-mares. "There's always a witch."

"I know." His gentle tone washes over Grethel, and she wishes she were at his cottage on the other side of Sage Hollow.

"Does anything feel off to you?" Grethel stands and paces across the carpet, pausing once to trace her fingers over the soft petals of a peace lily.

"Nothing unusual. Look, it's just the holiday. You'll feel better tomorrow."

Ding dong. Ding dong.

The resonant chimes reverberate through the cottage like warning bells.

Grethel's stomach drops to her feet wrapped in fuzzy socks. "You're right. Anyway, someone's at the door. I should go."

"Sounds good. I'll talk to you later. And Grethel?"

"Yeah?"

"I love you, little sis."

A lump forms in her throat, and she blinks away the tears. "I love you, too."

Grethel hangs up the phone and drags her feet to the front door. Bracing herself, she turns the knob.

"Trick or treat!" A little boy dressed as a vampire grins at her with fake fangs.

Grethel picks up the tray and returns his smile. "Take two pieces of candy."

The young vampire snatches a Twix bar and bag of Skittles. "Thank you. Happy Halloween!"

Before Grethel can respond, the boy runs down the sidewalk and toward the next house. Puffs of smoke spiral from nearly every chimney on the street, painting the sunset's fiery hues with strokes of gray. An owl's hoot joins the choir of laughing children.

The chilled October wind blows into Grethel's cottage, carrying the scents of pine and burning firewood.

Shivering, she closes the door and leans against it. This isn't so bad. She can get through the night and reward herself with a mug of hot cocoa.

Knock. Knock. Knock.

Grethel pulls the door open. Standing before her is a teenage girl wearing a black dress and pointed hat, broom in hand.

In a single blink, Grethel is five years old again. The woods crawl with shadows and spread out for acres like an inescapable maze. Fatal hunger claws at Grethel's stomach, threatening to devour her from the inside out. A cottage made from bread with a cake roof and sugarcane windows appears as a safe haven. The witch, with her bright red eyes like pools of blood, cackles and announces how Hansel will be cooked for her grand feast.

"Trick or treat."

Grethel jumps and almost drops the tray of candy. The teenage witch squints at Grethel from under her hat's brim.

I'm not in those woods. I'm safe. Hansel is safe. The witch is dead. She burned in the oven.

Grethel holds out the tray, her legs weak. "Choose a treat."

The witch picks up a pack of candy corn and drops it in her bucket shaped like a pumpkin. "Are you alright?"

"Yes, thank you for asking. Happy Halloween."

The girl tilts her head and narrows her clear blue eyes, but she doesn't press the matter. After giving Grethel a sweeping wave with her broom, she spins in her black boots and skips away.

Two young sisters dressed as princesses race down the mostly deserted street while a woman bundled in a coat and scarf chases after them. In the distance, someone shouts, "Boo!" Faint shrieks and giggles follow. Grethel's heart sinks. If only she had a childhood full of joy and fun.

A rustling sound drifts from the rose bushes lining the cracked sidewalk. Grethel freezes with her hand on the door, her stomach in knots. Was that an animal? It must have been. The red flowers glow like embers in the setting sun, and Grethel yearns to curl up by her fireplace. Maybe she can move the candy tray outside for the children and call it a night. She steps back but halts when something flashes among the roses.

Blinking red eyes.

No, she's imagining things. The teenage witch's presence conjured dark memories, like remains in a grave that refuse to stay buried.

A shadow shifts behind the bushes. Grethel tries to retreat into her cottage, but her feet are rooted to the spot. Snaps from breaking sticks mingle with the owl's hoots as a cloaked figure emerges from its hiding place.

The wicked witch grins with half her teeth missing, the rest cracked and yellow. Wrinkled skin on her face and hands is discolored and scarred from deep burns. Cadaverous fingers grip a wooden cane from under the sleeve of a torn ebony cloak.

And those eyes, just visible beneath a ripped hat flopping to one side, watch Grethel like a hawk cornering its prey after a relentless hunt.

A scream tangles in Grethel's throat. No, this can't be real.

"Hello, dear." The witch's voice sounds as though she inhaled volcanic gas. "Long time, no see."

"You shouldn't be here," Grethel forces out through chattering teeth. "You're dead."

The witch cackles, but it comes out more like a deadly wheeze. "I got out of the oven. Frightened children always forget to finish the job. You should have waited to ensure I was dead before you and your brother ran away. You may be taller now, but you're still that scared little girl."

Grethel's knees wobble. This shouldn't be happening. The oven's heat should have burned the witch to death.

But somehow, Grethel's worst nightmare has become reality.

"Leave us alone." Grethel's voice quavers, and she's back in the past once more, cowering in the witch's dreadful presence.

"No can do." The witch shuffles closer with her cane. "I've been waiting for my feast for seventeen years. You're not a child anymore, but you'll still be tasty. Once I eat you, I'll find that brother of yours."

Bile creeps into Grethel's throat. She has to get away from this monster and call Hansel. He's not trapped in a stable this time. He'll be able to help. She pushes the door shut, but the witch sticks out her cane just in time to stop it.

"Now, now, slamming a door in someone's face isn't polite. You should have learned your lesson after the stunt you pulled with my oven." The witch's burnt lips twist into a scowl. She knocks the candy tray out of Grethel's hands and forces her way inside.

Sweat drips down Grethel's neck. She bolts for the living room and fumbles with the phone. Each time she tries to dial Hansel's number, her trembling fingers slip and she needs to start over.

The witch stumbles through the doorway, crimson eyes gleaming with hunger. Grethel attempts to call her brother yet again, but before she can enter the final digit, the witch swings her cane and hits the coiled phone cord. The receiver flies from Grethel's hand and lands behind the pot of peace lilies.

"No." Grethel presses her palms to her chest. She can't face this witch alone. Not again.

"Now, where were we?" The witch adjusts her hat with a skeletal hand. "Oh, yes. We were discussing how you'll taste delicious all grown up. Perhaps I'll add pumpkin spice to the recipe for the festive occasion. What do you think, dear?"

Grethel flicks her gaze to the fireplace. Maybe she can shove the monster into the flames.

But if the oven didn't kill the witch, the fire may not do any good.

Heart pounding, Grethel races around the wicked creature and into the hall. She hurries through the kitchen doorway. Her socks slip on the tiles, but she catches herself before she can fall and crack her head on the tiny wooden table. She yanks open a drawer and pulls out a steak knife, its blade glinting in the sunset's rays that filter through the window above the sink.

"Yes, this is much better." The witch pauses in the doorway, her red eyes scanning the kitchen. "Your oven isn't nearly as big as mine, but once I chop you up into pieces, it'll work just fine."

Grethel raises the knife in her quivering hand. "The only one who's going to be cut into pieces is you."

"I don't think so."

Clunk. Clunk. Clunk.

The witch's cane collides with the tiled floor as she approaches. When the monster is within arm's distance, Grethel swings the knife. The blade slices a deep gash into the witch's cheek, and ruby blood splatters the table and floor.

The creature's shrieks echo in Grethel's ears as she rushes through the backdoor leading onto the deck. If she lures the monster out of the cottage, Grethel can take her down. She tricked the witch once. She can do so again. This time, she'll make sure the witch is dead.

The night wind whips Grethel's auburn curls from her face. She keeps a safe distance from the gaping hole, where warped wood and rusted nails litter the grass below. The construction workers haven't finished replacing the decking yet, lucky for Grethel.

She faces the open door, her fingers slick around the knife's hilt. A bat swoops down, and she screams, staggering back a step. The hole's open mouth yawns closer, the nails far below protruding from the wood like sharp teeth.

The witch hobbles into the doorway. Blood trickles down her face and drips onto her cloak. In her free hand, she clutches a knife.

Grethel's lungs constrict. She can't lose her focus now.

"Come and get me," Grethel taunts, her voice surprisingly steady.

Thump. Thump. Thump.

The witch inches onto the deck, her cloak rippling in the wind. Grethel stands her ground. The timing must be perfect. She won't get a second chance.

"Should I chop off your arms or legs first?" the witch wheezes.

Grethel grips her knife tighter.

"I asked you a question." The witch clunks closer, her eyes blazing like those belonging to a devil.

Grethel raises her chin but doesn't speak. Just a few more feet.

Closer. Closer. Closer.

"I think I'll start with your—"

Grethel kicks the cane, and the witch breaks off with a shriek. While she teeters on unsteady legs, Grethel lunges forward and plunges the knife into her neck before shoving her hard toward the hungry hole.

The witch flies over the edge and falls down, down, down, slamming into the wood and nails with a sickening crunch.

Grethel stares at her enemy, whose mouth is open in a silent scream of agony. Tremors zap through Grethel's veins, and she sinks to her knees.

"You'll never come after Hansel or me again, Witch."

Black smoke engulfs the witch and swirls into a tornado. Tendrils twirl this way and that, round and round, until the entire hole is full of darkness. With a climactic burst, the smoke disperses into the autumn wind.

Grethel blinks dust from her eyes and squints at the spot where the witch lay moments ago.

She's gone.

Tears cascade down Grethel's cheeks.

The wicked witch is finally dead.

An owl hoot breaks the silence.

No, not a hoot.

A soothing coo.

Grethel tilts her head back, squinting against the sunset's glow. A white dove soars from the sky and lands on her shoulder. She smiles through her tears as she runs her fingers along the soft feathers of the bird's wing. A dove just like this one carried her and Hansel across the lake after they had escaped the witch's cottage seventeen years ago. She must have been hearing this bird all along. Maybe this is a sign she'll be able to bury her traumatic past once and for all.

She continues petting the dove as the sunset's last light melts into the shadows. The full moon shines high above, surrounded by stars sprinkled across the canvas of the velvety black sky.

Tomorrow, a new beginning will dawn.

Tomorrow, the future will gleam bright.

Tomorrow, Hansel and Grethel will bask in golden freedom.

Curse Sealed with a Kiss: Sleeping Beauty and the Shadow Lord

By Julie Krohn

THE SUNRISE BREAKS OVER the horizon in the early morning hours. Colors of daybreak paint the sky, sending rays of light dancing over the treetops in the mountains to glisten across the streams. As water flows down the hillsides, the soothing, gentle trickle echoes in the air along with the soft chirping of birds in the distance. In the east, a shooting star blazes through the sky, leaving a fleeting blue streak in its wake. As I tilt my head up to watch, my shoe slides on the dew-covered slippery rocks on the riverbank.

In a fraction of a second, I tumble down the steep incline, gaining momentum as I weave through the scattered trees. Piles of fallen leaves swirl behind me until I finally stop at the bottom of the hill and fall into a rose bush thicket.

Ugh. As I move, wet leaves cling to my legs, their mildew scent permeating through the air. The thorny branches of the bush stab me, creating painful, jagged red scratches across my shins. When the cold air hits my open cuts, I wince and gently extract the wooden thorns buried beneath my skin. Exasperated, I let out a sigh and glance upward. The cliff edge looms high above me, approximately twenty feet from where I am. Across the stream, the riverbank slope on the other side appears to be less steep for me to climb.

Pulling myself up, I approach the water and hop onto the first exposed rock in the stream. The lapping waves soak my shoes. I try to step nimbly over the next three exposed stones poking out of the water. When I get to the fifth stone, it is much farther away. I leap forward and my foot lands on the slick surface and slips. My legs sink deep into the freezing water, reaching up past my knees, sending a jolt of pain through my body.

A startled cry breaks free from my throat, and I freeze as I adjust to the chill. As my balance wavers, I tighten my grip on the flowers I picked earlier. I try to take a step and I can't move my foot. My ankle is wedged underneath rocks in the water. I reach into the stream, getting my sleeves wet, and try to push the rocks. They don't budge. How did my foot slide in between them?

Panic takes control as my drowsiness creeps in. What if I can't get out of here before the curse takes over and I fall asleep? I grasp for the grass on the embankment, trying to claw myself out as dirt cakes under my nails. One of them breaks on the hard ground.

"No," I mutter in frustration, diving my hand back under the water to yank at my ankle. "Let go." The splatter of trickling water on the rocks echoes in the nearby cavern, making me more sleepy as the sleeping curse takes over. I'm so far away from the castle and I'm stuck in this ditch where no one can even see me. No one will be able to hear me cry for help. Father will be furious if I don't return by dinner and he finds out I left without telling anyone.

I yawn as my eyes get heavy. Trying to wiggle my ankle out from under the rock, pain shoots up my leg and blood swirls in the water.

"No." My voice cracks with desperate frustration and I kick forward against the rocks, making my leg throb.

From behind me, a hand plunges into the water toward my ankle. I whip my head to glance over my shoulder. A man with dark hair, a short stubble beard, and pointed ears is beside me, reaching into the water. With his dark tousled hair falling over his forehead, his thick, muscular arm stretches into the water, his hand grazing the curve of my leg. Finally, the weight of the rock shifts off my foot and my foot is free. Before I can stand up, his cold wet hands slide under my arms, giving me a shiver. His black feather wings flap and pull me out of the water, toward the shore, and up the embankment until we both land in the tall golden blades of the grassy meadow.

"Are you okay?" he asks, breathless as he crawls to my ankle. Blood runs across my foot, soaking the grass beneath it.

"I think so. I slipped and my foot got caught."

Without hesitation, he reaches into his pocket and pulls out a small glass vial of clear liquid. He twists off the lid and pours the solution onto my wound. The bleeding stops instantly.

"That should help with the bleeding." He tears off a piece of fabric from his black shirt and covers the gash on my foot, wrapping it around my ankle.

"What is that stuff?" I ask.

He smirks and his unique golden eyes sparkle with mischief. "Just a little secret magic."

"Magic? Do you always carry around magic in your pocket and use it on strangers?" I ask.

"Only pretty ones that get into trouble and almost killed." He twists the lid back on the vial and slips it into his pocket.

As I narrow my brow, the crack of rifles shoots in the distance, making me nearly jump out of my skin.

"What was that?" I glance over my shoulder, toward the thundering hooves of galloping horses.

"I have to go." He jumps to his feet.

"No, wait. What's your name?"

Shots fire past us again, hitting the trees nearby. I duck to the ground, covering my head with my hands as he dives into the grass, looking back at me.

"See you around, princess," he says, darting into the cover of trees in the woods, into the underbrush.

The court knights appear in the meadow from the opposite direction, charging toward me on their royal horses. I cower close to the ground as hooves pound, charging past me toward the opening in the forest where the stranger disappeared. Two horses slow and circle me.

"Princess Lucia? Are you injured, milady? What are you doing out here?" the lead knight asks.

"I was just picking some flowers from the meadow," I mumble, trying to stand up, my ankle sending crippling pain through my leg.

"You know better than to be out here in the middle of the day. It's much too dangerous for you. You should be in the castle getting your beauty sleep. Guard, place her on your horse and return her to the castle immediately."

I open my eyes with a slow blink. I am surrounded by layers upon layers of cream-colored pillows and blankets in my luxurious four-poster canopied bed. Outside the stained-glass window of my bedroom tower, the golden sun is setting in the west.

"Good evening, my sleeping princess. You're awake," Iridessa, my fairy godmother with iridescent wings, says as she flutters about my room, tidying things up as quickly as she can. She has been with me since the day I was born, protecting and guiding me. She is like my grandmother and nanny, but with special powers because of her Fae background. "You had quite an adventure earlier, didn't you? We didn't think you would make it back to the castle before your morning nap. You fell asleep on the way back with the guard. You really must be more careful, Lucia. Imagine if something bad had happened to you while you were out."

I smile with a nod. I hate that I can't stay awake for more than six hours a day; three hours in the morning and three hours in the evening. When I was born, an evil fairy cast a spell on me and two years ago it came to fruition, causing me to fall asleep for one hundred years. Luckily, the curse was prematurely broken by true love's kiss, a kiss from Prince Liam. I love him dearly and can't wait to see him again, but our kingdoms both decreed to hold off on any prenuptial arrangements until we were older. Unfortunately, although he woke me, the sleeping spell wasn't completely reversed by his kiss. Remnants of the curse still cause me to easily tire and require eighteen hours of daily sleep.

"It's time for dinner, princess," Iridessa says, laying a baby blue, floor-length evening gown on the bed. "Best get ready now, so you aren't late."

With a gentle hand, I move aside my blankets to check my poor ankle. Black and blue marks pepper my skin where the bones were wedged in between the rocks, but the cut on my leg is miraculously already mended back together. I limp to my closet to dress for dinner.

The quiet halls echo as I walk toward the dining hall. Downstairs, we are hosting notable guests to prepare for the anniversary ball next week. While dinner proceeds and the wait staff serves our meal, the court doors of the dining hall suddenly swing open and guardsmen rush in.

"Pardon the intrusion, Your Majesty," a knight dressed in armor says as his team rushes into the room, pushing a restrained man with his arms behind his back. Several more knights follow in after them, all equally strong and intimidating, holding a group of eight more men captive. "We found them trespassing on our land this afternoon."

"I demand you let my people go," the man in iron cuffs yells, his dark hair falling across his forehead. "All of them. Even the ones you have locked in your prison."

"He's the Captain of the Shadowed Woods, Your Highness," the knight says.

When I look at the man's angry face, chills prickle over my skin. Is that the man who helped pull my foot out of the creek?

"Lord of the Shadowed Woods Fae, you imbecile." The man grinds his teeth at the knight. "Not captain. I am a Lord."

"What is your name?" my father asks.

"Lord Barron of the Shadowed Woods."

My father pauses, staring at the man before setting down his silverware and placing his napkin on the table. "Interesting. We have had a few encounters with the Woods Fae in this kingdom. Are you from the local tribe?" my father asks.

"I am." The man proudly raises his chin, a defiant grin spreading across his face. "I believe my aunt was a childhood friend of yours, King. Until you betrayed her trust."

Annoyance fills my father's face as the crease between his eyes deepens. He clears his throat. "Your aunt was a friend of mine?"

"Queen Artemis was her name. Queen Goddess of the Shadowed Woods Fae until her premature death. A death you caused."

The King's face, usually stoic, momentarily loses color.

"I see. The Queen Witch herself." My father clears his throat again. "The audacity of you, thinking I would allow you anywhere near my territory. I prohibited all of her people from entering our lands. Banish these fools from the kingdom. If you set foot on my grounds again, I will have the heads of all your kingsmen placed on spikes around the castle. And yours... your head will sit right here in front of me as the blood still drips from your warm skull. Remove them now."

The knight guards seize the man's arms and grapple with him while they attempt to escort him from the room. The man stares over at me in desperation, and my heart races, thudding in my ears. I want to defend him, but I can't.

"This isn't the last you've seen of me," he yells, struggling to look back.

Over the next week, the anniversary ball arrangements move forward as scheduled, and the kingdom is excitedly anticipating the festivities. While making the necessary preparations and choosing the gala menu, the courtroom doors burst open with a loud bang, startling everyone in the hall. Slowly, a dark figure dressed in a black robe enters the room, his shoulders rolling back as he exudes confidence and strength. His footsteps echo through the hall as the room stays silent. Approaching the raised platform, the shadow lord takes off his hood, unveiling his face, his tousled dark hair falling across his forehead. He looks at my father, then glances at my mother, and finally meets my gaze. With a smoldering smirk, he pauses, making my insides flutter.

"You," my father says with disdain. "What are you doing in my courtroom again? Guards."

In a collective rush, the knights sweep in to grab him.

"I banished you and your people from our lands," my father continues. "Seize him. And seize the guards who allowed him through the gates."

The dark-robed man holds up both hands in surrender. "Your grace. Please." He bows in front of the king. "If I could have but one minute of your time, I will then go peacefully."

The knights continue trying to restrain him until my father raises his ring-laden hand and everyone stops.

"Alright," my father says. "You have one minute."

"Thank you, your grace. Please accept my apologies for our previous encounter. My behavior was rash and unbecoming of a lord." From under his robe, he draws out a long, narrow box and extends it to my father. "Please, accept this gift as a token of my sincere regret."

The guards focus on the king, who pauses briefly before giving a nod. The head guard takes the gift and swiftly transfers it into my father's waiting hands. After my father carefully removes the thick silver ribbon, he opens the box. The hilt of a sword reflects in the light, creating a dance with the facets of the green stones in the handle. As my father unsheathes the weapon, the sword's clang echoes against the stone walls in the room.

The blade of the sword blinds us with its mirrored silver finish and hushed gasps of awe fill the room as my father proudly admires the sword.

"My, what a wonderful gift. Where on earth did you ever find it?" the king asks.

"The people in my district made it. Only the finest artisans with extraordinary gifts can create masterpieces such as this. And this is, by far, the finest they have ever produced. The only one deserving of such a masterpiece would be the king."

My father's face lights up with a smile he can't hold back.

"I hope you like it, your grace."

The king eyes him suspiciously as he examines his prize.

The mysterious stranger glances in my direction. "If you don't mind, your grace, I also have a gift for your daughter."

My father narrows his brows. "No one but the king is allowed to accept gifts from outside factions."

"Oh, it's not really a gift then, per se. Just an offer of goodwill." The man in the robe retrieves a small box from his belt and hands it to the knight, who glances at my father. My father looks at the gift, then the stranger, and gives a curt nod.

The guard hands me a slender package wrapped in beautiful gold and silver embossed paper with a purple ribbon made of glitter and satin. I slowly pull the ribbon, and it perfectly falls to the side onto my lap. The hinge of the gift box creaks softly as I open the lid and the sparkle of light dances on a plum-sized stone in the center. The amethyst-colored jewel, flawless and gleaming, hangs on a gold chain against the velvet-lined case. When the light from the chandelier hits the stone, shades of purple on the inside move in slow motion, as if the gem is filled with a thick shimmering glittery liquid. It's mesmerizing to watch the flow tumble like waves of the sea.

"Oh, wow." I lift my eyes to meet his. "It's absolutely exquisite."

"Not as exquisite as you, my dear."

The stubble on his face enhances his perfect pink lips when his mischievous smirk spreads across his face, quickening my heartbeat. He has the most breathtaking heterochromatic eyes that sparkle with the colors of the sunrise; a central golden ring that changes from hazel green to a brilliant blue rim along the edge. I forget to breathe as butterflies flutter in my insides when he walks towards me. Taking my hand in his, he raises it to his lips, his breath warm against my skin. As his stubble lightly touches my hand, a wave of goosebumps washes over me. When he lifts his gaze to meet mine, a surge of electricity shoots through my heart when another smirk tugs at the corner of his mouth.

"My lady. Pardon my earlier behavior. Please accept this gift as a sign of my apology."

I can't look away, mesmerized by his eyes, and his smile widens. "The stone was retrieved from the deepest mines in the woods and set in one of the most treasured placements by the finest artisan. It's one of our most prized treasures and it's been in my family for centuries.

"I don't think I can accept this." My voice wavers and I break his stare, handing the box back.

"No, please. It's a token of my regret. I would feel better if you accept it, princess."

I can't help but be captivated by the trance of his unique eyes as rabid butterflies flutter in my stomach when he nods. Warmth fills my cheeks, and I want to fan myself from the concentration of heat boiling under my skin. I raise my chin, trying to take a deep breath to clear my mind.

"Very well, Lord."

"Please, call me Barron."

"Lord Barron of the Shadowed Woods." I stumble awkwardly on his name, heat is now inflaming my cheeks. "Thank you. Your generosity is noted and appreciated. I hope we can set aside what happened before and start anew."

"I do too, my lady." With seductive eyes, he smirks again. "Well, I should be going." He reaches for my hand and brings it to his lips again. I am now on fire.

With a nod, the robed man turns to walk out of the courtroom, surrounded by his following kingsmen. As murmurs start in the assembly, the king is quick to quiet them before he concludes the court and hurries out of the room, carrying his new prize.

An elder in my father's council hastily leans over my shoulder to whisper. "What a complete conman. It couldn't have been more obvious he was trying to bribe the crown. Here, give me that trash. I'll just throw out the junk jewelry. Is that okay, milady?"

Stunned, I take a moment and then nod. "Of course. What would I do with that trinket?"

"Exactly." Iridessa leans over on my other side as everyone starts to leave. "It's really for the best, princess. You wouldn't want such a cursed trinket anywhere near you."

The elder casually tosses the box into the trash while chatting with two others as they walk towards the exit. Quickly scanning the room to check that no one is watching, I slip my hand into the trash and retrieve the case and then drop it into my pocket. Iridessa turns around and smiles. "Shall we prepare for dinner, Lucia? You've had a long day, and you must be exhausted. You should eat before you get too tired."

Upstairs, I return to my room to dress for dinner. Alone behind my closed door, I pull the box from my pocket and open it again. With a feather-like touch, I run my fingertips over the purple stone. It comes alive as if smoke is swirling inside. A brief spark runs through my fingers as I skim over the smooth surface and pick up the pendant.

Underneath the stone, there is a note on the inside of the box.

When the haze of slumber rolls in,

Wear this stone to give you energy.

As you stare into the waves of lavender,

May your eyes be awakened by the power of the Woods.

"There's the princess I've been looking for all my life." The deep male voice makes my hair stand on end at the base of my neck.

I whip around to see him, a dozen yards away. It's been two days since I last saw him and he is standing with his hands in his pockets, his dark hair falling across his forehead, almost shielding one of his eyes. He has the most seductive smile that pulls on one side of his lips and the rabid butterflies that live in my stomach just for him come alive in a storm of nerves.

"What are you doing out here? Won't you be in trouble if they find you again?" I whisper as I scan the people roaming the gardens.

His smile broadens. "Nah, it's remarkable how friendly folks become when you give them lavish gifts. The king said I was welcome to stay on the grounds for a couple of weeks. Until we work out a resolution."

"A resolution to what?" I glance behind us at the walkway that leads up to the castle, searching for guards.

"To our war," he says. "Your king has held my people in captivity, enslaved here to work hard labor for decades. I don't think it's right and I want my people to be free. My people and I want them back home, where they belong."

Narrowing my brow, I nod. That doesn't sound unreasonable. "And my father doesn't want that?"

"No, princess." He shakes his head. "Unfortunately, he would like to keep them here. For himself. It's better for your kingdom if he can use the slaves to do the back-breaking labor so his people don't have to. But obviously, you can see my point of view. We just want our people to come home."

"How do you plan to convince the king to agree and release them?"

"I'm not sure yet." He suppresses a laugh. "I guess I'm hoping he'll show a little compassion, have a little empathy, and release them. But so far, it's a no. But I'm not giving up. I was able to get him to change his mind and let me stay here after demanding my severed head last week. So, I guess that's progress."

In an awkward moment, I nod with a little laugh.

"Has anyone ever told you how beautiful you are?" he asks. "The way the light bounces off the golden strands of your hair. Off the flecks of gold in your eyes. It's breathtaking."

I avoid his eyes and focus on the courtyard in the distance.

"You're not wearing your necklace," he says. "Can I ask why not?"

Scanning the gardens again for onlookers, I shrug my shoulder. "Like I said in court, the necklace is exquisite. Too exquisite to wear all the time. I want to save it for a special occasion."

"Hmm," he mutters, coming closer to whisper as he stares out toward the courtyard. "What if I told you that this pendant has the power to keep you awake?"

With a side glance, I meet his eyes, and his brows raise.

"Pardon me?" I ask.

"Remember the magic in the vial I used on your leg in the field?"

I hesitate with a nod.

"That same magic can help you stay awake. The necklace I gave you has inherent magical powers. Did you find the note under the pendant?"

I hesitate with another nod.

He leans in even closer to whisper in my ear. The smell of his cologne waves up to my nose and I take in a steady breath. "You know, I heard a rumor that the princess still has trouble with her sleeping spell. Someone said she can only stay awake for four to six hours of the day. Is that true?"

I stare at him, not saying a word.

"Look, it's not a secret Queen Artemis was my aunt." He stares out at the gardens. "I know about the original curse, the one used to put you under a sleeping spell when you pricked your finger. And I also know that when the curse was lifted, it wasn't completely removed. You still suffer from severe fatigue and an excessive need for sleep. But... if you wear that necklace, your curse will be lessened. Not entirely broken, but you will be able to stay awake 10-12 hours at a time."

My eyes widen in disbelief.

"Fine, princess." His smirk lights up his face and he nods. "You don't have to believe me now. But I already helped you once. What do you have to lose if you trust me again?" He brushes my golden hair away from my cheek and tucks it behind my ear. My heart speeds with the intensity of five hundred horses, and the warmth creeping up my neck might make me pass out.

"I do know another secret though. The curse wasn't completely broken because Liam isn't your true love. You need to find someone that makes your heart race."

He inches closer as he runs his fingertip along my jaw-line. "Someone who makes your temperature rise. Your blood thump in your ears. Your insides tremble." His nose is inches from mine. His heterochromatic sunrise eyes are hypnotic, and I drown in their depths. "When you find that person that makes you want them with the pureness in your heart, kiss him and he'll save you."

After I sneak away from the gardens, I rush back to my room and hurry over to the wooden chest at the foot of my four poster canopied bed. As I lift the lid, the heavy wood makes the hinge creak loudly and reverberate off the walls. I grab the pendant box again and open it.

A glow of golden sparkles twinkles in the purple stone in the center, and I gasp. It's incredibly beautiful. The lavender haze of smoke swirls, mesmerizing me. Picking up the necklace, I cradle it in my palm, staring at the three-dimensional depths of the churning smoke. Suddenly, footsteps echo down the hall. I shove the pendant back in the case, into the wooden chest, and shut it just as there is a knock on the door.

"Princess Lucia, may I come in?"

"Yes," I say, rushing to my vanity chair.

Iridessa, her iridescent wings shimmering with pinks and blues in the light, comes in and walks over to my bed to pull back the sheets. "I saw you downstairs in the gardens and then you disappeared. Is everything alright?"

"Yes, just fine."

"I thought maybe you were getting tired."

"Yeah, a little bit I suppose," I lie.

"I just wanted to remind you we are going to have dinner an hour later tonight. I know that won't do well for your bedtime, so when you feel tired, just let me know and we can retire you to your room earlier."

"Oh, I don't want to miss all the fun."

"That's alright, sweetheart. There will be plenty of good times for you beforehand." She gives me a pat on the shoulder and then leaves.

I bite my lower lip and rush over to the chest to take out the box again. The swirls of amethyst stir as I undo the chain and clasp it together at the back of my neck. Instantly, a sense of rejuvenation floods my blood. I take a deep breath; the burst of energy filling my insides and I turn toward the mirror. The gold chain sparkles like diamonds in the light. When I look at my reflection, I already think I look less tired.

I step out of my closet wearing an exquisite pink off-the-shoulder evening gown. Stones and jewels glisten on the tight bodice and the full puffy ball gown skirt sways with every step I take. Hanging from its golden chain, the large plum pendant swirls with shades of pink and white as it magically matches my dress.

"You look absolutely heavenly," Iridessa says. "Come now, princess. We don't want to be late."

Heading out to the festivities with Iridessa following close behind, we approach the landing at the top of the ballroom stairs. Swarms of people fill the room below, laughing and dancing, eating and talking. A ten-piece band is playing horns and drums at one end of the room. I spot my father on the dais sitting next to my mother on the opposite side of the room, being served by our servants and laughing as he talks to other heads of state. As I scan over the rest of the crowd, I feel a pair of eyes watching me and am instantly drawn to them. In the corner of the room, a man dressed in a crisp black and white tux and wearing an irresistible smirk nods when we make eye contact, and he strolls toward the base of the staircase. He reaches for two champagne glasses as the waiter walks by. When he gets to me, he offers one with a nod.

"You look lovely tonight, if I might say so, my Queen."

"I'm not the queen." I laugh, shaking my head, making him smile.

"I'd make you queen of my world, Lucia." He leans to whisper, his breath warming my ear.

My heart loses the ability to keep time as heat creeps up onto my cheeks.

"Would you like to dance, my lady?" He offers his elbow to escort me.

My hand slips around his firm bicep and the warmth of his body warms mine. He places our glasses on the tray of a waiter walking by and then we head toward the center of the dance floor.

We dance one dance, then two and three as the hours pass by.

"Are you tired yet?" he asks with a laugh as we walk toward the balcony of the ballroom to step outside for a break.

"No, not at all."

Outside, the fresh air fills my lungs as I overlook the courtyard below. The scent of roses and jasmine drifts on the gentle breeze as others walk by in conversation.

"You do realize that it's after midnight," he says.

"What? How can that be? I don't feel the least bit tired. My feet ache though."

"Your feet ache? What about mine? You've been stepping on my toes all night."

We both laugh.

"It's because of the necklace, isn't it?" I ask. "It's keeping me awake."

With a sad smile, he nods. "It doesn't take away the curse. But it lessens it."

"You're helping to give me my life back. Thank you." I reach out and put my hand over his.

As we stare out at the courtyard, an animated couple walks by laughing.

"You know, there is a way to reverse the curse completely," he whispers.

I glance at him over my shoulder as he stares at the gardens below. And then he meets my eyes.

"How?" I whisper.

Glancing over his shoulder, he moves in closer. "It's a secret."

"I won't tell anyone." I can't even breathe waiting for his answer.

He turns so we are standing face to face, nose to nose. His eyes are so intense, and the scent of his cologne makes me take a deep breath. "There is a stone that exists that would remove the curse completely. But I need your help to find it."

"My aunt's scepter, the wand she would use to wield her magic, and the one she used to put the spell on you, has a stone in it. That stone can reverse your curse with my help." He glances over both shoulders and then leans in closer. "The stone is here. Somewhere inside this castle. Hidden wherever your kingdom hides its treasure. With your help, if you take me there, we can retrieve the scepter and reverse the curse."

Despair fills my heart, and I slowly shake my head. "I have no idea where that would be."

His expression falls as he knits his brows. His anxious eyes sink in disappointment, and he sighs. "Maybe it doesn't even exist anymore. When Artemis was here, your father struck her down, wrapped her in iron, and destroyed her. We never heard anything more from her. I was hoping her things were not also destroyed."

Perplexed, I narrow my gaze. "I can search for it. There is one place I could look. It's a vault underground. I'm not really allowed to go down there, but I could try to sneak in."

"If you could get me into that vault..." He nods.

"No, I must go alone. If anyone found you snooping around with me, there would be too many questions. I don't know if I can do this, though."

He takes both of my hands in his and our eyes meet as I drown in the depths of his. "I need you to try. For me. I need that scepter," he whispers. He pushes back my golden hair behind my ears, brushing the backs of his fingers across my cheek. "You are so beautiful in the moonlight. The light sparkles like crystals on the lake in your eyes. My sweet Lucia, you shine wherever you go. Your name reminds me of the light of the dawn that shines on the horizon, but your eyes are like the light of the moon that shines in the middle of the night."

He slowly pulls away, his eyes still locked on mine.

"The scepter has to be here. Find it and then come find me."

"Princess Lucia," a voice says.

I whip around to discover Iridessa standing behind us, her brow creased with worry.

"Hi, Iridessa. I was just talking to our guest about the war on the Woods Fae."

Iridessa stares at Barron and then back at me. "I'm a little surprised that you're still awake. I would have thought you retired hours ago. You must be tired."

"I am feeling a bit sleepy," I lie. "I think I will retire for the night." As I turn back to Barron, I curtsey. "Thank you for the honor of your company tonight. It has been a pleasure."

Barron reaches for my hand and brings it to his lips. Electricity fires under his kiss as he slips a stiff piece of paper into my palm and curls my fingers around the folded note.

I creep down the hall with my lantern, the stone floor freezing my bare feet. There is only one spot I can think of where I'll find what I am looking for... the vault. As I tiptoe down the stairs, through the winding corridor, I finally approach a large heavy iron door with thick iron locks. As I pull down on the locks, they are heavy and solid. With a sigh, I scan the empty hallway. How am I supposed to open that without a key? Flanked on each side of the doorway, empty armor knight suits stand by at attention as if they are watching me, laughing at me because there is nothing I can do to open those locks. Could one of those knights be hiding a key in their armor? I reach into my pocket and the edge of Barron's paper note pokes into my palm. Slowly, I pull out the note and unfold it. Wrapped inside the sheet of paper is a three-inch metal skeleton key that shimmers in the low light. I lift the lantern to read the note.

Magic manifests in many forms.

Use me to unlock countless secrets.

"No. It can't be," I whisper, analyzing the key and shifting my gaze back at the lock. I slide the skeleton key into the keyhole and turn. Nothing happens. Then, after a few brief seconds, it magically shifts, clicks, and unlocks. It worked. I listen for any footsteps coming down the hall and then push open the door.

Inside, the room is dark, all except for an emerald hue of light emanating from the far side of the room. As I step inside the cold dank vault, gold and silver, from goblets and jewels to coins and gold bars, pour out of treasure chests that line the edges of the room. Rubies and diamonds reflect off the low light coming from my lantern, sparkling in every direction. I cross the room and approach the green scepter glowing in the dark in the most beautiful light that takes my breath away. Enclosed in a cage made of iron bars, the swirling emerald liquid inside the stone captivates me as I stare, its glitter dancing in the light. In the center, the stone clears into blackness, resembling a midnight sky. Twinkling stars edge the outside as a vision forms in the middle, an image of a spindle wheel with blood dripping to the floor. The face of Queen Artemis appears in the background, her arms up in a spell cast and the stone whispers the word "Barron."

The vision transforms into another image of my kingdom being stormed by the fae. Bodies lay across the courtyard of the fiery castle as the fae swoop in and destroy the people crying for mercy.

"Fulfill my wishes, Barron. For us. Destroy all of them."

Confused, I step back and the blackness dissipates as the swirling green haze closes in again.

"This can't be right. She wants him to destroy the kingdom?" I whisper.

I rush out of the room to the hallway and collide with someone.

"Princess! What are you doing here?" Iridessa asks, grasping my arms to catch me.

"Nothing." I wipe my eyes, trying to hide my tears.

"You're not telling the truth. Why were you in that room, Lucia?" She corners me up against the wall and tilts my chin up to stare into my eyes.

With a deep breath, I stifle the cry in my throat. "He tricked me, Iridessa. Barron told me if I helped him find his aunt's scepter, he would reverse my sleeping curse and I would be normal again. But the scepter showed me his real plans to destroy our kingdom. I can't believe what a fool I was to trust him."

Iridessa purses her lips and sighs, her kind eyes showing sincerity. "Shh, Lucia. We may be able to fix this."

With her arm wrapped around me, we slip back into the vault. At the nearby desk, Iridessa picks up a fluffy white swan feather quill pen. She holds it up to the light, the feather swaying back and forth as she waves her wand in front of it. Gold pixie dust sprinkles into the air, floating around the pen as she mutters a spell.

Inverse the slumber curse from the heart of pure,

And return the curse for the wicked to bear.

Iridessa meets my eyes. "The curse began in blood with the prick of a finger. It can only be reversed in blood. Have Barron sign this decree that will give power of the scepter over to you. Once he signs, we need him to prick his finger on the end of this pen and your original curse will be broken. Go to him now. Get him to sign the decree. Then prick his finger."

"My Princess, do you have good news for me?" the handsome shadow lord asks as I approach him at the banquet table of the ballroom. The gala in the room is dying down as the band plays slower songs in the distance and just a few people remain on the dance floor.

"I found the scepter." I reach for a small cracker from the impressive spread of hors d'oeuvres at the table.

"Wonderful! Where is it?"

"I can't give it to you."

"Why not?" He knits his brow.

"The stone showed me a vision. A vision of what you plan to do. And I can't let that happen." I shake my head.

Perplexed, he purses his lips in a smirk. "What did it show you?"

"That you plan to destroy my kingdom. That you want to take control of my people, seize our power, and rule."

He shakes his head. "No, my dear sweet princess. It's only showing you your own worst fears. Not the future. I told you what I want, Lucia. I want my people to be free. I want to reverse your curse. Isn't that what you want?"

As I get lost in his sincere eyes, I struggle to trust him.

"My dearest Princess. You are a vision sent from above. A kiss woke you from your slumber and only a kiss will eternally set you free from the curse." He reaches over and brushes his fingertips along my jaw, sending electrical signals down my spine. He leans closer and his breath smells of strawberries as it dances across my skin. As I stare at his soft bottom lip, I want to kiss him. My breath gets stuck in my throat as it closes up and I force myself to swallow, my veins flooding with adrenaline. I meet his eyes, his eyes that captivate me in their depths.

As he leans in and brushes his lips across mine, I close my eyes. Stars twinkle in the blackness behind my lids. His warm lips move against mine and I am spellbound by his heavenly scent, the baby-soft stubble above his lips gently tickling the skin of my upper lip. He slowly pulls away and with our eyes locked, he smiles.

"We could rule the kingdom. Together. We would be the most powerful couple in the world."

There is a sudden clang in the room when someone drops a tray. We both jump and turn toward the crowd.

The guests at the party begin to yawn, covering their open mouths and appearing sleepy. Some sit on the floor. Others start to faint. One lady leans against another man, her head on his shoulder as she closes her eyes.

"Barron, what is going on? Why is everyone falling asleep?" I reach out to catch a young servant woman before she falls to the ground.

He looks around with a smirk. "It appears everyone is ready for a nap."

"Did you do that to them?" I wrinkle my brow in confusion, my voice reaching a level of hysteria.

"No. You did that to them," he says. "When you kissed me. You think the reversal of the curse is free? There is always a price. I can't reverse the curse completely without the scepter."

"You never said that would happen. I don't want this. I want you to stop this." As another lady faints to the floor, I reach to catch her.

"I demand you reverse this," I say louder.

"I can't." He shakes his head. "Not without the scepter."

"I will never give you that scepter. Return my people." The necklace on my neck tingles and I rip off the golden chain.

Barron's eyes darken and his appearance starts to change. He seems to grow in height before my very eyes as dark shadows swirl around his feet.

"You're an angel, my dearest Lucia, but your kingdom has hurt my people for too long. I will not allow it to happen any longer."

"I'll let your people go. Just reverse the curse."

He shakes his head. "Your father stands in my way with his refusal to cooperate. I cannot be guaranteed that you will keep your word."

"Wait!" Iridessa screams. "We will give you the scepter. Princess Lucia is in charge and next in line to be queen. She will set your people free. But only after you sign a treaty of peace and agree to reverse the slumber curse on our people. Sign the decree and your people and the scepter are yours." She hands over the swan-feathered quill pen.

He smirks as he gives her a skeptical stare.

"Alright, fine." He takes the pen, holding the paper in his hand over the surface of his palm. With one brow raised in skepticism, he signs his signature in over-exaggerated large letters, and then to finish; he punctuates his signature with a period. The end of the quill pen punctures through the parchment paper and into the center of his palm. Startled, he pulls out the pen, and dark red blood bubbles in his hand.

With horror in his face, his eyes lock with mine. "What did you do?"

The green haze inside the scepter swirls, turning colors to a teal blue until the entire wand glows. Barron stumbles backward, reaching for the table to keep his balance as his eyelids grow heavy.

"I will let your people go," I say, "but you... you will suffer from your own greed. Goodbye Barron. Sweet Dreams." I lean forward and kiss his beautiful lips once more.

"And that promise is sealed with a kiss."

The kingdom returns to normal; the flowers bloom and the skies light up in the brilliant morning sunlight. My father woke from his slumber curse and resumed his reign as king, and now I am a part of his council, helping him to rule.

My curse has been completely broken. I can stay awake from the break of dawn until the moon rises high in the sky. And I feel more alive than ever.

I kept my word and we released the Shadowed Woods Fae to their own lands. A sleeping Lord Barron was also returned to his kingdom and I hope to never see him again.

For insurance, I kept the scepter. You never know when you might need it.

As I sit on my stool at my vanity and prepare for bed one night, brushing my long golden hair, a disembodied whisper comes from the corner.

"Luce."

I slow my brushing and shift my eyes in the mirror to look behind me. The usual green scepter sitting against the wall is glowing a greenish blue, the teal color reflecting off the walls. The whisper comes again.

"Lucy."

The faint turquoise grows brighter. Then the color turns blue. Another whisper comes. This one louder.

"Lucia. Barron wants to talk."

MOTHER KNOWS BEST

BY OLIVIA LYNN

In the hours of the morning dreary
I arose solemn and weary
At the window did I weep
Freedom for its bitter taste
Thrust into a world unknown
Curiosity killed by memories undone
Grey skies reflecting
The damage unrelenting
Anguish moved within me
Taking all, leaving me empty
Hollow was my body
Empty was my soul
Drifting into lifeless abandon
Mother, how I miss your falsehood
To a waif who desired adulthood

Whisk me away into a time
Where I am me, and you are mine
Contentment seems such a vain thing
What happiness can a girl like me dream
Allow me an escape from this waking nightmare
Where I exist and you surrendered
With my own hands, I mended
But the flesh had been offended
To her body, I lay by restless
Never slumbering, but drifting endless
A milky hand on your breast
There, beating, had come to rest
"In this hour I defy
The life that is my lie
What use am I to continue living,
When here you lay cold and unfeeling?"
The girl wept bitterly against
The woman she thought hers
Demise thick in the air
Putrid cunning and despair
With great force of will she did lift her face
Looking over yonder, to somber windowed greys
With resilience, she grasped
Her mother's pallid hand
Painting again at last
Excellent effort achieved
By moistened brow and rosy'd cheek
Pushing the window to sky
A mist caressed and enchanted by
A familiar voice resounded
Though strange and unfounded

"My dear daughter,
If you must weep, then cry for joy
We will be together, you must employ
Take one step, the rest without
With that, I forgive our ending bout."
The girl turning, saw the woman-thing speak
Head lolling, neck cracking
At angles clacking
Dark pus oozed from cracked lips
Her belly sprouted
Like a puppet, she moved
All at once the girl's anxieties quenched
And wrapping her in a cool embrace
She leaned back and moved into space
"Oh, I am blessed!
Mother knows best."

An Enchantment of Twelve

By Christine Letizia

As the oldest of twelve, I'd always been compared to what came after me. My next youngest sister was more beautiful and so was the one after her. By the time we reached the twelfth, and my mother died of exhaustion during childbirth, there could be no other belief than this final child was the most beautiful of all.

In that light, I was practically a hag.

I was also twenty-five and unmarried, which is the lowest a princess could fall.

An ancient, unwanted hag. And the servants wondered why I was snippy.

Hence, it was unsurprising that my father, the King, wanted to execute me once the truth of our nighttime adventures came to light.

The twelve of us listened in horror on the other side of the door as Calaen, the soldier I'd drugged for the last three nights, recounted how we went to an underground, enchanted castle and danced with twelve princes. At least, he didn't say what else we did with the princes.

"And Liette would clap her hands to open this portal?" King Thoren demanded. "She led them there?"

"They all deceived you," Calaen replied.

"But Liette is the oldest. She knows better than to disobey me. She knows what I expect of her."

I scowled. *Why do you think we snuck off, old man? Because you have your crown so far up your ass, you can't see that we long for more than your expectations of us.*

The king slammed a fist on his throne. "She will lose her head like all the men who came here before you. All the men she tricked!"

My sisters gasped. I swallowed as the noose tightened around my neck. My father hated my betrayal, but more than that, he wanted to rid himself of me. I was a failure.

We waited for the soldier to speak, but the room stayed silent until the king spoke again. "I will call my daughters in to confess. Then, you may pick your bride. Choose wisely. You will one day inherit this kingdom."

For a brief moment, I considered fleeing into the world below. Would my prince welcome me? He'd always been so dashing and attentive, always hinted at a future together. I'd begged him to meet my father countless times. But he'd claimed he couldn't leave his enchanted castle.

Was that a lie? I'd never know now.

The king's steward bolted into the corridor and stopped short when he saw all twelve of us listening at the door. The man's pale skin flushed. He waved us in, unable to meet my eyes. "Come, ladies."

We filed into the throne room. I lifted my chin, unwilling to give the courtiers the repentant princess they were hungering to see. Tears slipped down the face of my youngest sister. Her hair flamed red like our mother's. In fact, with her rosebud lips and blue eyes, she was nearly her twin.

I struggled every day not to resent her.

"Stop crying, Cressie!" I hissed.

She sniffled but heeded my order.

Our father glowered at us before launching into the soldier's story and presenting all the evidence against us—three enchanted twigs of gold, silver, and diamond plus a fancy goblet.

The goblet glinted with magic. Every moment in the world below had felt like a fairytale. For months, I'd pressed the brim of a goblet like this to my lips, pouring wine greedily down my throat. And every night ended with wine-flavored kisses with my prince.

A flush rose from my core. I hungered for more wine and kisses, even now when I was facing a death sentence. Perhaps I'd been enchanted. I couldn't care less.

The soldier remained silent during our father's tirade. He stared at the polished floor in front of him, until the king called his name. Then, his blue eyes met mine.

A fire burned behind them. The gilded walls of our cage pressed in on me. My breath quickened. I wanted to run from the room but not before beating him senseless.

He had every right to hate me for drugging him. It could have been his head on the chopping block. But I still wanted to scream at him for exposing us.

"What say you, Calaen? Which of my daughters do you wish to wed?"

I swore my father said, "to bed." For isn't that what this was about? He wanted a male heir. No more petticoats and dance shoes.

Calaen pushed away from the wall. My sisters called him old, but he was only five years older than me and quite handsome in a rugged, broken sort of way.

Cressie tucked herself behind the next oldest sister, Rowena. How arrogant to think he'd choose her because she was so beautiful. Though he probably would. The last thing I'd hear in this world would be their wedding bells.

I sucked in a breath and knotted my hands in the fabric of my dress.

His fiery eyes met mine again. "I wish to marry Liette."

A gasp sliced through the room. My shoulders slumped in relief. I couldn't imagine why, but he'd chosen me. He'd saved me!

My sisters cheered and crowded close. Tears sparkled in their eyes. Only Cressie stared at the soldier in disbelief.

My next youngest sister, Aliya, pressed her head of golden brown hair against mine. "You shall rule our kingdom, Sister. As you were meant to."

Her words fit in my heart like a missing puzzle piece. I'd always felt the call to rule. "Thank you," I whispered and hugged her close.

The king grumbled on this throne. "Are you sure Liette is your choice?"

A smile played on Calaen's lips, eliciting a pleasing warmth in my chest. "I will accept no other but her."

Calaen's words "No other but her" echoed in my ears during the ceremony in the castle gardens. Instead of the moonflowers in the underground gardens, morning glories spread open their purple petals and their vines embraced the trellis we stood beneath.

He looked rather striking in a white dress shirt and tan breeches. His hair was golden brown like Aliya's. It had been trimmed and his scruffy beard removed.

In an elegant, off-white ball gown, I wore a silver circlet in my raven hair. I felt like the princess I'd always wished to be as we stood under the trellis, our hands joined. Though I knew in my heart, I should have been marrying my prince instead.

A cool wind nudged me. I glanced away from Calaen and into the eyes of a gray-haired woman. She watched us from behind a hedge. A red, oval-shaped jewel hung from her neck. Shivers wormed their way up my spine.

I'd seen her before, but the details were blurry, like in a dream. Why was she lurking in the castle gardens?

But I didn't have time to wonder. For in a blink, she vanished.

We finished the ceremony, and applause carried us out of the gardens and into the ballroom where a grand party awaited. We ate and drank, nothing as magical as the food or wine from the enchanted castle, but it was a far cry from what they served at the gallows. Father even congratulated me with the memorable words, "At least, you've made yourself useful in the end."

This is my beginning! I wanted to shout it from the tallest tower.

As if he sensed my rebuke, Calaen led me away from the king and onto the dance floor. He drew me close, and I melted a little into his muscled chest. "Careful," I warned, my voice soft and velvety. "You might make a habit of saving me."

His chuckle passed through me, pleasant and strong. "I'm happy to make a habit of it."

I leaned back to look into his eyes. Their blue had darkened like the flames in the ballroom candles. "But why? I could have killed you like all the others."

We swayed together for a moment in silence. Calaen finally broke it. "You didn't create the law those men should die after three days if they didn't discover the truth. Your father did. You only meant to keep your secret." He wrapped a strand of my black hair around his finger. It felt possessive. A thrill coursed through me. "You always look out for your sisters. It's time someone looked out for you."

My heart stuttered. How could he grasp who I was after only a few days? What had he seen as he spied on us from under his invisible cloak?

I closed the space between us again. "You are a surprise," I whispered.

He squeezed our joined hands in response, continuing to lead us around the ballroom. A limp in his left leg added a lag to our dance steps. We made the turns awkwardly. My cheeks flamed. Several of my sisters looked away, embarrassed for me. Cressie smirked from the banquet table. In the enchanted ballroom, my prince and I led the dance. Here, things were different. It was hard to accept, but accept it I must.

His voice was strained. "I imagine my skills as a dance partner pale in comparison to the prince's."

They did, but I couldn't say as much to a man who'd served my kingdom and saved my life. "The prince from below was raised on dance lessons, like me. We spent hours beaten by instructors until our form was perfect." Or so I assumed.

"Then, why spend every night dancing?"

I mulled over his question. "Because it was fun and I never worried about anyone's expectations."

His cheek brushed against mine. It was already rough with the stubble from his beard. A quiet hum built between us as we progressed along with the other dancing couples. The music didn't sweep me away as it did in the enchanted castle. But there was a consistent pleasure in being close with him that made me not want the dance to end.

He cleared his throat. "Will you miss dancing in the underground castle tonight?"

Another unexpected question. But Calaen wasn't like my prince from below, who never asked me about the world above. He only poured me more wine and knew how to spin me around the ballroom and when to take me to the gardens.

Of course, I couldn't go back. How could I look my prince in the eyes and tell him I married someone else? It was unthinkable.

"I will miss it," I told him, knowing he sought my candor, not more lies. "But there's no going back."

The temperature in the ballroom seemed to dip after those words. The shadows on the periphery deepened, hiding those better who were indulging in each other. My scalp prickled as if thousands of eyes were watching me. I didn't want to be in here anymore.

Calaen rubbed his hands up my arms, now covered in goosebumps. A crease of concern appeared between his eyes. "Are you well?"

I blinked and looked around. Was someone watching me? There was the old woman in the garden, but that might've been a fluke. Now, it felt like something had its sights set on me. A creature in the corner perhaps? I'd never felt anything monstrous in the enchanted castle but here, it seemed possible.

"I think I've had enough of this celebration." I dragged him off the dance floor. "Can we leave?"

He gestured towards my father on one end of the ballroom and my sisters grouped throughout, dancing and laughing. "Do you need to wish anyone a good night?"

I snorted. "I've slept in the same room as my sisters my whole life. Or I've danced in an enchanted ballroom with them for hours. We can take an evening apart."

His eyes crinkled with amusement, but the blue depths smoldered. The heat in his gaze seared across my skin. Surprise fluttered through me as my lips parted, aching to be kissed. For once, I wasn't longing for my prince.

We wandered back to the gardens. Moonlight washed over the plants and shrubs, turning them ghostly pale. Their leaves looked waxy and fake. I glanced around. Beyond the moonlight, the darkness seemed to shift and grow. I wished I could direct the moon like a lantern and shed light on all that remained hidden.

The castle below was shrouded in constant darkness. Everything was illuminated by lanterns and candles. And yet, the darkness didn't feel as dangerous as it did tonight.

Calaen spoke, ending a prolonged silence. "It feels as though something is bothering you." He turned to face me. "Do you wish to be alone?"

Alone with the creepy, shifting darkness?

"No, not at all!" I squeaked.

He placed his hands on his hips. "But something is bothering you."

I stepped closer to him, almost as if someone or something might overhear us. Though to all appearances, the gardens were deserted and we were decidedly alone. His eyes dropped to my lips.

"I feel as though someone is watching me." A breeze passed between us. Goosebumps surfaced on my arms again. "It started during the ceremony. There was a gray-haired woman. Then, I felt it again in the ballroom."

Calaen studied the collection of shadows the moon couldn't reach. "And now here, too?"

I nodded, unnerved.

He guided me toward where the moon shined directly on an elaborate fountain my mother commissioned after my sixth sister, Genevieve, was born. We sat on the edge of a rectangular pool. Water trickled out of the sculptures of men and women; their blank gazes eerily focused on our backs.

"The gray-haired woman, is there anything you re-member about her?"

I brought a hand to my chest. "She wore a necklace with a red jewel, and she looked familiar. Like I'd met her before."

"But it was almost like a dream?"

I practically pounced on him. "Exactly! Like a dream." The word 'dream' drew forth a hazy image. It was of the gray-haired woman showing me the entrance to the kingdom below. "I think she may have revealed the portal in our nursery."

He nodded and took my hand in his. "Was the jewel like this?" He traced an oval shape on my palm, just as I'd seen. The sense of his touch lingered, and the darkness seemed to stretch closer.

"It was. How do you know all this?"

"Because it was the same woman who told me how the king's daughters danced in an enchanted castle." A small grin flitted across his face. "She cautioned me not to drink your wine and gave me an invisibility cloak."

"But why you? Why didn't she help the others?" A dozen men had died trying to uncover our secret. Perhaps it was them who were watching me, waiting to pull me into a different underworld, one for the dead.

Calaen shrugged, his expression growing distant. "Maybe she pitied me. I was in bad shape."

My fingers brushed across his left knee. He stiffened. "Because of your injury?"

He stood. "Um, no. That had healed by then. Best as it could." He rubbed the back of his neck and kept his gaze on the fountain. "I'd been drinking steadily in the days after the war. I was engaged, but she left once she saw my wounds. The ale took her place."

Calaen limped over to the other end of the fountain and plucked a leaf out of the water. He twirled it between his fingers. "The old woman found me stumbling back home. Asked me what I wanted." He smirked. "I could've said I wanted my girl back, but I was drunk and the latest man had been beheaded for not discovering your secret. I told her I wanted to know where the princesses go. Expose you and stop the needless deaths. I'd already seen so much death."

He knelt next to me again. "I would have believed it all a dream if I hadn't woken in my bed with the invisibility cloak in my hands." He held up the leaf. "She saved me from drowning. That's what she did. And now I'm here with you."

Placing the leaf on the edge of the fountain, he leaned towards me. The sound of his breath mixed with the bubbling water, wrapping me in a new enchantment that was quite different from the one in the kingdom below.

Calaen's story burrowed into my heart, for I'd never thought of those fighting in my father's battles and what happened to them after the war. But I'd wanted a say in sending those men to war, to fight an enemy who was near collapse. The Ironstead kingdom was teetering on the edge, and we'd given them the final push. Was war necessary? Yes, we'd doubled the size of our land, but what of the men who'd fought, who'd been injured or died?

Calaen weaved his hand through my hair. Dark strands tumbled over his fingers, and my breath caught in my chest.

Shadows only a stone's throw from the fountain seemed to pulse. For a moment, I perceived a hand encased in darkness reaching out to grab me. I swallowed a burst of fright and jerked away.

"Perhaps she did save you." I got to my feet and paced beside the fountain's edge. "And maybe she saved me, too, by showing me the door to the world below."

Saved me from the doldrums of a life I seemed born to live. I brought a hand to my throat. But why did it feel like I might end up on the executioner's block, nonetheless? Was something out to get me?

"But whether she intended to save us or not," I continued, "I think she was using us."

"For what purpose?"

My eyes skittered across the darkness. "I don't know. But she told me about the door and you about the wine. All so everything that happened came to pass."

He rose beside me and took my hand in his. His touch steadied me. "And I'm grateful that it has." A flush worked its way up his face. "I looked forward to each evening when you would come with a glass of wine for me."

I laughed. "So you could silently mock me while I attempted to put you to sleep?"

"Not entirely," he said with a wink. "You were quite charming. Regaling me with stories and castle gossip. As if you felt bad for what you must do to keep your secret."

"I did feel bad," I replied in a quiet voice. "I hardly thought..." I fiddled with the wedding ring on his finger. "I never would have believed you would choose me."

He tilted his head. "And who should I have chosen? Timid Cressie?" He chuckled. "I've faced men butchering each other without blinking an eye. So bent on survival, they forgot their own humanity. I probably forgot my own at times. I couldn't pick a wife who screamed every time I broke a twig off a tree."

A snort burst out of me. "You were under an invisible cloak. She didn't know you were there."

"I doubt she would've been much different had she known I was." Calaen ran his hands up my arms and tucked them around my elbows. Everything faded around me, including the darkness and shadows. There was only us, listening to the water trickle under the moonlight. "But as I said to your father, I will accept no other but you."

Our arms brushed against each other with an alarming friction as we walked to our new rooms. It sent my mind in all the anticipated directions of a wedding night, but I didn't have the nerves most did. Not after all of the nights in the gardens with the prince.

Curiosity replaced those nerves, especially after our time together near the fountain. What would Calaen be like in our marital bed? Would he be tender and passionate, or would it be another awkward dance?

We passed the grand nursery that I had shared with my sisters. Twenty-five years in a nursery! My father punished me for not being marriageable by keeping me in there. But when I'd discovered the portal beneath my bed, I'd stopped asking for my own room.

That door to the world below was so very close now. It pulled at me as if I was tethered to it. Something dark and willful inside of me yearned to go through again, to take the staircase down into the belly of the world and find the lake under a permanent black sky. It wouldn't take long to reach the lake and find my prince waiting for me in his boat. And only a little longer to tell him what had happened. That Calaen had saved me from being beheaded. That I was not only betrothed but married to him.

I turned my face away from the room, ignoring the tether even as it burned. He would have to hear it from one of my sisters if they ever snuck down there again. I couldn't face him.

Besides, I had a new beginning to focus on—a married life with our own private rooms and a role in ruling our kingdom. It was a life I'd dreamed of constantly before I'd discovered that secret entrance.

We left the nursery behind as well as the room beside it, which had been Calaen's so he could keep an eye on us at night. In the next corridor, we found our rooms. There was a main chamber with a fine table where we could dine and a set of plush chairs for reading and conversation. Candles were already lit, and a fire crackled in the hearth.

Calaen removed his boots as I went to investigate the bedroom. Rose petals were scattered over the sumptuous bed. It had to be my next youngest sister, Aliya's, work. Only she would be so thoughtful.

A silky, white nightgown lay folded on the bed, a gift from the castle seamstress. I thought she hated me. Maybe she hoped I would be more tolerable now that I was finally married.

I ran a finger along the thin straps, imagining Calaen doing the same. A deep ache awoke inside of me.

Sticking my head out the door, I took him in. He sat on one of the chairs, pulling at the sleeves of his dress shirt. It was rather endearing to see the hardened soldier, so determined to uncover our secret, now nervous at being alone with me.

I cleared my throat. He looked up, eyes wide and vulnerable.

"I've found a gift, a nightgown. It will only take me a moment to change."

"Of course," he said, his voice rough around the edges.

I left him to ruminate about my nightgown. With care, I removed the silver circlet from my hair and placed it on a side table. I'd saved it to marry my prince, having discovered it one night near a fountain in the enchanted gardens. He'd placed it in my hair then kissed me silly. Forgotten in my bliss, I'd brought it home with me. On one hand, it felt wrong to wear it for today's ceremony. But perhaps it was a way to keep a piece of that fairytale experience with me in the real world.

The nightgown poured over my body, soft and slick, rounding my curves in the sensual fabric. Pressing my hands over my breasts and belly, I felt far from a twenty-five-year-old hag.

I minced out to the main chamber in my bare feet. Calaen was pouring wine into two goblets. "I just found this," he said before turning to me.

His mouth dropped open when he saw me. He handed me a goblet, his eyes roaming over my every curve with a naked hunger that was startling. As if I were a five-course meal, rather than the scrap of bread my father had convinced me I'd become.

He clinked his goblet against mine, his gaze steady once more. Then, he rested his hand where the nightgown dipped down in the back so his fingers brushed against my bare skin. Without saying a word, we carried our goblets into the bedroom. I took a small sip before placing mine next to the silver circlet. He took a gulp of his and did the same.

Calaen's nerves seemed to have resurfaced. I sat on the bed, but he stared past me as he unbuttoned his shirt. "I think you need to see what I've become since we waged war against the Ironstead kingdom."

He removed his shirt and stood before me like I was his executioner. My eyes roved over the extensive battle scars cut into the muscles of his chest and others which wrapped around his torso. "I fought for our kingdom for four years until Ironstead fell. I've been wounded more times than I can count." He tapped his lame left knee. "I am hideous and a burden. Or so I was told when I returned home and the girl who'd waited for me left in disgust."

My hands twisted the bed sheet at the thought of some silly village lass turning up her nose at him.

Limping over, he grabbed his wine goblet and took another hefty drink. He set it down hard enough that some liquid splashed out. "I'm not perfect like your prince from below."

Surprise spread through me. I lifted an eyebrow. "How much did you see when you were spying on us under that invisible cloak?"

His lips curled in a mischievous grin. My breath quickened. He'd seen it all.

He gestured down to the floor as if the castle was under our own. It wasn't. I don't know where it was. "I saw you in the boat, being rowed across the lake. You would always skim your fingers across the dark water." Calaen stepped closer. "I saw your smile under the golden and silver trees. Heard your laughter under the diamond ones." He reached out and wrapped a hand around my arm. "I saw you twirl around the ballroom for hours." Gently, he lifted me to my feet. "And then I saw him take you into the gardens and kiss you."

I knew I wasn't the only one who went into the gardens. Aliya hinted that she'd ventured in there with her prince. But I still felt exposed and perhaps a little ashamed that I'd been seen.

Before I could wrap my arms around myself, Calaen released my arm and touched his fingertips to mine. I stilled. Cautiously, he slid his fingers up until ours were interlaced. "I didn't mean to embarrass you," he explained in a quiet voice. "Only to say that I know you're used to being close with a man without scars or calluses."

It's true, my prince's skin was smooth and unblemished. He always seemed perfect, maybe too perfect. Almost as if he wasn't real.

Calaen felt very real. And I didn't mind it.

"I'm the ugliest of twelve beautiful princesses," I quipped. "Surely, you don't think I would mind some scars and calluses."

He waited a beat then shook his head. "Whoever told you that you're the least beautiful of your sisters is a damn fool."

Any lingering resistance to this match floated away. I placed a hand on the closest scar embedded in the hair on his chest. The skin was sunken and stretched thin. Neither hideous nor burdensome, it only showed me how brave he'd been.

He sucked in a breath as I traced the scar.

"I wouldn't have left had you come home with these markings." I dragged my eyes up to meet his. "Will you kiss me now?"

A genuine smile split his face before he leaned in. My lips met his halfway, and I lost myself in the firm pressure of his mouth. It sent a wave of tingles across my body.

The kiss was more than pleasing. It felt natural. His mouth seemed to fit mine. Was that an odd thing to notice? Perhaps it was, but then, all thoughts flew away once my tongue found his.

A deep groan emanated from his chest as our tongues slid along each other. I ran my fingers through his hair then down his back, over more scars and old wounds, each mark reminding me of the sacrifices he made for our kingdom.

Calaen broke the kiss. His hands brushed across my hair, and his lips caressed the side of my neck.

"Liette," he murmured, his mouth flush with my skin. He teased the hollow at the base of my neck with the tip of his tongue. A low moan spooled out of me.

He straightened and stared deep into my eyes. "If I could give you reason to make that sound every day, I would be a happy man."

I opened my mouth to say something, anything but gave him another kiss instead. There were no words right now. Nothing about this felt choreographed or awkward. In fact, this was a completely new dance altogether. And we were making it up as we went.

Nudging his lower lip between my teeth, I gave it a soft bite. A growl rose through his throat, and with one movement, he lobbed me onto the bed with a wicked smile. I grinned back at him, enjoying the luscious texture of the rose petals on my arms.

Hunger returned to his gaze. He started to crawl towards me when I snapped my fingers. "You must remove those breeches immediately, sir."

With a solemn nod and a glint in his eyes, he said, "As you wish, my lady."

He unbuckled his pants, leaving on only a thin set of undergarments. His skin glowed in the candlelight and muscles rippled along his thighs. But my eyes drew to his left knee. It was a mass of scars. The skin was twisted and purple. The injury must've been excruciating.

I leaned up on my side as he lay beside me. Reaching out, I passed my hand over his knee. "She was a damn fool to call you hideous and a burden."

Relief, pure and sweet, drew his eyebrows up his forehead. The kiss that followed ached with passion. I followed the rhythm of our mouths, drifting down to the bed. His chest partly covered my own. His fingers skirted over the nightgown along the side of my rib cage until he reached my face and cupped my cheek.

He pulled back. Only it wasn't Calaen, and I was no longer lying on our rose-covered bed in a room infused with candlelight. A sky as black as pitch stretched above. Below me was a quilt stolen from one of the many bedchambers in the enchanted castle.

My heart danced a rapid beat as my prince hovered over me in Calaen's place. A lantern set on the grass revealed his honey-brown skin and short, dark hair. He wore an unbuttoned, blue ruffled shirt and black breeches. Every inch of him was devastatingly handsome, a true fairytale prince, aside from a rather vicious expression on his face. A sneer marred the perfect lips that had kissed me night after night, and his eyes were no longer green but like pools of ink.

We'd lain together at least a dozen times, but I never once felt uncomfortable. Until now.

I tugged part of the quilt over myself. "What has happened? How did I get here?"

"Good evening, Princess," he said between gritted teeth. "Or have you already forgotten that is how we greet each other every night?"

I started to apologize then waved off this nonsense. "We usually meet at the lake, and I'm fully dressed. I think we can forgo formalities. Answer my questions!"

The sneer dropped, and his lips drew into a pout. "You are not fully here because you didn't drink much of the enchanted wine that I left in your room." My forehead creased in confusion. He sighed and rolled his eyes. "The wine from this castle makes people sleep in the world above. That is why you and your sisters would always fall asleep instantly once you left."

I remembered how Calaen drank a good deal of it. "So, that means Calaen... is asleep?"

"Yes," he ground out, "the soldier you took to your bed is asleep."

I sat up further and secured the rest of the quilt around myself, rolling him off of it. "It wasn't that simple. I didn't just *take him to bed*. My father meant to execute me for coming here, and Calaen saved my life! He's my husband now. I had no intention of hurting you, and I'm sorry for it. Truly." I glanced around. There was no sign of my sisters. "But really, how am I not fully here but here all the same?"

"I was only able to bring your shadow. Your body is still in bed," he flinched, "with him."

My shadow? I held my hand up. In the light of the lantern, it looked normal. "I don't appear very shadowy."

He grabbed my hand and hauled me to my feet like a sack of potatoes, a far cry from his usual swoony, romantic self. "In the world above, you would be a shadow. Not here."

As his words sunk in, I pulled my hand away. Something clicked in place. "It was you, wasn't it? In the shadows. You were watching me."

He raised his hands to the black sky. "How is it any different than your soldier watching us the last three nights?"

It was a fair point. I started to say as much when he continued.

"I knew something was off. The boat was always heavy while we rowed back. And my youngest brother said his boat was heavy on the way to the castle." He wagged a finger at me. "I realized someone was spying on us. My brothers and I followed him back into the world above, shadows to his shadow."

He moved away from the lantern. His face turned as black as the sky. "And yes, I watched you. I watched you betray me."

The word 'betray' cleaved my heart. I dropped to my knees and sunk further into the quilt. "I thought about coming here," I explained, my voice hoarse. "Would you have welcomed me if I fled my kingdom? Could I have stayed? I didn't know! And when Calaen chose me, it was such a relief. He would one day be king, and I could rule beside him."

I picked at a loose string on the quilt. "I used to dream of ruling. Before I came here. Before I met you. It was like rediscovering a dream I thought I'd lost."

"And what of my dreams?" Darkness crept into his voice. I shivered. Why had I never seen this side of him before?

I almost said *What dreams?* But it's like he heard me. The muscles in his arms flexed beneath his blue ruffled shirt.

"Perhaps I dream of being free," he muttered. "Not lost in a bargain my mother made with a demon. Twelve princes were imprisoned in an enchanted castle for twelve years. She meant to protect us as Ironstead crumbled, so we wouldn't die in the war."

Ironstead. The name cut through me like cold steel.

My prince ran his fingers through his hair and gripped the short strands. "But she didn't realize the cost. That he would feed on us."

He turned back to me. The lantern on the ground cast a strange light on his handsome features. It appeared as though the skin around his right eye had deteriorated and what remained was the chill white of bare bone.

I gasped and covered my mouth, locking a scream in my throat.

He stepped toward me, anger sharpening what was left of his face. "We are only halfway through our prison sentence. And you mean to abandon me here!"

I scampered back in horror and finally released the scream. It echoed through the gardens. The shock of it sent a jolt through me. A rush of air blew past. I rose from the ground, and everything rippled around me until the world vanished.

Trembling, I shot up in my bed—back in my body, back in my bedroom, back beside Calaen.

I prodded Calaen's scarred shoulder, but he didn't move. His breathing remained steady, and his golden-haired head wouldn't budge from the pillow. At least he looked peaceful. I almost wished I could join him. But there were bigger concerns. My prince was furious, and the enchanted castle was a prison. Plus, some demon was feeding on him and his brothers because their mother made a bad deal.

In a blink, I knew who she must be. That damned gray-haired woman skulking about. I needed to find her!

I covered Calaen with a blanket and hastily dressed in my off-white wedding dress, for my other clothes were still in the nursery. My hand rested for a moment on the goblet holding the enchanted wine. He'd meant to keep me down there with him. Should I be helping him?

But in my heart, I knew I must. I would no sooner leave him down there than any of my sisters.

My gaze landed beside the goblet, and worry surged through me. The silver circlet, the one I wore for the wedding and found in the gardens down below, was no longer on the table. I glanced around but saw no sign of it.

Who removed it while Calaen and I were sleeping?

I didn't bother with shoes but rushed out our chamber door. My bare feet slapped against the cold stone floor. The sound echoed in the wide corridor. I rounded the corner and stopped short. The door to Calaen's room was open.

My throat constricted as I tiptoed closer. Peeking inside, I jerked back in surprise. The gray-haired woman lay sprawled on the floor, a silvery cloak in her hands. I eased closer and looked her over. A sizeable welt swelled on the side of her head, and the golden goblet from the enchanted castle rested on its side beside her. Someone had struck her with it.

I patted her face, unnerved to be so close to the queen of Ironstead. She didn't stir, though her chest rose with an inhale. Carefully, I pried the cloak out of her hands. It must be the one Calaen used to stay invisible.

There was more at play here, and I wasn't sure what was going on. But any tool to help was needed.

I made to leave when a wrinkled hand grabbed my wrist. My heartbeat spiked as the old woman looked up at me, her green eyes so like my prince's. "You."

Exasperation threaded through my voice. "Yes, me. Who struck you?"

She shrugged, not moving from the floor. I considered walking away and leaving her here. I needed to figure out what was going on and how to help the princes. She tightened her hold on my wrist, a mind reader like her oldest son.

"I never thought the soldier would choose you."

Nice to know you're like my father. I tried to pull my wrist away.

"I thought you would return to the world below. To marry my son. I sent you down there to fall in love with him and you did."

A soft exhale escaped my lips. I grasped her elbow and helped her up. Once she was settled on the bed, I sat next to her. "Yes, I did. But things are more complicated now. Besides, your sons are in danger down there."

Tears filled her eyes. "I think I made a mistake," she whispered.

No kidding.

I thought of how tonight I'd been a shadow in the world below while my body was up here. Could it be the same for the princes?

"Are their bodies resting somewhere in the world above? Perhaps I could wake them."

"It wouldn't be that easy, even if you could find them. They're in a hidden chamber far from here." She brought her hand to her chest. Her eyes widened, and she let out a soft cry. "My necklace!"

The necklace with the oval-shaped, red stone was no longer around her neck. I'd bet my entire set of dance shoes that whoever took my silver circlet also took the queen's necklace.

"What significance does it have?"

"It appeared after the bargain. All of our lives, my sons and mine, are tied to it."

Could the person who stole it have any idea of its importance?

"We should go to the world below," I suggested. "We'll speak with your sons. Maybe they know more about," I waved my hand around, "all of this."

"I cannot go down. I'm not allowed."

Probably so she couldn't see how the demon was reneging on their bargain. I got to my feet, holding tight to the invisibility cloak. "Then, I will."

She blinked up at me, the lines deepening around her mouth. "Liette, if it means saving them, do whatever you must."

Her words felt ominous. I nodded and then ran out the door.

I reached my sisters' room and cautiously pushed the door open. Moonlight pooled down on their sleeping forms. Gentle snores filled the room. I wished I could embrace each of them one last time, not knowing what was waiting for me in the enchanted castle.

My old bed was next to the window at the far end of the room. I covered the space, conscious of my bare feet squeaking on the wooden floor. But when I reached my bed, I found someone had pushed it aside and the entrance to the world below was wide open.

My eyes shot over to Aliya's bed, but she was curled under her blankets. I searched each bed until finally discovering one that was empty.

Cressie's.

Foolish girl! What have you done!

I sped back to the door leading underground. Lifting the skirt of my wedding dress, I grabbed the lantern hanging on the wall just past the entrance. I hurried down the long, spiraling staircase and through the stone tunnel into the woods beyond the lake. Dirt gathered between my toes as I ran past gold, silver, and diamond trees. Near the lake, the princes stood by the water's edge, their voices raised and angry. Perhaps they were waiting for my sisters and were upset because they hadn't come.

After abandoning the lantern, I covered myself with the invisibility cloak and crept past. Their argument reached a crescendo, and one struck another with his fist. I didn't stop to hear what they were saying, for my aim was to reach the boats they'd left unattended. Ten boats sat on the shore. Two were missing. One was probably my prince's. The other may have been the youngest prince's boat. If he'd rowed Cressie to the enchanted castle, then that was where I needed to go.

I climbed into a boat and pushed away from shore. I began rowing. Sweat gathered on my chest as I lifted the oars under the cloak. I strained not to splash the black water and alert the princes to my presence. My arms were limp by the time I reached the opposite shore. Raising my skirts, I staggered to the castle.

Inside, the ballroom was empty, though invisible musicians continued to play. I passed through another hallway and reached the throne room. Torches lined the circular room, casting light on paintings and tapestries. In the center, Cressie sat on a throne encrusted with diamonds. She wore the silver circlet and the necklace with the red jewel. Tears spilled down her face and her body shook. Her wrists were shackled to the armrests.

I swept closer, surveying the room. She was alone.

"Cressie, stop crying," I hissed, just as I had this morning when we walked into our father's throne room. How much had changed and hadn't changed in the space of a day.

She gulped and swung her head around. "Liette?"

I removed the cloak. "Yes, 'tis I. And you were very foolish to come here!"

"He told me I could be queen," she mumbled, her face beet red. "I just needed to bring the circlet and the necklace."

"Who said that?"

She glanced around. "My prince. He said someone as beautiful as me should have her own castle. And you had the one above."

I tugged at the shackles. "But you didn't wish to marry Calaen."

"No, but I couldn't believe he chose *you.*"

I stepped back, frustrated with the metal restraints and my sister.

A voice came from behind me. "She will be his queen, and he will release us."

My prince's youngest brother stood under an archway leading further into the castle. A thinner copy of his oldest brother, he stared at Cressie with reverence and hope.

"Is this an agreement you came to with the demon, or like your mother, are you making a bargain without knowing the end results?"

He flushed and twitched to the side when my prince strode into the room. His skin looked normal again. There was no evidence of the demon's price.

"What is all this?" he asked his youngest brother.

"I thought to offer her as his queen. She's the most beautiful. Perhaps he'd let us go."

My prince glared at his brother. "Perhaps?" He shook his head and held out a hand.

The younger brother scoffed but placed the keys there.

My prince strode over to us, all muscle and anger and gallantry. My heart raced. I had to remind myself to breathe. He was so dashing.

He unlocked the restraints. I embraced my sister. She sobbed against me.

He stepped back, guilt marring his handsome features. "You'd better go."

I removed the circlet from her hair and placed it on the throne. Then, I unfastened the necklace. I turned to the youngest brother. "Why this necklace?"

He shifted, uncomfortable. "The demon, he whispered in my dreams to bring it here."

I peered into the depths of the charm. The red substance inside appeared to boil like blood in a cauldron. The queen had placed their future in my hands, but I wasn't the one who should make this decision.

I handed the necklace to my prince. "Your mother said your lives and hers are tied to this. But if the demon wanted it, it must contain some power. Maybe the power to break the enchantment. I'll leave it to you to decide what should be done with it."

With that, I wrapped an arm around my sister and ushered her away from the throne.

"Liette?" His deep voice reached into the core of me.

Ever the gentleman, he bowed. "Thank you."

I nodded, resisting the urge to run into his arms, if only for one more kiss. But that wouldn't be fair to him or Calaen.

We left and made our way home. All the while, we talked and talked until I tucked her into bed and made her promise not to go into enchanted worlds without me.

Once back in my bedchamber, I lay down beside Calaen. Exhaustion settled over me.

He cracked a groggy eye. "Did something happen?"

"Let's talk on it in the morning."

Calaen gave a soft grunt and then wrapped an arm around me. I snuggled closer to him. My eyes drifted shut, while I held onto an image of his face and the prince's, both of them casualties of the war.

In this life in the world above, there were hard truths to face and difficult choices to make. But I knew Calaen and I would be better rulers than my father.

I would accept nothing else but this.

2 Cups Butter, 2 Cups Sugar

By Mary V. Jenkins

2 cups butter

2 cups sugar

It was no surprise, when she finally found the little house again, to find its skeleton. A lifetime had passed, after all, since that month in the woods.

4 large eggs

The foundation was solid, as was the brick oven.

The cage.

Forest creatures had gnawed away at the walls and most of the roof. The chests they'd emptied had filled with fallen leaves and rainwater.

1 quart molasses

Father had been so happy when they'd returned. Never mind it had been a month. Never mind he had thought them dead. They came back, her brother fat and merry, laden with gold, no pebbles or crumbs.

It had been a month and his wife, their mother, was gone.

They came back and Father had taken their treasure, and with it, bought a bigger house. He bought her brother a pony and bought her a dress, and then another. So many colorful dresses. It was only right, Father said, as they were now wealthy.

It had been a month, then a year, and Father had taken a new wife. She was young and pretty. They shared dresses.

2 and a half quarts flour

It had been a month and a year, and then another. Her brother forgot what it was to be hungry. His cheeks stayed rosy and his hands stayed soft. He counted coins with Father.

They never spoke of the month in the woods.

Father never asked where she learned to bake soft cakes or spin sugar into glass.

One day, Father asked for lamb for dinner. She taught herself to roast meats in the brick oven of their big house. The smell of roast lingered.

2 tablespoons baking soda

New families arrived and sold new wares, of which Father bought many, and their small village grew. A wider road was built, as was a bridge over the river.

One day, one month, and years later, she walked along a new path which followed what had been the edge of the woods. A white pebble caught her eye. She picked it up.

Her brother had moved into his own house, smaller than Father's, though still larger than what they had known as children.

The pebble was cool in her hand and then heavy in her pocket.

4 teaspoons ground cinnamon

Cinnamon was hard to come by. Father liked it baked in rolls.

She remembered when they had no rolls, when they had been hungry. Father had taken them into the woods. He had taken them into the woods and left them there.

One month and years later, Father had fallen asleep by the fire. His chair had been costly, made as it was of heavy wood and dark leather. He had not finished the meal she had made. The crumbs of the sticky sweet roll glistened in the firelight.

4 teaspoons ground ginger

She had learned to make every kind of sweet and all types of breads and meats. An old woman had moved to their village and taught her about herbs and roots, what could be gathered in the woods, and what never should.

One night she made a stew of roasted vegetables and mushrooms. She did not eat. Father and his wife slept for two days.

2 teaspoons ground cloves

One month and many years later, Father ran out of money. Her brother refused to pay his debts as he had his own family now.

Father's second wife left.

He asked about that month in the woods. Where had they had found their treasure? He did not ask why her brother had returned fat when she had not.

No question of baking or sweets.

Was there more? More jewels, more pearls? Was there any more gold?

She did not answer him right away. Looking around the kitchen of their big house, she saw the sacks of flour, of sugar, the rack of spices. She looked down at her hands, strong from kneading dough but starting to spot with age. A lifetime making sure they always had bread to eat.

2 teaspoons salt

Yes.

Yes, she told him. Deep in the woods, there was something.

He wanted to leave right away, of course, for his debts were due and he would lose their big house.

He had to wait, for she would need one month to go ahead and prepare. Father tried to argue, yet she stood firm.

Once he had gone to bed, she packed the contents of the kitchen larder and set off into the woods.

1 quart hot water

One month, many years, and another month later, the little house in the woods stood restored. She had replaced the roof with butterscotch and the walls with gingerbread. She had poured new sugar windows and swept the floors clean with a peppermint broom.

She had sent her father to follow the trail of white pebbles through the woods. He should be there soon.

The oven was warming.

Queen of Diamonds

By Sophia Alapati

"And if the weevils weren't bad enough," the miller said earnestly, "my girls won't stop fighting. They're fourteen and fifteen, and Rosie's always been annoyed by Marigold running after her. But now that she's courting, it's a hundred times worse, screaming matches every night. My wife and I are at our wits' ends with them, Your Majesty."

Elodie rolled the words around in her mouth like a pearl before she spoke. This was part of being queen she liked most—sitting in state with her subjects, listening to their troubles, and giving them something that would help.

"I have some experience with sisters not getting along. They both work in the mill, yes?"

No pearls formed this time. Instead, a few pieces of gold fell from Elodie's lips, followed by a small citrine.

Two years out from the fairy's blessing, she could demurely drop the metal and gemstones that appeared in her mouth when she spoke. She caught them in her lap and transferred them to the grain sack the miller had brought to catch her advice.

Unlike some of her subjects, he didn't watch the riches. His eyes stayed on her. It made her want to give him diamonds, though she couldn't control what minerals came out of her mouth. Gold was typical, enough that her attendants gathered it to be smelted into bars and coins. Some sounds made different stones with occasional reliability, but she hadn't solved diamonds yet.

"They do," said the miller. "Marigold bags the flour and Rosie takes it from her to load into the wagons."

"Give them separate tasks. Rosie's learning who she is outside your family, and Marigold needs to learn who she is besides Rosie's little sister." Emerald and malachite joined the gold and citrine in the sack.

The miller rubbed his chin. "Now there's an idea."

"But make sure the tasks are about the same. Don't stick one girl with all the hard work when the other's lounging around all day."

The words tasted bitter in her mouth, but gold and garnets were unharmed by old pain. Elodie was beyond not being good enough, beyond competing with her sister for love that would never come her way. She had the king's love now—the entire kingdom's—and if that wasn't worth more than her mother's disdain, she didn't know what was.

(Meanwhile, her mother and sister had all manner of disgusting creatures, slithering and leaping and buzzing from Honora's mouth with every word. Elodie kept waiting to hear that the town of Everwell had fallen to snakes and toads and insects, but if it had, the news hadn't made it to the castle.)

"No lounging in the mill, I assure you," the miller chuckled. "I'll have Marigold feed the grain in and I'll take over the bagging. Then they won't be working in such close quarters. Thank you, Your—"

The gilded double doors swung open, admitting two more royal guards. They parted to make way for the king.

She still thought of him that way—*the king*—even though he was her husband. It seemed to Elodie sometimes that she had two husbands. In public, she was married to the king. But at the end of the day, relaxing in their rooms after dinner, she was married to Benoit. Benoit read to her, and sang songs with her, and asked what she thought about issues of government, even though she was only a peasant he had polished and set in his crown.

Today, in the receiving room, his eyes softened when they found her. "Ah, my dear," he said. "We'll be ending advising hours early today, I'm afraid."

The miller bowed. "Your Majesty. Thank you very much for accepting my petition."

"There are still three people waiting," Elodie said. She spat two bits of jade and a piece of lapis into her palm.

"We've had a change in plans."

"Thank you for your time, Your Majesties," the miller said. He held up the grain sack. "This will make up for what we lost to the weevils. And thank you again for your advice on the girls. If there's any trouble, I'll tell them they can take it up with the queen!"

He laughed and left, escorted by the guards.

"Is something wrong?" A diamond the size of a grain of barley. She wished she could run after the miller and give it to him.

Benoit was two decades her senior, with grey streaked through his beard and hair like bands in a tiger's eye, but he did not usually seem *old*. Right now, though, he looked tired. He sighed and took her empty hand in his. "I'm afraid you cannot counsel the people anymore."

Elodie's mind raced. Until she left home, her mother needed little excuse to steal small joys from her. Elodie's favorite blue hair ribbon, taken because she had stained her dress with soot—and never mind that she'd stained it sweeping out the chimney as her mother had ordered. It was proof that she could not take care of nice things, and so Mother had taken the ribbon and given it to her sister.

Now she had as many blue ribbons as she could ask for and a husband who would not take them from her. But Elodie's heart clenched all the same. "Did I do something wrong?"

The question fell from her mouth as a piece of quartz, rough-edged and clouded. Benoit caught the stone before it landed. "No, no, of course not! But we must protect our economy."

"Our economy?" she echoed. Small pieces of gold dropped into her lap.

"Yes. You see," he said, in a tone more patient than the tutor who was teaching her reading and etiquette, "your gifts have made it so everyone can afford more. Now the merchants are raising their prices."

She did not understand what made it so complicated. "Then tell them not to raise their prices," Elodie said, in another shower of gold.

He patted her hand. "I'm afraid it is not that simple. Besides, this would not solve our other problems. The gold miners and the jewelers' guild are angry at their wares being devalued. Our trade alliance with Gentia is at risk if we no longer need to barter for silver with them. No, I'm afraid this is the best way."

"Then we can just keep the jewels, and I could still speak to them," she argued, scattering sapphires. It made her feel sick, but at least she would still get to talk to ordinary people.

"You have such a generous heart, my treasure." He rarely called her *Elodie*. The pet names were sweet when he was Benoit. When he was the king, they made her feel like a little girl, scolded for not pulling water from the well fast enough. "But we must keep you safe, and my advisors worry the people will be angry at the change. They don't understand big ideas like economics, you know."

She wondered if he, too, was thinking of Everwell's modest homes, and the fact that Elodie had never held a book until she came to the palace. The fact that even when given the run of the royal library, she'd needed months of tutoring to tease even the simplest words out of the cloth-bound pages.

"I could join the meetings with your advisors," she suggested. "We could find a way to explain it to everyone." And perhaps she would understand better herself, hearing it from those learned advisors whose counsel the king kept.

But Benoit shook his head. "I know you want to help, but for now, we must give the decision time to settle. In the meantime, I have something for you."

He drew a piece of cloth from his coat and gave it to her. A veil, the edge beaded with pearls. Her pearls. Only the round, white, perfect ones, the ones that came from cheerful songs and words like *swoon* and *autumn*. Elodie preferred the iridescent lumpy pearls that came from *rattle* and *harrier*.

"Just for a little while, until things are more stable," the king said. "Try it on."

She did. The top of the veil lay across her nose and draped down below her chin. "What do you think?" A stone pushed itself out of her mouth and fell into a fold of fabric at the bottom of the veil, which caught it.

"It's perfect," he said. He pressed a kiss to her forehead.

If Benoit said it was perfect, it was. And, Elodie told herself, it would not be forever. They would fix the economy—she would ask her tutor what exactly that meant—and things would go back to normal.

Ending her advising sessions did not fix the economy. Beyond the palace walls, the merchants kept raising their prices. Gentia and the guilds were still angry. Cutting off the steady stream of gold and jewels only made people resent the loss of abundance. Some had stopped spending, waiting for a time that an opal could buy more than a loaf of bread.

These household hoards had, in turn, given rise to a new faction: jewel thieves. People woke to find their houses burgled from the inside, as though the renegades had simply slipped through the crack beneath the door and let themselves into the house.

Inside the castle, people were unhappy too. Elodie's handmaidens, who she used to tip in shining moonstones, were dour now, their once-cheerful chatter replaced with resignation every time a stone clinked into her veil.

It was harder to tell whether her tutor was upset. He always looked like he'd just smelled a cow pat on the bottom of his dyed-leather shoe.

"Of course, we cannot predict when inflation will cease," he said, looking down his nose at her. "We must weather the situation until the value of gold stabilizes. And then, of course, we must ensure this does not happen again."

"But Benoit said I'll get to speak to the people again." A faceted oval gem fell from her lips. With the veil, she couldn't always tell what she'd made. This one felt like a peridot, though she couldn't explain how. "I want to help."

He eyed the bottom of the veil as another stone fell into it. "You're helping the kingdom by keeping your jewels to yourself."

"That's not the way I want to help people." Gold chips.

Her tutor sniffed. "Your gift has far too much impact for the lower classes to be allowed its fruits. Why do you think you're here?"

"I don't understand."

He tutted. "Your Majesty," he said, in a tone that suggested he would be more frank if she weren't the queen, "you are an incredible asset to the king." *Asset.* Like a fine ship, or a fruitful field. "It helps him to have you here, yes, and it equally helps him that you are not elsewhere. Giving your jewels to others."

The hurt was exquisite, presented to her on a little covered plate like one of the layered desserts the palace's pastry chef made. She could choke on it.

Of course she'd known the king wanted her for a queen because of her gift. She wasn't a fool. The fairy had promised the king's hand. The gold and jewels were the steppingstones across the moat and into the palace. But she had them because she was kind, and if the king loved her for the gold and jewels then he must also love her kindness. It made sense in her head.

It had never occurred to her that even that could be a fragile lie. That the king might want her, not even for her jewels, but so other people couldn't have her. Like the blue hair ribbon, locked tight in Honora's jewelry box, never worn again after it was taken.

Not something to be cherished. Something to be controlled.

The "oh" fell from her lips as a tiny, perfect seed pearl. The veil caught both the pearl and the tear that escaped before Elodie scrubbed her face dry.

Very well. She was still the queen, and if she couldn't help people with her jewels, she would have to help them as a normal queen would: by reviewing treatises and writing correspondence and understanding the laws that bound her country together.

"Should I read aloud?" It was her favorite part of their lessons, even if she only got to read primers and etiquette books.

Her tutor eyed her veil as it caught another gem. A gem he would not get to keep today. "I'll leave you to it."

He didn't stay to correct her pronunciation while she read. Fine. If she had to learn the words herself, she could remove the veil. She could choose her own books. Dictionaries. Long lists of uncommon words with too many consonants and unlikely sets of vowels. If she was given only a few words, then she wanted the most beautiful, the most interesting, to crystallize.

Cherish gathered into a rounded ruby on her tongue. *Climate* dripped tiny topazes onto the page, golden beads that gleamed in the lamplight. *Crepuscular* brought out half-born amethysts, a horizon of white crystals separating the black geode shell from jagged, sparkling twilight.

By the time she finished reading, she had a pile of remarkable gems she wasn't allowed to give away. She carried them back to her room and hid them in one of her hatboxes. When things went back to normal, she'd share them again.

The economy did not recover. The king, under counsel of his advisors, took Elodie's words back from the people.

Clinking chests, armored carriages, and pallets of gold bars crawled up the road to the castle. Once past the gates, the gold and jewels would disappear into a vault, where only the king and queen could use them.

But Elodie had no use for gold and jewels now. She wanted her people to have her words, in whichever form they took. She had hoped the advice was worth as much to them as the treasure, but she'd been a poor widow's daughter once. Kind words did not fill empty stomachs or mend leaking roofs or heal dying fathers.

She had tried to help people with her gifts, and in the end, all she had done was broken the kingdom. The thefts continued. People were starving. People were struggling. *My fault.*

Elodie watched the ant trail of stolen wealth from her bedroom window. Guilt and anger and resentment burned inside her, spitting sparks in her chest.

She thought of the word *renegade*, of the way it had solidified into a red tiger's eye with a band of fire streaking through it.

Walking along that brilliant band took her to her husband's strategy room. The murmur of his advisors leaked through the heavy door.

"I need to speak with the king," she told the guard.

She was the queen, so he let her in.

The king and his advisors turned as one when she entered. "My dearest," Benoit said, "it is wonderful to see you, but we are a bit in the midst of things."

Elodie thought of her sister, who barreled through Everwell like a runaway bull heedless of what she trampled. Honora had been cursed for shunning a person in need, the way she acted every day of her life, and yet she'd still blamed Elodie for it.

("You told me the fairy looked like an old woman!" she'd screeched, face red, arm pulled back to strike. A fleet of toads hopped out of her mouth. "If I had known the stupid fairy would change her disguise, I would have helped her. This is *your* fault!")

Elodie had been glad, after the wedding, not to see Honora again. But now she needed her sister's brashness. Her inflexibility. Her indifference to what other people thought of her.

"I'm sure you are busy, which is why I belong here." Stones clinked into her veil. She refused to taste them. "I have worked hard with my tutor so I can best serve our people as queen." She turned her gaze on Benoit and willed it to be hard as diamonds. "I will have a seat at this table, as we said in our wedding vows."

They had stood in front of the nobility, Benoit in his ermine-trimmed cape and Elodie in a jewel-encrusted gown made from cloth of gold. She'd repeated after the officiant, gold scattering at her feet. *I will be the treasure of your heart, and you will be mine. I will serve you and defend you. You will always have a seat at my table.*

Then they'd said, "I do," and her first diamond had formed in her mouth. It was so large she'd been afraid she wouldn't be able to get it out and already cut to a point that sliced her tongue on the way. Benoit had a new crown made with the diamond as the centerpiece.

He was wearing it now as he said, "Oh. Um..." He looked at her, then at his advisors.

Elodie knew what they saw: a diamond pulled from the muck, cleaned up for palace life but stained by her origins. The jewels were all they wanted of her words. And her husband... Benoit listened to her, but the king listened to these men.

Elodie rested her hand on his shoulder and said, "You've always asked my thoughts in private. If I cannot speak to the people, allow me to be your counsel here as well."

Benoit's hesitancy broke. He straightened, shoulders back and chest out. "Quite right. Let us hear what the queen has to say."

Before any of the advisors could reply, Elodie pressed forward and seated herself. "Excellent. Now, where were we?"

By the end of the meeting, she had certainly achieved Honora levels of popularity with the advisors. The longer the conversation went, the more Elodie could see that the king's advisors were concerned with keeping the peasants poor rather than with helping people. Otherwise, they'd focus on limiting prices and establishing new trade agreements, rather than taking riches back.

Her husband, for his part, showed Elodie a mix of the king and the private Benoit she knew. When other advisors interrupted her, the king asked for silence so she could finish. When one scoffed at her notion of regulation, the king demanded he apologize to her. Benoit did not dismiss her ideas outright, but he was cautious and leaned toward agreement with his advisors. He patted her hand when she was frustrated, in a way that felt both fond and patronizing.

She would talk to him about that later.

But she had won some victories. The castle would open its gates to feed the hungry at a weekly banquet, and Elodie could resume her advising, one person per day, if she kept the jewels.

It was not enough. Only the people in the city, or those few who could make the journey to the castle, would benefit. What about her subjects in Everwell, in the other poor towns scattered across the patchwork countryside? They were beyond her reach.

At least the banquets and advising would aid a few people. Elodie held these promises in her heart like treasure in a vault.

"Your Majesty," said the advisor who Benoit had forced an apology from, as Elodie rose to leave. "I understand that you want to help. But these are complicated matters."

"Yes, I know," Elodie said. Her veil was so heavy from hours of arguing that she had to work to hold her head up. "But as we've established, the king has hired me the best tutor in the country, and I can keep up perfectly fine with the rest of you."

The advisor turned the color of carnelian.

Elodie was grateful the veil hid her smile. "Now if you'll excuse me, I must put these gems in the vault, as you suggested."

She hoped the room was large enough to hold her words. She would not be silent any longer.

Three dozen servants had spent the day carrying the riches into the vault at the center of the castle. Now, the room was a landscape of locked chests, loose stones, and gold bars, glimmering in the torchlight like sunrise on fresh snow.

Elodie emptied her veil, letting gems cascade to the floor. Instantly lighter, she examined the pile. Mostly gold nuggets and semiprecious stones—one particularly spectacular turquoise, sky-bright and veined with black. What had made that? *Correspondence*, perhaps, when she had offered to write to her recent friend, the queen of Gentia, to discuss the value of silver. Or maybe *responsibility*, when she'd demanded they do more for their citizens.

Movement flickered in the corner of her vision.

Elodie looked up. There, again—one of the chests. There was something in front of the lock, almost brown enough to blend in with the wood, but for the line of splotches.

A snake.

It clung to something that jutted from the lock. Elodie stared as it shifted its body, and the unmistakable sound of a key turning echoed in the vault. The lid of the chest opened, and Elodie saw—

Her face. Herself. Stretching, scowling, standing, and climbing out of the chest.

"Honora?"

A pit opened in her stomach. A stone dropped into her veil. All at once, the fabric felt an encumbrance, smothering her, trapping her, making her voiceless. Elodie tore it from her face. The sapphire slipped from the pouch and clattered to the ground.

Her sister froze. "Elodie." A toad pushed past her lips and dropped onto the ground.

If Honora kept talking, they'd soon be in a bog of creepy-crawlies. "Don't speak," Elodie said quickly, "or I'll call the guards."

Honora's mouth snapped shut.

Selfish Honora. Belittling Honora. Arrogant Honora. Stopped in one sentence. A bright feeling, like power, like a crown, like *renegade*, sparkled inside Elodie.

"You're behind the thefts," she accused. Honora nodded. Elodie wanted to laugh. After all of the advisors' plotting, Honora hadn't even had to break into the castle. She'd simply locked herself in a chest and let the king's men carry her past the moat and the walls and the guards, directly to the kingdom's golden heart. "You can control your creatures. You slip them in through a window or under the door, and they let you into the houses." Another nod. "And you came here to rob the vault. How were you going to get the jewels out?"

Honora mimed, one hand crawling like a spider with the other fist balanced on its back.

"They can carry things? Hmm. And how were you going to get yourself out?"

Honora pointed at the snake, now lying on the floor in front of the chest, its neck coiled back to hunt. As

Elodie watched, it lunged at the toad, striking but not catching it. The toad hopped a few times before falling still, paralyzed by the bite.

Well. Elodie would be sure to stay far away from her sister's snakes.

But what to do with Honora? Elodie could call the guards and be rid of her, and yet—and yet—

The gems, the threat of the guards, her ability to debate, all the tools Elodie had to make people listen, were not hers alone. They were given by the fairy, by her husband, by her tutor. But she could use them all the same. If these were the rewards for her kindness, she would take them and be kind on a larger scale.

And she could use her sister's audacity too. In the strategy room, Elodie would have to fight for every carat of respect. But here—here she need not endure the king's paternalism or the advisors' sneers to help people.

Renegade.

"Very well. I will help you. But I have rules." Honora arched her eyebrows, but she didn't argue. Treasure scattered before Elodie as she spoke. She barely noticed it. "First, you can only take gold and silver. The gems are too obviously mine. Agree?" Reluctant nodding. "Second, you have to share them. Every family should get a little. Especially the ones you robbed, and especially the ones outside the city. If I find out you have kept everything for yourself—and I promise, I will find out—then I will turn you in."

She had no idea how she might make good on that promise, but Honora nodded all the same.

Elodie tingled with the power, with the anticipation of her third request. "Third, if you are caught, I will not protect you, just as you never protected me from Mother."

"But—"

"I won't take any arguments from you," Elodie said. A jade green frog fell from Honora's mouth and hopped across the floor to Elodie. "Are you making it do this?"

Honora shook her head.

Elodie picked up the frog. It was cool, with big onyx-black eyes, and surprisingly fragile in her hand. Its heart beat against her palm, a quick, steady pulse.

She had spent her entire life being kind, and now it was time to be kind to herself. Honora could not blame or control her any longer. "That is my offer. Have your creatures take the gold and silver and give it to my people. I'll cover your escape. Or I can call the guards. Your choice."

Elodie could feel the force of Honora's irritation from where she stood. But her sister only curtsied. "I accept, Your Majesty," she said. An oily black toad fell to the floor with a wet *plop*.

"Wonderful. Then you'd better get to it," Elodie said, and all her words were diamonds. "We have a lot to fix."

The Tailor and the Elves

By Tom Elmquist

It had only been a few weeks since Eric's grandfather passed. The wound on his heart was still very open and very raw. He loved his grandfather as a father because that's what his grandfather had been since he was twelve. Eric's parents died in a car accident just before his twelfth birthday, and so Eric went to live with the only family he had ever known.

Eric's grandfather was a tailor and a cobbler. He loved watching his grandfather make beautiful clothes for all walks of life. His grandfather learned his trades from his father, his father learned from his father, and so on through the generations. His grandfather worked and owned the same shop that his great-great-great-grandfather opened so many years before.

Eric stood in front of that store with keys and a large envelope in hand. The shop was all his grandfather had left him when he passed. The lawyer said there wasn't much more than that in his grandfather's estate.

"I wish I had better news for you, Eric. Your grandfather's estate was modest, to say the least. All he left you was the shop and this envelope," the lawyer had said.

When the meeting was over, Eric walked to the shop. He peered into the window and saw the shop was just as his grandfather had left it. It was neat and orderly but was also warm and inviting. He could imagine seeing his grandfather taking measurements for his next client's suit.

The thought brought Eric to tears again. The wind blew, shaking the envelope in his hand. He sat on the step and opened the envelope. In it was the deed to the shop and a letter.

Eric,

If you are reading this, I am gone from this world. I am sorry, I will not be there to see your family grow. I'm leaving you the shop, everything in it, and the apartment over it. Do it as you see fit. I will not fault you for selling everything and trying to make a better life for you and your family.

If you decide not to sell, I hope you follow in my footsteps as I followed in my father's. Your father never understood the business, so I felt like I was going to be the last generation to open the shop. Then, when your parents passed, and you came to live with me, that gave me hope.

It gave me hope for the future, hope that you might pass your skills on to your kids, and the hope I would have some form of immortality in the world.

I always believed there was something magical about that place.

Never doubt that I am proud of the man you've become and of the family you have started.

I love you, Son. The shop can benefit you and yours no matter what you decide to do with it.

Love,

Papa

Reading the words brought new pain to Eric's heart, and tears welled in his eyes. He stood and turned around toward the door. He saw his reflection in the window, but it wasn't the man he was today. It was his younger self. It was almost like he was looking into the past, to the day he came to live with his grandfather.

He shook off the vision and walked up the steps. The key slipped into the lock effortlessly. He turned the key and heard the bolt slide free from its locked position. The lock turned and moved so smoothly you would think the mechanism had been oiled.

The silver bell tinkled when Eric opened the door. The tiny sound beckoned him to enter. It welcomed him as if to say, "Welcome home, my friend. It has been a long time."

Eric closed the door and gave the shade a little jerk to raise it. It slipped from his fingers and flung wide open. There was a shrill sound as it went up. It was like one of those toy cars you had to use a pull string to get it racing. It made a loud pop as it hit the top, breaking the place's near silence.

Eric first noticed the sound or, more importantly, the lack of sound. The suits and clothes lined the walls, and the racks made an almost perfect baffle. He could barely hear the street noise even though it was less than ten yards away. The quiet was oppressive, and it felt like it would crush him if he didn't break it.

"Is anyone here?" Eric asked out loud. He knew no one would answer but wanted to break the silence.

He went behind the cashier counter and turned on the shop P.A. system. His grandfather had loved everything about the fifties and had the satellite radio tuned to the fifties channel. The sound of Johnny Mathis singing poured from the speakers.

He flipped the lights on and looked around. The nostalgia hit him like a ton of bricks. He saw his grandfather taking measurements of a man who stood on a stool. His grandfather would call out the measurements, and Eric would write them down. This memory made him smile.

Eric made his way up the stairs to the apartment where he and his grandfather had lived as he grew up. Everything was just as his grandfather had left it. It was neat as a pin and organized perfectly. Much like the store downstairs, everything had a precise order. It gave him a sense of comfort to be in such a well-ordered place.

Eric went from room to room, turning lights on and off. He made a mental checklist of everything that needed to be changed, moved out, or sold. He intended to live here with Katie and Cory, and he wanted to make everything perfect for them.

He went up the second set of stairs and checked all four bedrooms and the bathroom. Most people would pay millions for such a home in the city, but this one was his now.

His phone rang. He pulled it from the pocket of his jeans. He looked at the screen and saw his wife's picture.

"Hey, Babe," Eric said, answering the phone.

"Well?" Jess asked. Her voice already sounded annoyed.

"Well what, Babe?" Eric asked.

"How much do you think we can get for the place?" she asked, sounding greedy.

"Honestly? I was planning on moving us in. It's ours, free and clear. All we have to do is furnish it the way we want. Then Emmy can go to the best schools in the area," Eric said.

"No way in hell. I'm not moving across the country to live in some old man's house. I don't care that he was your grandfather," Jess snapped.

Eric became furious. "Look, this place is huge; you will love it here. We are doing this. It will be good for us and Emmy," Eric said, putting his foot down.

"What are you going to do to pay the bills? I mean, taking care of Emmy is a full-time job," she said, sounding like the spoiled rich girl she was.

Eric thought, *the least she could do was show a little gratitude. I mean seriously. We were just handed a huge home and a business that used to thrive. What more does she need? As for Emmy, she leaves Emmy at daycare all the time while she goes out and spends all our money.*

The two argued for the next two hours, going back and forth. Jess finally relented with the caveat they would move back to California if things didn't work out in six months.

So, that's what they did. Eric, Jess, and Emmy moved to Mason City, and he took over making suits and shoes for the City's elite businesspeople.

The business was slow at first because word had spread quickly about the death of Eric's grandfather. They had been there a month, and not a single customer walked through the door.

"See, I told you this wasn't going to work," Jess said. A snide tone poured from her lips.

"Fuck! Are we really going to go through this again? It's only been a month," Eric retorted.

"Well, it's not going to work. You know it, and I know it. We will be going—" the sound of the door chime cut Jess off.

A man walked in and asked, "Is this the shop Henry Gerber used to own?"

"That was my grandfather," Eric said with a smile.

"My condolences. My father suggested I come here for a few suits and some shoes. He raves about your grandfather's work," the man said with a smile.

Eric stepped from behind the counter, "I'm Eric Gerber. Pleased to meet you," and shook the man's hand.

Jess stormed up the stairs and slammed the door to the apartment in a display of dramatics.

"Matt Larson," the man said, firmly shaking Eric's hand. A grim look crossed his face as he watched Jess leave,

"Sorry about that. It was just a little disagreement between my wife and me. So, tell me, what are you looking for?" Eric asked.

Matt told Eric he was looking for suits and shoes for a new job. So Eric started by asking appropriate questions about what material, style, and colors Matt wanted. More importantly, he asked how many suits Matt wanted. Then, he took Matt's measurements.

So, after an hour and a half, Eric had his first order for five suits and three pairs of shoes. The estimate for the order was over two thousand hundred dollars.

When Eric told Jess about the order, she scoffed, "Luck. That's all it was. Fucking luck, and unless you can do that consistently, we are screwed."

"God dammit, Jess, why can't you just support me or, even better, why don't you get a job and help out around here," he shot back.

This went on until Emmy started crying. Eric pushed past Jess and tended to Emmy.

"There's daddy's big girl," Eric said, smiling.

"Da da da da da," Emmy squealed with delight.

"You believe in me, don't you? You know Daddy can make this work to give you a better life," he said, cooing at Emmy.

Eric settled Emmy for the night and went down to the shop. He started working on the suit order. Eric worked until three in the morning, cutting and pinning the material until he couldn't keep his eyes open. He made his way to the living room and fell dead asleep on the couch.

Eric awoke to Jess shaking him. "Hey, wake up. How did you manage to get two suits and a pair of shoes made in one night?"

"Hmm?" he questioned

"Down in the shop. There are two suits done and a pair of shoes," she said.

Eric and Jess went down to the shop, and there were indeed two suits. Both were made to perfection. He couldn't believe his eyes but hid the amazement from Jess.

"Are you really this good?" she asked again, sounding greedy.

"My grandfather taught me well," he said, trying to sound nonchalant.

"But if you can do this, you can make our lives so much better. You could put away for Emmy's future and get us a big house in the country. You could make us millionaires." The greed in her voice was unmistakable.

"Slow down, Babe. It's just two suits."

"I had no idea. I'm so sorry to have doubted you," she said, and her apology sounded genuine.

Later that night, Eric worked on the next two suits. He worked late into the night, and just like the night before, he crawled up the stairs and passed out asleep on the couch again. The next morning, Jess woke him up the same way.

When they went downstairs, they found all the suits and shoes complete. The suits hung neatly in a suit bag, and the shoes were perfect and polished in boxes.

Eric called Matt to let him know the suits were ready.

"Incredible. My dad said your grandfather was good, and you appear to be just as good. I'll be there in an hour," Matt said, sounding overjoyed.

As promised, Matt was there within the hour. He opened the bag with the suits and opened the boxes with the shoes.

"Can I try them on?" Matt asked.

'Of course," Eric said.

When Matt came out of the dressing room, he wore a suit that fit him so perfectly it appeared as though it were a second skin.

"Amazing. I have never had a suit that fit so well. Your family's reputation is well deserved. I will be telling everyone I know to come here for suits and shoes," Matt said with overwhelming excitement.

"Thank you. I would appreciate that," Eric said, smiling.

Matt returned to the changing room and hung everything back up neatly. He came out and immediately moved to the cash register. Matt pulled out his wallet and paid with a card. When the payment went through, he lay five crisp $100 bills on the counter.

"That is for how fast you got this done. I will tell everyone I know about you," Matt said, shaking Eric's hand.

Matt was true to his word, and business rolled in. Within weeks, Eric had more orders than he could handle. At least, that's what Jess thought. Jess loved the money coming in. She was able to put Emmy in the best daycare in the city. She was also able to live the lifestyle she had always dreamed of. She didn't have to work, and she could essentially do as she pleased, especially with as much work as Eric had on him.

Eric would stop work long enough to eat and sleep and put Emmy to bed. No matter how much work he had to do, he was happier than he had been in a long time. Each day, he woke up with a sense of purpose, and each night, he slept in blissful peace.

Weeks turned into months, and months turned into a year. Eric and Jess found a routine that suited them. Eric worked, Jess played, and Emmy grew as children do.

On Emmy's second birthday, Jess threw her a lavish party. Eric stopped working long enough to spend time at the party with his family. He spoiled Emmy with all the affection she could want. Emmy smiled and laughed. She babbled gleefully at all the bright colors and presents.

It was a joyous day for everyone until they got to Jess's final gift. She pulled out a leather-bound box. The box looked far too sophisticated for a simple child's birthday present. Jess opened it to reveal two silver tiaras. They were identical in their design. Dozens of sparkling clear jewels adorned the loop and swirls of the silver metal. One sizeable, pinkish-hued jewel sat in the center of the tiaras. The tiaras were far too ostentatious to be authentic, or so Eric thought.

The only difference between the two was the size. One was small enough that Eric knew immediately it would fit Emmy perfectly. The other tiara was larger and was obviously meant for Jess.

As Jess tipped the box for all to see, a small slip of paper fell from the box. Eric was the only one to notice the paper fall to the ground. Eric moved to pick up the piece of paper. He bent down and picked it up, trying to be as nonchalant as he did it.

No one paid any mind to him. The guests were all too busy oooing and aahing over the tiaras to pay any mind to what Eric was doing. He opened the slip and saw the jeweler's receipt. What he saw on that little slip of paper simultaneously caused his heart to sink and his blood to boil.

The tiaras were indeed real. The metal was rhodium, probably one of the most expensive metals in the world. Eric knew this because some of his most recent clients requested rhodium cufflinks for their suits.

What Eric thought were fake crystals were actually ninety-six diamonds with a string of letters after them. He had no clue what those letters meant, so he assumed it was their grade.

The thing that made his blood boil the most were the center stones. On the receipt, they were listed as Padparadscha sapphires. Again, he knew very little about what that meant, but he assumed they were probably the most expensive sapphires.

When he saw the price, his jaw clenched so hard he almost cracked a molar. Two hundred thousand dollars plus tax was the final sale price. A note on the bottom of the receipt finally made his blood run cold. It said, *"Custom pieces. Final Sale. No returns or Exchanges."*

Millions of thoughts flooded his mind.

I'll kill her.

No. What about Emmy?

Fine, I'll make her life miserable, so she leaves.

She will take Emmy with her.

Every imaginable scenario went through his head in the span of a few seconds. All of them were shot down because they all wound up with Emmy being without both of her parents or him never seeing his daughter again.

He snapped himself back to reality as Jess put the more petite tiara on Emmy's head. Jess place the larger tiara on her head. As she did, he positioned himself with his back to the guests and his shoulder touching Jess's

"Can I talk to you in private? Now!" Eric whispered with a low growl in his voice.

"What? Now? Can't it wait until after the party?" she asked defiantly.

"No! Now!" he said loud enough for the guests to hear.

Eric stormed inside, shoving the receipt in his pocket as he went. He heard Jess ask someone to watch Emmy.

"Excuse me, everyone. My husband needs a moment of my time," she said, trying to seem like the perfect hostess. Then, she followed Eric inside.

"What the fuck is so goddamned important you would embarrass me in front of our guests. Are you trying to ruin Emmy's party?" she snarled at him.

"First, knock off the perfect little hostess routine. You only act like this to appear like we have this perfect little life," he started.

"Well, I—" Jess tried to defend herself.

"Shut up, you gold-digging bitch. Explain this now," he ordered, pulling the receipt from his pocket and slamming it on the table.

A look of fear flashed on Jess's face, but it was replaced by another, a look of anger and defiance.

"Knock it off. We can afford it. So what if I went a little overboard," she said.

"A little overboard," he scoffed and threw his hands up. Jess said nothing. "A little overboard would be renting a pony or a petting zoo for the backyard. This is insanity," He said and pointed at the receipt.

"Again, we can afford it. Now put on a happy face and get your ass back out there to help me entertain our guests," she commanded.

"No! Fuck you and fuck every last one of your guests. I have to get back to work if I am going to support YOUR lifestyle," he said and returned to the shop.

"You know what, fine. I'll make up some excuse for you," Jess snapped back.

"Fine," Eric snapped back.

"Hey, Mister Tailor, man. How have you been getting things done so quickly anyway?" Jess taunted.

"I work my ass off," he retorted.

Eric turned to go back to the shop and then turned back to face Jess.

"I want a divorce," he said as he felt his resolve steel in his gut.

"Fine. Just know I'm going to take everything from you. You're gonna wind up penniless, homeless, and you sure as shit will never see Emmy again," she snapped back.

Jess was right about one thing. Eric never saw Emmy again.

Later that night, Jess lay awake. She couldn't sleep because of the fight earlier. She heard Eric moving around for a few moments, and then a resonating snore came from the living room. She decided to go down to the shop and try to find the secret of Eric's success.

Jess thought, "*I know Eric has a secret, and I intend to figure it out.*"

Jess crept downstairs. Eric's snore told her it was safe to pass the living room. She got to the stairs down to the shop and heard strange sounds coming from there. She crept down the stairs, and the sounds got louder. She heard the rustling of fabric, the sound of a sewing machine working, and a low murmuring like children whispering to each other in a game of hide and seek.

Trying to stay in the shadows, she peeked around the corner. She saw nearly a dozen figures milling around the shop. They were doing this and that, but they all seemed to be working on Eric's most recent order. They appeared to be half the size of ordinary humans, and there was something else about them that Jess couldn't quite put her finger on.

"You may as well come out of the shadows. We all know you are there," a voice came from the shop.

Jess stepped into the dim light from the lights over the suit racks.

"Ah, the lady of the house. How can we help you this evening?" the voice asked.

Jess turned to see a young woman who stood no more than three feet tall. Her long, thin hand extended to Jess. Jess reached and shook the small hand. Upon closer inspection, Jess noticed the young lady's features were perfectly proportioned. Her eyes and ears were the only two things that didn't look quite right (besides her size).

The young woman had long, pointed ears, and impossibly violet eyes.

"Would you please stop referring to me as a young lady? I happen to be three hundred and twenty-nine years old," the woman said as though she heard what Jess was thinking.

"I'm sorry. Are you?" Jess asked and trailed off.

"Elves? Yes, we are elves. I am Raina, and this is my family," the woman said.

Jess looked around and noticed the rest of the figures paused momentarily to wave.

"What are you?" Jess again tried to ask a question.

"Doing? We are here to help as we have done through the generations of your husband's family. We are here to help his family prosper. Your husband's ancestor made shoes for the townsfolk, and we have stepped in to help your family prosper. That ancestor and his spouse gave us clothing in return. So we decided to return and help the family as much as possible," Raina explained.

"But," Jess started.

"We have returned in secret. No one else has ever known we were helping until now. We would like to keep that secret," Raina continued.

"I understand. I think," Jess stammered.

"Listen, what would it take for you to keep our secret? What would make you happiest in the world?" Raina asked.

Upon hearing the question, her sense of greed replaced the awe and wonder of what she saw.

"What can you offer?" Jess asked.

"Anything you want. All you have to do is ask." Raina said in a hushed voice.

It took less than a second for Jess to respond.

"I want Emmy to have the best of everything for the rest of her life. I want my husband out of my life forever, and I want to be taken care of for the rest of my life," Jess said, the greed and excitement oozing from her words.

Raina sighed.

"Very well. Go to bed and all will be well when you wake," Raina said.

Jess did as Raina told her.

The next day, or so Jess thought, she woke to the sun stinging her eyes as she opened them. She looked at the window and thought, *It seems so late. What time is it?"* She turned to her phone on the nightstand. The clock on the phone showed 11:46 am on Monday, June 6.

"What? Did I sleep for a full day? How? Wait, why didn't Emmy wake me up?" Jess asked aloud.

Jess ran to Emmy's room. She looked and saw nothing but an empty crib. Her next thought was to wake Eric up, so she ran downstairs to the living room in a panic.

"Eric!" she screamed as she turned the corner, but Eric wasn't there.

The only thing she saw was a discolored patch on the carpet. Upon further inspection, she saw the discolored patch formed two words: "It's done."

She touched the discoloration, and a faint copper smell rose to her nose.

"What the hell?" she breathed.

She ran down to the shop to see if Eric was working. He wasn't. There was nothing in the shop. All the suits and shoes were gone. The only thing that remained on the tailor's dummy was a leather coat. She touched the coat. The leather was supple and fine grade. She knew a coat like this would go for thousands of dollars. She looked closer at the lapel and noticed a strange discoloration about the size of a half-dollar.

When she held the discoloration to the light, she saw something she had seen thousands of times before. It was the shape of a tattoo Eric got when he was younger. It was a dragon head with flames all around, placed on his right forearm. Eric said it was some flash art he thought was cool. The coat also faintly smelled like his favorite cologne.

Jess screamed as she realized it was the very tattoo she had seen all those times and the scent of her husband's cologne. She put things together and made the startling realization this coat was made of her husband's skin.

Jess called the police and she was immediately arrested when they arrived. The police had received several complaints of screams the day prior. The investigation found that the coat was made from Eric's skin, and it was Eric's blood on the floor that spelled out that chilling message.

The police interrogated Jess for hours. They mainly wanted to know what she did to Emmy. Jess told the story over and ove of what had happened the night she saw the elves, always keeping the details the same and never wavering.

Emmy became listed as a missing person even though the police knew she was dead. Jess was found not guilty by reason of insanity for the murder of her husband. Jess lived out the rest of her days in a mental health facility, telling the story to anyone who would listen and was taken care of as per her wish.

So, you may ask yourself, "What really happened to Emmy?"

Raina and her family raised her and taught her the ways of magic and ways of the unseen world. She lived happily ever after.

There are two morals to this story. The first, greed will ultimately take everything away from you. And the second, watch what you wish for. You may just get it.

KINGDOM OF ASH

BY ADELE LILES

The glass that fit, the love we swore
Lies abandoned on the floor.
I needed a partner, not a queen,
Who rules a castle of forgotten dreams.
We speak of treaties, lands, and war,
But not of us, not anymore.
The girl I loved drowned in gold,
In ways royal, in manners cold.
Yes, I strayed, I sought the fire—
The warmth.
The touch.
The vanished desire.
Where's the one who danced in rags and wishes,
The one I trusted with midnight kisses?
You gained the crown but lost your soul.

An empty heart, truth be told.
A charming life crumbled into sand
When you cherished the throne more than my hand.
I hunted for comfort in faces strange,
Bodies in the dark to dull my pain.
Yes, I strayed. I found others new—
The men.
The women.
Anyone but you.
More attentive to your throne,
Leaving our love to die alone.
The queen you are, the maiden you were—
I loved the latter, not the first.
The crown fits well, the velvet glove.
You're queen in name, but what of love?
Now you're lost in royal pride,
And left me empty, cast aside.
Yes, I strayed. The clock struck—
The dance.
The magic.
It's all fucked.

The Castle Lacrimosa

By Sasha Ravitch

Latin	English
Lacrimosa dies illa	*Full of tears will be that day*
Qua resurget ex favilla	*When from the ashes shall arise*
Judicandus homo reus.	*The guilty man to be judged;*
Huic ergo parce, Deus:	*Therefore spare him, O God,*
Pie Jesu Domine,	*Merciful Lord Jesus,*
Dona eis requiem.	*Grant them eternal rest.*
Amen.	*Amen.*

– Dies Irae sequence, Requiem Mass

I: THE MOAT

Water is a Witness. Sometimes it is a graveyard and sometimes it is a womb, but it is Water and it is always a Witness.

This Water has not always been what it is; it is un-natural. You must understand that once upon a time a

Lord with too much money and too much pain came to this place. He liked it, for it was a beautiful meadow surrounded by an even more beautiful forest, and there was an abundance of foxes and hares for his hounds to hunt. It was isolated and he liked that too, for he was a paranoid man and he feared the covetous eyes of his courtiers falling upon his wife and daughter. He left and returned with many more men and many more tools, and the men built a castle for the Lord. It was a great stone fortress for just a single family and their servants, but otherwise unextraordinary.

Once the castle itself was completed, the Lord had the men build the Moat. They dug deep—much deeper than one would think to look at it—and they dug wide. They lined the bottom with jagged stones from the local mountain and from the faraway cliffs. They purchased large iron spikes from the neighboring smithy and arranged them between the rocks so their sharp ends faced upwards. The Lord was pleased. He believed that trespassers attempting to ford the Moat would impale themselves and bleed out or drown. His wife, the good Lady, had furrowed her brow when she saw these spikes being put in. What if there is some accident or some emergency, she had questioned. The Lord remained expressionless. He did not care much for anyone outside of his family and his Sovereign.

Soon after the Moat was dug out and lined with instruments of brutality, a party was sent into the forest to fetch water to fill it. At sunrise, the men left with their wagons and pails, and at sundown, they returned without a single drop. The Lord was furious and demanded to know how they had wasted an entire day only to return empty-handed. They declared they could not find a single drop of water. One of the laborers spoke out of turn, sharing that the men were confused to not find a single river or stream, as they could *hear* the sound of living water everywhere they searched. The Lord dismissed them for the night to sleep in the stables. He commanded them to search the forest in the other direction at sunrise.

At sunrise, the men went back into the forest, this time returning before noon with their wagons heavy with water. The Lord was pleased and asked where they found the river. They corrected him that they found no river, but that there was a modest lake that would have just enough water to fill the Moat. The same man who had spoken out of turn the previous day wondered aloud if maybe it would be unkind to drain the entire lake of its water to fill the Moat. He asked if they might search for an additional source of water to fill the ring-ditch around the castle. The Man Who Spoke Out of Turn cited the many animals in the forest that likely relied on this water, to speak nothing of the spirits there, too. The Lord rolled his eyes at the superstitions and sympathies of the worker. The Lord proclaimed that if he had an issue with the work, he was welcome to dismiss himself and return home without pay. The Man apologized.

There were many days which followed with many men journeying back and forth to the lake in order to fill the Moat. The Lord watched the work from the castle's gatehouse. He thought the castle's silhouette looked rather like the hoary teeth of a grimacing giant—something he appreciated. A castle should appear dour and uninviting, the Lord believed; there was nothing worse than unwanted guests—and for the Lord, all guests were, truly, unwanted.

On the final day of filling the Moat, the Man Who Spoke Out of Turn sighed at the edge of the empty lake. It was a shame, he thought to himself, wondering how the forest creatures would find the fresh streams to drink from if a whole team of workers could not. The Man Who Spoke Out of Turn reached into the left pocket of his trousers and dropped a single coin into that desiccated lake. The Lord had no time for superstitions, but the Man Who Spoke Out of Turn did and he knew he had contributed to the draining. The rusty coin glowed against the mud at the bottom of the lake, which was swiftly drying out in the late afternoon sun. The Man frowned and then rejoined the others.

The drawbridge was put in last. When all was complete, the Lord retained around six of the men to live in the servant quarters and maintain the castle. The Man Who Spoke Out of Turn was amongst them.

The Lord sent for his daughter to come and join her parents in their new home. The Lord had not wanted the young Lady to stay with him while so many laboring men had been about, for he was very aware of how beautiful his daughter was. And the Lord was very aware of the age his daughter had become. She was no longer a little girl, and this concerned him as she was most precious to him. Many might have called into question the Lord's capacity for feeling at all if it were not for how obviously he cherished his daughter. So the young Lady with thick mahogany curls and large, doe-like eyes of the same color arrived at her family castle.

Things were only idyllic for a fortnight; you see, this Moat was not a conventional Moat, and it was not filled with conventional water. They had drained the local Fairy Queen's lake. This water was sacred to her, as it was where she took her baths and fed her wells. This lake was where she kept the prized souls she had lured into service from the neighboring villages. This lake was where she kept the souls of women who wandered into her forest unwitting, of babes she stole from their cradles and raised beneath the waters. All of these unfortunates gestated beneath the lake until it was their time to wait on her as a handmaiden.

Those who lived in the bordering villages knew this about the lake and kept a wide berth from it. When fate and fortune left them no alternative but to pass its perimeter, they would bow and apologize or leave offerings by the base of an old Hawthorn. The locals would make the journey out each midsummer and midwinter, arms heavy with loaves of bread that had been slathered in butter, their backs bent over from the weight of jars of honey and pitchers of milk. There they would leave their gifts to the Queen—who was said to be extremely beautiful, though no one could admit to having seen her—in hopes that she would not recruit another handmaiden from their own bloodline.

When the Lord had sent a team of men to survey the land for construction purposes, some of the neighboring villagers had warned them to not build in that meadow. The woods and all things in it belonged to the Queen, the villagers said. When they shared this information with the Lord, he had scoffed and replied that the only thing a man of his rank would bend a knee to was his own King. The men looked nervous, and so the Lord had ceded to blueprints that relied heavily on extra iron.

The Moat's waters were Otherworld waters and they were not meant to be appropriated by man. Invisible bodies undulated around the castle in a thick band of restlessness; the cries of babies seemed to bubble up to the surface, to splash against the banks. The moans and wails of phantom women were captured by errant winds, which slapped against the castle's parapets. The Lady and her daughter began to develop a very un-pleasant habit of sleepwalking. The Lord would awake around midnight to witness his daughter with her feet dangling in the Moat, his wife demanding the draw-bridge lowered. A priest was called to address these nightly visitations, and for a while, it seemed to work.

What the Lord did not see was the diaphanous figure watching him from the forest's hedge. She was getting so close. The Lord was clever enough to respond to each of her moves, but not clever enough to recognize whose moves he was responding to. The Queen knew that she needed to become more creative in her machinations. She could not cross into the castle for the conspicuous overabundance of iron was an uncomfortable and effec-tive deterrent. Instead, she sent a bird of bad omen to perch upon his Lady Wife's bedchamber window. The bird cradled a strange seed from a strange plant in its beak. When the Lady laid down to rest, the bird flew into the bedchamber and hid the seed beneath the Lady's bed. The seed emitted a faint violet light and soon began to sprout roots.

Each night the seed remained beneath the Lady's bed, the roots growing further upwards into the frame, knotting themselves into her mattress, and eventually into her flesh. A physician was called to attend to the Lady's ailing health. She became weaker and weaker, and spent less and less time awake, existing mostly in a state of fever. Her Daughter sat by her Mother's side as often as she could, until the Lord decreed they be separated. He could not risk his daughter becoming ill.

The Lady perished shortly after this with her physician by her side. He reported to the Lord – with a certain amount of astonishment—that in the last moments of her life, she had begun to choke up large amounts of water. It was as if she had drowned to death, he quietly remarked, aware of how ludicrous he sounded. The Lord sneered, but later in his grief, he entered his wife's bedchamber after her body had been removed. He felt a great unease when he witnessed how the straw mattress was heavy and swollen with water.

Grief mildewed the walls of the castle. The Lord and his young daughter wept, and they wept, and they wept. Their loss did not compel them closer together in desperate pursuit of comfort but pushed them further apart. Despair became a climbing plant which tore them in twain. The Lord spent more and more time alone in the Tower with his books, and the young Lady sought connection and kindness from wherever she could find it. The Queen wondered if the Lord would realize the consequences of his actions and return the water in the

Moat to the lake. He did not realize, but the Queen was patient, and so time choreographed a new performance of its danse macabre.

The Man Who Had Spoken Out of Turn had been a great friend to the young Lady as she mourned for her Mother; he had taken her for many strolls in the wild apple orchard to the left of the forest. The Queen had watched them, for this was her orchard, too, and deliberated on the next phase of her plan. The Queen understood humans very well—after all, the acquisition of so many human souls had taught her a great deal about their foibles and fallibilities—and so she assisted nature in taking its course. The young Lady and the Man Who Spoke Out of Turn became besotted with each other. All the Queen had to do was wait.

One day the young Lady came to her father with the Man Who Spoke Out of Turn by her side. The Lord was confused to see his daughter standing by his servant. She declared that they were in love and they sought to be wed. The Lord was stunned into silence for a brief moment before pounding his fist on the table and forbidding her to marry him. The young Lady wept and wept and wept, begging her Father for mercy, for permission. But the Lord was not the merciful type and he refused to lose his daughter to marriage—especially marriage with a commoner in his employ and so soon after his wife's death. The Lord exiled the Man Who Spoke Out of Turn. Hunting dogs chased the Man out of the castle.

There was no time to lower the drawbridge, and so the Man Who Spoke Out of Turn steeled himself to cross the Moat with all of its iron spikes and jagged rocks. The

Queen remembered the Man and his protestations at draining the lake, remembered him and his regret and his kindness. Turning the coin he had left in the lake in her hand, she made sure that he safely crossed the Moat by commanding the many spirits she had trapped within its boundaries to help him. When he got to the edge of the forest, the Queen sent a hare to distract the Lord's hounds and he was free to escape. By evening he had become lost in the woods, but the Man Who Spoke Out of Turn found a small, dancing flame that directed him to the safety of the village. On the threshold of the forest and the village he had grown up in, the Man found a coin beneath his feet—a rusty coin he had left at the bottom of a dried lake years prior.

It goes without saying that the young Lady's fate unraveled expeditiously from this point. So too did the Lord's. She wept, and she wept, and she wept. Her sleepwalking recommenced, though the priest could do nothing for her this time. Grief is its own type of haunting and the Queen knew she had very little work on her end. The Lord awoke time and time again to see his daughter swaying limply from the top of the watchtower or the highest point of the keep. He would rush out into the dark night in his nightclothes to pull her off the precarious perch. Sometimes he would find her on the ground by the Moat listlessly gazing toward the spot the Man Who Spoke Out of Turn had swam through. Occasionally he would hear her speaking to someone, or something, in that dark, glacial water, or at the edge of the still forest. The Lord made a new bedchamber for his daughter in the forebuilding and locked the door. He stationed men outside her room, as well as on the stair turrets and the gateway to the upper bailey, to ensure that she could not escape.

It mattered little. By the following full moon, one of the men in the arsenal tower noticed something strange in the Moat below: a body floating face down. He called a party down to investigate the Moat. Every man, the Lord included, searched the area of the Moat where the body had been witnessed. They were relieved to find nothing there. As they were returning to the keep through the inner ward, they heard a distant wail—like the cry of a loon—and a foreboding splash. The Lord realized that all the men had abandoned their posts to inspect the phantom body, leaving no one to watch for the young Lady. They ran to the opposite side of the castle—the shallower part, while one of the men went to check on the young Lady's room.

The surface of the water was entirely still except for elegant ripples where pale, slender fingertips bobbed in a small, lifeless waltz. The watchman who had checked on the young Lady's room informed the Lord that his daughter was nowhere to be found. But she was found, the Lord whispered, as a team of men dragged the pallid corpse to shore. She had fallen feet first, the men informed him. The iron spears had pierced the soles of her feet, pinning her there to drown. The Lord, numb with his shock, gazed into the quiet, lurching forest.

The Lord was kept alive for many decades after his daughter's death by the sheer bitterness in his soul. At night, he wept, and he wept, and he wept. By day he would mount his horse and take his hounds into the forest, endeavoring to hunt and destroy every living thing which had the audacity to breathe when his wife and daughter did not. Sometimes he would catch very little, sometimes he would catch quite a lot, but always the Queen watched, and always the Water witnessed. When he became too old to hunt he spent his days in the library pretending to read while staring out into the forest or gazing into the Moat. Occasionally he swore he heard his daughter's voice, and she wept and she wept and she wept.

When he died it was no spectacular affair; indeed, its cruelty was in how normal it was. He simply went to sleep in his reading chair on an autumn afternoon, never to arise from it again. The men buried him in the family plot with his wife and daughter, plundered the castle of any valuables, and moved on to seek their fortunes elsewhere.

At least half a century had passed, and the legend grew throughout the kingdom. They referred to the abandoned estate as Castle Lacrimosa, so haunted was it by the sound of weeping. The teenagers in neighboring villages would challenge their peers to sneak into the grounds and bring back water from the Moat—presumed to be cursed—or to carve their names into the drawbridge. No one endeavored to move in, though the castle was still very habitable. It appeared that the reputation it had amassed, between the curse of the Queen and the hauntings of such melancholic ghosts, made it unattractive to prospective buyers.

One day a Man arrived through the forest and stood at the threshold of the meadow, gazing at the castle.

The Queen noticed him because he so reminded her of another man she was familiar with. This Man carried an old, rusty coin in the palm of his hand, turning it over and over like a strange amulet. His father had recently died from a bout of typhoid that had ransacked their village. Before he passed, he had given his son the coin and told him a strange story about a beautiful young Lady, a bitter Lord, and a strange castle he had helped build by hand. He confessed to his son about the cursed Moat, and how he was spared from death by strange and invisible hands. The Son of the Man Who Spoke Out of Turn came to the forest in pursuit of the castle, and the forest erupted into gossiping whispers. For the Son of the Man Who Spoke Out of Turn looked so much like his Father that it was hard to distinguish the two, and he held in his hands a coin which had been charmed by the Queen.

Water is a Witness, and they recognized the Son of the Man Who Spoke Out of Turn as he entered the meadow and stepped closer to the Moat. The Water wept, and they wept, and they wept, for they knew what was coming. Water is a Witness, but the things which incubate inside them are actors of their own accord.

II: THE MONSTER

A wet and terrible thing she had become. A wet and terrible thing the Queen had made her. So long her teeth had grown, and how sharp their points now were. How long and spiny her fingers, and how thick and crooked her nails. Once the loping curls of chestnut had hung about her soft, heart-shaped face like a well-suited picture frame. Now rotting tangles of mottled brown clung to the nearly translucent whiteness of her flesh.

Bits of duckweed had grown its roots into her knotted tendrils, freckling her body with signs of its habituation to the water. The warm mahogany of her eyes had been eclipsed by sticky black baubles which seemed too large for the sockets which housed them. And always, always, her feet bled from their strange stigmata. She did not know this, though; the young Lady had not seen her mutation into a Monster, for she cast no reflection in the surface of the water, and there was not a single soul to speak her condition aloud to her.

Around in circles she swam, for this is what they all did. Like a school of fish, these rot-maidens and water-women churned the perimeter of the castle, their cold bodies gliding against one another, contorting and twisting into strange braids. Some had webbing like waterfowl beginning to grow between their fingers and toes; others groaned in pain as gills sliced their way into their necks over the decades which passed. Others, still, moaned and wept as the skin of their thighs seemed to melt their legs together into one grotesque, crooked limb—a tailfin of sorts. Occasionally, one of this dreaded throng would get pushed too close to the bottom of the Moat, and the iron stakes would rip her open from mouth to foot as if gutting a fish. The mutilated body would trigger a feeding frenzy, the swarm of the creatures feasting on the viscera-strewn water.

It had taken some getting used to, but the taste was acquired swiftly for there was nothing else to eat. Eventually, she could not imagine anything else in the world she wished to eat more. Those who abstained did not mutate in the same way and they became weaker, frailer, and their visages seemed to dim as if slowly disappearing. They were often the ones most easily pushed to the bottom of the Moat to be staked and gutted and turned into dinner for the rest.

Those that chose to eat became stronger and hungrier. They experienced their bodies changing into aqueous demons of unique appearance. She was a recent acquisition for the Queen, relatively speaking, and her changes were slow at first. The eyes, the teeth, and the nails had been consistent. But recently small spikes of bone had begun to push their way out of her skull and ruptured the surface of her scalp. They dripped with a viscous yellow-green emulsion, which mirrored the same sticky oils her pores secreted whenever she was hungriest. She was not conscious of these changes and so she had not realized what had become of her tongue. But if she had been aware, she would notice how whenever she parted the gray cleft of her lips to devour some floating bit of intestine or a fluttering piece of lung, her tongue shot out long and fast as an arrow coiling itself around the organ meat and dragging it back into her mouth.

The mercy the Queen had granted the women she kept in the water was that they were ignorant to their transformations. She had no intelligent thoughts of her own for these many long years, there was only the pull of the throng and their unending circles – broken up by the occasional feasting. The Water became increasingly comfortable, and soon she could not remember a time where she had ever been anywhere else, nor had been anyone else. This was the way of things until the day he arrived.

Something stilled the mass of monstrous bodies from their circumnavigation—something was different. Things were very rarely different. Sometimes there would be an errant teenager who would throw rocks into the water, but if they kept swimming he would not be able to see them. It was only when they stopped their perpetual gyrations that they became visible. It was only when they dared to emerge from the water that they could be witnessed for what they were. But this feeling was different, and though they did not possess the capacity to know it, the Queen knew it, and the Water knew it, and so they knew it, too. The women in the Water began to crush against each other in an attempt to reach the surface. She was amongst them, using her talons and teeth to hook into the flesh of disparate bodies and propel herself upwards faster.

She could see long, strong fingers just barely submerged beneath the water, and past them, the whirling and rippling visage of a figure crouched over. Faster she swam and thrust herself past the others until she reached out one of her slimy gray hands and curled her fingers tightly around his. She was not sure which dire compulsion compelled her to do this: only that there was an instinct she could not deny. The figure with the hand dangling in the water was frightened by this, and he sprung backward onto the land, dragging her with him. She felt the gelatinous stretch of her flesh slap against grass and dirt, and she gasped desperately before looking at him.

Half a century she had swum in the waters of oblivion; half a century she had sunk her memories and the heart which held them to the bottom of the Moat, let it disintegrate there. Half a century she had not thought of her father, the Lord, nor the Lady, her Mother, and she had not even thought of her heartbreak over the Man Who Spoke Out of Turn. But in an instant she remembered him, as she gazed into a face she believed must be his.

From between her lips, a maddening, guttural sound began to unspool, a cursed, waterlogged howl which so terrified the Son of the Man Who Spoke Out of Turn that he began to scream in response. As he attempted to crawl backward away from the Moat she grabbed hold of his ankle so that each inch backward he crept, he dragged her with him too. She wept, and she wept, and she wept, but the sounds that came out were croaks and gurgles and vomiting mouthfuls of water and half-digested organ meats. She was becoming conscious of her monstrosity in the mirror-trap of interaction with this man she remembered. The throbbing black spheres of her eyes, the lancets of her teeth, the bestial quality of her voice, the long quills of her nails, the sticky substance oozing from her discolored skin—she recognized them for the first time. And she screamed afresh, she wept anew, louder and more ghastly as the terrified Man struggled to break loose.

III: THE MAN

Horror choked the air out of the Son of the Man Who Spoke Out of Turn's lungs, his desperate screams going from ear-shattering pleas to whining, gagging whimpers. The Monster's fingers had burrowed beneath the lining of his boot, and its nails shredded the flesh around his ankle. Droplets of steaming blood sank into the earth, the scent of ichor only exciting the creature as its swollen, waxy tongue shot itself out of its mouth like that of a frog's. The tongue lapped at the blood-spotted dirt and scrupulous grunts of exertion interspersed the staccato of swallowing. He took this moment as an opportunity to attempt escape, wrestling his ankle free and kicking the Monster back with the heel of his boot. There was a crude, wet cracking sound, followed by a hoarse noise of pain. The thing began to claw its way back toward him with slow, heavy tugs. Its nails repeatedly plunged themselves deep into the earth to drag its wet belly and limp legs in his direction – but it could not move very fast on shore.

He was transfixed, staring at this creature. All of his animal body screamed to turn and run, but the same brutal curiosity which had called him to this haunted place kept him standing and staring at the Monster as it dragged its pallid body toward him. He witnessed the exposed patches of skull where strange bony spikes wept an unnaturally colored liquid. He witnessed the bulging black marbles of its eyes, reflecting back his frozen visage within them. He witnessed the trail of vermillion that led back to the Moat by way of this thing's feet. His eyes lingered for a moment on the Monster's feet—the story of the young Lady who had lived here, and his father's first love immediately conjured in his mind. His father had not wanted to say much of it, but there were no shortage of rumors throughout the countryside regarding the tragic demise of the beautiful noblewoman who lived at Castle Lacrimosa.

The Son of the Man Who Spoke Out of Turn felt his heart constricting and his vision obscured by tears. Grief clung to the scaffolding of his ribcage like a burial shroud, so possessed was he by the unimaginable tragedy of the Monster before him and the sudden knowledge of who she had once been. But she was no longer that young Lady and she did not think as such. In his hesitation, she had reached him once more and both her hands closed around his ankles and yanked him toward her. He fell with so much force that the wind was knocked right out of him.

As his eyes fluttered open he felt the steady lurching of his body as he was dragged back toward the Moat. He could not conjure the same will to resist this time; her strange venom had begun to saturate the wounded flesh of his ankle and he was numb from the waist down. They were so close to the water that her feet dipped back into its dark surface, her bulbous eyes spinning around in their sockets with ecstatic emotion. He knew the more she was submerged in the Moat, the greater strength she would have. There was no point in resisting.

A sudden disruptive rustling on the edge of the forest became noticeable enough for even the Monster to stop and look toward the noise. The Son of the Man Who Spoke Out of Turn heard the porcelain voice of a woman in his head directing him to reach into his pocket and retrieve his father's rusty coin. Struggling to shift his weight just so, he managed to grab the coin in his palm. This action elicited a shrill scream from the Monster who released him instantly. Before the Monster could orientate herself, the porcelain-voiced woman gave him another command: *run*. Having recovered sensation in his legs, the Man began to clumsily scamper his way back from the Moat and toward the forest until he finally gained enough balance to run. The Man did not stop running until he was at least a mile into the forest. But once he stopped running, he wept, and he wept, and he wept.

The Man made his way back to his village, back to his home, back to his family. There he held his son for a long time in his arms, and there he kissed his wife and did not let her leave his side. His family had been alarmed to see him return with his clothing shredded and damp and stained with strange streaks of unnatural colors. He said nothing to them about what had happened or where he had been, only that he had run afoul of the forest. They knew better than to push him and the Son of the Man Who Spoke Out of Turn did not bring the subject up again for nearly forty years. Over time his ankle healed, though it maintained a rather remarkable scar. While his family agreed to pretend nothing had happened that day, occasionally his wife and his son would exchange concerned glances when the Man refused to go near bodies of water.

The Man had grown old as men are wont to do and eventually took to his bed to die. The Grandson of the Man Who Spoke Out of Turn had grown into a man himself and sat next to his father. In the feverish hallucinations of incipient death, the Man had begun to mutter nonsensically. While it was challenging to extrapolate from, his son eventually parsed together that the thing which troubled his father had to do with the day he had run afoul of the woods. Such bizarre musings fell from the old man's dry lips: ravings about a Monstrous woman, stories about the son's Grandfather, and something about a cursed castle. The son listened patiently, knowing better than to try and set a dying man straight, but did not think much of it. Shortly before his father's final breath, the old man grabbed his son by the wrist and looked him directly in the eye. With shocking clarity, the Man told his son that upon his death, his son must return the coin to the forest but that he must not go near the cursed castle no matter the temptation. The son nodded and promised his father he would do so, though he relegated this information to more fantasy.

His Father died shortly after, and over the following days, his son helped his Mother attend to all of the belongings. Some things they would sell, some things they would keep and some would be buried with The Son of the Man Who Spoke Out of Turn. One day while clearing out his father's garments from the armoire, he found a small leather satchel. The Grandson of the Man Who Spoke Out of Turn opened it and overturned the soft and worn deer leather satchel into his hand. In the center of his palm fell a small, round, rusty coin.

The Grandson of the Man Who Spoke Out of Turn fetched his warmest coat and his sturdiest boots and made his way into the forest.

Beauty of a Beast

By Hannah Saal

Her reflection was visible in the windows, but she looked beyond. Past the castle grounds with their budding trees and bushes. Past the stone benches and sculptures, dotting the greening world. Her eyes were fixed on the surrounding wall, high and made of stone and covered in brambles and roses. The front gate was locked, a thick chain wrapped twice around with an iron padlock. She couldn't see through the bars of the gate, the ivy and thorns making it impossible. She knew there was a forest on the other side and a path through it, though she couldn't remember what that road and those trees looked like anymore.

Sophie rubbed her arms where the thorns had scratched her, her hands bandaged. She had gotten further up the wall than her previous attempts, before the pain had become too much and her strength failed her.

She almost wished the injuries were worse, rather than a simple nuisance, a torment reminding her she was still trapped.

"Let me go."

Every single day, she said this. Every single day, the Beast answered this.

"I can't."

But today, Sophie didn't accept it. Maybe it was because of the burning in her hands. Maybe it was because it was three months exactly since she'd taken her father's place. Maybe it was because she was simply tired of the same answer. Maybe it was because of everything.

"It's not that you can't. You won't."

She turned around to face the Beast, his huge, hairy body almost comical as he tried to appear and act civilized. He sat at the long dining table, gripping his fork and knife in his paws, the claws clicking against the silverware. Sophie's place setting was at the other end, her food already eaten. She realized early on that starving herself would only make it harder for her to escape. But she didn't enjoy the Beast's company, despite his obvious attempts to make himself pleasant. She preferred to eat quickly and return to the castle's library where the books provided a necessary escapism as she plotted another escape attempt.

The Beast looked back at her. She found his eyes uncanny, the rich green staring out from the face of an animal. They were his only human feature. The rest of his body was a hybrid of wolf, a boar, and a bear. She tried not to think about who could have ever thought of, let alone make, such a creature.

"I can't. I love you."

She scoffed, irritated at the cheapness of his words. "You don't know what love is."

The Beast bristled. She wasn't scared of him or his anger anymore. The last time he'd gotten angry and had been standing too close to her, she'd grabbed a nearby candlestick and hit him on the head with it. Now he knew to keep his distance.

"I know what love is. I love you."

"You only love yourself."

He stiffened. "I do not. I love you."

"You don't. If you did, you'd let me go."

"How could I let you go? How could you let go of someone you love? Maybe *you* don't know what love is!"

"You can't control the people you love. You let them go and you hope they stay. And if they love you back, they will."

Sophie held his eyes. They both knew what would happen if those locked gates ever opened. She could not deny the pain she saw in his eyes, but she refused to let herself be moved by it. She understood that pain. If she left, he would be all alone. In quiet moments, she could almost feel sorry for the Beast, being all alone in this castle with no one for company, but not sorry enough.

"How could I let you go?"

His voice suddenly seemed weak, though it was still a deep guttural rumble. She could hear the child she sometimes felt he was. She occasionally wondered what kind of childhood he'd had, how he'd gotten to be this way. She'd never asked, and he'd never volunteered.

Maybe there was an explanation for the way he was. There were no excuses.

She sat down in the chair next to him. "Because it's what I want. What I need. I need to be free, and I want to go home. When you actually love someone, you do whatever you can to make them happy, even if it may hurt you. I took my father's place here, knowing I would be trapped. Have you ever done something like that for someone else?"

He looked away. She kept her eyes on him. Maybe he would hear and listen this time.

"If I didn't look like this—"

Sophie leaned back in the chair. "It's not that. Most of the time, I don't even notice the horns and the claws and the fur. You're a man."

He looked at her. She could almost see human eyebrows lifted in astonishment, though his animal face could not show them. "I am?"

Sophie crossed her arms. "Aren't you? You talk like one. You think like one. You certainly act like one. So be a good one. Let me go."

He stared at her and Sophie began to smile. She reached out her hand to touch his paw. His fur was soft.

"I can't. I love you."

Sophie withdrew her hand as if she'd been burned. She stood up. "You're already a beast. You don't have to be a liar too." She headed for the doors.

He stood up, the chair screeching against the tiles. "You said I was a man."

She whirled back to look at him. "You're not a beast because of what you look like. You're a beast for what you've done. You've kidnapped me and caged me here. Only monsters do that, even the human ones. Claiming that you love me when you refuse to let me go? That just makes you a liar as well."

She flung the double doors open, leaving the dining room. There was a shatter of dishware just before the doors swung shut behind her.

She went to the library. Books covered every inch of the walls and ladders positioned to help reach the higher shelves. When the Beast had finally let her out of her room and given her this place for her use, she'd almost cried at the sight. The library in her town was small. She'd read every book in it by the time she was fifteen. This huge library became her sanctuary, the books her new best friends. But it didn't matter how big the cage was; it was still a cage. She grabbed the book she was in the middle of and sat in the window alcove and let her mind escape.

The candles had burned low by the time she returned to her room. Her maid had turned down her bed for her. She thanked her and the maid smiled. This was the extent of their conversations. Sophie had never heard her speak. She hoped it was a personal choice, not an edict from the Beast. Her maid was the only person she'd ever seen in the castle. Though she'd searched the place from basement to attic for any possible way out, she'd never seen anyone else. It would have been nice to speak with her, to converse with someone other than the Beast. But she was glad for the company, even if it was silent.

She had a dreamless sleep. She felt lucky every morning after a night with no dreams. Dreams turned to nightmares here. The sun slashed across her face, burning her eyes. She rolled away from the window. When she opened her eyes, her gaze fell on the bedside table where a book and a ring of iron keys lay.

She jolted up and grabbed them. They were real, not a figment of her imagination. The keys were cold and hard and beautiful in her hands.

Her maid was laying out her clothes for her. When Sophie looked up, she saw the dress was the one she'd worn when she first arrived. Her own clothing had disappeared after her first night here. A new dress had been laid out every day for her. But there were her old clothes, the blue apron and white dress. It had been her mother's dress before her death. She'd been distraught when it had disappeared. Seeing it back again, it felt like a part of her family returning to her.

"He's letting me go?"

Her maid nodded. She pointed towards the bedside table. The book was about different cities in the world. She opened the front cover and saw that the Beast had written her a message. The writing was ugly but legible. She could imagine the painstaking care he had taken to make sure she would be able to read his last message to her.

Sophie—I give you your freedom and I give you the world. Please remember me some time. Be happy. Be free. You deserve it.

—Beast

She stared at the words for a moment. Was this a trick? She felt the book in her hand, the keys in the other. Her dress was lying at the end of the bed, waiting for her.

"Is this real?"

Her maid nodded. Sophie smiled. She got up and twirled around the room.

She was free. She was going home. She would see her father. She would be home. She would be free.

Sophie turned to her. "Come with me."

The maid looked sad and shook her head.

"Why not? There's a whole world beyond those walls. It's not perfect, but it's there."

The maid pointed to herself and then gestured to the room.

"It's your choice to stay here?"

She nodded. Her eyes were sad but determined.

Sophie took a deep breath. She wanted to argue with her, but she couldn't, not if this was her choice. "I guess I have to respect that."

She maneuvered to put the book and keys in one hand so she could clasp the maid's hand with the other. "Thank you for everything you've done for me. I wish you every happiness."

The maid squeezed her hand back.

Sophie washed up and got dressed. Her maid packed up the few items that Sophie had into the satchel she'd brought with her from home, some food for the road, the Beast's book, and the keys. When Sophie came out wearing her own dress, she could feel home on her skin. She took the satchel and ran through the castle's halls and down the staircases until she burst out into the early spring air. A horse was saddled and waiting by the trees. She greeted the horse and grabbed the reins and walked towards the locked gate.

She took the heavy keys out of her bag. One of the keys had a rose-shaped handle which matched the padlock. She'd attempted to pick the lock several times and had failed, so her fingers were familiar with the padlock's rose design. The key clicked, and the tumblers shifted and then the padlock opened. She unwrapped the chain and the gate doors swung out and open. The trees beyond were thick with green leaves, the sunshine filling the forest with life. The road was wide and clear. Leaving the keys in the padlock, she mounted the horse and trotted through the open gates. She didn't look back.

The Beast watched her disappear from his window. He felt the hollowness returning to him, an emptiness that had been chased away when this young woman had entered his life. Sophie had given him a purpose, something to be better for, to fight for. But now that she was gone, there was nothing left. He would be a beast always and always alone.

He raked his claws down the window, screeching as he went. The sound faded. She was gone from sight. He looked at the scratches in the glass. Would he get it fixed? They started out deep but lessened as they went down the pane until where his hand rested against the window and—

He stared. It was a hand resting against the glass. Not a paw, but a hand. He looked ahead and focused his eyes on his reflection. It was a face looking back. His face.

No horns, no fur, no fangs. He stepped away and looked down at his body. There were his legs and his torso and his arms. He felt his face.

He was human again.

"You learned what it really meant to love someone else. The spell is broken."

He whirled around. The maid stood in the doorway.

She sighed, walking towards him. "It's good to speak again."

"Why didn't you all these years?"

She shrugged. "I couldn't. Punishment for cursing you. We're not supposed to cast spells like that on unsuspecting humans. Even if they deserve it."

He scowled. He'd despised the enchantress's presence in his household all the years of his curse, and they'd avoided each other for the most part. When Sophie had arrived, he'd been glad the enchantress was there to help make Sophie more comfortable. But now she was gone. He turned back to the window. He couldn't even take real delight in being human again. He'd wanted to be human for her. There was no one to care now.

"Do you think she will come back?"

The enchantress came up and stood beside him. "No."

His shoulders slumped. He knew it too. He'd given Sophie her freedom. She wasn't going to give that up again for anyone.

"But that doesn't mean you can't go after her."

He looked over at her. She smiled back.

"Not right away, mind you. Give her some time. Give yourself some time. Decide what you want to do with your life. Who you want to be. Maybe then would be a good time to see her again." She turned to face him. "You have a chance to start over. Take it."

"Do you regret doing it?"

"No. Being silent for so long was certainly not ideal, but if you've truly learned what it means to love someone else more than you love yourself, then it was worth every moment. Love is a powerful and wondrous thing. It can make men beasts and beasts men. It can make anything and anyone beautiful or ugly. Don't waste that power."

He nodded. She'd said this to him right before she'd cast her spell on him all those years ago. He had not understood then. He understood now.

"I wish you every happiness." She turned to leave.

"Wait... please. What's your name?"

She laughed. "Miranda. Why do you ask now?"

"I never knew it."

"Well, now you do." She kissed him on the cheek. With a swirl of glittering air, she was gone.

He looked back out the window. They were both gone now, and he was alone. Utterly.

But the hollowness within him was lessening. For the first time in a long while, he felt something he thought might be hope.

Her reflection was just barely visible in the watch's face. She sat behind the counter in her father's shop, as she pried open the watch and looked over the inner work-ings. Taking a thin pair of pliers, she pulled at the gears where they were stuck together. She felt a strange thrill at the mundane work. She remembered feeling like this after she had successfully fixed a clock for the first time all by herself when she was young.

Sophie had fallen back into her life the way she fell into a dream, slowly, but cautiously, waiting for some-thing to shift. She had come home a few weeks ago. She rode into town and the villagers looked, looked away, and looked again. She'd been gone for three months. No one had expected to see her again, least of all her father. She ran into the repair shop, which was in the front room of their house. Her father just stared at her, unable to speak, unable to move. Then they embraced and cried.

The shop had closed early that day and remained closed for two days as the father welcomed his daughter home. There had been so much to tell and to under-stand.

It had been strange at first to see her village outside her window, not the walls and the bushes and statues she now realized she'd grown accustomed to. She joined her father in the shop and neighbors who had never stepped foot in there before found things they needed to fix. The questions and looks were kindly meant, for the most part, Sophie knew, but a lot of it was plain curiosity. They wanted to know where she'd been. Her father had not told anyone, and she saw no reason to share.

The library became her sanctuary again. No one stared at her there, mostly because it was just her and the librarian haunting the shelves. He was a widow who'd fallen in love with books after the death of his wife. Sophie was a friend, another person in love with the written word. He didn't bother with questions, just happy to have his fellow ghost with him. So, she took refuge there from the stares and the questions and books were once more her escape.

She'd considered donating the Beast's book to the library's meager collection. New books were rare in their part of the world. But she'd hesitated and ultimately decided against it. It now lay beside her on the counter as she fixed the watch. She read passages about foreign countries and faraway places in between repairs and customers.

The shop door opened. Sophie looked up from her work, a smile ready on her lips for a costumer, but the smile froze. Julien was one of the last people on earth she wanted to see.

It had not been until she'd returned that she realized there had been some good things about being locked away with the Beast, primarily the advantage of not having to deal with men like Julien, not having to even think about them. He was one of the village's eligible bachelors and heaven's gift to women, according to him. Sophie had always tried to avoid him whenever she was out in the village. He'd somehow managed to interpret her avoidance as an invitation to flirt and woo. She had feared he'd been on the verge of proposing when she'd taken her father's place with the Beast. In her three-month absence, not one thought of him had crossed her mind. Now she was back, and she feared he would pick up where he thought they'd left off.

"Hello, Sophie."

"Hello, Julien. What can we do for you today?" She doubted that he was here as a customer, but she could still hope.

"Oh, nothing. I just came to speak with you."

"I'm sorry, but I'm very busy today." She turned back to the watch she was almost done fixing. She might have to break a piece of it to have something to continue working on.

"Well, take a break for a minute and listen to me." He pushed the watch in her hands down to the counter.

Sophie bit back her first response. Maybe it would be better to just get this over with. "Only if you make it quick."

"Feisty. I like that." He grinned at her.

Sophie had to admit he was handsome, especially when he smiled. It was really too bad that a pretty face couldn't make up for the rest of a person. "What do you want, Julien?"

"I was wondering if you would go on a walk with me this evening."

"I'm sorry, I can't." She tugged the watch out from under his hand.

"Tomorrow evening then?"

"Can't." She examined the gears again.

"You know, there are many women in this town who would kill for the chance to walk out with me." He shifted his weight.

"Then you should go ask them."

"But I'm asking you. Let me be blunt, Sophie. I want to marry you. Will you be mine?"

She took a deep breath and drew herself up on her stool. She looked him in the eye. "Julien, thank you for the honor of your proposal. My answer is no."

He still smiled though his eyes shifted as the message finally got through from his ears to his brain. It took a while.

"I'm sorry. I think I must have misheard you."

She shook her head. "You didn't. I said no. I'm not going to marry you, Julien. Have a good day." She looked back down at the watch.

He grabbed her arm, pulling her towards him over the counter. "No one says 'no' to Julien."

She yanked her arm out of his grasp, brandishing the pliers at him. "I just did. Now you can either be gracious about it or not, but you will accept it and leave this shop."

He leaned away from her. She wasn't sure whether it was because he actually took her words seriously or whether it was the sharply pointed pliers aimed at his face. "No one in this town will ever marry you. You mysteriously go missing for three months and then return out of nowhere. Do you expect any man to want to marry a woman with that kind of taint?"

"If I cared what the men of this town thought, then I'd be concerned. But I don't and I'm not. Good day, Julien."

He backed away towards the door, his eyes on her face. "You will regret this."

She smiled at him. "I may regret many things in my life. This will not be one of them."

One last look and he turned on his heel. The door slammed shut behind him. She watched for a moment to make sure it remained closed before returning to the watch. Her hands shook slightly. Aggravated, she pushed out of her chair and opened the back door of the shop that led to the rest of the house.

Her father was sitting at the kitchen table on the other side of the threshold. One look at his face and Sophie knew he'd heard the whole conversation with Julien.

"Are you sure, Sophie?"

There was a kettle on the fire. She poured herself hot water and made some tea. "I didn't escape one beast to marry another, Father."

"People have been talking though. About where you've been."

She sighed, sitting down at the table with him, her hands warm against the mug. "All this town does is talk." This too had been another realization upon her return, which was harder for her to reconcile, since her village and the idea of home had been built up so magically and heavily in her mind. "This place is so stifling, Father. I want to be free."

"I know, my dear."

She took a sip of her tea and studied him over the rim of her mug. His brief captivity and then hers had taken its toll on him. He now looked as old as he actually was.

"Father, I've been thinking about leaving."

"Leaving?"

She instantly wished she had not mentioned the idea, but she knew she had to continue. Her father would get it out of her somehow if she tried to back down now. "Yes. I want to see the world, Father. There's so much out there. And I want to see it all. I want to see everything. I can't do that here."

He considered silently. Sophie waited. He didn't look at her, his eyes passing over their small kitchen. Her mother had loved to cook and bake, her favorite pastime. This had become her father's space after her mother had died until Sophie was old enough to help out. They then divided the labor. She'd occasionally caught her father watching her as she moved about the kitchen. She knew she looked like her mother. She'd wondered if in times like that her father saw his dead wife and not his grown daughter.

"There's nothing I can do to stop you... is there?"

Sophie shook her head. "No. But you could support me."

He looked at her. His eyes were sad though he smiled at her. "I will always support you, Sophie. Just... just promise me you won't go right away."

She stood and hugged her father tightly. He hugged back. "I won't go for a while. I promise."

A while passed, slowly and quickly in its turn. She saved money and planned her trip. She would start in Paris. She would mail letters home every chance she got, one of her father's few stipulations. She was happy to comply if it kept him content. She didn't plan to be gone longer than a year. That was the other stipulation. She was to come home no matter what. Perhaps she would choose to leave again and permanently, but for now, she was to come back home. She didn't mind. She knew she would want to make a proper goodbye to her childhood home if she were leaving for good. This was just an extended holiday.

She was working on a local family's broken music box a week before her departure, when the door of the shop opened, and a stranger walked in. He was a handsome man, tall and swarthy, with dark hair and green eyes. He held out his watch. Sophie took it and saw that it had stopped. She set to winding it up.

"Are you going on a trip?" His voice was deep.

She looked up from her work. The book the Beast had given her was lying open on the counter to the section on Paris. She smiled.

"Yes. I'm going to Paris. Have you ever been?"

He stared at the picture of the city on the page. "A long time ago."

"Did you like it?"

"Very much. It's a beautiful city."

It was a simple repair on his watch. She gave it back to him and he paid her. She asked if there was anything else he needed, and he shook his head.

"Well, then safe journey and have a nice day."

He nodded slowly. "Thank you. You too. I wish you every happiness. You deserve it."

His words were odd coming from a complete stranger. He looked at her, uncomfortable, as if he had said something he shouldn't. He turned on his heel and left the shop.

She stared after him, the music box lying forgotten beside her. The words rang in her ears, oddly familiar, like the lyrics to a song known long ago. Her eyes widened. She dashed out the door. She ran down the road, ignoring the stares she still got from her neighbors, until she saw the back of the man on the road heading out of the village.

"Wait!"

He stopped in his tracks and slowly turned to her. She halted in front of him and stared at him. She met his eyes, so green and human. Her heart stopped.

"How..."

He swallowed and looked away. "I learned what it meant to love someone. The spell broke."

"When..."

"Right after you left."

Sophie couldn't help staring. He was human. The green eyes fit in perfectly with the rest of him. It was hard to believe this was the Beast she'd known. She wondered if she was making a mistake. He looked at her. Those eyes were the same, whatever else had happened to the body.

"What are you doing here?"

He shifted from foot to foot. "I sold my property. I just donated the books to your town's library."

"You did?" Her eyes widened. She could just imagine the librarian's face at the sight of all the books the Beast owned. She wanted to race off to the library to see if they were really there.

He nodded. "Yes. I think the town will use the castle as a school of some sort."

"But then... where will you go?"

He shrugged. "I thought I'd see a bit of the world for a while. I was stuck in that castle for years. It's time for a change."

She smiled slowly. "I know what you mean. I'm leaving as well."

"Paris, right?"

She nodded. "At first. After that, who knows."

He smiled. "That sounds wonderful. I hope you enjoy it." He looked down at the ground for a moment before looking back at her. "I want to apologize for what I did to you. You were right. About everything. And I'm sorry. I hope you'll be happy, Sophie. You really do deserve it." He started to turn away.

"Would you like to stay for dinner?"

He turned back to her, eyes wide with surprise. "What?"

She'd asked the question before she could really think about it, but she wasn't going to take it back. She didn't want to.

"A stranger passing through town...you probably don't have a place to eat tonight."

He stared at her. "You would have me over for dinner? But what about..."

"Are you the person you were before?"

He swallowed. "I'd like to think not. I hope not. Miranda put that curse on me for a reason. The curse broke because I learned my lesson. I'm trying to be better than I was."

Sophie wanted to ask who Miranda was, but she curbed her blatant curiosity. "Well, if you're not the beast you were before, then I think my father and I can give you at least one meal. If you would like, that is."

He smiled and Sophie smiled back. Turning, they began to walk back together in silence. The shop was just in view when she stopped. "I don't know your name."

She'd never asked his name, never wanted to know it. He'd always been the Beast to her and nothing more.

"Tristen."

She held out her hand. "It's nice to meet you, Tristen. My name is Sophie."

He took it. His hand was warm against hers. "It's nice to meet you, Sophie."

They let go and walked back toward her home.

The Bona Fide Princess Pea

By Jacque Vickers

A MUSEUM SHOWPIECE FROM 1835, beholding a pea,
A lady, proving herself a true Princess, she holds the
key
Betrothing a finicky Prince she's been married to ever
since.

Delighted with other ladies failing the Princess pea test,
the lady's claims had always proven to be
true,

Sleeping on twenty mattresses and eiderdowns on top
of a pea, she was a princess through and through,
The lone green pea, a small nimble weight, a blessing to
the Prince and Princess's fate.

Years onwards from meeting, their souls joyfully yearn-

ing to travel,
The truthfulness and honesty of which put early to the
test, not to unravel
Thanks to a pea, the most glorious love which there ever
could be.

THE ROSE RED CAPER

By William J. Connell

Princess Shahrazad sat at a marble vanity, stroking her rich black hair with a pearl comb, gazing at her husband's reflection. The Sultan, clothed in white robes which barely covered his belly, sat cross-legged on the floor, hands pressed together.

"Please, Shahrazad. It has been so long. Tell me another story."

Shahrazad's smile was sly. "It has been. And during that time, I have borne and raised you three strong sons and a lovely daughter. I think that more than compensates."

"You know how much I love the boys. And you, dearest. Your stories are so entertaining. Please, one more."

Long ago, her tales of Arabian Nights had kept the Sultan so entranced he would not execute her until she had finished each one. At first, despite being in constant peril, she'd found his childish ways endearing. Over three years of such storytelling, he'd become completely enchanted by her, and in turn, her endearment waned.

"Why, Dear, there is one I can think of I never revealed. But if I tell this 1002nd tale, you must promise me something."

"Anything, my love."

"I will decide *after* I've told the tale. Agreed, my sweetheart?"

The Sultan nodded like one of their eager puppies.

Shahrazad twirled around.

"Picture a small fire, burning at night in the deep dark woods. Two men, and a woman with flowing golden locks of hair, seated in a circular clearing. Their heads are bowed. The exterior of the circle is in darkness, but you can make out creatures stirring in the shadows."

The man on the right, lean and wiry, spoke in a hushed voice.

"Nice to see you, Goldi, present circumstances notwithstanding."

"Glad to see you still have a sense of humor, Jack. Think you're nimble and quick enough to get out of this one?

The second man, who had sharp features and flawlessly coiffed black hair, cried "We're doomed! Doomed!"

"Don't blow your horn, Charming," Jack remonstrated. "And keep your head down."

Something stirred outside the circle. Jack heard heavy-footed thumping on the forest floor. A large rabbit settled onto a wooden throne just outside the firelight.

"Jack. Goldi. Prince Charming. Thank you all for accepting my invitation at this late hour."

The voice was soft and raspy.

"As you requested, Mr. Fufu," Jack said.

"Our pleasure, Mr. Fufu," added Goldi.

"Invitation! I was walking through my pumpkin patch, and I was attacked by a zillion bunnies out of the dark. Then I'm knocked out and wake up in a coach with a bag over my head. And I get dragged here and—"

"The prince loves to jest. He's happy to see you too, Mr. Fufu," Jack interjected, and then murmured, "Tread lightly, Charming."

There was silence for several beats.

The raspy voice continued.

"I have a soft spot for humor. Mrs. Fufu says it is my weakness. But my friends, I have another mutual associate to whom I am indebted. She came to me with a problem. She has a plan which uses each of your unique talents. I hope you will perform a favor for her, which I would consider a favor for me."

Jack heard Prince Charming breathing heavily. "I just want to go home to my pumpkin patch!"

Goldi whispered, "Won't he shut up?"

Jack said, "We're grateful to express our gratitude, Mr. Fufu."

"Thank you all. I am going to have our mutual friend explain the situation. Ms. White?"

A pleasant-looking, black-haired woman, dressed in a light blue dress, a violet bow in her hair, and white boots, stepped into the firelight.

Though his head was still bowed, Jack recognized the footwear. "Hello, Snowy. Let me guess. This is about your lovely sister, Rose Red."

Snowy White nodded. "You know my sister is always chasing the most eligible bachelors. Princes, Dukes, doctors, shipping magnets. Marriage, divorce, marriage, divorce, always working her way up. She wrote me saying she was in Italy and finally met THE prince, someone with a fortune and military might to match. Her whale. I wrote back it sounded like a matter that needed caution. I have not heard from her since. But I did hear from The Little Sea Maiden. She told me while her husband Prince Daryl had been in Venice on diplomatic business, he was at the castle of Duke Alfonso. The Duke showed Daryl a portrait, a fresco hidden behind a curtain, purporting to be his last duchess. According to Prince Daryl, it was the image of Rose Red. Alfonso spoke as if she were no longer—"

After a pause, Snowy White's voice trembled.

"The Duke is notorious for repeatedly seeking a new bride, whom he falls in lust with very quickly and marries. His wives all come to a bad end.

They disappear within a year of marriage and are either found or declared dead, and he marries again."

"I've heard of this Duke Alfonso," Jack recalled. "A powerful warlord. Purported leader of the criminal underworld throughout the western Italy city-states."

"I do not appreciate the man's methods, Jack" the raspy voice interjected. "Alfonso is without honor. But this presents for me a delicate matter. I cannot intervene directly without creating a complete war, which I do not wish at this time. You know I am a simple carrot farmer, and we are in the middle of harvest season. I require discretion."

"This Duke Alfonso," the Sultan exclaimed. He marries a new woman and kills her every year? Barbaric!"

"Imagine that," Shahrazad replied.

"Snowy," Goldi asked, "if your sister married him and she's in the painting then – what can we do?"

"I have a plan," Snowy White snapped. Then, "Sorry Goldi, I'm feeling stressed. The Duke's pattern, once he tires of his new wife, is he forcibly hides her in his home, the Doge Palace in Venice. There is an order of cloistered nuns inside who remain mostly unseen and veiled when they do appear. We have it on good authority that he secludes his wife in their nunnery for a couple of months until just before he weds his new wife. Then the former one is secretly 'disposed.'"

"Oh no, no!" yelled Prince Charming. "That Doge's Palace is a fortress. It's impenetrable."

Jack snuck another glance at Snowy White's acknowledging look.

"The palace is a massive edifice," Snowy agreed. "High thick walls and heavily guarded. But we do have a plan."

A pair of large hares brought an easel with drawings and set it beside Snowy White.

"Mr. Fufu, may they look up? "

"Of course, my dear."

Those in the center looked towards Snowy White who held a pointer to touch the illustrations.

"The Doge's Palace sits at the top of the Grand Canal, which is the central waterway through Venice. Duke Alfonso has one thousand Spanish Moor soldiers on the premises. Refugees from Iberia. They serve as his personal guard and are fierce warriors, battle-hardened from fighting on the Iberian Peninsula."

Jack processed everything. "But—if the painting was shown to Prince Daryl, then—"

"Duke Alfonso follows a strict process. He first has the artist Frau Pando paint a fresco of his wife and keeps her alive in case Pando needs more. Then Alfonso hides her away. The only way in and out of the nunnery is through a brass door with a lock built by Claus of Innsbruck."

Charming exclaimed, "He's the finest metal-smith in the world!"

Snowy wrung her hands. "The wife has forty days after the Duke first reveals the painting. The Duke bragged to Prince Daryl that this was the first time he'd displayed the image. That was three weeks ago. We have nineteen days left."

"We can't get there in time," Charming whined.

Jack reluctantly added, "Charming has a point. England to Venice is over three weeks under sail."

Mr. Fufu's voice broke in. "Daryl returned on a conventional boat. We have a special transport with an impeccable captain who will get you there in seventeen days."

Snowy White added, "We have flying carpets."

"How fast can carpets get us there?" Jack asked.

"Three days." Snowy paused. "But you need to learn how to drive them. That will take time. You'll be taught while traveling at sea."

Goldi nodded. "I've heard carpets are not easy to control."

"We will need them to get my sister out. And to avoid the Rocs."

"Oh sure," Prince Charming blurted. "The place is surrounded by giant sharp boulders."

Snowy White shook her head.

"No, not quite. *Rocs*."

She flipped the paper to a drawing of a great hawk-like bird, with sharp talons and a hooked beak, flying over water and clutching what looked like an elephant.

"Check out the tiny pachyderm," Charming said.

"No, that *IS* an African savannah elephant, largest in the world."

More silence, until Snowy continued.

"Duke Alfonso has four Rocs under his control. Patrolling the skies of Venice."

"Giant frickin Rocs? Are you kidding me?"

Jack sensed Mr. Fufu's dissatisfaction.

"Prince Charming, you seem unenthusiastic about this, not in the spirit of things. Would you prefer to not participate?"

"Giant Rocs? Hell no, get me out of here. Please!"

"There is no need to beg. It is unbecoming. You wish to leave. Then you should leave. My associates shall assist you."

Out of the corner of his eye, Jack saw rabbits, hedgehogs, shrews, rodents, and other mammals of assorted sizes descend upon the Prince. Charming's shriek was muffled as the animals placed a sack over his head and tied him to his chair. They raised the chair and carried Charming out of the clearing. It was done in fifteen seconds.

"I sensed Prince Charming was not feeling esprit de corps. Anyone else?"

"I'm in, Mr. Fufu."

"Me too," Goldi chimed.

"And me."

This voice came from Jack's shirt pocket.

"Thumbelina?"

A brown-haired faerie with coppery-red accents poked her head out. "It's me, Jack."

"Ms. Thumbelina, I almost forgot," said Mr. Fufu. "As a winged water sprite, you will find Thumbelina has a particular set of skills that may be useful. But time is at a premium. I entrust you to Ms. White's capable hands. My charges will escort you to a safe place for boarding your ship. Expenses are not an issue. I wish you good fortune and speed."

With that, another group of rabbits and rodents picked up the chairs (providing one for Snowy White as well) and began to move them.

***

"What does Snow White need them for? Doesn't she have seven dwarves hanging around?"

Shahrazad maintained her smile.

"Different Snow White. Snowy White is the nice, pleasant sister, and her gorgeous, completely full-of-herself sister is Rose Red. You need to read up on the Brothers Grimm. Shall I continue? Picture our group on a caravel, a small sailing ship with triangular and square sails rigged up, rapidly sailing over the water. Jack admires the view.

***

Jack leaned over the railing at the aft of the ship.

"Jormungandr," Jack whispered, reading the letters emblazoned on the sterncastle.

"An appropriate name for a ship that, like the Midgard Serpent, has circled the world." Sinbad laughingly added. "Unlike the serpent, this boat has done it seven times."

"I've heard you're a great sailor, Sinbad. The wind is blowing against us, but we're moving exceptionally fast. How do you do it?"

"This my friend is a caravel, designed for speed." Sinbad pointed above. "Those sails? Lateen. With their triangular shape, they catch the wind even when it blows against us. We also have square rigs when the wind is with us. We never stop."

"And when there is no wind?"

Sinbad laughed again. "I'll show you."

Jack followed Sinbad. They passed The Steadfast Tin Soldier, staffing the helm. Sinbad patted the soldier's shoulder and said, "Steady as she goes, my friend."

They continued through the aft hatchway and under the poop deck.

"Sinbad, just curious. How does a tin soldier steer when he gets wet?"

"We oil him as needed. Let me assure you, he's the best helmsperson I've ever seen."

At the rear of the ship, three figures were lying in hammocks. To the left was one with the body of a strong burly man, but with the arms and head of a bear. On the right, two men dressed in mufti outfits, with large domed heads, identical in appearance, were sleeping. A three-handled apparatus that looked like a windlass was in the middle of the floor.

"Meet our propulsion team," Sinbad said. "This is Mark. Also known as the Bear Prince."

The bear looked up from his hammock, then slipped out, hunching over to fit in the space.

"Thank you for helping us." The Bear Prince's voice was rich and textured. He extended two paws/hands and hugged Jack.

"I break easily," Jack said.

The Bear released Jack.

"Sorry. I'm a hugger."

Jack looked puzzled.

"The Bear Prince. Snowy's husband. I heard your curse was lifted."

"It returned. I will remain like this unless Rose Red is freed."

Sinbad pointed to the others. "And these two stalwart gentlemen are Mr. Dee and Mr. Dum. Good workers. When we have no wind, these three spin that winch, which operates two propellers outside the ship, besides the rudder. We never stop."

Sinbad gathered several long sticks with hooks on their ends which flared outward.

"Shepherd Crooks? What are those for?"

"Flight training time," Sinbad answered. "Trust me, you'll be glad we have them."

"Magic carpets. How hard can they be?"

***

Twenty minutes later, Jack found himself tossed about in rough seawater. His arms ached from treading afloat. The waves were too high. A towering one was approaching. In the distance, he heard Goldi yelling for help.

Before he could act, the wave crashed. Jack felt the force of the water sucking him down.

He could not believe this was how it would end.

Something grabbed his pant's belt and hauled him up. He somersaulted into the air and fell onto a plush black Persian Carpet. Sinbad stood over him, hands on his hips.

"Not quite as easy as you thought, I presume?"

Jack knocked some water out of his ears.

"Just bad luck. Where's Goldi?"

"We have her. Let's get back to the ship and start again."

****

Jack soon sat on the deck with Goldi and Prince Charming, all shivering under blankets. Sinbad sat cross-legged on his floating black carpet. Snowy had her easel. The others were off to the side, save for the Tin Soldier who remained at his post.

Sinbad addressed them.

"Magic carpets respond to commands immediately. They aren't familiar with you.

So they watch where you look. If you change your gaze they follow that. You must know how to command them. Lose focus—lose the carpet."

Sinbad patted his finger on his carpet. Its edge curled towards his hand.

"Is that thing purring?" Jack asked.

"Pinta is an old friend. Once they get to know you—and if they like you—they may help you. Right now they'll do just what you command and go where you look."

Jack spoke angrily. "Charming—thought you were leaving."

"Mr. Fufu t-t-tendered me a proposal I c-c-could not turn down."

"Why ARE you here?" Goldi asked.

"Mr. Fufu said I know how to give commands."

Sinbad stood up on his carpet.

"The prince does. Now you're getting it. Each of you has an assigned magic carpet. You must direct them, and they will fly for you. But they don't trust you yet so if you mess up, you're in the water."

Thumbelina flittered to Jack's ear and whispered, "You can do better Jack."

"I'm nimble, but I don't have wings," Jack retorted.

"That's why Jack, you are training with Thumbelina. Goldi, you and Prince go on your carpets. We're going to keep working."

"I'm c-c-cold and tired," Charming complained.

Sinbad clapped his hands together. "All the more reason to get back in the air. Oh Snowy, you had something to add?

Snowy White had her flip chart out.

"We just got word by lobster. Prince Daryl's trip was longer than we thought. We only have thirteen days left."

The deck was silent, until Prince Charming exclaimed, "That's it, we're d-d-done."

Jack's eyes met Snowy's, and he could see tears welling up.

The Bear Prince spoke. "Me and the boys, we'll work double time. We'll get there in ten days. Right?"

Jack thought the twins had expressionless faces, but they were large-armed. They nodded in unison.

"It's agreed," Sinbad announced. "There's an old saying among Persian sailors, 'Seek Allah's help. But catch more wind in your sales.' Unfortunately, that cuts your training time. You'll all have to learn carpet riding quicker. We try again."

The group dispersed to their duties. Snowy grabbed the Bear Prince's arm as he passed. He gently patted her hand.

***

Winds were blowing through Jack's hair. He was lying on his carpet and plunging into the sea.

"Keep looking Jack," said the voice in his ear. "Don't turn your head."

The ocean was coming up fast. Jack couldn't stop from glancing aside.

His carpet turned just above the water, then cut hard to the right. Jack was thrown into foamy waves. The currents buffeted him (again). He managed to swim to the surface.

Thumbelina fluttered overhead.

"You're getting there, Jack,"

Another wave knocked him underwater.

Jack was disoriented. The long Sheperd's crook wrapped his waist and yanked him high onto a deep black carpet floating above the waters. Jack could not tell which was sky and which was water and felt himself tottering. A hand on his shoulder steadied him. He heard Sinbad. "Again."

***

After several spills into the ocean, it was time to rest. There was a small space under the forecastle deck with hammocks for the men to sleep in and a separate space for the women. Jack slept extremely well and dreamed of—

"Time for training!" boomed Sinbad's voice.

***

Over the next several days, Jack spent a lot of time in the water. Thumbelina had many suggestions, which at first did not make much sense. But on the fifth day of training, Jack was sitting on his carpet as it hovered over the water.

"Jack, talk to it."

"Talk to what?"

"Your carpet."

"Ok. Well, fella, how are we doing?"

The carpet spun over and dropped Jack into the water.

The water was rough, but not so much that he could not get to the surface.

"Aaah. Thumbelina what kind of advice was that?"

"Your carpet is she. Her name is Nina."

The carpet's tassels fluttered in the wind.

"Ok, Nina. Can you help me out of here?"

Nothing.

Jack added, "Please!"

The carpet sank under the water, wrapped Jack up, and then shot skyward. It flattened. Jack looked down.

"Woah. Hey, where's the ship?"

Thumbelina alighted on Jack's shoulder and pointed westward. "There. You can see the others flying below."

"I'm soaked."

Thumbelina flew in front of Jack.

"Are you?"

"Yeah look I—"

Jack felt his shirt and pants. They were—barely damp.

"Nina flew us high. She has to warm herself too. She often does after you fall. But this time she took you with her because you asked nicely."

Jack felt the sun burning his skin. He felt the plush fibers of the carpet drying too.

"Ok. Maybe I am starting to get this. But Nina, I'm human and can only take so much time this close to the sun."

Jack felt Nina shift underneath him.

"But of course take all the time you need to dry. Just—please don't let me fry."

After a few minutes, they returned to Jormungandr. Sinbad, Charming, and Goldi were all standing on the foredeck, with Snowy off to the side. Goldi squeezed her wet hair.

"This seawater is ruining my curls. And you said we need them as part of the plan."

Snowy produced a decanter. "This is a magic curl conditioner. We'll restore all your hair's luster once we dock. We need those curls to attract the Duke's attention!"

"Well done everyone," Sinbad said. "Consider the basics of training completed. Now we move to more complicated maneuvers."

Snowy had another chart out with an illustration of a Roc descending on a ship.

"Rocs like to fly straight. They are extremely quick in the open air. With those wings, they accelerate faster than any other airborne creature. They also like to dive and snatch things out of the water, like ships or swimmers. But they do have weaknesses."

Snowy showed drawings to illustrate her points.

"First, while they can overtake anything directly in front of them, they aren't built for sharp turns. They can be confused when they have to make a cutback. Second, they concentrate on their prey intently. Once they go after it, they generally don't notice what's to their sides. Third, they are drawn to rich colors. You'll notice all our carpets have vivid coloring. We can capture their attention to follow us and then do maneuvers. Lastly, they will grab things out of the water. But they don't really swim well. Get them to dive under the water, we'll confuse them."

Charming whined. "Great, so we race around on these magic rugs and if Rocs don't snatch us out of the air, we can survive. And if they catch us?

Sinbad answered. "You're eaten. Which is why tomorrow we have new exercises."

Under the tutelage of Sinbad, the intensity of maneuvers increased exponentially. Each person knew their flying carpet. Jack's red Nina, the fastest. Sinbad's black Pinta, wise and experienced. Goldi had golden Santo, the slowest but the strongest. And Charming had violet Maria (who was reliable but a bit weak in hearing). Practices were usually ahead of the ship. Buoys with high masts attached were deployed, which the riders and rugs had to maneuver around. At first, there were simple back-and-forth slalom movements. After a day of this, Jack said, "Thumbelina, I think Nina and I are getting the hang of this."

"That's good Jack. Nina might be the fastest, but she is certainly the most stubborn."

The back of the carpet swatted tassels at the fairy.

"It's true, Nina. Flicking me off won't change that."

They heard Sinbad's voice. "Down here, everyone."

The three carpets returned to a spot ahead of the ship. Jack noticed the buoys floating farther apart.

"Sinbad, the markers are drifting."

"Yes, as I set them. You can do simple zigzags. Good. Now this is going to get challenging."

Goldi gave Jack a tired look. Charming complained again, but Goldi told him to shut his mouth.

The new movements *were* harder. Turns broader and sharper. Flights went straight up and divided down. Much time was spent in the water. The practices grew more dangerous.

Late one afternoon, Jack found himself in a thick cloud.

"Now what?"

Thumbelina told Jack, "Sinbad said this is a test. Find him."

They moved outward. The mist cleared. From this vantage point, the speeding caravel was a speck on the water.

"Holy—"

"There he is, Jack." Thumbelina pointed toward Sinbad, meditating on his black carpet, Pinta.

Jack heard a voice. "Fly at me."

"Don't take your eyes off him," Thumbelina warned.

"Ok, Nina. Let's go. Slowly."

Nina moved cautiously toward Sinbad.

"Too slow!" Sinbad remained meditating, but his voice was in Jack's head.

Jack hesitated, but Thumbelina reminded him that HE controlled the carpet. He patted it and whispered, "A *little* quicker."

They moved closer. Almost upon their target, Sinbad called, "Now jump Jack!"

Jack clutched his carpet but said, "Jump?"

Nina flipped him into the air. Their momentum carried Jack over Sinbad, while Nina passed underneath. Jack landed on Nina.

"Whoa! What happened?"

Sinbad flew beside them. "That's a double dip-flip. You may need some fancy maneuvers in Venice. Maybe even going through a church steeple."

"A steeple!" Jack yelled. "Listen, Sinbad, this is going to faaaa—"

Thumbelina flew to Sinbad. "He was doing well. You baited him to look at you."

"The Rocs will be unforgiving. We're not going into a pillow fight."

Jack plunged further from their view.

Thumbelina sighed. "Come on, Nina, we better get him before he hits the water."

***

More days. More training. Less frequent falls in the water. Jack found it never-ending.

Until he stood on the forecastle while the Doge's Palace rose into view. It was imposing, a solid wall with few windows, occupying a huge space that faced the Venetian Lagoon. The stone had a pink hue that Jack found amusing. Armed guards formed a wall of shields stretching the length of the palace.

"The Palazzo Ducale," Sinbad said, leaning over the deck. "Five hundred feet across. The wings off the sides go back three hundred feet. The prison at the rear forms a courtyard."

"A pink palace?" Jack asked.

Sinbad laughed. "Yes. Pink Verona marble. Symbolizes blood. That's where Duke Alfonso proclaims public death sentences. The condemned is tied to a raft and sent into the lagoon."

Sinbad pointed to the left where a brick obelisk, capped by a belfry with windows and a pyramid-shaped spire, rose into the sky.

"That tower is St. Mark's Campanile, three hundred and twenty-three feet high."

Deep bongs started ringing from the tower.

"Noon. Those are the bells in the belfry," Sinbad said. "You may get an up-close look at them."

A Roc circled the tower. Another landed atop the Palazzo and spread its wings. Jack's heart jumped.

"Sinbad, you fought one of those things?"

"Several times. They're not that tough."

A fleet of striped dolphins had been swimming beside the ship. As one dolphin breached the water, a third Roc, larger than the others, swooped down and grasped it. The dolphin squealed and wriggled as two talons squeezed. The Roc tossed its prey into its beak and settled atop the palace to eat. The dolphin's squealing stopped.

They watched the Roc pick at the dolphin's flesh.

"That's the fate of a condemned prisoner, Jack."

"I hope it isn't ours."

Sinbad smiled.

"Maybe the ones I fought were a little smaller."

Jormungandr passed by the palace and continued under the stone colonnade that formed the gateway to the Grand Canal.

"You sure we won't run aground?"

"Caravels have a low draft. We can get through the Grand Canal, but we're stuck if we turn down another one."

Not far past the Palazzo, the caravel pulled to a dock in front of a more modest but still beautifully adorned Venetian mansion.

Jack turned to see the Bear Prince escorting Goldi towards the gangplank. The Prince wore a large, brimmed plume hat to cover much of his face. Goldi's locks were more flowing, more golden, more luscious than Jack had ever seen. Her hair cascaded onto a shimmering pink dress which matched her toenails, visible through her glass slippers. Snowy White followed in a drab cloak, her posture indicating subservience to Goldi. Mr. Dum and Mr. Dee trailed behind Goldi, in ill-fitting formal attire.

"Guess Snowy's hair potion worked," Jack observed.

"We got that dress from Briar Rose. You know who the slippers are from. Time to follow, Jack. To the plank."

Jack stopped at the top.

"You think this will work?"

"Start walking. Steal a quick glance at the Palazzo's corner tower closest to us."

As Jack walked, he raised his eyes briefly. A tall figure appeared in a window at the top of the palace tower nearest them, with a smaller figure behind him.

Jack looked down quickly. "Duke Alfonso, I presume?"

"You presume correctly. He got word of a minor diplomat arriving by boat today, accompanied by his niece, an exceedingly fetching maiden from the Kingdom of France. I believe a sea sprite got into his ear."

They reached land and followed the entourage into the house. Once inside, Jack asked, "We're sure he's going to go for Goldi?"

Snowy White threw back her hood. "Rose is a flaming redhead. The Duke is on the lookout for a ravishing blonde. We should be getting an invitation soon."

Jack heard marching feet approach. A string of guards came by the window. Three guards armed with round shields and strong sabers appeared in the entranceway. Accompanying them was a well-adorned emissary dressed in formal attire, gazing over the group, stopping on Goldi. Jack thought this was the man he'd seen behind Duke Alfonso in the tower.

Charming hesitated, then gestured.

"I am Prince Charmed. From Avignon, Kingdom of France. On a business trip. This is Princess Falalalala."

Goldi, fussing with her hair in front of a mirror, said, "You can call me, Princess Falalalala."

The emissary eyed the Princess, dismissive of the others.

"Duke Alfonso requests your appearance immediately. Come with me."

Charming stood paralyzed.

The emissary grabbed Goldi's shoulder. She shook off his hand and slapped him. The emissary grasped a dagger in his sash. Jack stepped forward and punched the emissary, who stumbled backward. The guards drew their swords and moved forward. Sinbad jumped in with his own saber drawn. The guards swung at the Sailor. There was a quick clash of slashing metal. In another moment, the guards were staring at their weapons on the floor.

"Gentlemen, please assist the Duke's envoy to his feet. Proud sir, I am sorry you fell. And guards, please, allow me to help you retrieve what you accidentally dropped. I am Princess Falalalala's guardian. We are most grateful for Duke Alfonso's invitation and are happy to accept."

Sinbad flicked one sword, then another, to two guards, who caught them. Sinbad stepped on the third sword. He lowered his own saber. As the guards picked up the emissary, Sinbad added, "I believe you said ten o'clock in the morning. Two days from now. The Princess shall require time to prepare. We shall be there at eleven am. Please convey our warmest regards to the Duke."

The guard whose sword Sinbad stood over stared at Sinbad until the others pulled him back and exited. Jack heard the boots of the guards marching away.

"Shahrazad, why are you stopping?"

Their three sons and sole daughter huddled at the room's entrance. Shahrazad beckoned their children to enter. Each gave her an embrace. Shahrazad told her boys to "sleep happily," and wished her daughter the "sweetest dreams." In turn, each child gave their father a dutiful bow, then went off to their bedrooms.

Shahrazad yawned.

"I think that is enough for one night."

"No, my sweet, the story is not finished."

She rolled her head back and stretched her arms. "Not now."

"Please. I will—whatever you wish for telling the story—I will double it."

The Princess grinned, snapped forward, and continued.

"I will hold you to that, my love."

Now, the group was mildly scared at Sinbad putting things off, as two days were the fortieth day after the first reveal of the painting. But coming too soon would appear too eager. They needed to keep up the proper façade. That night was spent furtively moving items from the caravel, especially the carpets. Then the caravel, crewed by the Steadfast Tin Shoulder and the capable Mr. Dee and Mr. Dum, left in darkness to continue down the Grand Canal. The next day, Jack and Sinbad took a jog around the Palazzo and scouted all the windows, which were high from the ground. They also noted where the nunnery might be—at the rear of the Palazzo. Several times Jack noticed the shadow of a Roc passing over them.

"Do not be concerned," Sinbad assured Jack. "The Rocs won't attack until the Duke commands them."

Upon return, they finalized their plans. You could feel the group's tightness, but Goldi made special porridge that helped everyone sleep.

On the fortieth day, just before eleven am, a retinue of soldiers and diplomats from the palazzo came. Sinbad greeted them warmly on behalf of the Kingdom of France. All were dressed in formal attire, save for Jack. The entourage—Goldi, Sinbad, Snowy, and the Bear Prince—was escorted through the high-arched Porta della Carta into the Doge's Palace. Jack slipped in with the soldiers wearing mail hauberk, a coned helmet that concealed much of his face, and carrying the saber Sinbad had disarmed from the guard. Once inside, Jack fell back. Thumbelina, who was right in his pocket, directed Jack up three flights of stairs, through spacious passageways, and finally, stopping at the nunnery, located at the back of the Palazzo, several floors over the prison. Jack made a gesture to relieve the two guards standing there. Thankfully, they were happy to comply.

"Pretty empty up here," Jack mused.

"Everybody's in the main hall for the reception," came a voice from under his chainmail.

Jack touched the steel door. A handle sat atop a large bronze box. Jack grabbed.

It would not budge.

"Yup, that's impregnable. Thumbelina, you're up."

Thumbelina flew to the box and entered a keyhole. Jack turned his back to the door.

"Thumbelina, what's happening?"

"Real tight and dark in here. I'm using faerie dust to see. Lots of tumblers. Gears instead of springs. Not easy"

Sinbad stood with hands clasped behind his back in the middle of a winding staircase. He had spent the last twenty minutes accompanying Duke Alfonso slowly down the steps. The Duke was a large broad-shouldered man, clad in military dress. A curved-blade scimitar dangled from his waist. Periodically they would stop in front of drapes, which the Duke's assistant pulled back to reveal exceptionally like-life paintings on walls—frescoes—of young, vibrant women. Their expressions were generally neutral, though Sinbad saw a hint of sadness in each countenance. He also noted the hair colors. Black or perhaps dark brown, followed by red, and then blonde. This repeated several times. The Duke bemoaned his lack of fortune in finding a suitable long-term mate. Sinbad listened carefully but said nothing. They stopped. Another set of curtains parted.

Rose Red!

Sinbad maintained a polite, mildly interested look.

"My previous Duchess," Alfonso began. "She had a beautiful smile. Perhaps too enchanting. I shall miss her, though."

Sinbad's eyes must have betrayed something, for the Duke said, "I speak of her in the present as if her fate could be undone. Nevertheless, your ward could, perhaps, fulfill the void left in my heart. Does that interest you? I see it does. Forgive my boldness, I am a fighting man, sir."

The Duke leaned closer.

"I understand you are, too."

Sinbad opened his arms and said, "My Duke, what a wonderful note on which to leave these stairs of sadness and visit my ward."

A throng had gathered in The Chamber of the Great Council, the largest room in the Palazzo Ducale. The ceiling and all the walls were adorned with exquisite frescoes and paintings, except three large windows on the exterior wall. Goldi, Snowy, Prince Charming, and the Bear Prince sat on spindly gold-plated seats built into the walls. Nearby were two golden thrones positioned atop a dais.

"This is taking forever," Goldi whispered.

Snowy said, "Just wait. It's according to plan."

Charming was rocking back and forth. The Bear Prince waited patiently.

The emissary from the other day appeared from double doors and announced, "Duke Alfonso d'Este."

A hush fell over the crowd as the Duke entered, followed by Sinbad. The Duke strode over to the throne and sat down. Sinbad walked over to Goldi, took her hand, and they both went before the throne.

The Duke's face showed interest. He called his emissary over and spoke to him quietly. The emissary nodded, turned, and quickly exited the chamber. Returning his attention to the crowd, the Duke proclaimed, "I had to give some orders. Now, I am ready to meet your ward."

"Duke Alfonso—presenting my ward, Princess Falalalala."

Goldi shook her curls, which caught the Duke's eye.

"Pleased to meet you. You may call me Princess Falalalala."

Thumbelina had tried. And tried.

"JACK! I can't open it!"

"Thumbelina, we are running out of time." Jack saw a group of guards turn the corner and march towards them.

"We got company. It's now or never."

Thumbelina quietly said, "Oh Faerie God-mother, I don't know what to do. I've failed. I've always believed in you. If you do exist, please help me this time."

Thumbelina pushed on a tumbler.

It did nothing.

Thumbelina felt the tears coming. She cried. Hard. Her tiny body crumpled over. Her backside bumped into a tiny spring, which moved ever-so-slight-ly.

A sound explosion of grinding, spinning, and whirring. Thumbelina flew out of the box. The door swung back to reveal a dark chamber. It was adorned with religious artifacts, but there was no group of clois-tered nuns. Just one figure, sitting in a far corner by an altar. The figure looked up.

Jack and Thumbelina exclaimed, "Rose!"

Jack noticed a small square window far up the exterior wall.

They ran inside and slammed the door shut.

Outside the back wall of the palace, the Steadfast Tin Soldier leaned by a tarp-covered cart. The soldier feigned efforts to fix a broken wheel. From a window high above came a cry of "Nina!" At this, the tarp was thrown back. A brilliantly red tasseled carpet flew out, carrying three other rolled-up carpets. Nina flew into the window. A Roc passing overhead seemed to take interest, but the carpet ducked into the window before the bird could swoop.

Sinbad had been extolling the virtues of how a union through marriage between France and Venice would be mutually beneficial. He was about to discuss the various wines of the two regions when Goldi turned him to one of the floor-to-ceiling open windows.

High outside, Nina hovered carrying Jack, Thumbelina, and Rose Red, with three rolled carpets beside them.

"Pinta, Santo, Maria, now!" Sinbad called. The three carpets unfurled to life and swooped through the windows. Santo first scooped up Rose Red and raced down to Goldi. Black Pinta went to Sinbad, and violet Maria went to Charming. The Bear Prince jumped on Maria with Charming, Snowy and Rose Red (after a quick embrace) sat on Santo with Goldi, and Sinbad stepped on black Pinta alone. The carpets rapidly ascended the way they entered.

Goldi yelled, "Sorry Duke, but you're a two-timing bastard!"

Silence in the Great Chamber. Broken by Duke Alfonso clapping his hands. Cries ring from the audience as the Rocs circle above. The Duke's voice booms, "Find ALL of them. Bring me their DEAD bodies!"

The carpets regrouped outside the Palazzo. Sinbad pointed where two Rocs were flying. Jack saw another one on the horizon. The fourth was not visible. The Bear Prince jumped on Goldi's carpet, Santo, the strongest of the flyers, and held Snowy and Rose from falling. Santo flew low, just over the narrow canals. Charming steered to the outside of the Venice boundaries and turned sharply, a Roc following him. Sinbad and Pinta flew straight for the clouds, approaching the direction of the Roc coming on the horizon. Jack took Nina to a medium height above the Grand Canal.

The Rocs closed.

"Slight left. Slight right. Slight lift. Quick dip!"

Jack's command directed Nina through the gondolas and masts of boats on the Grand Canal. As the canal which went through the entire city, this was the most crowded waterway. It was wide enough for a Roc to pick off something in the water.

"Good job, Nina. Thumbelina, anyone chasing us?"

"Not that I OH SHIT THERE'S ONE RIGHT BEHIND US!"

Jack saw the Roc's reflection in the canal.

"Steady Nina. Wait. Wait. Hard left! Hard left and straight!"

Nina took a sharp turn onto Rio Marin, a smaller, narrower canal. The Roc's claws grasped water instead of its prey. The bird flapped its wings and began to ascend.

Jack looked over his shoulder. The Roc was heading away from them, but with a few flaps of its wings turned quickly.

"The reports of their poor agility have been greatly exaggerated," Jack said. "Nina, another hard left."

The carpet turned down another narrow passage. The Roc saw them and adjusted its flight. This game of cat and mouse continued. Nina made her way, under Jack's direction, until they came onto the larger Giudecca Canal. Jack brought Nina above the water and briefly paused to rest. But a few moments later the Roc appeared at the same level they were. Then Nina was racing up the canal, in the reverse direction Charming had gone.

"I hope, Nina, we are the fastest."

Ahead, Prince Charming approached from the opposite direction. Nina had gotten ahead of

Charming, and they were doubling back. Charming's eyes were bulging. His Roc was closing.

"He's terrified," said Thumbelina.

"Hope he remembers what to do," Jack said. The two carpets, with the Rocs right behind them, raced towards each other. Just before contact, Jack commanded, "Hard Up!" Nina drove steeply skyward while Jack hung on, as did Thumbelina.

Charming—panicked.

"WE'RE DONE!"

Fortunately, Maria had the weakest hearing of the carpets and heard "We're Down!" She dove under the water.

Jack heard a pair of shrieks and felt the collision beneath him. Feathers floated by.

Jack and Thumbelina yelled "Hooray!" as they leveled the carpet to where Charming was floating on Maria.

Sinbad and Pinta appeared beside them. "Santo and the women are on their way to the ship. Maria's too wet to outmaneuver the Rocs, but she can make it back with Charming if we take care of the others, Jack. Time for you to go to church."

"Damn," Jack said. But there wasn't time to argue as another Roc had seen them. Nina flew off. They stayed low in a narrow alley. Jack watched the shadow of the Roc. It was pursuing them, keeping pace above, waiting for enough room to ambush them. Up ahead. the narrow alley opened to the Piazza San Marco, the largest and most open courtyard in Venice.

"Nina, the moment we have space, hard right and then way up!"

"That's two commands, Jack."

"I trust her."

They hit the open plaza. Nina hugged the corner of the buildings on the right. Jack saw the shadow overhead continue in a straight line.

"Nina, climb to that Roc's level," Jack ordered.

They did.

"Now stop."

They did, and were floating, a couple of hundred feet in front of the towering Campanile, high over the courtyard.

The Roc circled, somewhat confused by the suddenly stationary object. This confusion quickly abated as it made a large arc.

"He's coming," Thumbelina cried .

"I hoped so," Jack said. "Nina. Like we practiced. Slowly."

They approached the top of St. Mark's Campanile tower. Three windows opened on each of the four sides of its belfry, where the tower's church bells were housed.

"Jack, that Roc's getting closer!"

"Wait," Jack said. "Wait. Wait." Nina inched forward. Jack looked straight ahead.

"JACK!"

"Full speed Nina!"

Nina flew straight at the tower.

The Roc's jaws snapped, clipping one of Thumbelina's wings.

"Ouch!"

Part of Nina's fringe was also bitten off.

They were running into the tower.

"Hang on Thumbelina. Nina—Side roll—Now!"

Nina furled herself up, wrapping Jack and Thumbelina. The carpet slipped through a central upper window, gliding between the hanging bells, and flew out the corresponding opening on the other side of the tower.

Unfortunately for the Roc, it could neither change its size or direction, nor pass by the bells. Jack felt the force of the trailing Roc's head colliding with the bells.

Citizens on the outskirts of Venice were surprised and wondered why St. Mark Basilica's campane were ringing three minutes before noon.

Nina, Jack, and Thumbelina were flying over the Adriatic Sea. Jormungandr floated on the horizon.

"You did it Jack," Thumbelina said.

"We all did," Jack said, giving Nina a pat. She flipped tassels towards him.

"My wing is sore but—Oh no!"

She pointed skyward. Sinbad and jet-black Pinta were flying downward at a sharp angle towards the water, a Roc in pursuit. Jack recognized it.

"That one snatched the dolphin two days ago."

This was the largest of the four by far. The Roc was gliding about three body-lengths behind Pinta. Jack watched the creature flap its wings and close ground. Sinbad and Pinta switched into a complete nosedive.

"They won't make it," Thumbelina said.

"We're too far," Jack added helplessly.

Pinta and Sinbad made no effort to change their trajectory. They disappeared into and under the water. The Roc emitted a deafening screech before following them into the Adriatic Sea.

Then the sky was silent.

Nina floated in place for a while.

No one spoke.

And then—

"Jack—over there—"

Sinbad broke the water's surface, holding onto a rolled up, floating Pinta. Nina flew over and picked up both. Pinta remained furled. Sinbad took deep breaths and patted Pinta.

"Good job old friend."

Sinbad turned to Jack.

"You three didn't do too bad either."

Jack smirked. "You know, Sailor, funny thing about magic carpets. You must direct them, and they will fly for you. But if they do not trust you and you mess up, you're in the water."

Sinbad rubbed his forehead. "I'll try to remember that."

Jack assessed the mood on Jormungandr as quite celebratory. The Steadfast Tin Soldier, having been picked up in Venice by Santo, was having Snowy and Rose Red lubricate his joints with the richest Venetian oils. The Bear Prince, who had reverted to his human form (*Was that Brad Pitt?*), steered the helm, and smiled at his wife. Charming was sobbing with joy. Sinbad dried himself with towels. Jack thought even Mr. Dum and Mr. Dee had mild smiles on their faces. The magic carpets? They were sunning themselves on the deck.

As for Jack, he and Goldi were both tending to Thumbelina's bitten wing (which would regrow with enough seawater treatments).

"Ouch! Easy! Wings are sensitive."

"Sorry Thumbelina. These will need a lot of seawater. But we've got plenty. And Jack." Goldi touched Jack's shoulder. "I guess you are still nimble and quick."

"Not bad for an old guy."

Goldi's smiling expression darkened.

"Jack—there's something stirring in the waters ahead."

The water swirled and boiled. A serpentine head rose slowly from bubbling waters, until it towered above the caravel. The monster's wake rocked the boat, which began spinning.

"Jormungandr!" Sinbad yelled, slipping on the deck. "The Midgard Serpent."

Even the steady Steadfast Tin Soldier fell.

"What's he doing here?" Charming protested. "He's a Norse fable!"

Jack grabbed Goldi from falling overboard. "Tell him that!"

The serpent roared, a forked tongue darting from its jaws.

Jack saw Snowy sliding across the deck calling, "Hold tight! I may have a plaaaaaan."

Shahrazad stopped, stood up, and walked towards her bed chamber.

The Sultan called, "My dear, please, you can't stop there! I can't wait! What happened next? And what is your price?"

Before disappearing behind bedroom curtains, Shahrazad coyly said, "I did, you must, and the answer to your questions are Tales 1003 and 1004 of the Arabian Nights. Night Honey."

Every Rose Grows Merry in Time

By Kristen Argyres

I stroll across the moors toward town, the hem of my belted plaid kissing the purple heathers as I pass. The late summer breeze carries the sweet sounds of musicians practicing their songs and scents of freshly baked bread and treats. The wind sweeps my braid from my shoulder in its wake. Tents are pitched below in the hollow of the hills, people milling about like ants.

Of course, the Fair starts tomorrow. I must have lost track of time out in the wilderness. I cannot afford to have people who knew me from my previous life recognizing me in public, and the Fair is likely to draw at least a handful of my old neighbors. I could get arrested.

I spin on my heels toward the trees when a voice calls out to me.

"Leaving so soon, lass?"

I pause and rotate to better see the solicitor: an ancient woman with a cloud of wispy white hair protruding from her hair veil. She leans on a sturdy wooden cane, her back bent forward from years of labor.

No doubt she wants to sell me something. "The Fair isn't for me." I frown. I never particularly cared for chatting up strangers, and now that I live alone, I am disused to small talk.

"Scarborough Fair's got something for everyone, if you know where to look." She winks, dipping her head toward the activity below.

I ignore her. Supplies can wait. Winter has not yet come, and the crowds will disperse by September's end. I can always walk to another village if needs must.

The crone chuckles, amusement crinkling the corners of her misty eyes. She prods the gnarled knot at the end of her cane in my direction. "Come visit my tent tomorrow, lass. And bring that heart you carry with you."

A chill skitters down my spine. *How did she know?* I reach for my satchel, making sure my prized possession remains in its rightful place. A familiar lump fills my hand. I sigh with momentary relief, then whip around to confront the woman. "Who are you?"

No one hears me, not even the wind. She is gone.

Puzzled, I retire to the hills, nibbling the inside of my cheek. I rest my hand on my bag as I recall the fateful night I became the Maiden of the Moors. The screams, the flash of my blade, the way the light faded from Hendrie's eyes. I have no regrets. *I took what he owed me.*

A smile tugs at my lips, and I sing a line fit to the melody of the song the bards all sing about Hendrie and me. A tune which fails to recount his misdeeds, despite me accomplishing the impossible to please him: "Ne'er did he intend to be mine."

Come morning, the soft glow of my cambric shirt fades with the rising sun. People only recognize me at night, when the fabric fashioned by faerie magic casts a gentle light like the moon.

As I prepare to break my fast, my ears are assaulted by shouting vendors and tinkling bells, resonating as if I were in the thick of the Fair. I am comfortable with silence, but the sound of other people together carves me hollow.

I stir my oats with a wooden spurtle, my mouth set in a stubborn pout. *I will not go.* I mutter the words like a prayer, casting away spirits with malicious intent. Yet, as the sun rests upon the rowan branches overhead, I find myself on the road toward town, staring down the rutted dirt path.

Just for a moment, to satisfy my curiosity. That woman must be like me, treading the fine line between realms. How else could she disappear like that? I draw the hood of my cloak over my head and hug my bag close to my body. I do not worry about my prized possession being stolen, but rather, the panic its discovery would cause. Despite the rumors, the Maiden of the Moors can still be killed by a mob of angry townsfolk, and I intend to live a long life—if only out of spite.

Fair-goers flow down the aisles of tents and stalls like a current down the river. Ignoring the protestations of my growling stomach, I search for any signs of the old woman who approached me yesterday.

Tradesmen with brightly colored fabrics, exotic spices, and shining armor contrasted by more sensible bulk crops, boots, and tailored garments. I scrunch my nose at the intense odor of ale and spirits penetrating the air, complemented by buttery baked goods. My mouth waters.

A minstrel plucks the strings of his lute in a bawdy love song, eliciting tittering laughter from passers-by. I hop to one side to avoid a questionable puddle, keeping my belted plaid wrapped tightly around my body.

I wander the Fair in its entirety with nothing to show but new bruises from being jostled along with the surge of the crowd. Still no sign of the old woman. *She didn't give me any directions*, I groused. *I shouldn't have come.*

But then my attention is tugged toward an unmarked tent at the mouth of the final aisle of vendors' stalls.

I sucked in my cheeks, considering my options. This entire trip will have been a waste if I do not at least peek inside.

I push the flap aside, enter the dimly lit shelter, and wait for my eyes to adjust.

"Welcome, lass! I've been expecting you," a familiar voice greets me.

Shapes begin to take shape in the darkness. "You were hard enough to find," I huff, crossing my arms over my chest.

The crone extends a hand, inviting me to sit on a worn cushion across the cooking fire in the center of the tent. "Yet you still found me." Her wrinkled cheeks stretch in a mischievous grin. "I expect nothing less from the Maiden of the Moors."

I sit, keeping a wary eye on the old woman. "How did you know?"

"Like sees like, lass," she cackles, stoking the fire with a stick. The charred end tumbles into the flames, crumbling to ash among the burning coals.

My gaze flickers toward the wizened woman. Though her plaid is worn by the elements and constant use, it has held up well. Her stiff, jerky movement is natural for someone advanced in years. Try as I might, I do not sense anything out of the ordinary about her. "Who are you?"

The woman stares at me, eyes unflinching. "A friend," she says. "Or, at least, one in the making."

I purse my lips. I try from a different angle. "*What* are you?"

My host chuckles. "That, lass, is a question I can't quite answer." Her shoulders quirk. "Who knows what I am now? Certainly not a mortal woman anymore, but neither am I one of the Folk." She juts her chin toward me. "Same as you, dearie."

My heart sinks. I knew, of course. With so much time spent among the Folk, I must have lost pieces of my humanity along the way. I twirl a loose lock around my fingertip. "Why me?"

She leans forward, her wispy hair framing her face like a cloud. "Because you'll do anything to get what you want."

My chest tightens, her sharp tone like a knife in my periphery. "I made favorable deals, that's all." Nothing more, nothing less.

The crone tilts her head. "And what of the lover who scorned you after all you did to prove your devotion?"

I grind my teeth at the mention of Hendrie. She approached me, knowing who I am. Does she want me arrested or killed? My muscles tense.

"You killed the lad, plain and simple."

I did. My blood boils at the memory of the night I found Hendrie with another woman. The glint of my blade in the moonlight, the heat of his innards as I cracked bone and severed flesh and tendons. Jaw set, I crumple the skirt of my plaid in my hands to restrain myself. "I only claimed what was rightfully mine." My tone brooks no argument.

"Of course, lass." The crone's smile spans her entire face. With a wave of her hand, she cuts the tension in the air between us. "That's exactly why I chose you!" She draws back the tapestry behind her to reveal a pallet covered in white cloth. "I hope we can both get what we want."

I raise an inquisitive brow and angle my head to better see. "A corpse?"

"A fresh one." She withdraws her cane, allowing the curtain to fall back into place. "This person wanted to find true love before they died." The woman's pale eyes linger on my bag. "You have a spare heart. Perhaps you'd like a companion?"

I blink. "You think I can raise the dead?"

"You've made a shirt from moonlight, called rain forth in a drought, and found an acre of land at sea." The woman shrugs. "What's a little necromancy?"

I scoff. No one knows I received help from the fae for each impossible task: the little Folk of the moors, a cantankerous kelpie, and a troupe of playful selkies. I school my face, but my pulse thrums, thrilled at the prospect of a proper challenge. "Why should I?"

The woman exhales, puffing out her cheeks. "Owing a favor to a corpse gets complicated. To cast aside my debt, I must find a way to bring back the dead." She reclines against a crate behind her. "You're my best bet." Her pale eyes rest upon me, gleaming in the firelight. "I'll pay you handsomely, lass - and if we're lucky, this person just might fill that cavernous hole in your chest."

I rake my teeth over my lower lip, meditating on the knot in the pit of my stomach. I would not go so far as to hope for love. In the time it took me to accomplish my three tasks of faithfulness, Hendrie found another lover. A lass with flaxen hair and dimples when she smiled.

When I found them together in the field upon my return, rage stained my vision red. I unsheathed my dagger and plunged the blade into his chest to claim what was rightfully mine.

My pulse pounded like a war drum, drowning out the woman's screams as she fled toward the village. Hendrie's blood splattered hot against my skin as I carved out his heart. *My* heart. I severed flesh, cracked the ribs, and tore through glistening red muscle. The coppery tang of blood coated my tongue as I held my prize aloft, panting and grinning with satisfaction. I tilted my head and laughed, admiring the way the organ fit so perfectly in my palm. As if it was meant for me.

But my own heart stopped beating that day, too. As if Hendrie's betrayal broke it beyond repair. *I'm already branded a criminal, what do I have to lose?*

"I'll see what I can do."

The old woman claps with delight. "Marvelous! I've got most everything you'll need."

Bubbles burst on the surface of the thick poultice in my cauldron, a clay-colored reduction of eclectic ingredients my new friend supplied for the ritual. The mist clings to me, cool and damp against my skin.

I inspect my pile of components, double-checking everything is prepared. I will only have one shot at this, so I cannot afford to make mistakes. I glance toward the pallet, the body still concealed under a snow-white pall. The crone warned me not to peek. My fingers itch to unveil the corpse, but I have come too far to ruin my chances over something so trivial.

I never promised to keep him. If he's a nuisance, I can drop him off at the Fair – someone will make use of an extra pair of hands.

I turn to my brew and toss a bundle of herbs into the cauldron, breathe to life a spell of my own design, draped over the frame of the bards' song.

I shall make me a Scarborough Fair
Parsley, sage, rosemary, and thyme

As I stir in the leaves, I recall Hendrie's careless vow and my desire to escape its shadow.

Remember me to one I've slain there
Ne'er did he intend to be mine.

I think of how free I felt after murdering Hendrie. Among the glittering jewels of dew, my cambric shirt laid unsullied on the grass, despite the gore at my feet, plastered upon my dress. I tucked the garment away in my bag and wandered to a nearby stream, slipping out of my clothes to wipe the grime and blood from my skin and hair and from under my fingernails.

Once clean, I wrapped Hendrie's heart in my soiled frock and donned the cambric shirt instead. I sauntered through the moors on bare feet with the gentle light of my faerie gown guiding my path. I have wandered these hills like a lonely ghost ever since that night.

Bolstered by the memory of my resolve, I grab fistfuls of grain to add to my potion and chant, binding the ingredients with magic.

Barley, oats, wheat flour, and rye
All to blind the wandering eye

Never again will I suffer another man's contempt. All that worthless Hendrie did was green a woman's gown while I achieved greatness. I deserved more for my deeds - and I would claim all I desired within my grasp.

Flame and rain, fair breeze, and stone
To bind all flesh, muscle, and bone

I already have the flame, rain, and breeze, so I drop a few round stones into the cauldron. After a few rounds with my spurtle, the rocks skim the bottom of the pot with a sharp clink. Compared to commanding the ethereal light of the moon, crafting a body of human flesh is not so difficult. Of course, having an extra heart to spare makes things easier.

I gather my foraging basket and gently fold in handfuls of berries to the brew.

Rowan, sloe, blaeberry, and crow
To tend love's seed and make it grow

Tendrils of colored steam rise from the cauldron, snaking their way toward the pallet on which the body lies. *That's my cue.* I extract Hendrie's shriveled heart from its wrappings and gently place it into the cauldron. The organ absorbs the surrounding moisture, darkening to a deep blood-red. The heart beats to life.

I suck in a breath, the blood in my veins resonating with its pulse.

Every rose grows merry in time
Will you be a true love of mine?

The heart glows bright in a flash, then fades like a falling star.

I leap to my feet, cradling the heart in my hands. Kneeling beside the pallet, I slope forward, pressing the heart above the corpse's left breast. With each beat, it burrows deeper into the flesh until it disappears from sight.

I rock back to rest on my heels, anxiety clawing at my chest, stealing the breath from my lungs. Seconds become hours; I am a prisoner of time.

Then, the body beneath the cloth stirs - first the fingers, then an arm.

A soft sigh tickles my ears. I clap my hand to my mouth, stifling a gasp.

The woman sits upright, pressing the pall to her chest. Her dark eyes round, lips parted as she scans the scene. Our eyes meet as the first light of dawn dances across her face.

Ensorcelled by her stare, my mouth hangs open like a bronnie out of water. Never have I beheld anyone so beautiful.

She beams, her dark eyes twinkling, and caresses my cheek with slim fingers.

My heart thumps heavy in my chest, revived by her touch, and the sweet sound of her voice. I am overwhelmed in all the best ways. I assumed the person would be a man, but nothing in my life has ever felt so right.

Her laugh is clear and true, like a bell. "Aye, I'll be your true love." She pecks my cheek with her warm, soft lips. "You can call me Mary."

Rising Cinders

By Thony Mintz

I whisper in the swirl of cinders
By your sleeping little head.
Like I spoke in the scuttle of mice
To your mother, before she was dead.
You answer me when you kindle my hearth
And clean my walls and floors.
You carry me with you in singing, my girl,
Even beyond my doors.
Now, these step-people on my steps,
Traipsing along my halls:
Rude, to you, my pumpkin, my doll!
No.
I'll rouse all the glamor I've got, girl.
I'll magic you off to that ball.
Just set one last fire when you leave them.

I'll lock them in, and end your hassle.
Then you and me, think what we could do
With the stone and fire of a castle.

No Flower of Her Kindred

By Sasha Kielman

IT WASN'T SLEEP SHE feared. It was the nightmares.

She saw things she couldn't possibly remember. Bonfires. Not just spinning wheels and spindles, but whole villages, soldiers putting them to the torch for suspected rebellion or witchcraft. Women running, screaming, holding babies to their chests.

Her father, late at night, pored over documents, or sat hunched over a crystal ball, shadows creeping in the corners of his chamber, his study, even with a fire blazing.

Her mother, weeping, alone in her bed. She would never bear another child.

Aurelia could hardly look at them. What they did, they justified in the name of protecting her. She wanted to scream, but screaming was unladylike in general and particularly unbecoming of a princess whose parents had massacred their own citizens to ensure her survival. Screaming would do nothing to help those who were killed, those who lost their loved ones. And she could say nothing to her parents, who kept such violence far away from her by sending her to live among fairies in the forest.

So she avoided them. Barely met their gazes. Spent long hours in the chapel, clutching her rosary so hard her knuckles turned white. It was one of the few places she could find peace, where no one would disturb her. Where she could turn off her own mind and focus on breathing and repeating the words of the prayers over and over, feeling nothing save her own shaking.

The healthy forest girl was gone. Rosy cheeks, flowing hair, sparkling eyes? Princess Aurelia had none of those. The castle confined her as much as the bed had.

No one knew how long they had been asleep. Phillip claimed it was a few days, perhaps at most a week, but the magic--spells--curse--turned time such that Aurelia felt like she slept for a hundred years and still she was exhausted. She hardly even wanted to sing when she was allowed out of the castle and into the forest. The fairies did their best to cheer her, but she could barely eat. The juice of fresh berries, which she once loved so much, reminded her too much of blood.

"I do not fear magic." She snapped her book shut and rose from the table. "What I fear is once more being used as a pawn in someone else's game. Atrocities being done in my name. The vulnerable suffering while the nobility live life unaware."

"Is that how you felt, in the fairies' cottage, Princess?"

"That the nobility were generally unaware of our existence? Yes. And I was fine with that, at the time, not knowing the truth of my identity. But a sovereign is responsible for the care of each creature in their kingdom. Perhaps Maleficent would not have cursed me if the fairies had made overtures to her in the past. Or my parents. Or Prince Phillip's parents. Do you disagree, Lord Montblanc?"

The old Duke's title was fitting, for his hair was white as snow, and his skin nearly as pale, though with tinges of pink in his cheeks. He was kind, and wise, however, and Aurelia was grateful it was he who was assigned her politics and history tutor rather than some of her parents' other advisors. Though she could name nearly every plant that was safe to eat in their lands, her parents found her schooling lacking. She did not know the history of their House, nor anything of how to flatter courtiers and foreign nobility. She was a princess but did not know how to act like one.

"I do not disagree, my Princess. You must remember, however, there is conflicting advice on how to treat our magical brethren. Some prefer to be left alone, as you were with your godmothers. Others, like Maleficent, prefer to be flattered. It is hard to say how any particular witch or Fae will react until it is happening. And then, as you well know, it is far too late to make apologies."

"Are there no records of previous diplomatic engagements? Or lists of what has been previously given as gifts, so as not to give the same gift two years in a row?"

She knew there were records of other things. Such as the villages that were burned. The so-called witches and followers of Maleficent.

Lord Mountblanc chuckled. "You are wise beyond your years, my Princess. You will do well as Queen. It is well that you were raised among the fair folk, for you understand their ways and how they are like to take offense. I daresay King Hubert would never tell your mother if she gave him the same gift two years in a row."

"He'd laugh about it with my father though, I think. Or it would come out when they'd been drinking."

"That is true, I suppose." Lord Mountblanc's eyes twinkled and he stroked his chin. "I'll ask about records for you. I think that is enough for today. Until next time, my Princess."

She nodded as he bowed and kissed her hand before leaving the room.

She sighed. What had her parents been doing for the past eighteen years? Besides persecuting alleged followers of Maleficent or black magic users.

She would find out. And she would be a better queen.

Dear Philip,

Please do tell me all about your days. I want to hear every detail! Perhaps not every detail. But I missed so much of a so-called normal life, and I still have so much yet to learn. Tell me more about how your father governs your kingdom. I cannot wait to see you both again for Christmas. I know you are busy with your duties, and I treasure your letters. It is less than a year now until our wedding—I count the days.

Until the next, with all my heart, I am yours.

Aurelia

She enclosed her latest drawing, a mother bird in her nest with her eggs. It seemed silly, but Briar Rose wouldn't have given it a second thought to ask Fauna to give the bird her blessing, so Aurelia prayed for her in the chapel, that her eggs would hatch safely and her babies would be healthy and strong and that they could all grow up together as a family.

She missed the fairies. Or were they witches? Or Fae? Lord Mountblanc used all three terms in their lesson the prior day. There was still so much she needed to learn. And so few people willing to teach her. To even talk to her on an even level. So many people were either frightened of her or thought she was strange. And she knew she was. The cursed princess, raised in the forest by her fairy godmothers.

But the curse was gone, and here she was, no longer in the forest. She tried not to complain too much about how restrictive the heavy gowns and shoes and jewels were, and how difficult it was for her to be indoors so much. She was grateful to be alive, truly.

But she was so lonely.

The bonfire blazed in the town square, not too far from a fountain. The water wasn't flowing, but at least it was there, should the fire spread. The air was thick with smoke, and she tried to breathe quietly, blend in beneath her dark cloak. Her shoes, at least, were back to normal, thin dark leather suitable for the forest.

"Are there any witches in this village? If so, now is the time. Declare yourselves, register with the King and Queen, and we will leave in peace." A man, richly dressed on horseback, spoke from near the bonfire. He was well guarded by knights in full armor, some on horses, some on foot.

"There are no witches here, my Lord." A man, apart from the crowd, spoke up. He was eyeing the bonfire and the knights carefully. "We are honest, law-abiding citizens. But how will our women produce enough yarn to mend our clothes and keep us warm in the winter with no spinning wheels? Will the King and Queen send fabric to help?"

There was indeed a chill in the air. Aurelia could hear the wind whispering through the forest behind them.

"You will be compensated for your losses, yes, Monsieur Mayor," the Lord replied. He tossed the man a bag of coins. "Distribute this among your people."

"Thank you, my Lord." He clutched the bag to his chest, still looking back and forth between the bonfire and the knights. "Will that be all for tonight, my Lord?"

The Lord looked from the Mayor to the crowd.

"You have no witches here, Monsieur Mayor?"

"No, my Lord. We all attend Mass every Sunday. Abbe Pierre will attest to that."

"What about maidens? There is a mix of old and young in this village, is there not?"

"Yes, my Lord. We have maidens, and children, and widows, a mix of old and young, as you say."

Aurelia did not like this Lord's line of questioning. The Mayor was an honest man, it was plain to see. The crowd was growing restless; not just the wind was whispering around her.

"Very well. Bring me your most eligible maiden. I do not wish to sup alone tonight."

The Mayor swallowed. "My Lord, your offer of supper is very kind. Will you and your knights bring the young lady back home to her family at such a late hour tonight?"

The Lord slapped the Mayor in the face before Aurelia even realized it was happening. The slap was so loud the entire crowd heard it, and there were anguished cries and gasps.

"And here I was thinking you were a shrewd man, not bad for a country Mayor." The Lord sneered. The Mayor was cowering on the ground, still clutching the money bag to his chest. "Learn to do as you're told and keep your mouth shut in the presence of your betters. If you ever meet any of us again."

Before the Mayor could respond, the Lord was talking to the knights, and the crowd was running as the knights approached them.

Aurelia ran, too, not knowing where she was, or where she was going. She ran for the forest, even though it wasn't her forest. This forest's trees pointed in warning rather than in welcome. A raven looked down upon her as she entered. She ran until she could no longer hear anything except her own heart beating.

She stopped to catch her breath.

Something reached for her in the dark—

She woke up screaming.

The maidservants always tried to cheer her up the morning after a nightmare. Aurelia never told them what happened in her sleep, but upon looking in the mirror, the truth was plain across her face. No cosmetics could hide the dark circles under her eyes or replace the health she had lost, and they felt unnatural on her face anyway.

Getting lost in books would do her no good after such a nightmare. She needed to ride, to breathe fresh air, to feel as free as she once did. The harvest moon soon approached, and she could do so much more good helping a village than sitting in a castle.

She knew her way around the castle well enough by now. Would anyone notice she was missing, though? She asked for her hair to be plaited back, and dressed as simply as she could. No jewelry.

Once her ladies left, she hurriedly hid her journal and sketchbook under her dress, crept out of her room, and followed them to the servants' quarters. She only had to hide behind a tapestry once, and couldn't believe it actually worked.

From the servants' quarters, she found her way to the laundry, which was no longer fully staffed due to the hour. She grabbed a plain headscarf, and an apron, hiding her own shoes, and taking simple leather ones. From there, she headed to the kitchens, filling a basket with bread, cheese, and apples. No one stopped her; hardly anyone even looked at her, so set upon their tasks were they. Nor were they expecting to see a princess, one they hadn't seen grow up as they should have.

She made her way to the stables without incident. No groom was there; she did not stop to question her luck but saddled her favorite horse.

They flew through the yard and out the gates before anyone could stop them. Aurelia only breathed once they were approaching her beloved forest.

She breathed and with her exhale came her tears. She felt trapped by the fairies' worries while she was living with them, but that sensation was nothing compared to physically being trapped in the castle all the time. It was not befitting of a princess to wander around talking to strangers, especially those below her station, as she'd been informed many times. Plus the restrictive clothing—she could not go barefoot or underdressed—and the etiquette expectations, and the weight of history.

She tied her horse to a tree limb and sank to the ground, not even taking out her sketchbook or snacks before she closed her eyes and fell asleep.

A dark castle loomed in the distance. Ravens cawed overhead.

A great queen held court in her throne room. A group of women stood before her, bent by age or fear. Their clothes were threadbare, their eyes bloodshot.

"How many villages have been burned so far?" the queen asked. No, she was not just a queen—she was a fairy, a dark one.

What were these women doing with Maleficent?

"Five villages are represented among us," an older woman at the front of the pack answered. "There may be more with no survivors."

"That damn fool," Maleficent replied. "Burning people will not stop me. Nor will it save his kingdom." Her gaze was not upon the women before her, but off into the distance.

Slowly, she turned back to the quaking humans before her, her right hand gripping her scepter. "I cannot give the gift of magic to those upon whom it was not bestowed. But I can offer you shelter in my lands, such as they are. Women have no need to fear violent men here."

"Thank you, Your Majesty," the lead woman said. "I accept your offer of shelter for myself. I cannot speak for everyone here."

Maleficent only nodded, keeping the elder woman's gaze. "There is work to be done here in my castle for those who wish to serve. Otherwise, there is land you may farm. My servants and subjects will not harm you. I declare it so." She brought her scepter down against the ground, and magic went out from it. A raven flew down and landed on her throne's left arm.

"My servant here will escort you out of the castle and to safe lands." She gestured, and the raven flew around the throne to Maleficent's right, then turned back and cawed at the women. They followed, some shuffling, some crying.

Maleficent sighed, her eyes glowing.

Aurelia awakened. She looked up to the sun to gauge how much time had passed. Only about two hours, she surmised. Sighing, she tried to collect her thoughts. Was she touched by magic? How was she seeing these scenes from the past in her dreams? Was this part of the curse?

Her horse lay beside her, and she reached over to stroke it before grabbing an apple and biting into it. There was no one in whom she could confide save Phillip, and she could write none of this in a letter. Christmas was still months away. Who could she trust besides kindly old Lord Montblanc? He was wise, but he knew little of magic.

For the first time, she regretted that Phillip had killed Maleficent to save her. She could not have trusted the witch, but she would have answered her questions, even if the answers were skewed in her own favor.

Aurelia sighed. How would her parents react if she told them she was touched by a magic of some sort? She had already been touched by magic when her fairy god-mothers gave their blessings when she was born. And when Maleficent cursed her in turn. And again during the enchanted sleep.

But she never had nightmares growing up in the cottage, and the enchanted sleep had been peaceful and dreamless.

What had changed?

Maleficent's defeat. Her entire life.

If Maleficent was dead, who reigned over her lands to the north? Who was protecting the women who sought shelter there?

Aurelia stood, brushing off her skirt. She swallowed some water before untying and mounting her horse once more. She had not brought enough food for such a journey, but she would make do with what she could find in the forest. She had a good nose for mushrooms, and she could eat berries without having to look at them.

She rode as hard and as fast as she dared push her beloved mare. They rested close together at night, and though she bore no sword and shield, she feared no evil.

She had already faced evil.

She would not say she defeated it. Not yet, not while she still did not have the answers she sought.

Three days and three nights passed before she reached the edge of her parents' domain, following the path Phillip had told her about. Thankfully, he, unlike her parents, never questioned her curiosity. Maleficent's lands lay directly ahead to the north. The mountains loomed over her as if daring her to cross the veil and approach.

Aurelia swallowed, straightened her spine, and urged her horse forward.

Crossing the veil was not as unpleasant as she feared; the hairs on her arms stood on edge, her ears rang and then popped, and she had a sense of a sort of current running through her body as gossamer passed over her.

It was over in an instant. She blinked, taking in her surroundings. Though the terrain was rocky, and the trees already shed most of their leaves, the land was not as desolate and unfamiliar as she feared. It did not match Phillip's description. Perhaps the landscape had changed since Maleficent's death.

Or, perhaps, the veil created a glamour or spell.

It was quiet as she rode towards the castle. Ravens cawed overhead, but she saw no other living creatures. All her senses were on alert. She could feel the magic emanating from this place. And yet she was unafraid. She had been cursed. She would be queen. She had nothing to fear from whatever may have lurked in the shadows.

The castle wall's doors opened as she approached, though she saw no one upon the walls, or within the bailey. She did not dare search for a stable; she dismounted and stroked her horse's mane, trusting that she would not abandon her.

And if there was no one around, no one could harm her.

Taking a deep breath, Aurelia stepped inside the castle.

The great hall was empty; the passageways leading to other rooms and towers dark. Yet it was clean; no vermin skittered about, nor were there cobwebs lurking in the corners.

She stepped forward into the center of the great hall, a dark throne looming ahead.

She tried to imagine the hall like that of her parents'. Full of life and courtiers scurrying to and fro, colored banners strung from the rafters and rugs upon the floor to help keep out the approaching winter chill.

It was easy to imagine the castle was beautiful. It did not match the image of its prior occupant, however. She could not imagine Maleficent welcoming many courtiers to her home.

She was certainly not being welcomed now, not that she expected she would be. But for the castle to be completely empty? No castle was ever empty, not even in a time of war.

She stepped forward, at first tentatively, then more confidently. She held her head high, imagining she was wearing a crown and beautiful robes.

She sat upon the throne, and for the first time since she had learned the truth of who she was, she felt powerful. She was a princess. She would be queen.

Magic went out from the throne. How it happened, Aurelia could not say. A bright light and wind sped away from her, disappearing into the darkness.

All was silent for a moment, and then around the room, torches in wall sconces began to glow with an ethereal light. The walls and floor seemed brighter, as if dust and dirt were wiped away.

Aurelia considered the magic for a moment. It did not match the kind of magic for which Maleficent had been known, which all accounts agreed was dark magic.

The sounds of footsteps and voices began to enter the room.

"Is it true? Can it be?"

One older woman and one younger were at the head of the crowd, a group of about ten women ranging in age and size.

"Who are you to dare to sit upon Maleficent's throne?" the older woman demanded, drawing herself up straight, although she was not very tall.

Aurelia stepped down from the throne. "I am Princess Aurelia," she replied, her voice sounding more confident than she felt. "I came here looking for answers."

The older woman was not impressed. "Answers you shall have, Princess. As best as we are able. And then you shall depart henceforth. Those of your House are not wanted here."

"I can understand why. But I had nothing to do with my father driving you out from your lands."

"So you do know something, at least." The older woman put a hand on her hip. "Tell us, how do we know you won't banish us from here as well?"

"I won't. I have no reason to do so or to harm you at all. My father does not know you're here. Nor does he know I'm here."

"You expect us to trust you with just those words?"

Aurelia resisted the urge to sigh. She held out her hands. "I have no weapons. I came here alone; my horse is tied outside. I barely have any food provisions left. Should I not have prepared better if I wanted to do you harm?"

"Let us hear what she has to say, Nora," the younger woman at the front of the crowd said to the elder. "We can at least do that before sending her away." A few of the others nodded.

Nora turned back to her. "Very well, Princess. Why are you here?"

Aurelia met her eyes and took a breath before she began. "I've been having dreams. Visions, really. Of spinning wheels burning, villages burning, of women being persecuted. I would have no other way of knowing any of this happened. I was raised in seclusion by fairies in the forest. I had no idea there was such suffering after Maleficent's curse until I started having these dreams."

"Well, now you know," Nora replied. "Almost all of us lost loved ones in your father's witch burnings."

"I am sorry for your losses." Aurelia bowed her head and placed a hand to her heart. "I grieve that I was the cause of such horrors. But I don't understand why I'm having these dreams now. Why I'm seeing things I couldn't possibly have seen. How I was even able to pass through the veil and find you without a fairy helping me."

"You've been touched by magic more than once in your life, Princess," the younger woman said, eagerly. "Perhaps it has finally unlocked your own latent gift."

"There is no history of magic in my family, though." Her brow furrowed. *At least of which I know.* Those records could be disguised or destroyed as well. Paper burned even more easily than wood.

"You were able to bring the castle back to life," the younger woman continued, gesturing around them. "It's been dormant since Maleficent died."

Aurelia swallowed before asking her next question. "And you all have been alone here without your queen? How have you fared?"

"Many of her followers with whom you'd be more familiar have moved on," Nora answered. "The ogres are all gone, having left to find a new master. Anything she conjured with her magic died with her. The wards, and the veil, as you say, have held and kept us safe. At least until now."

Aurelia nodded. "I am glad to hear you have been well protected. No one will do you harm here, I promise."

"And how will you explain to your father where you've been when you return to your lands?" Nora retorted.

Returning to the castle filled Aurelia with dread. The heavy dresses and jewelry, the confinement, the expectations... She was not in a hurry to return, though she was certain her absence had long been discovered. Perhaps sharing this with the women would help her gain their trust.

"I am not going to return with haste. I miss the forest, and my freedom," she began. "I will tell my father most of the truth: that I feel too confined in the castle and wanted to spend time in the forest to clear my head. He does not need to know that I came here, nor will he."

At this, Nora's hard eyes indeed seemed to soften. She nodded, though not as stiffly as she had been holding herself.

"Let us show you our lands," the younger woman said. She reached a hand over to Nora and one out to Aurelia. "Come, see for yourself what we have built, away from the cruelty of the wider world."

"I would very much appreciate that," Aurelia said in reply.

Nora sighed. "Very well."

"I am Lucy," the younger woman said, smiling widely as they walked from the throne room. She eagerly introduced Aurelia to the rest of the group; some were more friendly than others, but Aurelia was grateful she managed to get at least Lucy to welcome her.

As they walked from the back of the castle out into fields leading up to the mountains, Aurelia found herself more at ease. There was a vegetable garden behind the castle's kitchens, and she could hear the ravens cawing overhead. Nature seemed more welcoming than it had leading up to the castle, a clear deterrence for outsiders to never reach this place of peace. There was a small village where the women built their homes, with children playing outside and others tending to daily chores. Cows and goats grazed in a patch near the village, and a vineyard was not too far off.

It was a peaceful life, and one Aurelia could not help but envy. This was what she thought her life would be, before her fateful birthday. A quiet one, where she sang in the forest and tended to the lives around her.

She swallowed and realized her eyes were beginning to fill with tears. "It's beautiful," she managed to say softly to Lucy. They were at the back of the group, trailing behind some of the others who were returning to their homes, their interest in what was happening in the empty castle sated.

Lucy reached over and squeezed her hand. "It's a simple life, Princess. But it's what we've built for ourselves."

"It's the life I thought I would lead," she said, looking down at the ground for fear her tears would give her away. "I can't bear the thought of being trapped in a castle for the rest of my life."

"So don't be," Nora said, turning around to face them. "Prove yourself to us. Work hard, and we will allow you to stay."

Aurelia's eyes widened. "You said those of my House were not welcome here."

"They're not," Nora replied flatly. "But you're not one of them, not really, since you were raised in the forest. And you clearly have a magical gift, whether you know what it is or not. There're a few healers and midwives among us who might be able to teach you their ways. Perhaps you'll learn something from some of Lady Maleficent's old books. Who knows?" She shrugged. "I may not be trusting, not after what I've seen. But the more women we can protect and welcome here, the more I think we should."

Next to Aurelia, Lucy's grin was radiant. "Come, Princess, let us see what else you can do in the castle. Perhaps its halls will be welcoming to all manner of magical creatures once more."

Aurelia managed to nod, while Lucy grabbed her hand, dragging her back inside, with Nora and a few others following.

They went from room to room, asking Aurelia to try different hand gestures and thoughts. Wherever they went, the castle awakened; flames sprung to hearths and candles, and dust and cobwebs disappeared. Several books in the great library called out to her as if begging to be released from their shelves. One woman brought blankets and made up the queen's suite, although Aurelia's choice of decor would have been vastly different from Maleficent's. It was of no matter, however; she had slept under trees and the open sky, and if she was indeed to stay, she would have plenty of time to fashion a home of her choosing.

It was a thrilling thought, one that also frightened her. What would they do if they were discovered by her father? Would magic she didn't even know how to use be enough to help?

After a long day, she fell into the bed with even more questions than answers she had received. But her dreams were quiet, and her heart peaceful.

The next morning, she awakened feeling refreshed and energized in a way she had not since she began living in her parents' castle. The color had returned to her cheeks, and there were no dark circles under her eyes.

As she went about the day, greeting the women she met the day before, meeting many of the other villagers, and learning about magic, she felt at peace. She could help these people, unlike her feelings of powerlessness over the past few months. She felt centered in the earth, helping work the soil and clean the castle. She felt centered in herself and her capabilities--here she was not constrained by courtly roles.

She went to bed that night realizing she had not missed her family at all.

Her crown was made of berries and branches; flowers were twined in her hair. Her feet were bare, and her dress had no trailing sleeves, nor overflowing skirts. The throne room was filled with joyous faces, fairies, and even a few animals.

"All hail Queen Aurelia."

She sat down on the throne that was now rightly hers. The new queen smiled for the first time in months.

The Beauty of the Beast

By Emily Rozmus

SHE HEARD HER SLEEVE rip and felt a breeze cool against her shoulder. His hand was heavy on her neck now, squeezing her throat just a little, almost in tempo with his rapid breath. She met each kiss with her lips, tongue, and teeth, but he always pushed more. He was the predator.

Mary had agreed to go in the closet with him, after all. When the green glass bottle pointed to her, she shrugged, looked across the circle, and held out her hand. Dolph took it, and they walked like royalty amidst the cheers of their court. She turned once, glancing at Drew and Lacy still sitting cross-legged in the circle. Drew's face was mostly hidden in shadows, but she could see her mouth twist in a sneer. Mary realized what they thought didn't matter, turned, and focused on their destination.

Playing spin the bottle had been Hef's idea. He was wearing a red bandana on his head. After the dance ended, he had shed his jacket, and he looked like a pirate with his white shirt unbuttoned and untucked, his black pants low on his hips. And a bandana tied on his head. "Let's play a game," he said, smirking. His side-eye caught Dolph, who sputtered, spitting out the champagne he guzzled from the bottle. The label itself was worth more than Mary's dress.

"A game? What have you got in mind?" Dolph laughed.

Hef took the empty bottle from Dolph's hand. He held it aloft and shook it. "We've got a bottle. Any ideas?"

Dolph grinned and grabbed it back from his friend. "We're not twelve anymore, Hef. We don't need to play games to get laid, do we?"

Everyone laughed at Dolph, his dark complexion flushed with the effects of alcohol, but his demeanor was poised as ever. In the end, he was the one who decided the game was worth their time. Even if they didn't need to play a game to get laid, they could still use it to fuck around.

Which was how Mary ended up with Dolph in the closet. Their breath steamed the space filled with fur coats and ski equipment. Playthings of the rich.

He was bold, but she was just as determined. It didn't matter how much he pushed. Mary knew how to handle a boy. She wasn't shy.

She had arrived at the afterparty with Clint, but it didn't take long to realize who she showed up with didn't matter. Not at Fox Hall.

Clint was nice and all. They sat next to each other in geometry, and he was a math wiz. Not that Mary couldn't hold her own. She only acted stupid. She had found over the years, in new school after new school, that smart didn't win friends or invite popularity. So she hid her brain and flaunted her beauty instead.

"You mean this formula works for any right triangle? No matter what the other angles' measures are?" She didn't need false eyelashes. She could flutter her own like butterflies caught in a hurricane. Clint leaned over her desk, his pencil scratching the theorem out, his blue eyes like puddles in the morning after a rain. He was sweet and dull, but he was also a date to the Fall Formal. Though she had plenty of new friends—Drew and Lacy were top-notch—she had yet to score when it came to boys. She was a junior, and this year at Piedmont Prep was the first she was without the most popular, good-looking male at her side.

Clint would do. And he did. She let him unbutton her shirt on their first date, his hands soft and cool. She pushed him away before her bra came off, though. Mary knew how to play the game. She had a strategy.

As sweet and soft as Clint was, he hadn't been her first choice. Oh, no.

Her first day at Piedmont, Dolph Fox caught her eye, leaning against the hall outside the gym. He was dark-haired and had coal-black eyes. Her own Dad would call Dolph "Black Irish," heralding her with the story of her great-great-grandparents leaving Donegal and taking with them their Spanish blood and Irish hunger. Whether Black Irish or not, the Foxes had never left anywhere hungry. She could tell by the way he tilted his head, listening to the girl who was in a deep discussion with him, her hands spiraling and long blonde hair moving like waves of wheat.

Oh. You, Mary thought. *You'll do.*

But he was as emphatically engaged with the blonde girl, Simpson Malley. They weren't dating, she learned. But Simpson was in Dolph's court. Mary was barely over the drawbridge.

Mary wasn't jealous. She was persistent. She had to be. She knew her place in the halls of places like Piedmont Prep. She was new. Her family was well-to-do, but newly so. They moved a lot. She had learned a long time ago how to make sure she made her way to where she belonged.

Moving from one school to another had taught Mary that survival wasn't the prize. She only played to win. In fifth grade, Mary had beat out Stacy Murray, Friends Ambassador of Foster Prep Primary, the student everyone looked up to. Mary didn't hold back on Stacy. She assessed her opponent, watching her in action to learn how to beat her. It only took one error, and Mary made her move. When Stacy scowled at Janah Garcia because she answered a question correctly after Stacy couldn't, Mary tearfully shared her disappointment with the teacher. The teacher watched Stacy after that, writing notes now and then when she observed Stacy's face in reaction to her peers. Many notes later, Stacy was asked to step down. Of course, Mary accepted the title of Foster Friends Ambassador, representing their school at the next tri-city summit.

And now, at Piedmont? Simpson Malley wouldn't know what hit her.

Mary's Dad told her that she was as good as anyone else. He bought her whatever she wanted, intent that she fit in. No—not just fit in. Frank Riley made sure his daughter stood out. She was a beauty after all, some of the Black Irish blood still evident in her dark skin and hair. The night of the Fall Formal, Mary donned her dress, posed with Clint, and smiled for photos in the front hall of their house in the best neighborhood in the town. Mary's father watched her slip into Clint's Porsche, slim and svelte in a simple blue velvet dress.

Her mother, God bless her, stood quietly by. Pamela's approval was nice, but Mary didn't need it. She waved at Dad, blowing a kiss through the window.

Mary turned and smiled at Clint, his boy-next-door good looks highlighted in the ultraviolet blue light from the radio. Clint was a gentleman. He was nice. But he wasn't Dolph.

Clint lifted her hand, kissing it with those dry, cool lips, and Mary looked at the blood-red rose on her wrist.

When her father traveled for work, he asked what each of his daughters wanted. Her sisters asked for dresses and jewelry. But Mary only wanted his attention. She asked for the same thing each time he left on a trip for the Hunt Company.

"I want a rose, Daddy. Just a beautiful rose." And every time he left to travel the world, he promised her he would bring just that.

Mary smiled at the flower Clint had brought her. It only confirmed that she was on track. This was her night.

Simpson Malley had the flu. She slid down in the seat, relaxed and sure that her path to dominance would be established before the night was over.

When the bottle pointed at Mary, she wasn't surprised. All night, she had seen Dolph looking at her. She danced slowly with Clint, her face tucked between his neck and shoulder, but she felt eyes on her back and she knew. When the lights came on in the gym, Dolph came to them. "After Party at my house," he said. "No need to bring anything. I've got it all." He smiled at them, but Mary saw his dark eyes slide to her.

Clint was used to Piedmont afterparties. "C'mon, Mary. Let's just go back to my place. My parents are in Europe. We can be alone all night."

Mary could have laughed in his face. She had already told Lacy and Drew she'd be at Dolph's. Instead, she simpered, "Let's just go for a little bit. I don't want anyone to think I'm rude!"

Clint agreed, of course.

And the party was all she expected to be. Mary hid her awe at the gate surrounding the estate, the intercom entry system. Fox Hall was massive, and the entrance hall was full of life-size portraits of men with Dolph's graveyard black eyes. The party was taking place under their noses, but somehow, Mary knew the Fox men didn't mind.

There were a slew of people, all from the right crowd. Lacy and Drew pulled Mary to the side when she and Clint arrived, giggling. They were both relatively new at Piedmont too but had established their place in the hierarchy. She had met both of them at the meet and greet at her father's new high-profile sales job for the Hunt Company. The small but elite company had recently been bought out by Fox Conglomerate. Drew and Lacy's fathers worked for the Hunt Company too. Mary had sipped Shirley Temples with the two girls while they gave her the lowdown.

Drew was a blonde, but her brown eyes were ringed with dark black lashes that she had to trim when they got too long. She had arrived two months before Mary. "Dolph Fox is the hottest guy at Piedmont," she said. "He has the best parties. I haven't been yet, but the rumor is the Fall Formal party is the one." Mary could tell she was interested in Dolph. Her eyes narrowed and she smiled.

Lacy jumped in. "She's right. Dolph's dad runs Fox Conglomerate. He's the reason we're all here. Our dads, I mean." She finished her Shirley Temple and pulled the stem off her maraschino cherry. "Dolph Fox is the biggest catch you can make. And thanks to Hunt Company, we get in on the chase." She winked. Lacy was as outgoing as Mary, but Mary had noticed earlier how she hung on her dad's arm, and he cuddled her as if she were just a child.

Mary always assessed her competition. Lacy and Drew were pretty and rich, just like Mary. But as the two other girls shared their accomplishments, trips to Europe, and hopes for Ivy League schools, Mary knew they were very different from her. She didn't have any *hopes*. Mary was already a legacy at three of the top schools. She spoke French and German after she studied abroad. Mary had her own accomplishments memorized. She didn't have to worry when it came to Drew and Lacy, especially not about Dolph Fox.

As Mary walked through Randolph Fox IV's palatial home, she took note of every girl there. She noticed what they wore, and who they were with. Clint disappeared to find her a drink, and she stood to the side, watching. Waiting too. She noticed one girl who was unfamiliar. Definitely not from Piedmont. She had silky auburn hair and a golden slip dress. When she smiled at her date, Mary felt something twist inside.

Hef sidled up to her, his shirt undone and the red bandana low over his brow. "So, new girl. Tell me a little somethin' about yourself." He was a step in the right direction, Mary knew. She was quiet before she turned to him. His green eyes flashed. "This is the fourth place I've lived in 17 years." She watched Clint approach, two beers in his hands. "I have three older sisters. They're all in Ivy League schools. I don't like beer," she said taking the bottle from Clint. "But I love champagne." She turned, winked at Hef, and then drank the whole bottle. "But in a pinch, this'll do."

Clint, ever attentive, made note of what his date really wanted and left to find champagne. And luckily for him, there was plenty. Just short of a fountain, the bartender (bartender, Mary noted) popped cork after cork. "Kind of like you, Hef!" another member of the pack, Trystan Martin kidded. "Poppin' cherries and corks wherever you go!" The party cheered as one, and the bubbles floated them all to the ceiling and beyond.

Turned out that Clint didn't like champagne. He was kneeling by the toilet before two AM. Mary gave him a wet washcloth and made sure he was propped up and not flat on his back. Clint was like a little puppy, and Mary loved a sweet little cuddly pet. When she was sure he was safe, she left him, checking her makeup in the mirror. She could handle her champagne, and despite several glasses, she looked as fresh as she had when she climbed into Clint's Porsche. Her black hair was sleek and shiny. Her green eyes were perfectly lined. That Black Irish blood gave her skin the perfect glow. She liked sweet puppies like Clint. But she craved the wild animal she sensed lived inside of Dolph Fox.

And now, in the closet with the very prey she had hunted, she knew she had been right. He was exotic. He was not tame, not domesticated. Simpson may have the public version of Dolph, but Mary knew that the real Dolph was with her now, hungrily kissing her and tearing the blue velvet dress.

"Mary," he said, pulling away from her, "I believe I have found my match. Where have you been all my life?" In the dark closet, she could feel his warm breath and could see his dark eyes flashing. She ran her hands through his thick black hair. A low growl came from deep in his throat and it made her knees weak.

"Doesn't matter where I've been. Only that I'm here now, Dolph. Seems like this was fate, you know. "She sighed as he nuzzled her neck, his teeth grazing her flesh and his tongue finding the pulse of her carotid artery.

"I could eat you alive," he whispered. A loud knock on the door pulled his hot mouth away from the delicate skin of her throat. "Damn," he said. "I guess our time is up."

"Hey, stop hogging the closet, Fox!" It was Hef's voice, but Mary could hear the rest of the remaining party members yelling catcalls. It didn't faze Mary a bit. She had earned her spot in the closet, and when she was done, she'd earn her place outside it. By Dolph's side. Running with his pack.

Dolph pulled back but didn't let go of Mary. "If I had my way, we'd stay in here all night. But we have to play by the rules, right? Else what's the point in playing games?"

"If you say so," Mary said. She straightened Dolph's collar. "Who knows, maybe we can play for real when the game's over." She raised her green eyes to his black eyes. There was a flash, a moment where he seemed like something else, more feral. Wild. Not a boy.

When they opened the door, Hef jumped on top of Dolph, tackling him to the ground. Dolph, grinning, turned over, pinning Hef underneath him. "Where's your ascot, Hef?" Dolph asked.

"Lost it in a game of spin the bottle," he said. "Good thing I still have my smoking jacket. Wouldn't want the bunnies to forget who I am." The two wrestled until Trystan poured his bottle of beer on them.

"Are we done with this game?" He leaned over and pulled Hef and Dolph up. "Thought there was gonna be other... entertainment." Trystan turned and looked at the people left at the party. Most seemed to have left while Mary was in the closet. Drew and Lacy were still there, but where was Clint? Mary turned to Dolph who stood close behind her, brushing himself off after his tussle with Hef.

"Looks like I'm stranded," Mary said. "My date left!"

Dolph didn't seem surprised. "You're right. Hef suggested he leave. He got a ride with Paisley and Demitri. Terrance and Shanna. Yep, they all went home."

Mary wasn't surprised either. She looked around, pleased with the thought that she was left standing after so many had fallen back. "So, what do we do now? This has to be the elite group, right?" She smiled at Drew and Lacy. Behind them, Mary could see the graceful girl in the golden dress. Dolph's hand, warm and smooth, wrapped around the back of her neck, pulling Mary gently to him.

"This *is* the elite group," his mouth was close to her ear. His breath was hot against her skin. Mary was barely aware of Hef with his arms around Lacy and Drew. Trystan stood to the right of the girl in the back, and Mary thought she saw at least one other boy in the dark shadows of the room.

"Hef and Trystan love this part of the elite group, don't you?" Dolph pulled back from Mary, but his hand stayed firm, his thumb pressing against her shoulder. It felt good, until it hurt. But she wouldn't pull away. This was what she wanted. "We've been forming the group for a while now." Dolph said, "but it used to be just James and me."

The shadowed figure stepped forward and Mary saw that the other male looked just like Dolph, tall and dark. "Meet my little brother. He's too uncivilized for school," Dolph grinned, and his incisors seemed sharper than usual. "Our father has a tutor for him here, at Fox Hall. Right, James?" Mary watched James as Dolph spoke and noted that he seemed less than impressed by his older brother. Despite James' size and frame, he looked smaller in stature, almost rodent-like next to Dolph, his eyes narrowed and his mouth moving though there were no sounds.

"Just you and me, Dolph," James said. "Until Father decided otherwise." Even in the shadows, Mary could see that James was wary of Hef and Trystan. She wondered what their father had to do with who Dolph's friends were. Maybe it had something to do with James. Mary thought about the word Dolph had used to describe his younger brother. Uncivilized. In a house this big, this grand, what did that word mean, exactly?

Abruptly, Hef grabbed Mary around the waist. She was startled, but didn't pull away. She wanted to be sure they knew she was up for anything. "So, you all ready for a different game?" He asked. "There are four girls and four boys. Just what this game needs." Mary glanced at Drew and Lacy. Trystan stood between them, his arms draped around their shoulders. The girl Mary didn't know stepped forward.

"Lana," Dolph said, "I forgot. You probably don't know the others. He walked over to her, and Mary was instantly jealous. It wasn't often that Mary felt insecure, but this girl was definitely competition. Her long auburn hair framed her flawless face, almost angelic in the candlelight of Fox Hall. Her golden dress glowed in the night, a taper in the dark.

"Lana's dad works for Fox Conglomerate too, but she doesn't go to Piedmont. She's over at Excel Prep." Dolph held her hand, pulling her into the circle. "So, everyone here is a Fox, in some way or another." Mary heard James in the shadows, sighing or laughing. She couldn't tell. It was strange the way the brothers seemed at odds. Even she and her sisters, despite their competition, could cooperate with each other when the situation called for it.

"So, the game," Dolph said. "It's pretty simple. We don't need anything special. There are very few rules. We'll go over them later." He was holding Lana's hand, and Mary felt Hef's arm tighten around her waist just as she saw Dolph pull Lana closer. "It might seem strange at first, but trust me, this game will be the best you have ever played in your life." He grinned and Mary noticed that his incisors were big. Kind of long. Had it always been that way?

"We call it Fox Hunt. Funny, huh? My family has been playing it for generations. Before we even came to America. My Dad taught it to James and me when we turned 13. And since Trystan and Hef's dads work for Fox, we taught it to them." Trystan made a sound low in his throat, and Mary watched as Lacy pulled away—or tried to—and he pulled her closer to him, pinning her to his side."

"What—how do we play?" Mary asked. She was up for this. "I'm ready." She shook her long, black hair and stepped forward, pulling away from Hef.

Dolph was handsome in the low light, his eyes intense. "I knew you would be, Mary. I've been watching you for a while." She felt his words in her stomach, a slow burn.

Of course, he had, she thought. *It always goes my way.*

"There's always a winner, even in Fox Hunt." Dolph's eyes were darker now, like a bottomless loch. "To start, ladies, we have to blindfold you. Don't worry. You can trust us." He nodded to Hef and Trystan, who pulled scarves from their pockets. "James," he said to his brother who still hung back," come over here and blindfold Lana. I've got Mary."

She walked to him with no argument, but Mary heard a commotion behind her. "I'm not sure I want to play." It was Lacy.

Figures, thought Mary. *Lacy was a child.*

"I'll just sit this game out. Okay? I think I'm getting a headache. Is there a place I can call my dad to come and get me?" Dolph continued to tie the scarf around Mary's eyes, even as he replied to Lacy.

"Your Dad wants you to stay, Lacy. He knows all about Fox Hunt. In fact, he may be invited here someday to play it too." So intent was she on getting Dolph, in being number one, Mary hadn't blinked an eye at any of the night's events. An aggressive make-out session with Dolph in the closet? Perfect. Clint conveniently leaving her behind? Ideal. Being singled out in the elite group. Dreamworthy.

But what did Dolph mean about Lacy's dad knowing about Fox Hunt and wanting her to stay? Mary was confused, and though she was in the dark now, she could still hear Lacy's heavy breathing. "But I really...I mean..." Lacy said. Mary heard a little gasp and then a small whimper. What was happening?

"Dolph," Mary said, "maybe we can let Lacy just sit this game out." She spoke in the direction she imagined Dolph to be, but his answer came from behind her.

"Sorry, Mary. There's no sitting this game out." She felt hands grab her arms and let out a quiet "oh" of surprise. With the scarf tied around her eyes, she could see light, but no images. She heard similar sounds around her of the others being blindfolded, quiet murmurs of dissent, but then Lacy screamed.

"Let me fucking go! Right now. I said I didn't want to play!" Then there was the sound of muffled cries. Someone pulled Mary by the hand, and she walked in obedience. But a part of her wondered if she should scream or try to run.

The sound of others walking assured her that they were all being led to the game. The game. This was no big deal, she thought. Mary realized how dumb she was being about this. They all were. This was just boys being boys. Scare the girls and get them all emotional and then reassure them with a makeup session. She realized she was slouching, and stood up straight, pushing her shoulders back and holding her head up.

"Oh Mary," Dolph said quietly. "I knew you would be the one to beat in this game. Just you wait. You'll have more fun than anyone." She smiled at his encouragement.

"I've never been one to turn down a challenge," she said blindly.

"Good. I knew I could count on you." She felt his lips soft on hers as they stopped walking. "Keep that in mind.

I'll see you in a bit." With that, he gently pushed her back. She could sense the other girls nearby.

"Just be calm," Dolph said. "As soon as you hear the door shut, you can take off your blindfolds. We'll be back to get you soon."

The sound of the door clicking shut seemed like a finality. It was quiet, but firm. As she took the scarf away from her eyes, she felt one of the girls push past her. In the dim room, she saw Lacy, turning the doorknob and pulling it, willing it to open. Lacy had a scarf tied around her mouth as well. She was sobbing and making high-pitched groans.

The girl Lana stepped up to Lacy, placing her hands on her shoulders. "Come on, now." She untied the scarf from Lacy's mouth and put her hand up instantly to quiet her. "Just stay calm. This is no reason to panic. We have to stick together, and if we can keep our wits, no matter what happens, we'll all be okay."

Mary was instantly annoyed by Lana. "It's just a game. I'm playing to win," she said. Mary wasn't a pushover. Her older sisters had teased her constantly. As the youngest, she was the target of bullying and verbal abuse from three older sisters who were constantly vying to be the best and get Daddy's attention. Mary was used to challenges from other girls. "Scary Mary, Hairy Mary." Her sisters taunted her. "Geez, why don't you just jump off a cliff? You can't possibly be one of us," they said. Her older sisters were blonde and petite. They played the piano and rode horses. Mary was the opposite with her dark looks and tall form. She had never let them get the best of her. She wasn't going to let this girl beat her either.

Lana turned to Mary, her angelic face stern and stony.

"Ok, I hear you. I get that you are sure this is just a game. We don't know much here, but we do know that we are being forced to play and that we are currently locked in a—" she looked around at their surroundings "some kind of chamber?"

It did look like some kind of chamber from a castle, but then, Fox Hall looked like a fortress. The walls were stacked stone. Mary could see the door they came through—broad and wooden, but directly across from it was another closed wood door. Lana walked to it, tugged at the handle. It was locked. The girl walked past Mary, who stepped back as if to let her pass by without sullying her. Tugging on the handle of the door they had used to enter yielded the same results. Locked. It still didn't faze Mary. "They're just being boys. Trying to scare us. I am not falling for it." It was chilly in the chamber, and Mary rubbed her arms to get warm.

"What did they mean? That my dad knows about this? My dad wouldn't want me to be treated this way!" Lacy's voice rose, ending in a sob.

"Don't worry. They're going to come and let us out and then laugh. Try to get us all emotional and then get some ass from it." Mary laughed. "It's a joke!" She thought about Dolph's words, his assurance that she hadn't let him down.

Drew hadn't made a peep the entire time. Now she stood, arms crossed in the damp, dimly lit chamber. "You're an idiot, Mary. You think you are so freaking *smart* and *better* than the rest of us. Truth is, the minute you showed up, I knew exactly who you *are*. Boys just being boys? Great. Whatever this is, it's absolute bullshit. I want out of here now. You can stay, be Dolph's lay, and believe it's gonna get you somewhere." Drew turned and took Lacy's hand. "We are leaving. As soon as this door opens—"

And it did.

The other door, the one they hadn't used to enter the room, opened. A man walked in. *Of course*, Mary thought.

Drew immediately rushed to him. "Let us out. We don't want to be here. Lacy told them while we were still in the house that we don't want to play." She tried to push past him, but he put out his arm to stop her. He was tall and broad, and it was easy to stop Drew. She was half his size. She was wearing heels. She was just a girl.

Mary almost moved to help her, but then pulled back. She didn't need any other girls. They were competition. Drew had mentioned more than once she was interested in Dolph. Mary was sticking to her game.

Lana moved instead, and she pulled Drew back. "Hey, we just wanna go home," she said to the man. "We're cold and tired, and we're just not up for any games..." The man seemed to be listening. He nodded his head, standing still in front of the door.

"Of course, I understand. You see, I can't let you go right now—" He was interrupted by a loud screech. It was Lacy.

"Get me out of heeerrreeee! I want to go home!" She sank to her knees, and Drew knelt by her.

"Ladies, if you follow me, I'll take you outside. And I'll go over the rules. You see, we've gone past any point of turning back." He was stoic and Mary knew it had to be part of the act. This was all so dramatic. She practically rolled her eyes. All she knew was she was out to win. She remembered Dolph's warm, hungry kisses. Drew might think this was all bullshit, that Mary was just a piece of ass. But Mary *was* smarter. She *was* better. This night belonged to her.

She stepped up to the man, "I'm ready," she said. "Let's play."

He turned to the other three girls. "Come on, now. If you come ready to play, you'll get a head start. You're going to want one. *Toose mawh lah na hib-reh.*" His voice had a slight accent. Maybe Irish. His tweed jacket and the dark cap on his graying hair fit the lilt of his commands. Mary didn't fear anything from him. He looked like someone's grandpa.

"Here's the thing. When I open this door, you need to be ready. Take your shoes off now. You'll need to run, you see. Split up. Do not stay together. You'll only make it easier—well, easier for them to win. And ladies, there's always a winner. The Heir chooses, you see. If he wants you to win, you'll know." He stopped, took his hat off, and wiped his forehead.

"Please, mister. My dad wants me home. He said 'don't be late...'" Lacy tried one last time.

"Girl, your da knows what you're doing tonight. You see, his role at Fox Conglomerate is all contingent on tonight. You're a pawn in a bigger game." He seemed sad, speaking softly. Mary felt a moment of uncertainty, wondering what he meant. "Now. Run."

He opened the wide door, stood to the side, and raised his arm to urge the girls forward. Mary strode through the opening, out into the dark November night. She didn't look to see what Lacy, Lana, or Drew did. If her father was relying on her, she would make him proud. There was a winner in this game, and Mary didn't lose. Her blue velvet dress was the same color as the post-midnight sky. It was cold, but there were worse things than a little frost.

And the minute she stepped outside, she heard one of those things.

It was a howl. An animal's deep throaty cry. As if that weren't enough, the first was followed by several other howls. Mary's own voice was frozen. She was unable to speak or move.

This was the game.

A dark figure ran by her, to the left of the girls. Drew turned and tried to get back inside, but the door was shut and the grandfatherly man was gone. "What—what's going on?" She said. She sniffled softly, but her tears were nothing compared to Lacy's sobs.

"Daaaaddddy!" she called, falling to her knees. She had taken her shoes off, as the man had said. They stood on gravel and the tiny rocks cut into Mary's feet through her strappy sandals. They had to be rough on Lacy's legs. "I want to go home!"

At that moment, two shadows emerged from the dark around them, becoming the outlines of the boys. At least that's what Mary thought. But as her eyes focused in the night, she realized that what she thought were the boys didn't appear to be the same as she had last seen them. They stood upright, sure. They were wearing some semblance of the clothes they had on originally. One still wore a red bandana. But in the light of the moon, full and bright, Mary realized something wasn't right.

The boys weren't boys anymore. They were covered in hair—fur? They stood on haunches, like a wild animal. In the moonlight, she could see their snouts with mouths full of white teeth, long, sharp. They glinted in the night's dim light, like icicles on frozen trees. It was strangely beautiful. She stood with the rest of the girls, colder than the air around them. Four girls were entranced by the sight before them.

"It's like a fairy tale," she said, and her teeth chattered in the cold night air. She felt rooted to her spot, watching the beasts close in on the girls, but adrenaline kicked in when another howl ripped through the night. "Run!" The grandfatherly man's words echoed in Mary's brain.

Mary turned away from the wooded area to their left and headed for the road. All she could think of was escape. She would run. This was like a fairy tale, but she wasn't going to wait to be rescued by any knight. She bent to finally remove her shoes but stopped at the commotion she heard in the dark.

She could hear a scuffle in the gravel behind her and turned her head briefly. Drew's silver dress sparkled in the moonlight, a spotlight for her final act. One of the creatures—*not Hef, Mary thought crazily—he's not wearing the bandana*—was dancing with Drew. Dancing? No, not quite. He held her up, his arms... paws clutching her closer. But his snout was buried in her neck and there was a sound of something wet and messy, like a dog chewing on a bone. This was beyond any competition she had imagined.

Mary stood with her stiletto heels in hand. She saw how Drew seemed to fall into a silver puddle in the gravel, how the creature's long snout rose to the full moon above. She considered attacking it, stabbing it with her silver heels, but there was no time, and Mary left Drew behind. Lacy had already disappeared, and Lana's golden dress was a blur near the tree line. This was the game, she thought. Run. Run. Run.

It seemed she ran forever when her feet finally found a grassy surface. She felt a sense of relief when her sore feet, bleeding now from the rocks she ran on, were cushioned in the lush grass of Fox Hall grounds. She tried to remember the layout of the estate, but in her excitement, she hadn't paid attention while Clint drove them down the long and winding lane to the house. She vaguely remembered a fence. More like a gate, iron, tall with spikes. There had been a small cottage near the entrance. A caretaker's house? Was that where the man lived? Was there someone there who could help?

She ran on in the dark, aware of the sounds around her. She heard howls, but nothing else. No screams, no cries for help. And thankfully, she didn't see anyone. Or anything.

In the midst of flight, she found herself crying. This night was crazy and unreal, but she didn't cry because she was scared. Mary was crying because she was damn disappointed. This was supposed to be her night! The night she finally came out victorious. She would go home and let her father know she was dating Dolph Fox.

Daddy didn't play favorites, but it was clear he had expectations of his daughters.

Now, she ran, ran, ran through a garden of rose bushes, bare of everything but their thorns in the cold night. For a moment, she could swear she smelled roses, the ghost of their aroma. She felt the thorns grab at her legs and tear and puncture the skin. She was bleeding. *It will only make it easier for them to smell me. To catch me*, she thought.

In the dark, she saw a light. It wasn't far, maybe thirty yards. She remembered winning the 100-yard dash at Foster, pushing past every other girl in her class. Mary could do this. In the distance, she heard someone yelling. It propelled her forward, closer to the light so she could see it came from the small cottage near the gates. She would get help here. She had to.

Someone inside extinguished the light as Mary approached the house. She was at the rear of the small, stone structure, and the windows were dark now, heavy curtains pulled over their panes. Mary ran to the front, beating on the solid wood door. In the drama of the moment, she noticed the trimmed bushes by the front door, a door knocker shaped like a harp. "Help! Help me," she screamed.

It occurred to her as she was begging for help that whoever was inside this neat and tidy house was more than likely involved in whatever this game was. She had a moment of rational thought—the first since she had seen that animal eat Drew. Animal or just a boy being a boy. It no longer mattered. She felt helpless being hunted, with no way to protect herself. No means of escape. Everyone here was in on the game.

She pounded on the door several more times, but it did no good. Mary looked around her. She thought she remembered the gate surrounding the estate being close to this cottage. She imagined the inhabitants were in charge of opening and closing it when the intercom buzzed. She ran in the direction she believed to be the way out, the sound of her breathing nothing compared to a long howl. It broke the night's cold silence, the last note of it trilling over the screams of another girl. One more down, she thought. There were only two left in the game.

The night was bright, and Mary had no doubt she was making herself an easy catch. The thought made her stop, lean over, and laugh hysterically. *Hadn't that been the plan all along?* she thought. An easy catch. The beauty who would rule Piedmont on the arm of its king. But Dolph wasn't a king. He was nothing of the sort. He was a beast. A killer. An animal.

But Mary felt his kisses, his bites on her neck. In the midst of their time in the closet, its playful and teasing roughness, she had felt as beautiful as she ever had been. That she brought out such wildness in him made her feel in control.

The old man had said there was a winner. He said the Heir would choose the winner.

It could be me, Mary thought, her breathing slowing. *I can still make this the night I've waited for.* The heir had to be Dolph. He was the oldest Fox. And he had hinted all night that he had his eye on her. That she stood out.

She was the winner. He would choose her.

She stood tall, pushing her hair back from her face. The last scream had come from the woods, and Mary headed that way, intent on facing the pack that hunted her. She knew Drew was gone—she had witnessed her failure. And another scream not long ago. So at least two were dead. Could be more if the third girl was caught unaware.

She strode, no longer running blind, her eyes and ears were in tune with the night's velvet stillness. There was no sound other than her own harsh breaths. She could see dark shadows, bushes and trees. But there was nothing else around her. No one was near. She kept walking, her feet sore, but steady in the cold, wet grass. The bright moon didn't matter to Mary. She had her own quarry now. If this was a game, she needed the light to play.

"Dolph!" she yelled as she approached the edge of the woods. "Hey, Heir! I'm here!" she stopped and looked around, turning a full circle in the moonlight. "Dolph," Mary was quieter now. "Who wins this game?"

In the shadows, Mary saw a shadow crouching, close to the ground. She turned, and there were two more shadows walking on four limbs, coming from her left. "Yeah, come on. Let's play." She whispered. She saw one still had the absurd bandana on, so she knew it was Hef. It was clear the other had killed someone. She could tell by his red, bloody muzzle. Trystan?

The lone shadow, close to the ground crawled to her, its back hunched and the fur quivering in the night. It crept closer, and as it neared, she could see its mouth, open and slavering, teeth white and wicked sharp. The monster spoke, its voice gravelly and grating.

"Un-civ-i-lized." Its long tongue lolled, cynically and teasing.

James. Mary knew this was Dolph's little brother. *Uncivilized.* This beast before her was more dangerous than any of them. She breathed in deeply, and in the frigid cold, Mary smelled summer. Once again, the sweet scent of roses seemed to linger in the air.

Autumn returned with a loud crack to her right. The sound of brush and bushes breaking made her swivel her head. In the dark, she could make out a figure on two feet, golden and glowing. It was Lana in the yellow dress, she realized. It was just her and this girl, an unknown enemy.

"Hey," Lana hissed, her eyes moving from Mary over to the creatures in the shadows. "Come with me. Let's see if we can climb the fence." Lana held her hand out to Mary, reaching. Mary could see sticks and leaves in her long, silky hair. She could see one of her hands was bloody and had smeared across her dress. She looked pathetic. She looked like the loser of this game.

"Go on. Try to escape." Mary shrugged. "There's one winner of this game. You can run while you realize who it is, but I'm staying right here." Mary yelled out the Heir's name again. The animals to her left growled. The crouching beast in the dark let out a sound that eerily seemed like laughter.

Mary ignored the sinister sound of a beast laughing. She watched Lana shift from one foot to the other, nervous and unsure. She was a loser, Mary realized. So weak.

"Dolph," she called again. "We're here!" she would show Lana what confidence looked like. She would prove to the brothers that she was certain of victory.

"I'm here, Mary," Dolph's voice called. She turned toward the house to see him as she had always seen him. His dark good looks were masked in shadow, but he was a boy—just a beautiful boy. "You're ready for the game to end, I take it." He walked closer to where she and Lana stood.

"You told us there's always one winner. I'm done with running. Just end the game. Choose the right girl." She glanced over her shoulder and watched as a shadow moved behind Lana. She knew Hef and Trystan were still on her left side, away from Lana. The creature stalking behind her had to be James. In the moonlight, the figure stood on its hind legs over the girl in the yellow dress. She could see its snout, its ragged ears starkly against the glow of the moon. The monster's silhouette was ghastly, wild, and raw. She felt a thrill at the thought of besting this beast.

"So smart, Mary, "Dolph said. She turned to him, the boy she wanted to impress. He was in a white sweater and black pants, no evidence of a beast. She walked closer to him, making her intentions clear.

"I'm tired of playing around. Let's finish." Mary pivoted so Dolph's line of vision fell on Lana. Mary's eyes stayed on his face, so handsome. He smiled, and his teeth were sharp, like knives. The rest of him appeared as it always did, but even now, there were signs that he couldn't be trusted.

"We're both here, but there's only one winner," she said. Mary waited for James to make his move and attack the girl in the golden dress. He was fully visible now, towering over Lana, and Mary could tell from her hunched posture that her final opponent was aware of the monster behind her.

Her father's last trip was two weeks ago. They never knew where he went. Mary wasn't really even sure what he actually did for work. But he always came home, his hair greyer, his face more lined. As always, he had gifts. Her older sisters, complaining over glasses of wine, took the necklaces he offered. Always so greedy.

For Mary, he had a single rose. It was lavender, golden at its tips. "So rare," her father told her. She received it gratefully, bringing it to her nose. But there was no scent. It was as if the flower was a void. She looked at her father, her eyes showing disappointment.

"Sometimes beauty comes with a price," he said. "Sometimes the loveliest of all lacks what we most expect from it." She put it down on the table and pushed it back toward him.

He could always see her better than anyone else.

"You are a confident girl. A heck of a player, Mary." Dolph said. He walked toward her, and she straightened waiting for him to recognize her as the winner. Daddy thought she was shallow. Lacked inner beauty. Well, the heir of Fox Conglomerate didn't think so. She smiled as he stopped next to her, reaching out her hand. Dolph took it. And pulled sharply. She pulled back. Dolph grabbed her by the arm and yanked—dragged her toward Lana and James.

Mary slid on the wet grass, her heart beating like a bird in a cage. "Wait! What—"

But Dolph didn't wait, even when Mary lost her footing and fell to her knees. They were steps away from Lana, still hunched, her arms around her torso. Behind her loomed the beast, and the moon shone on them all.

"*Tá tú caillte, Muire.*" Dolph walked away from Mary, still on her knees. She watched him walk to Lana.

"*Buaiteoir gealgháireach.* Come with me. We'll get you inside. Warm and safe." Dolph gently took Lana's hands and pulled her to him. He leaned over, swept his arm under her legs, and carried her away.

In the dirt, Mary watched their departure. Behind her, she knew the beast waited, and as it came closer to kill her, she could smell it. But it wasn't the scent of death—blood and musk.

It was roses.

Following the Breadcrumbs

By Avery Timmons

Here goes.

Hansel raised a fist to the wooden door, his knuckles just barely skimming its splintered surface. His stomach twisted itself into knots. His mouth was dry and sticky. If it hadn't been for Alma and their children standing just behind him on the stoop, he might have lowered his fist and walked away.

But instead, he rapped his knuckles against the door three times.

It immediately opened.

There was no mistaking that the woman standing in the doorway was his sister Gretel. She was no longer the eighteen-year-old girl she was when Hansel saw her last, of course—the years had clearly taken their toll on her. Her gaunt face no longer had any of its youthful softness, and her once long, thick hair was now thin and fragile, falling to her shoulders.

But when she smiled and it lit her big, blue eyes just as it did when they were children, before their relationship began to crumble, guilt squeezed his heart. Maybe he hadn't done either of them a favor by keeping his distance.

"Hansel." Even her voice was the same: low and warm. "I was worried you didn't get my letter. Come in, come in."

She stepped off to the side so the family of four could walk into the cottage, the skirt of her long dress swishing across the tops of her bare feet. Distantly, Hansel could hear introductions being made, but he couldn't bring himself to join the conversation. He was too distracted by the cottage.

It wasn't at all what he expected. Guilt snuck its claws deeper into him.

Clearly, his sister had been doing well for herself. While just big enough for one person, with every room visible from the living room they stood in, it was… warm. Homey. A fire crackled in the brick fireplace. The rich, mouth-watering scent of cooking meat drifted in from the kitchen. Decorative vines were draped across the walls.

But the one big difference Hansel couldn't help but notice was the lack of photos. Unlike his own home, where Alma had littered their walls and any flat surface, really, with framed photos of the family—Hansel and Alma on their wedding day, young and grinning from ear-to-ear, the children at each stage of their lives.

There were even photos of Alma when she was young, with her parents. Everywhere you turned, there was a reminder that you stood in a home where family was cherished.

Gretel's alone-ness was starkly obvious.

Despite it, she stood back and clapped her hands together, grinning from ear-to-ear as her gaze roamed over her nephew and nieces.

"Well," she said. "You arrived at the perfect time. Why don't you take your places at the table? Dinner shouldn't be but a few more minutes."

"Would you like any help?" Alma offered, but Gretel waved her off before darting into the kitchen. As the children ran to claim their places at the tiny, circular dining room table that appeared to be for two but had six chairs crammed around it, Alma sidestepped toward Hansel.

"She seems nice," she whispered.

Hansel just nodded. He had never intended to imply otherwise. His sister always *had* been nice. There were just things that he couldn't get out of his mind when he looked at her—nothing that was even her fault.

Once they were all situated around the table, practically sitting shoulder-to-shoulder, Gretel came out with plates of steaming food balanced on her arms like a seasoned waitress. The meal of meat, green beans and carrots, and a glistening buttery roll looked delicious; Hansel's mouth watered as Gretel set the plate down in front of him.

"Thank you." He managed to get his first words to her out, lifting his gaze to hers, but she didn't look back at him.

Only once Gretel was back with her own plate did they dive in. The group settled into quiet as they ate, with nothing more than the sound of forks clinking against ceramic plates. The meal tasted just as beautifully as Hansel imagined, and even the children—notoriously picky eaters, all three of them—devoured their food.

Yet as he ate, Hansel couldn't shake the feeling that something just wasn't right.

"The meat is excellent," Alma said. Her hand lingered in front of her mouth as she chewed. "So tender. Any chance you could give me your secret recipe?"

Gretel's eyes glimmered, her lips stretching into a toothy grin. Not quite pride, no. Something darker.

Something that Hansel didn't like. Something that reminded him of...

No. He shook the thought from his head and forced himself to swallow. Of course, being reunited with his sister after all these years, he would be reminded of what drove them apart in the first place: the witch. Yes, Gretel had obsessed over it, while Hansel had chosen to bury it deep down and never speak of it again, but Gretel was nothing like that wicked woman.

"It wouldn't be a secret, then, would it?" Gretel asked.

She met Hansel's eyes across the table. A chill slithered down his spine.

No, *no*. He couldn't let himself go back there; not now, not while they were trying to enjoy a meal. Not while he was trying to make up for so many years lost and repair his relationship with his sister, which he never should have let crumble in the first place.

He just needed a moment to clear his head.

And if that included taking a look around to be absolutely sure something wasn't wrong, then so be it.

"Um, Gretel," he said, slowly lowering his fork. "Where's your restroom?"

She pointed over her shoulder. "Through the kitchen, to the left, and down the hallway. I can show you, if you'd like."

Hansel was already standing. "No, no. I'll manage."

Through the kitchen, to the left, and down the hallway. The instructions were simple enough. But when he reached the doorway where he was supposed to turn left, his gaze pulled right, and that same chill crept over him, lifting the hair on his arms.

At the end of the hall was a wide, silver door. A walk-in freezer, from the looks of it. Hanging off the handle was a golden padlock, but it was unlatched.

Why would one woman need such a large freezer?

It wasn't necessarily malicious. It was an impressively large freezer; if Gretel came to check on him, he could just tell her he wanted to take a look because he was thinking of getting one himself. But it sounded like she was occupied; the girls were babbling, telling her about school.

As he stepped closer to the door, memories flashed through his mind like a film reel: shiny, silver cage bars; piles of smooth, yellowing bones; the heavy, black door of a brick oven.

Gretel wasn't the witch.

But what *if...*

A gasp pulled itself from Hansel once he opened the freezer door. He quickly realized his mistake as silence fell over the other room—they heard him. Yet even as his mind begged him to go, to shut the freezer, gather his wife and children, and get the hell out of there, his body wouldn't cooperate, his limbs remaining frozen. Bile burned in his throat. Even his eyes couldn't draw themselves from the severed human limbs that scattered the freezer shelves.

"Hansel."

He didn't turn at the sound of his sister's voice. He couldn't.

"Hansel. We don't have to turn this into a big fuss. Alma and your children loved the meal. You wouldn't want them to know the truth, would you? You wouldn't want to traumatize them just like we were, would you?"

Hansel whirled. But when he spoke, he kept his voice hushed; he hated it, but she was right. He would rather be the one to bear this newfound knowledge alone. He hadn't worked all these years to make sure his children had the childhood he and Gretel never had, only to screw it up.

Gretel had done that. Sick, twisted Gretel.

He had coped with their near-death experience by locking everything in, by distancing himself from all reminders of the witch, including his own sister. But his guilt dissipated now—now that he realized that Gretel had coped by turning into the witch herself, moving out to a secluded cottage and— and *eating* people.

Had she killed them herself, too? Had she invited Hansel and his wonderful Alma, his three beautiful, incredible children, to drive them to the same fate?

Was he about to relive the worst experience he had ever been through?

"We are going to walk out of this house right now," he hissed. "And we are never going to come back. I should've never brought them here in the first place. I should've burned that letter of yours."

Gretel smiled. But this time, Hansel didn't second-guess the wickedness in it.

"I already invited everyone for Christmas. You aren't really going to tell your children why you made poor Auntie Gretel spend Christmas all alone, are you?"

"You're sadistic."

"Or should I tell them? Actually, *maybe* I should tell them how Daddy runs and hides when things get hard."

Hansel's hands shook. His stomach churned. He didn't know quite what to do, but he did know three things:

All of this was his fault, but he had to do *something*, because those limbs in the freezer—

They were far too small to be from an adult.

Hansel stepped out of the freezer. Gretel smiled, triumphant, but her smile vanished when Hansel grabbed her by the upper arms and spun them around.

"No!" Gretel snarled. "Let me *go,* you bastard!"

She was stronger than Hansel had expected. They struggled for a long moment, but when Hansel pictured Gretel tying up his own children, adrenaline burst through him. He shoved her into the freezer; she stumbled back and fell against a shelf, an arm and a limbless torso falling to the floor with her. But by the time she managed to scramble to her feet, Hansel was already shouldering the door shut and securing the padlock.

"Hansel!" Gretel's scream was muffled and transported him back to when they were children. "Let me out *now*, Hansel!"

In her blood-curdling scream, he could hear the witch's howl.

Free Fall

By Kristen Argyres

THE BREATH IS STOLEN from my lungs, my clothes and hair lashing above me as I plummet toward the ground. In my stomach, the fragile wings of butterflies tear from their tiny bodies, my fears fluttering away with them.

I tumble to the earth as memories crackle past as if lodged within bolts of lightning. A spindle. A sprawling valley of lush greenery, viewed from high above. Smooth, polished stones that sparkle like gems in the moonlight.

Enormous boulders below beckon me, but we never collide.

I dream of terrifying bliss every night—and every morning, I wake in my ivory tower with the rosy dawn spilling in from the very same window which calls out to me in sleep.

At first light, servants arrive to dress me in my finery. Soft silks and gleaming gold and jewelry in every color, an elaborate crown of twisted metal high upon my brow. I am a queen now, though I have no memory of meeting my esteemed spouse for the first time. When I woke to find him there one night, he acted as if he knew me. As if I ought to know him.

The prince whisked the twins and me away in a carriage one day, surrounded by a legion of armored soldiers. My husband claims he rescued us, though from what danger, I could not say. All I know is I must not remove the wedding band on my finger. So, why do I yearn to return to those ruins?

Two children who call me "mother" greet me each morning. Their pleasant smiles, flaxen hair, and shining eyes reflect my own. No doubt they are mine. Yet, just as I lack an image of my wedding or exchanging vows with my husband, I have no recollection of the twins growing in my belly or the pangs of childbirth.

Why?

No one answers my questions. Servants flash me pitying smiles and offer kind, gentle words as if I am a wounded animal at risk of flight.

Sometimes, I believe it. I must truly be mad to not recall such important things. So, I eat and drink and smile and dance when prompted despite the insistent tug at the back of my mind that something is wrong. I ignore the itch between my shoulders and the dreams in which I never hit the ground.

Perched on a throne beside my husband, I stare blankly at the ring he gave me upon our alleged engagement. Wrapped around my finger, a filigree of gold contains a garnet, whose deep red hue stokes an ember in my mind, casting familiar shadows across the backs of my eyelids.

A sharp ache overcomes me like a dagger. I shift my crown to rub my temples, my vision growing hazy.

He turns and smiles. "Is something wrong, darling?"

I shake my head, my stomach somersaulting with violent knots at the sight of him. A glimpse of a figure looming over me, a pressure on my hand. A shiver of nausea coats my skin with gooseflesh.

Why?

I stumble to my feet and excuse myself. I am queen; I can leave whenever I please. Or, so I thought.

Servants lead me straight to my room in the tallest tower of the castle. They draw a bath with aromatic oils and scented soaps. A woman offers me wine from a crystal carafe.

I guzzle it down to dull the pain.

Another pair of women pat me dry and braid my long hair and dress me in a nightgown. As the sun dips to kiss the western horizon, heads bow to dismiss themselves from my presence.

I should be pleased, surrounded by luxuries and delicacies, but I cannot drown this nagging dread in strong wine. I blink, finally recognizing this place as a gilded cage.

My gaze falls upon the eastern window with its high stone arch. I grin and snatch up the crystal carafe. With a crash, glass shatters in a tinkling symphony of falling stars.

A gentle breeze summons me, and I step upon the sharp shards without a care. My blood sings as a gust sweeps my skirts out over the ledge, thrumming life into my veins. I am drunk on a sensation far more potent than wine. *This feels right.*

I lean forward, and my dream begins anew. Air sweeps my locks from my face with a pleasurable sting upon my skin. No memories dart across my vision, but sunlight catches the glittering facets of garnet on my left hand. I pry the gem free from my finger and let it fall.

The sun dips behind the mountains, shrouding me in the jagged shadow of their peaks.

My skin stretches too tight as memories flood my mind.

My false body yields, snapping and tearing to reveal scales and fangs and claws. I unfurl my wings, catching the wind to sail over the stark-white tower of my captivity. Flight lifts my heavy heart high, and my spirit ascends toward the clouds.

Voices cry out in alarm at the base of the castle. Arrows and flames bounce off my beautiful scales and litter the ground like kindling.

I do not look back, not even when the king shouts demands for my return.

Instead, I soar on strong, leathery wings into the dusky plum sky. I taste the crisp air as I bellow an ecstatic refrain of freedom. I am not the sleeping beauty the mortals so desired. I am the dragon - and I shall not be kept.

THE LEFTOVERS OF LITTLE RED

BY A. WELLS

Little Red was never the same
Not after the accident
Not after the Wolf

She still looks the same
Small for her age
Supple skin
Dark eyes

But she's different
Quiet and alone
Never quite present
Ever observant and aware

There's something else
Something churning
Waiting and wanting
Longing for something

No one cares to know
No one wants to know

But it's there
It will be forever
If anyone were to ask Little Red would tell them

She would say it's an envy
A boiling rage
A nasty abyss inside her

She would say she hates the Woodsman
For he killed the Wolf
He got to cut its skin
Hear its cries
Not her

DOES SHE MISS IT?

BY A. WELLS

Does the little mermaid ever miss the ocean?
Does she ever look into the vast sea and yearn
to feel its cool embrace?
When she hears the crashing of waves,
feels the droplets splash her cheeks,
does she crave?

I mean, she must, right?
It was her home for
years
That water holds all of her memories,
Everything that she once was is in that ocean

Not just that, but her family still
calls the sapphire water their home

She will never see them again,
not after the choice she's made

Do you think her family holds some type of anger?
Do they lay awake at night wishing
that she had chosen them?
Whenever they miss her,
does that sadness turn to rage,
do they avoid the ocean's surface?

I couldn't blame them
Humans stole away their home,
Killed their people out of curiosity,
Polluted their waters without a second thought

And yet, she chose the humans
She chose to live amongst
murderers, polluters, takers
Traded her fins for legs in hopes of something new

 I wonder if it was worth it?
If she ever regrets her choice,
If she dreams of what once
was

Does she ever feel alone?
Living amongst creatures alien to her
Going through everyday knowing that she's different
It must be very painful

But it's what she chose

And she can never go back

ABOUT THE AUTHORS

KRISTEN ARGYRES

Kristen is from the Midwest, USA. Her loves include family, TTRPGs, and chocolate. She lives with her wife, their two children, and their clumsy cat.

Kristen is published in several Dragon Soul Press and Wild Ink anthologies. Her romantasy, "My Thorns For Your Roses" debuts through Conquest Publishing Spring 2026.

Amie Glazier

Amie Glazier works in content marketing by day, wrangles four kids by night, and writes about fantasy worlds after bedtime. After following her husband's military career around the country, Amie and her family now live near Seattle where she is pursuing an MFA and working on her novels.

Lindsay Schraad Keeling

As the cliché goes, Lindsay has been writing her entire life, graduating from SNHU in 2022 with her MFA in Creative Writing. After winning awards for several pieces, Lindsay published her debut novel, *The Funeral Director's Wife*, with Conquest Publishing in September of 2024. 100% of the proceeds are being donated to the Oklahoma Homicide Survivors Support Group (OHSSG).

Erin Jo Eldry

Erin Jo Eldry is a central Florida author, dabbling in both poetry and adult fiction. Her short works have been featured in various literary anthologies from Wild Ink Publishing and Bunker Squirrel Magazine, and her debut novel, A River Like Mine, is slated for release in July of 2026.

Kendra Ann Keplinger

Kendra is a graduate of Seton Hill University's Writing Popular Fiction program where she received her M.F.A. She currently resides in her "home among the hills" in West Virginia where she was raised with fairytales. She dedicates this to her friends and family who encouraged her writing journey.

Bruce Buchanan

Bruce Buchanan is the communications writer for an international law firm and a former journalist. But he's been a fan of fantasy and heroic fiction for most of his life. His influences range from the novels of Margaret Weis & Tracy Hickman and Terry Brooks to the Marvel Comics stories of Stan Lee, Jack Kirby, and Steve Ditko. Bruce has short stories appearing in the upcoming Wild Ink Publishing anthologies Tenpenny Dreadfuls, Clio's Curious Dash Through Time, and UnCensored Ink. He lives in Greensboro, N.C. with his wife, Amy Joyner Buchanan (a blogger and the author of five non-fiction books), and their 17-year-old son, Jackson.

Jade Lebzelter

Jade Lebzelter has always been proud of her last name, which means gingerbread maker. Though her own gingerbread houses crumble, she thought it only natural to write a story about Hansel and Gretel.

Erica Duarte

When Erica Duarte is not writing, she is reading or listening to audio books—her newest obsession. Erica lives in Tennessee with her husband and two children. She has stories in two other Wild Ink anthologies and hopes to have the privilege of writing pretty stories as a full-time career.

Maple R. Nowark

Maple Nowak is a writer who explores the chilling depths of horror, the mysteries of the occult, and the boundaries of belief. Her work delves into the unknown, challenging conventional views with tales that haunt and provoke. Through each story, she brings readers face-to-face with eeriness and fascination.

Colleen S. Harris

Colleen S. Harris enjoys studying poetry and mythology. A three-time Pushcart Prize nominee, she is the author of The Light Becomes Us (Main Street Rag,

2025), Babylon Songs (First Bite Press, forthcoming 2026), These Terrible Sacraments (Bellowing Ark, 2010; Doubleback, 2019), The Kentucky Vein (Punkin House, 2011), and God in My Throat: The Lilith Poems (Bellowing Ark, 2009).

Charlotte Bennardo

Charlotte is the co-author of Blonde OPS, Sirenz, and Sirenz Back in Fashion. She is an author and publisher of the Evolution Revolution trilogy: Simple Machines, Simple Plans, Simple Lessons. Her other works include short stories, articles, and blog posts. Currently, she is working on several speculative fiction and romance novels.

Adele Liles

Adele Liles has been a high school English teacher for 25 years. She has been a finalist in the Writer's Workout Fiction Potluck contest and published in multiple short stories and poetry anthologies. Her young adult novel, Among the Whisperings, debuts with Wild Ink in 2025. She lives with her husband and their "tiny panther" in Virginia.

Rebecca Minelga

Rebecca Minelga is an author and speaker who uses the power of words to navigate the liminal spaces between who we are and who we are becoming. She raises Guide Dog Puppies and two sons - in that order - with her husband just north of Seattle.

J.K. Raymond

Infinite Mass by J.K. Raymond, pub. 12/23. The Carnation Collection, a Greek Goddess-inspired anthology, contributing author,10/23. Clio's Curious Dash Through Time, a middle grades anthology, contributing author, 7/24. Tenpenny Dreadfuls, a horror-inspired anthology, Anthologist, contributing author, 10/24. Uncensored Ink, a banned book anthology, contributing author, 10/24.

Arwyn Sherman

Arwyn Sherman lives in the woods of Maine where they tend to their menagerie of animals and write fiction. Their work has appeared in anthologies, on a few stages, and is probably tucked away in the chapbook you forgot you bought at a late night poetry show.

Their debut "We, the Missing" will be released from Conquest Publishing next year. For more visit www.hopp.bio/arwyn-sherman

Charleigh Frederick

Charleigh Frederick has signed ten novels, including published works DEMON SCOUT and RULE 25: DON'T FALL FOR THE TARGET. She was a Vocal+ Fiction Awards 2022 Challenge finalist. Her poetry is in Brimstone and Venus and Behind the Vision LLC, as well as the upcoming anthology I LOVE YOU UNCONVENTIONALLY.

Matthew Crabb

Matt Crabb lives in the Green Mountains of Vermont with his wife, two daughters, and an overzealous boxer named Flynn. He received his MFA from Vermont College of Fine Arts, and spends his days writing creepy tales, cleaning the house, and shuttling his daughters to various activities.

Demi Michelle Schwartz

Demi Michelle Schwartz is a Pittsburgh-based author and holds an MFA in Writing Popular Fiction from Seton Hill University. Her work appears in anthologies, and she's the host of Literary Blend, a freelance editor through Amethyst Ink Editorial, and an award-winning songwriter.

Julie Krohn

Julie Krohn is an author and engineer who lives in Ohio with her husband and four children. When she's not analyzing computational models, she is engineering her own worlds of fantasy and romance through her writing. She especially enjoys concerts, tall rollercoasters, theme parks and all things Disney.

Olivia Lynn

Olivia grew up writing on a Windows '95 laptop in her youth. This passion led to her love of gothic literature and put her on the road to studying English in higher education. Emily Bronte and Edgar Allan Poe are two of her major inspirations.

Christine Letizia

Christine Letizia (she/her) writes middle grade books but enjoys dabbling in young adult fiction, cozy fantasy, and romantasy. She has a cultural anthropology degree from Stanford University and a master's from Southwest Acupuncture College. Christine lives with her family in Colorado and is a mom to four amazing kids.

Mary V. Jenkins

Mary V. Jenkins an Idaho-based writer whose senior thesis on Star Trek fan fiction earned her a bachelor's degree from Boise State University. When not hunched over her laptop, she can be found defending her trivia team's league title or baking thematic snacks for her next Dungeons & Dragons session.

Sophia Alapati

Sophia Alapati grew up in a public library and has been hooked on books since her first Storytime. She is a therapist specializing in anxiety and OCD. Her previous work appears in The Razor, Voyage YA by Uncharted, and Electric Spec journals. She can be found at .

Tom Elmquist

Tom Elmquist has always had a passion for writing. He started writing in middle school with a Christmas play. Then many school related projects followed. In October 2022, was first time being published in I'm Not The Villain, I'm Misunderstood. The story A Conversation with Death was nominated for a Pushcart Award. He later turned that short story into his first novel by the same name due out October 2025.

Sasha Ravitch

Sasha is an author, educator, consultant, and critic of Occulture, Literature, and Film. She professionally presents at conferences, and writes speculative fiction and film and literary criticism. She has been published by Hadean Press, Asteria Press, and soon Revelore Press, and is an editor for Lumina Literary Journal.

Hannah Saal

Hannah Saal is a graduate of Harvard and The New School's MFA Creative Writing Program. Her work has been published in the Saturday Evening Post, Thin Air

Magazine, and the 2022 National Flash Fiction Day Anthology, among others.

Jacque Vickers

Jacque Vickers is a graduate of Newtown High School of the Performing Arts. Her writing has been published in Anthology Angels 2023 anthology: Hot Diggety Dog! Tales from the Bark Side, UnCensored Ink: A Banned Book Inspired Anthology (Wild Ink Publishing.)

Jacque lives in Sydney, Australia.

William J. Connell

William J. Connell is a practicing attorney and teacher in Rhode Island and Massachusetts. Most of his non-fiction work is in the legal field and has been published in many law journals. His fiction tends to run to a mix of historical adventure, classic literature, and a dash of horror.

Thony Mintz

Thony Mintz writes speculative fiction and poetry. His piece "Grim Prognosis" is slated for production on an upcoming episode of the *Tales to Terrify* podcast.

When Thony isn't wandering among twisty oaks on a misty coast, he's revising a book about giant, sentient bugs trying to make it in America.

Sasha Kielman

Sasha Kielman is an attorney in Washington, DC. Her short story BETWEEN HEART AND HOME was published in *Living With Demons*, a mental health-focused charity anthology, and her short story YOU TRANSFIX ME QUITE was published in *Crimson Bones*, a Gothic romance anthology.

BlueSky and Tumblr: @SashaKielman\

Emily Rozmus

Emily Rozmus grew up in the old house on her family's farm listening to the scary stories her father shared at the dinner table. Add in an English teacher mother, and it was inevitable she embraced books, literature, and writing. She has been an English teacher and a school librarian, pushing books to young readers.

Currently, Emily works for an online library with eBooks accessible to all Ohio students. She lives in her hometown with her husband, three children, and grandson, not far from the fields where she grew up.

Her debut novel, The Fullington Road Monster, was published by Conquest Publishing.

Avery Timmons

Avery Timmons is an Illinois-based writer holding a BA in creative writing from Columbia College Chicago. Her short fiction can be found or is forthcoming with Querencia Press, Wild Ink Publishing, Fiery Scribe Review, and other digital and print publications. Her debut novel, Thicker Than Water, will be published with Wild Ink Publishing in 2025.

A. Wells

A. Wells is a college student in Northern Michigan. Ever since she was little, A. has had a vivid imagination, which she tries to capture through writing and art. She hasn't quite figured out how yet, but she's getting closer through every piece.

www.ingramcontent.com/pod-product-compliance
Lightning Source LLC
Chambersburg PA
CBHW061036310726
48969CB00004B/969